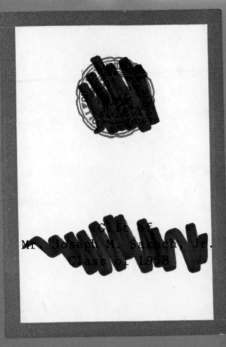

Perfect
TIMING

Perfect
TIMING

a novel

PHILIP LEE WILLIAMS

PEACHTREE PUBLISHERS, LTD.
Atlanta

Published by
PEACHTREE PUBLISHERS, LTD.
494 Armour Circle, NE
Atlanta, Georgia 30324

Jacket Illustration by Eileen C. Blyth
Book design by Candace J. Magee
Composition by Kathryn D. Mothershed

Manufactured in the United States of America

10 9 8 7 6 5 4 3 2 1

Library of Congress Cataloging in Publication Data

Williams, Philip Lee.
    Perfect timing / Philip Lee Williams.
        p.   cm.
    ISBN 1-56145-024-3
    I. Title.
PS3573.I45535P47   1991   90-28260
813'.54—dc20   CIP

For Lillie Mae Kirby Sisk

(1898-1988)

Beloved

THE SECOND COMING OF CAMILLE MALONE was a shock to me. I had thought she was long gone, dissolved in the irretrievable past, a filmy ghost on the battleground of old lovers. When I found that she was alive, if not well, it changed me.

I certainly needed changing. I was enduring a North Carolina spring, lost in a sorry state of affairs that found my wife and kids moving to Macon after my stupid and very brief affair with a red-haired harpist named Starr. Jill's parting shot was aimed for my soul, and it hit:

"Ford, you're a pitiful, wretched fool who's throwing away his life for nothing at all," she said calmly as she and the kids got in the Volvo and headed for her sister's. "I don't think you know what you're doing anymore."

Well, she had me there. I had been watching my kids' eyes as they got into the car. I wanted to tell them something intelligent, but intelligence was apparently slipping away as my stock-in-trade. I merely stood there while she waited for a response, and Kathy and Jay looked at me from the back seat with a numbing mixture of disgust and disbelief.

"I don't know what to say," I muttered. Jill's tongue fled around the inside of her lovely mouth for a moment, as if seeking the right word´s for farewell, but nothing seemed to capture her particular feelings, so she climbed in the car and drove off. I watched to see if she'd glance back at me in her rear-view mirror. She didn't. I felt a creeping devastation as they drove off. My affair had been over for weeks, but the damage it had done lingered. The fault was entirely mine.

Only a few months before, everything seemed fine. I was teaching my musicology classes in the mountains of Asheville and enjoying a professorship at McCandless Conservatory. This place was my haven. I'd gone to school here years before, then returned as a professor after graduate degrees at Columbia. That link seemed important, as if I'd forged safety from its anchor. The voluptuous safety of academia enveloped me, and I worked, as I had for ten years, on my magnum (and nearly only) opus, an opera based on *East of Eden*. Why I had picked this particular book seems obscure to me now, since I don't particularly like Steinbeck. Privately, I believe it was the James Dean movie that really got me, and the guilt I always felt over not dying young. My mother once hinted that if I died young, somehow magnificently, she would not be displeased. But maybe I misunderstood her.

Camille, twenty years ago, wrote a piano trio in a single weekend, and it was staggering, an engaging mélange of Bartók with a hint of Shostakovitch. I was wild for her, hanging outside the chapel and listening to her practice Brahms and swear like a longshoreman each time she missed a note. She'd be leaning into a ballade, and then she'd hit a wrong note and stop and scream "Shit!" at the top of her lungs. When she sat at the keyboard, her breathing nearly stopped, her eyes narrowed to slits and her face flushed.

By the time I met Jill, I'd long gotten over Camille. I left her in New York to make her fortune at Carnegie Hall, to tour the world, become famous. She wanted me to come with her and be her manager. I refused.

"You're a gutless lizard," she'd said as I was getting a cab for Penn Station and a train south. "You are no better than H. R. 'Bob' Haldeman." God, she hated Republicans, and anytime she wanted to fling down her most stinging bile, she'd say I was no better than H. R. 'Bob' Haldeman. That detail seems quaint now, like knowing some minor functionary in Neville Chamberlain's cabinet or Herbert Marcuse's hat size, but then it seemed important.

"Camille, I'm not going to spend the rest of my life basking in your glory," I said wearily. We'd been through it for days. She'd taken me to the top of the Empire State Building for dramatic effect and started shouting that I was a traitor.

"That's your role, Ford," she said. "To bask. You'll never generate enough limelight to pop a flash bulb in an Instamatic." She was right, of course, and I knew my role already: the handmaster to someone else's fame, the footnote in another's history. I had this theory that the wages of sin are boredom, and that the sins of my life would be secured by a life of unceasing routine and Rotary Club luncheons. But when Camille said it while I was holding up the cab, something in me turned brittle like an old grommet, and my soul began to leak out, and it bled all the way south, and I pretended I was over her.

She told me the first time we met that "no one ever gets over Camille Malone," and she meant it. But she changed. At first, she was flamboyant, cheerful, manic, funny, intemperate, and a frightening polemicist. She hated Nixon and country music, and she loved Mozart and Wagner and Nietzsche and junk food and bad television. If her tastes were food, they'd rot your teeth. And yet they were rich, and she was unquestionably the most exciting woman I'd ever met.

Years later, I sent her a copy of my book, *Rachmaninoff and the End of Romance*, but she didn't even acknowledge it.

I never told Jill that I worshipped Camille when I was young, although she knew we'd once been lovers. Jill had already spent too much time around musicians, who are always wavering between sobriety and indescribable crisis.

But the world was different when I came to college in the fall of 1968. I was the first boy in my high school to grow sideburns, and when I got to the Conservatory, to Tarmot Hall, I found that all the homilies I'd learned in the family breast were often untrue, that the world was sometimes a rather bilious place full of deceitful, lying mental dwarfs.

I believe now that humankind is improvable, though not perfectible. Camille was an atheist when I met her, but when we were juniors, she had a breakdown and came out a bead-toting Catholic. I used to go to mass with her and mumble along.

She made me read James Agee because he was a Catholic. We went to see *The Song of Bernadette* several times when it came to the student cinema. She wanted us to take vows for or against something. I tried to follow in her spiritual path, but it was ablaze with her gift for obscurity, and soon we were arguing over which modern people might one day be saints; just then, she was holding out for Eugene McCarthy. I told her she was becoming a fanatic, and she threw a plaster Saint Francis at me, missing my head but breaking a window.

A cooling fervor is a sad thing to watch if you live in that reflected glow. But Camille did cool toward religion, though she became a philosopher, arguing with every aspect of the world, alienating all her friends and going on terrifying binges of piano practice. She was sometimes thin and pale as a martyr. She'd play an E-flat major scale ninety times in two octaves without stopping. She would find a piece that spoke to her heart, like the first movement of the *"Pathetique"* Sonata, and she'd play it for an entire night, not stopping when she got to the end, merely starting over like *Finnegans Wake*.

Still, at least in the first three years of college, she was a dazzling gift to me. By the time I'd finished at the conservatory, I'd become more iconoclastic, withdrawn and serious about art, but I never got over a minor obsequiousness toward authority.

"Why do you think you feel this way?" asked Ricardo Lumpkin.

Ricardo was my analyst, at least I say he was because it made me feel very Hollywood, or wealthy. Actually, I met him through Jill. He taught psychology at Buncombe Community College, where Jill taught remedial math. I found he liked Vivaldi, and we hit it off at a party for the faculty at the College. Those of us in the Conservatory across town here in Asheville are supposed to feel genetically superior, and Jill never forgave my generally snotty attitude toward her work.

"About authority?" I said. "I don't have a clue."

This was about three years ago, and I remember sitting in his office and watching a bat make lyric circles around a street light outside in the twilight.

"Perhaps it's because you were overprotected as a child," he said.

"Ricardo, my parents adored me," I said. "They still do, as far as I can tell."

"Why is that, do you think?"

Ricardo had a goatee, surely one of the world's dumbest affectations, and he smoked a heavy Latakia. Its aroma drifted from his well-worn pipe as he puffed.

"I chose my parents well," I said sarcastically. "Is that permissible in psychology these days? I was a little nervous as a kid, that's all."

"What do you think caused that?"

"How would I know?" I said. "I'd have to stand up in front of the class, and I'd have an attack of nerves. I was reciting 'The Village Blacksmith' in the third grade, and I started wheezing and choking."

"Was it more frightening than your wedding to Jill?" he asked. "I remember you saying how scared you were there."

"Pretty low, Ricardo," I said.

He just chuckled. A lost art in America, chuckling, but Ricardo had mastered it, could have chuckled with Zubin Mehta and the LA Philharmonic. I talked little with Ricardo about authority or about Jill, to be honest.

I was thinking on all those things when, one Sunday night, I saw a television program on the homeless. It was on public TV. I was alone and drinking Sanka. I had only one light on in the house, and I could hear the clock ticking on the mantel, a Bavarian cuckoo clock that had belonged to my grandmother.

The program was set in New York City, and I was looking at the buildings, marking my own memories, when a woman on screen pushing a grocery cart seemed oddly familiar. She wore boots and a stocking cap, and her eyes had the twisted, concentrated look of a zealot on a mission. I sat forward and spilled my Sanka in my lap and did not even shout or curse when I was burned.

The face on my television belonged to Camille Malone.

FIRST AND ALWAYS, THERE WAS MUSIC. My mother had come out of the genteel Southern tradition of the arts, filled with dreams of Mary Garden and Adelina Patti, with old scratchy recordings of Caruso, soaring romantic ecstasies. Her name is even musical— Clarice—and as a girl, she played the piano beautifully and could sing dozens of arias along with the Metropolitan Opera broadcasts every Saturday.

She was also by nature undefeatable. As I have grown older, and she has aged gracefully, I have found that this quality is virtually nonexistent among most humans, the ability to keep rising above the stench of battle and defeat, to cheat the small deaths of humiliation, as it were. And I know, now, that this quality was what Camille had and why, when I came to McCandless, I fell so hard for her.

My father managed, with near genius, the Gallant-Belk store there in Jamesburg, interested in the arts as well as in commerce. He has pale blue eyes and a mustache stained from heavy smoking and coffee drinking. He is tall. When I was a boy, he liked to take us to church, get seated in the pew then rise, wander out front on the stone steps and sit there, smoking and thinking. He was often gone to the store, and I'd come up and help during holidays.

When I was ten, they went to Savannah and came home with an armload of new LPs, and we sat in the dark, comfortable music room Mom had created on the second floor of our house. I remember I'd come home from school, and it was cold and raining.

I do not know the month. But I recall every texture of that moment, the deep shadows of the room, Poe-like, a small coal fire in the grate, heavy carpet, dense Victorian chairs, and my mother standing over the record player.

The first thing she played was the *Symphony Number Five* by Anton Bruckner, then shifted to a Bach cantata, the Franck *Symphony in D minor*, and then to Eileen Farrell singing arias from Puccini. When Eileen got to "Un Bel Di," from *Madama Butterfly*, my mother dramatically placed her hands upon her chest and turned to the rainy window.

I did not yet know what the words meant, but I knew that Eileen was tragically sad, that she had been hurt, and I sensed that my mother felt the same way. That changed me. Each day when I got home, I'd listen to records and then practice the piano and try to write music myself. I came out of my shyness. I began to be popular with the other kids at school, and I started my endless fascination and love of girls, spurred by the nutty romantic notions of Bruckner and Franck and Dvořák and Puccini.

When I was eighteen, Mom gave me, for my birthday, the Bernstein recording of Mahler's *Symphony Number Eight*. I did not even go to school that next day, nor did I dare admit how it all made me feel, exalted, special. I could hardly explain to my beer-drinking buddies how I felt about the galactic mysteries of Mahler.

My father listened to Artie Shaw and Benny Goodman and Tommy Dorsey, too. He almost never drank, but when he did, he'd invariably take out the Glenn Miller records, and Mom would dance with him, laughing and happy, and I would walk by that room and see them, and he'd whisper in her ear, and she'd giggle like a girl.

I worked summers at the store, and Daddy had bought a tape system and played stuff like Patti Page and Jerry Vale on it, and he'd hum as he worked the floor, but I could not wait until I got home to listen to Schubert and Brahms, to work on my own compositions as well. By my senior year in high school, I had composed a full symphony, a string quartet, and a song cycle on poems of Theodore Roethke. I considered myself something of a pocket genius, and I headed away for school, sure that I was bound for the sublimity of being the most talented person on campus.

It was therefore a profound shock when I got to McCandless and found that I was in the bottom ten percent of the talent pool, that most of the students were dazzlingly talented, while I had far more ambition than genius. That discovery, more than anything, led to the slow fading of my high school dreams. Sometimes now, when I'm trying to work on *East of Eden*, I summon those days like one calls a ghost in a seance. I beg. I pray. I try to see my mother's tears as she listened to "Un Bel Di." But it's no good.

The campus at McCandless was not much different in those days. I was assigned to Tarmot Hall, and my roommate was a large, funny boy named Ronny Favors. My parents had taken me to Asheville, and my father had helped me drag my trunk and suitcases to the second floor. Tarmot Hall is gone now, bulldozed for a parking lot, and it's no great loss, even for nostalgia's sake. It was steam-heated, clapboard, two-story, with rusty plumbing that knocked all night and inner, mysterious workings that made the place groan and creak even in the slightest wind.

Named after Charles Brandywine Tarmot, a minor benefactor, the building's sagging floors and flaking paint were unworthy, in my eyes, of housing the South's newest musical star. My parents left. Ronny showed up several hours later.

"Let's go get into something," he said right after we'd introduced ourselves.

"Get into something?" I asked.

Ronny, I was to find, had a cheerful disregard for everything, and he easily swayed me into minor larcenies. He also loved to swear, and on my first day, I followed him right into a new brick building not far away. He walked in as if he owned it, stalked up a flight of stairs and down a hall. The term was just beginning, so not many students were around, but when we came to the third door on the left, I knew we were in the girls' dorm because we both saw, through an open doorway, a beautiful brown-haired girl clad only in a pair of pink panties. The shock on her face probably matched mine as I stared at her medium-sized but beautifully shaped breasts. Ronny, on the other hand, whistled at her. She covered her chest with her left arm, ran toward us and shut the door.

We did not get into trouble. The girl did not report us, and later, she and I became passing friends, and she would joke that I must do things for her since I'd seen her chest.

Ronny was from Memphis, had grown up in the sultry Delta tradition of its landed gentry, and was forever stumbling into trouble of one kind or another. He was taller than I, with black hair and blue eyes that drove women crazy. More than once I got back to Tarmot Hall only to find our door locked and the sound of the bedstead bumping furiously against the wall inside. I envied that.

Ronny was also a conservative, which isolated him some-what; most of us were quite liberal, and a coterie of juniors and seniors was absolutely radical, and I soon fell into a band of philosophical journeymen who would gather to discuss Hegel and Marx and Franz Fanon. The place was ninety percent white, but we read the plays of Leroi Jones out loud and hated ourselves for being white and middle-class. We shunned all middle-class pleasures. We did not watch television. We practiced and sang and composed and argued with unified hostility. When Camille had her conversion to Catholicism, she brought *The Confessions of St. Augustine* to one meeting of aggrieved atheists, leading to a verbal brawl that was even reported in the school paper, *Campus Notes*.

I think of Ronny Favors sometimes. After we graduated, in 1972, he got a job as a community choral director in California, some small dusty town in the Salinas Valley, and we heard later that he was fired for some unknown indiscretion.

When I think of Tarmot Hall, I smell the sweeping compound the old janitors used early in the morning when we were stumbling toward the showers; I hear record players with a mix of Bach and Sly and the Family Stone, Mozart and Cream. I recall the foul smells of poor plumbing, the pleasant time of Sunday morning when the halls were silent. I'd rise early and go out to The Meadow, a large expanse on the side of our mountain overlooking Asheville, and I'd pretend I was Thomas Wolfe, bound by the glories of my talent, write poetry (mostly bad) by the ream, wait for some girl to see me there. It did finally happen, but not before I was already enmeshed with Camille.

Those first months, in fact, are resurrected each fall when the new ones come in, but it's always a disappointment, for I can't bring my youth back at all. Now, they're all better than we were, better pianists, better composers, better singers.

The entire episode with Starr, I believe now, was triggered by my mid-life meditations on the past, which happened months before I saw the lost and pitiful Camille on television. I opened the door to my youth and found that it was lost, and I became moody and morose, unwilling to respond to Jill's most tender advances. She took me out for a romantic dinner after shipping Jay and Kathy off to a neighbor's. Nothing happened. We went to the art museum in town and saw some paintings by Andrew Wyeth. I started to see Ricardo, but he only confused me.

"You're trying to prove that death is only an illusion," said Ricardo.

"You mean it's not?" I said sourly. This was six weeks before Jill and the kids left in the station wagon.

"No," he said, puffing on his pipe, "death is not an illusion. I'm going to die, and you're going to die, and your children are going to die, and their children are going to die."

"Why not," I said, wanting to sob but not having the energy. "Mozart died. In a world where Mozart can die, anything's possible."

I left his office that day and drove back to our campus, thinking about my life and how I'd failed to find my vision. My piano playing was comic, indifferent. The day after Jill left, I felt a numb anguish. Each day at work, teaching musicology and history, going over the same life spans, of Louis Spohr and Luigi Nono, of Respighi and Reger, was boring, more evidence that I was adrift.

And so, when I saw Camille on television, it was an omen, a message from an idealized world that included my youth.

And in a fit of nostalgia, I called The Homeless Hotline in New York City and left this message: For a woman named Camille Malone who was in the special on CBS-TV, come and meet me at the Circle Beech! Come and tell me where we all went wrong all those years before!

But after I'd hung up, I realized she'd probably never get the message, and even if she did, how could she afford to leave? I therefore decided that I would go to New York and save her. I had no other choice.

"SHE COULD ALLEGE MENTAL CRUELTY, YOU KNOW, Ford," said
J. Thomas Brackett, Jill's lawyer and my former tennis partner. We
were sitting in his office (lawyers never leave their lairs), which was
in a structure in downtown Asheville. The room was huge and
sterile, and Thom was sitting behind his desk acting professionally
indifferent, fingers tented, staring at a spot on the wall behind me.
His nameplate said "J. Thomas Brackett," but the letter inviting
me to this auto da fé was signed "Thom," an affectation that made
me edgy.

"Come on," I said, "you know no jury'd ever buy that I was
cruel to Jill. In fact, I still love her."

"Have a funny way of showing it, Ford," he said. His voice had
dropped half an octave. "She said you are becoming deranged, that
in the past six months you began to talk to yourself out loud, forget
appointments, and completely ignore your children."

"Forget appointments!" I cried. "My God, was I that bad?"

"Go ahead and make fun of her," he said. "There's also the
matter of a Miss Starr Coventry. Need I bring that up?"

"You need not," I said. I got up guiltily from the chair,
blanching at Starr's name, which sounded like that of some hopeful
chorine or even a stripper. The name was entirely real, which tells
you something about her parents.

"Then how are you going to respond to these charges in the
proceedings?" he asked.

"I told you I'm not contesting the divorce, Thom," I said. I pronounced it like it's spelled, and when I came back and sat opposite him once more, I could see his face had reddened slightly. In a profession where composure is all, a slight blush is a crack in the carapace. "I'm just not going to play ball with you on the mental cruelty issue. I'll go for incompatibility."

"You sure that would be doing the right thing, Ford?" he asked, gathering himself again.

"No, the right thing would be for me to give her everything and go live in a cave and eat berries and roots for the rest of my life," I said. "What do you want me to say? 'I'm not who I was' or something like that? The fact in this case, Thom, is that I still love Jill, and that I really don't want a divorce at all. I want some time to think about this. I know I've hurt her, but I'm in a maze. I woke up one morning, and I was lost."

"I understand the man who's been doing your analysis is really an academic and not a registered therapist," he said.

"Jesus, Jill told you about Ricardo?" I put my hand over my eyes, not for drama but because I could not bear to see this pathetic little scene unwinding around me. "This is humiliating beyond belief."

"I think you might get thirty days, Fordy," he said, stepping into an intimacy between us that never existed, "but after that, we're going to court. Now I've done this before, and let me tell you quite candidly, Jill can virtually wipe you out."

"Thanks, Thom," I said. I stood and shook his hand across the desk. "I'll be in touch."

I went back out into the hall, dark spots circling around in my eyes like crows, my breath shallow and unformed. The place was cool, odorless, tasteless, nearly colorless, as if you were drowning in invisible water with each step.

I came outside and inhaled the rich April air of Asheville, the thin tonic I'd come to love so much in the years I'd been there. I stumbled toward my car. It was an ancient MG Midget, black with red leather seats, top down.

I started the car and drove back toward McCandless, and I fiddled with the radio until I found the station broadcast from Mc-Candless. It was playing the Brahms *Sextet*.

I was locked, antlers and all, in a deep struggle with my conscience. What did it mean to see Camille on television?

My fling with Starr had lasted two weeks. She clearly was no Camille. What would she have thought of Marcuse or Fanon or the *Obras Escogidas* of Lorca? Could she discuss Rasselas or Hardy, or James Agee's letters to Father Flye? Camille could, all these and a hundred more, discuss them, dazzle you with her opinions of them. We were intellectuals then, and Starr was not an intellectual.

I went into Roberts Hall, a three-story white clapboard structure built in 1887. Its rambling charm was repeated all over the McCandless campus. I had parked in the faculty lot behind it and come in the rear entrance, which immediately rises up three flights of stairs with iron railings. My office is on the third floor, but all over the building you can hear the faint notes of pianos, trumpets, and strings, some working through scales, others proffering snatches of melody. The hall off the third floor landing had been carpeted, but it tended to bunch badly over the old tile. My office was third down on the left, and I unlocked it and went in.

Here am I, Lord: desk piled five inches deep with papers, an old whistle, scabrous coffee cup, unmailed bills, magazines, the score of *Die Meistersinger*, Grout's *History of Western Music*, empty tape dispenser, empty stapler, postcard from Jay with a picture of Macon, a hockey puck a student from Montreal had given me, small portrait of Joseph Conrad, newspapers; two bookcases, one behind the desk, which faced a wall, the other in front; two chairs, old overstuffed things, inappropriate, but I didn't care; a dead shamrock plant Starr had given me with two plastic angels stuck in the soil holding a banner that said "Lovers Forever!"; and on the floor in the corner, my friend Barry Gutman's cornet, with the sticking valves which I thought I might be able to fix but couldn't.

I had two windows, both overlooking the deep green quadrangle where flowers were in riotous bloom. I had a small table on which I'd put my Realistic radio-stereo cassette player.

I came in, leaving the door open, sat down in my creaky desk chair and surveyed my ruins. My God! It hit me then with some kind of nostalgic force: I had unconsciously recreated my father's office in the Gallant-Belk in Jamesburg, the same baroque clutter, the same eccentric comfort. I'd been home not long before, and the office looked as it always had.

I was working through this, barely remembering I had a musicology class to teach in half an hour when I noticed that Miranda Terrell was standing in the doorway. Her office was two doors down. Once she had been a fine soprano, and she still sang for interminable faculty recitals, but she'd gained a shocking amount of weight and now waddled around in the amber-tinted glow of academia.

"So, Ford, how is it living all alone?" she asked with a pleased grin. Miranda took pleasure in misfortune. Lately I'd been her chief source of entertainment.

"You asked me that Monday," I said. I shuffled papers, pretending to look for something.

"So I did," she said. "Could I bring you over a quiche or a ham or something?"

"No thank you," I said.

"Oh, I guess you're just eating whatever pops up, then," she said.

I glared at her.

"That's an egregious slur," I said. "Nobody talks to me like that."

She stared at me for a moment and then laughed, a gut-trembling guffaw that made me feel nearly ill. Then she came into my office, approached me very close and pinched me on the cheek with her fat fingers.

"Oh, for God's sake, Ford," she said, "lighten up."

"Reasonable advice for all of us," I muttered darkly. She took it as I intended, as a tacky comment on her weight, and she shrugged with more grace than I had exhibited and was suddenly gone, leaving her cologne lingering around the edge of my desk like a pudgy ghost.

The day passed without memorable incident. My classes were boring, I ate lunch at a small Italian restaurant near campus and, that evening, I got back home, alone, left with mementos of Jill and the kids. I was drifting. I had an anxiety attack for about twenty minutes until the bourbon and water kicked in.

My house is my castle. From our salaries, Jill and I had saved enough to build a copy of a Plantation plain style house, two stories, with a gallery on the second floor. Around it were several gardens, but I was not the gardener; that was Jill, and this year, the roses would run wild, be eaten petal by tender petal because I was not going to mess with them. I had reached the stage in my life where wild things had a dangerous intoxication. To me, wilderness had the same fascination it may have had for Cortez or Neil Armstrong, the "other," the delicious alternative to the ordinary.

I walked through the empty house, room by room, here the blue-and-cream sectional set Jill had bought two years before, there the sideboard which had belonged to my grandmother, dark wood burned with my grandfather's cigarette stains. Here the large kitchen with the food island and ice-maker fridge, there the laundry room where Jill would sort and fold our clothing every Saturday morning.

I missed the rituals of family, and yet I could not dismiss the power of Starr's sweet body. I was a fool, no doubt, an Invisible Man, maybe no different from Ralph Ellison's novel or the increasingly nutty Claude Rains in the movie of that name. I was Dante, lost in midlife, stumbling farther and farther into the labyrinth of age and stupidity, and I had not the faintest clue who I was or how I'd get out. I had obviously lurched in the wrong direction, hurting everyone I loved.

I sat on the sofa in the living room and put on a CD of the Vaughn-Williams *Mass in G Minor*, a lovely, suitably lachrymal piece. Good stuff for a meditation.

And so Camille was a bag lady, now living on the streets. What could that mean? Had she become Little Dorrit or part of some fanciful waste from Harriet Beecher Stowe? She always told me about the symmetry of the universe, illustrating her talks with examples from thirteenth century Mystery Plays, this being in her Catholic stage; by the time she'd turned agnostic again, she was quoting Genet and Sartre and from *Waiting for Godot*.

Now, at this point in my life, I had a warm feeling for her religious conversion, since my own battles with religion had been shallow and capricious. Oh, we went, all of us here, to the

Mountainside First United Methodist. I found Methodism a suitable compromise between immoral maunderings and death. Camille talked of us as great lovers for a time when we were seniors, but I knew instinctively we were no Paolo and Francesca. We would never lose our lives or go to hell for love. We might kneel in some dark sanctuary for love. We might commit timeless rituals for love. We would not, however, die for it or of it.

I felt as if I might die of love. I loved Jill. Now, separated for some months, I knew that profoundly. Would I really go to New York and look for Camille? Yes, I would. Why? I couldn't actually ask my father these questions, but I could imagine his advice anyway.

FORD: Dad, I'm nearly forty years old, and I'm a complete mess.

DAD: Well, that happens, son.

FORD: I'm thinking of going up north to find my old girlfriend who's lost on the streets of New York. Do you think this is a reasonable thing?

DAD: Of course not, Fordy. Never do anything reasonable.

Dad said things like that, though this time the speaker was merely me. It was therefore ironic that as I sat on the sofa, daydreaming and listening to the end of the *Mass*, the phone rang, and it was my mother.

"I just wanted to let you know that I'm completely bereft that you haven't been to see me in so long," she said with a slight sniff. "How are Jill and the kids?"

I knew too well that fools died but once, yet I had not been able to call her, to tell her that my life was heading toward the inelegant conclusion of, say, Robert Schumann. I took a breath and decided to let it out.

"Mom, Jill and the kids left me and moved to Macon with her sister," I said. I heard this strangled sound on the other end, an inconclusive glottal.

"Oh, Ford, this is inconceivable," she said finally. "What happened?"

"I say that I'm in a period of redefinition," I said. "I'm trying to find my way out of the growing knowledge that I won't get out of life alive."

"And what does Jill say?"

"She says I had a short-lived but unforgivable affair with a red-haired bimbo named Starr," I sighed.

"And?"

"Mom, have you ever seen 'Star Trek'?" I asked.

"Is that the one with that cute man with long ears?"

"Yeah," I said. "Sometimes people in that show wake up and find everything changed. Do you know what I mean?"

"Ford, you need to come visit me," she said. "I'm aging, and you don't care about me anymore."

"Thanks for your poignant assessment of the situation," I said. "Okay, Mom, I'll try to get down soon. First, I've got to go to New York."

"Did you get some work up there?" she asked. "Is the opera finished yet?"

"The opera is not finished yet, Mom," I said. "The opera will never be finished. I think I equate completion with death."

"Then you'll leave it uncompleted like *Turandot*," she said.

"I'll leave it essentially unbegun," I said. "Look, I've got company coming in a minute, and I need to get off the phone. I love you. I'll call when I get back, okay?"

"Are you eating enough eggs?" she asked. "Your complexion sounds bad." A slight thrill of familial horror went through me with that sentence, but I could not face its implications.

"I'm fine," I said. "Stay well. Tell Dad I said hello. I'll see y'all soon."

I hung up and went into the kitchen and poured myself a drink. The truth spills out when you speak to your mother as a middle-aged man.

But not the whole truth. I wanted to tell her about religion, about the cyclical nature of history, both the world's and our own.

I wanted to transcend myself. Right here, Camille might throw in her latest interpretation of Bronson Alcott or Margaret Fuller, both of whom she found superior to either Thoreau or Emerson. All she needed was a word like "transcend" to fly off on one of her crazy speeches linking natural philosophy, the over-soul, and the divine sufficiency of the individual.

I went to my Steinway baby grand and sat at the stool, adjusted it, and began to play the Chopin *Ballade in G Minor*. I played poorly and with passion, but it was not like Camille, who assaulted the piano as if it had wronged her. When Camille played, even the birds in the trees nearby stopped their singing and listened, transfixed, aghast, in wonder. Her first concert in New York (and I was there, of course) was greeted in *The New York Times* the following day with a puzzling review that criticized her eccentric tempi while shouting to the skies her manic involvement with the work. They didn't use the word "manic." They said that she "played with an interior fright or rage that, instead of grabbing the audience by the heart, took them forcefully by the throat." To her, that review was as good as "hats off, gentlemen, a genius," but I wasn't so sure; there seemed disapproval in it.

Later, I ate a light dinner and then I fell into a profound sleep on the sofa in which I dreamed that I was traveling west with the Joads. Henry Fonda was sitting in this dusty truck, talking about how he was going to hit it rich in California then spend the rest of his life on a pond in Vermont. I was puzzling over this when Ma Joad's alarm clock, which was packed in the truck, went off. I waited for Henry to answer it, but he was giving some speech when I realized it was the phone beside the bed. Some dream. It wasn't even the right Steinbeck book for my opera.

I sat up and glanced at the clock, and it was 2:12 a.m. I grabbed the phone from its cradle and croaked something like a greeting. That was a mistake, but I know now that it was part of the inevitability of life.

For the second time in one night, it was my mother.

IN MY BOOK *RACHMANINOFF AND THE END OF ROMANCE*, the crucial thesis is that the twentieth century brought about a neo-classical revival, and that when style changes, with its roughly seventy-five-year cycles, the Romantic Age will return. I tinkered with establishing this date of Romantic death as 1913 at the performance of *The Rite of Spring*. Finally, though, I pushed it forward to 1922, the year of *The Waste Land*, a poem that defined and shaped the age. That means, in perhaps 1997, another Rach-maninoff will come along, full of dreams and dark emotions. *The Times* derided that part of my book with such scorn that colleagues began to needle me, asking if Romanticism had returned yet.

It did not return that night when my mother called. As soon as I knew it was she, I knew that the message was urgent. All mes-sages from my mother were urgent.

"Ford, you must come home immediately," she said. "I have a terrible problem."

"What is it?" I asked.

"He's here," she whispered into the phone. "I can't let him know I'm calling you. He's asleep on the couch downstairs."

"Who's there, Mom?" I said. "Are you sure you're awake?"

"I'm filled with terror and mortifications," she said.

I always hated it when she talked like that. Once she was guest speaker to some class at my school, and she referred to me as her "delectable and most talented offspring," and I nearly died from the embarrassment.

"You're losing me, Mom, and it's 2:13 a.m.," I said.

"He's here," she repeated darkly. "Clarence Clayton is here!"

I threw my legs over the edge of the bed and turned on the lamp.

"Clarence Clayton is there?" I said. My voice was rather high. "I thought he was still in prison. Where's Dad?"

"Your father's at a convention in Charleston. Clarence is supposed to be in prison," she hissed. "He escaped, the larcenous fool, and now he's forced me into harboring a fugitive. You've got to get down here."

My cousin Clarence was the dark side of the Clayton clan. My father's sister's boy, Clarence had gotten drunk one night in 1984 and robbed a liquor store and managed, through reckless insolence at his trial, to draw a twenty-year sentence. I never liked him anyway. My late Uncle Claude tried to help him, gave him money and preached the values of Rotarianism to him. But Clarence had a fine sense of his place in familial history, the potential catalyst of the Fall of the House of Clayton.

"How in God's name did he escape?" I asked.

"He says he made a gun from Ivory soap and blackened it with shoe polish," she sighed. "You'd think he'd written *La Traviata*."

"Why don't you just call the cops?" I said.

"Because I'm afraid of him, Fordy," she said. "He said that despite his escape, he's gotten religion, though God knows what kind of warped theology he must have inherited in that den of iniquity."

"All right, all right," I said. "I'll come down first thing in the morning, but this doesn't make me happy."

"How do you think I feel?" she said testily. "Like Debbie Reynolds? You must get up by five-thirty, Ford, shower and eat at some quick-food place on the way and arrive here by noon. By then, the beast will be stirring."

"The beast," I said as I hung up.

I keep a large blank book at my bedside table to record my dreams, having heard on some television show that this was therapeutic. Early the next morning at 5:30 sharp, I awakened, just as my mother had commanded, and wrote this:

Was with Catholics all night long. Link this to Mom's talking about Clarence getting religion. Me and Camille and Gerard Manley Hopkins, and he was reciting "The Windhover," but it was unintelligible, then he launched into a sermon on his alienation from God, and then Camille told him, to his face, that Cardinal Newman was better. Hurt Gerard's feelings. Perhaps relate sprung rhythm to Clarence being sprung from the pokey.

"Get dressed," I told myself. "There's trouble in Jamesburg." I began to laugh like I was mad.

I'D BEEN AT McCANDLESS FOR ABOUT THREE WEEKS in that fall of 1968 the first time I walked by the Chapel and heard the sounds of sweet music and curses coming from inside. The day was blessedly autumnal, with bright leaves blowing off the trees, swirling in eddies along the sidewalks of the old campus. I was uneasy. Already, I knew that something was badly amiss here; I was out of place, overshadowed by the least of the students in the freshman class. In brass methods, I was an embarrassment. In history, I said on a test that *carpe diem* meant "Then, the Lord created the fishes," a response I tried to hide but which escaped somehow. They laughed at me. My sight reading in voice class was improper.

Ronny Favors, on the other hand, could do anything. He played the piano easily, if without inspiration. He could play the viola and cello passably. He wrote a three-part fugue just for fun the first week we were there. He was glib. The girls loved him. Ronny had read Kafka. At my mother's behest, I had read much of Marie Corelli.

"You know, Ford, that her real name wasn't even Marie Corelli," said Charley Barstow, a tall, goggle-eyed boy who lived in the room next door. Charley was a violin major, and he later formed part of a quartet that is still touring Europe.

"What?" I said. "How could you know something like that?"

"My family is bookish," he said. "Her real name was Mary Mackay, probably a better name for somebody who wrote that drivel."

"I thought *The Soul of Lilith* was a good book," I said, defending my mother's taste.

"Oh my God," said Charley.

I never mentioned Marie Corelli again. My mother read many fine things, but I swallowed her weakness for turn-of-the-century popular authors with unfortunate eagerness. I'm probably the only man of the late twentieth century to have read most of E. P. Roe, for example, or Hallie Ermine Rives. There was no place for E. P. Roe in an atmosphere where most of the students were quoting *Blues for Mister Charlie* or *The Wretched of the Earth*.

That day I was feeling the uneasiness of my inferior training when I came behind the Chapel. The Chapel was (and is) a lovely antebellum structure of two stories, with three hundred wooden folding seats, a thrust stage beneath the proscenium arch, a balcony of delicate proportions, and a fine pipe organ. In pleasant weather, the thirty-foot-high windows would be opened, letting the cool mountain breezes mingle with Bach or Wagner or Vivaldi. At one Vespers concert, a mockingbird flew through the open window into the Chapel and sat like the Raven above an exit door. In the middle of a Beethoven trio, it began to sing wildly, and the antiphony between players and bird became legendary.

The windows were open. It was early October, and the day was cool. I was walking behind the Chapel when someone inside launched into a section somewhere more than halfway through *Claire de Lune*. I stopped on the sidewalk and listened. A squirrel was noodling with an acorn. The music had some kind of edge, because I slipped into the stage door, ascended the stairs, and found myself backstage watching the most beautiful girl I'd ever seen play the concert grand on stage. The place was empty but for her.

She had long dark hair, blue eyes, high cheekbones. She wore a peasant blouse and blue jeans with familiar anti-war patches on them. She opened and closed her eyes and breathed oddly as she played. She did not just play, however. She caressed the piano. I was bewitched. She got to a pitch of emotion on a passage, balled it up and slammed her open palms down on the keys, and with flaming, now wide-open eyes, screamed.

"I can't play this motherfucking piece of shit!" quoth Camille Malone. She stood and glared at the piano as if it had betrayed her. Her face reddened. Her beauty was translucent. She looked around angrily and saw me. I was holding a stack of books to my chest. Her anger immediately softened a bit, and a wry smile creased her lovely face.

"You're too hard on yourself," I said. She came walking over to me with a grin. Her jeans were tight. I desperately wanted to say something profound or witty.

"Who are you, a critic?" she asked. She came close to me and looked me over, up and down.

"I'm a freshman," I said. "I don't think I'm a critic, because I don't know what in the hell's going on."

"I'm a freshman, too," she said. "I'm Camille Malone from New Orleans." I shifted my books to my left arm and we shook hands.

"I'm Ford Clayton from Jamesburg," I said.

"Jamesburg what?" she said. "Is that in Virginia?"

"Georgia."

"Holy shit, you're from Georgia?" she said. "Maybe no one will notice if you don't say much." She smiled beautifully, and I wanted to kiss her.

"What's so good about New Orleans?" I asked with some heat.

"It's the cultural crossroads of the West," she said, throwing her hair over her shoulder. She was silent for a moment. "So, did you catch *La Chinoise* at the Godard Film Festival last weekend?"

"I must have been doing my laundry or something," I said. Her lips were a shade too dark for her face. They twitched like halves of a ripe plum, and a brief smile told me that she liked the answer. It had a certain cheek.

"So where do you live?" she asked.

"Tarmot Hall."

"Jesus, what a freaking dump," she said. "No Joyous Gard, I'll tell you that."

"No what?"

"Joyous Gard," she said with disgust. "Sir Lancelot's castle. Haven't you ever studied *Morte d'Arthur?*"

"Not this week," I said. "So are you a piano major?"

"Yeah," she said. She shifted from one foot to another and tried to find a way to say it. She finally just blurted it out. "I'm, like, a genius, okay? I could play the *Pathetique* when I was eight. I've been on TV nine times back home."

"Wow," I said. "Next they'll invite you on Ed Sullivan."

"They already did," she said coldly. "I told them to eat shit. I'm not going to be on a show with a mouse named Topo Gigio."

Amazingly, she was not lying. Ed himself had seen a film of her playing at seven and had invited her. Actually, it was Camille's father who said no.

"Well, meeting you has been a real sensation, but I need to be going," I said.

"Wait a minute," she said. "Give me a chance to show off for you."

She dashed back across the stage toward the piano, and my eyes never left her perfect, heart-shaped rear. She plopped down on the bench and launched into one of Rachmaninoff's *Preludes*.

Her playing was more than inspired. It was overwhelming, even frightening. I was lost forever, madly in love on the spot. I slowly walked across the stage and glanced toward the empty Chapel. She did not seem to notice me approach. I came over and stood at her shoulder, so close that I caught the fragrance of her, something like fading soap and sweat.

When she finished, and the last chord had died away, she turned slowly to me. I felt my eyes fill with tears. I didn't know what to say or do. My mouth was open, trying to ingest some oxygen. There was no oxygen left on the stage. It had all been consumed by the passion of her music.

"I may never get over that," I said.

"Nobody ever gets over Camille Malone," she said.

I once blurted out to Ricardo, in an unguarded moment, my belief that sanctimony has the power to ennoble. He scratched his goatee with the eraser of his Eagle Mirado pencil, then tapped his upper incisors.

"Ford, that's very interesting," he said.

He was always doing that, steering me obliquely around myself, pointing out the landscape of Ford Clayton with the Baedeker of psychology. But I meant it, because my involvement with both sanctimony and true nobility began with Camille.

The next time I saw her was a few days later in Jumper Hall. The money for the place, an ugly brick cube built in the late fifties, was donated by an industrialist named Morris Jumper. He was still alive, and the story was that the night before its dedication, when Mr. Jumper was to arrive on campus in the glory of his philanthropy, someone had painted a ten-foot-high kangaroo on the side of the building where a platform had been set up. At the last minute, a hysterical administrator had the brilliant idea to cover the kangaroo with a sheet on which "Thank you, Morris Jumper!" was inscribed, along with some stylized artwork depicting musical instruments. Unfortunately, a gust of wind billowed the sheet from the wall and it blew away like a sail, revealing in the middle of the event the kangaroo which had been painted with an obvious phallus under its pouch.

I loved the story. I took Kathy and Jay to a concert once several years ago, and when we walked by Jumper Hall, Kathy said in her seven-year-old voice that Jumper Hall was the place where they'd painted the kangaroo with the weenie. I got home and told Jill, who was delighted. Maybe Kathy would be a humorist.

Jumper Hall held some minor administrators, a small theatre and the student center. I walked into the student center one evening, feeling lost and homesick, wondering what in the hell I was doing at McCandless. Camille was holding court on some sofas in a corner. A few girls, all with long straight hair, looked irritated and severe. A few boys were trying to look irritated and severe, but in fact, as I saw immediately, they were leering at the girls. I was not far away, and Camille saw me and motioned me over. I went.

"Settle an argument for us, Georgia boy," she said. "Did Demosthenes influence Quintillian or not?"

I had seen *The Graduate* at a movie house in town the night before and had spent part of the day meditating on the humpability of Katharine Ross. I had not given much thought to Quintillian, since I'd never heard of him. I acted like I was considering the question. I took too long.

"Well?" said a boy with shoulder-length black hair. I stared at him. His eyebrows grew together in the middle.

"That depends on what you mean by influence," I said.

"He doesn't know," said another girl, this one heavy and mean-looking. "He's just jerking off."

I was shocked. Girls in Jamesburg didn't talk like that, at least not out loud or to boys. Still, I wouldn't show it. So I smiled with world-weariness at her, implying that she was ignorant and foolish.

"Try the other question on him," said the eyebrow boy.

"Okay," said Camille. "What's the central thesis of *Eros and Civilization?*"

"It's by Herbert Marcuse," said the fat girl with a preening disdain.

"Hey, don't tell me your reading list," I said. Camille grinned as the fat girl bristled. I'd never heard of book or author. "Look, I don't have time for your games. I'm late."

"He doesn't know," said a thin young man, taking a fanatical drag off a cigarette. "You could tell right away."

"Goddamn," I said. They seemed impressed. I walked away, feeling a rage for those pseudo-intellectual creeps. I went out a side door. It was early evening, not yet dark. I got a hundred paces from the building when I heard footsteps behind me. I looked over my shoulder and saw Camille.

"Hey, Georgia," she said. "Hold on."

I stopped and turned toward her, and saw the thin light trapped in her hair. She wore patched jeans and a blue bandleader coat with golden braiding on the shoulders.

"Forget the name of Robert Frost's grandmother?" I said irritably. She smiled and came up beside me. Across the quad, a shaggy boy and a gangly Dalmatian jangled by. The boy sang softly to himself or to the dog.

"You sure are pissy tonight," she said.

"Your friends are creeps," I said.

"They aren't my friends," she said. "They're undereducated morons. They didn't even know who wrote the *Metamorphosen* for strings."

"They didn't know our old buddy Dickie Strauss?" I said with mock horror. "The servile oafs."

"Come on," she said. "You're going to buy me a hamburger over at the dining hall. I'm starved."

"Why would I buy you a hamburger?" I asked.

"Because I'm Camille Malone, and I'm the queen of this place, or will be soon," she said brightly. "Also, you like my ass. I could tell it right off."

"I never noticed," I protested.

She laughed at me and threaded her arm through mine and steered us off toward the dining hall.

She was the first girl I'd touched since I'd left Jamesburg. Ingrid, my high school honey, was planning a career at a local grocery store, and she violently argued that college or conservatory was just a waste of time for me, that we needed to pick out a silver pattern, get married, and have babies. "We'll need a lot of practice making babies, too," she said in my ear, an effective but ultimately unworkable form of blackmail.

But that night with Camille, any lingering thoughts of Ingrid finally faded from me. Not that Camille felt much for me. I soon found out that she treated everyone the same, veering like a pinball from near-intimacy to pop-eyed accusations of faithlessness.

So we walked arm in arm to the dining hall. She was lovely, and I was young, and I felt suddenly as if I were a big man on campus. We passed a classroom building where windows were open. A trumpet player was fiddling with the "March" from *Love for Three Oranges*. A quartet was playing Schubert's *Death and the Maiden*. A sax player was doing something by John Coltrane. No matter where you went at McCandless, in the dewy light of early morning or the stillness of midnight, you heard music, live or recorded.

The dining hall was nearly empty since it was almost eight, the hour they quit serving. I bought us hamburgers, and we sat at a table and ate.

"You're from where?" I asked.

"New Orleans," she said.

"Oh yeah, the Crossroads of the West," I said.

"That's a lie," she said. "It's a provincial little backwater burg, actually. You know, Catholics, and Cajuns and alligators, moonshine and steam. I saw a man beaten to death with a lead pipe in the French Quarter one night."

"Jesus," I said.

"Yeah, that was one hell of a thing," she said. "Like being in a Clue game or something, this bizarre, choking, reconfigured Clue game, you know? Anyway, my mother, the Duessa, found out I was in the vicinity with some of my friends, and she freaked, thinking I was somehow involved. Ah, Duessa, you fool."

"What's a Duessa?" I asked with a sigh.

"Oh, just an evil enchantress from *The Faërie Queene*," she said, waving away my ignorance. "A symbol of evil, stands for people like Mary, Queen of Scots. Are you going to eat that french fry?"

"Help yourself," I said. "Why would you refer to your mother as an evil enchantress?"

She laughed brightly, yet her eyes seemed flat and hard. She looked away from me and reached in her purse and dug out a crumpled pack of Salems and lit one and blew the smoke violently away from us.

"Because she is," she said. "And my father is this kind of demented intellectual saint. He goes on retreats with his doctor colleagues. He's a gynecologist. So what's your family like, Georgia?"

"My father owns the Gallant-Belk store back home," I said with mild pride. "Mother is a housewife and amateur musician. I'm an only child."

"Are you into the Harlem Renaissance? Have you read *Cane*?" I had no idea of what she spoke so I smiled. "The war? What are you for or against, Georgia? Your mother must be the one who turned you into a musician."

"Both of them," I said. "Who turned you into a pianist?" She crushed out her cigarette and lit another. I noticed that her hands were shaking.

"It wasn't the Duessa," she said. "And it wasn't the doctor. They've been acting out this morality play for twenty years now. When she's not Duessa, she's Blanche DuBois. She's a hare. Did you know in medieval days people feared hares crossing in front of them because witches could turn into hares?"

The conversation swung back and forth like this for nearly twenty minutes as I finished my hamburger. She was driven and indiscriminate. She talked of Vachel Lindsay's suicide, of Mahler's state of mind when he wrote the *Kindertotenlieder*; she referred to herself twice in the third person as Brünnehilde. I was dazzled, and yet her startling range of interests was less education than escape. She'd read fanatically all her life, she said, to escape the dreck of her home. She practiced piano the same way. Hours and hours. Not until a couple of years later, when I took the train with her to New Orleans, did I realize the ferment and chaos of her home life as a girl. In later years, she felt terribly alone, kept saying that no one would remember her, that no one remembered Nicodemus, and *he'd* helped bury Jesus (this was after her conversion to Catholicism, of course).

We finally left the dining hall and came outside. Rain had begun to fall. One thing about Asheville: plenty of rain in the spring and snow in the winter. I went home summers.

"You never told me where you live," I said.

"Mary Grandville," she said. An older dorm a block away from Tarmot Hall. "I'm going to my practice room now. It's been fun, Georgia. Thanks for the burger." She thrust out her hand, and I shook it, wanting instead to press my lips to her wine-colored mouth. We were getting wet.

"Ford," I said. "My name's not Georgia. It's Ford." She smiled beautifully in the lamplight.

"Right, Georgia," she said. She backed up two steps and turned and ran off down a sidewalk toward the Practice Hall, an older building with dozens of small rooms. You signed up for specific times at the beginning of each semester. I walked in the growing rain, then ran back to Tarmot Hall, thinking only of Camille, that I was in her spell in some profound way. Perhaps she was, in fact, the Duessa; if she was a witch, she had ensnared me with her brilliance and disorder.

I came up to our room on the second floor and opened the door with my key. Ronny and Charley Barstow were listening to

Simon and Garfunkel, and Ronny was extremely drunk.

"What's the problem?" I asked.

"He's really down tonight," said Charley solemnly. "He got drunk. Angela dumped him."

"Who's Angela?" I asked.

"A fucking whore," said Ronny.

"She was his girlfriend back home," said Charley, whose words were slurred.

"Are you two drunk?" I cried. "It's illegal to have liquor in Tarmot Hall."

Ronny stood up and staggered toward me, struggling with his balance. He got in my face. His breath was flammable, and I tried to back up, but he kept coming at me until I was against the wall.

"Clayton," he said. He paused. In the dim light of the room, lit by a single forty-watt red bulb Ronny had bought somewhere, his eyes seemed huge, mad. "Clayton, you're a weenie."

"Why'd she leave you?" I asked, hoping to get his mind off of me. He stepped away and looked down at the floor.

"She's a fucking whore," he said, but "whore" came out more like "hoor," and so he tried it again, and this time it sounded like "whar." He seemed perplexed.

"Jesus, Ronny," I said, "don't be so down about it. I said on a test that *carpe diem* meant, 'And then the Lord created the fishes.'"

Charley was sitting on the bed. Paul and Art were like a rock, an island. Charles screamed, a curdled shout of drunken glee, then he stood and fell to the floor cackling and holding his sides, almost like certain pictures I'd seen of religious ecstasy. Ronny struggled to the window, opened it, and stuck his head out into the rain and proclaimed to the campus that Angela was a fucking whore. He then puked into the hedges below.

"Then the Lord created the fishes!" screamed Charley. "Aaahhhhhh!"

I fled. Out in the healing salvation of rain, I walked for a long time until I felt sleepy and confused. When I got back to the room, Charley was gone, the light was out, Ronny was snoring on the bed, and the needle of his stereo was bouncing silently just past the record's final grooves.

I CROSSED THE OKALATCHEE RIVER into James County, ninety miles inland from the Georgia coast. The river, a molasses-slow stretch of black water a hundred yards wide, was covered with hovering insects. I passed a newly cultivated field where crows and cattle egrets, black on white, hopped in the furrows looking for bugs and worms.

The trip down had been pleasant. I left just after dawn and drove for six hours straight. It nearly midday, and the top was pleasingly down on my MG.

The roll call of history, of my own history, began to come around me as I plunged into James County. As always, it was that smell, a fermented, yeasty, fecund smell of dank earth and black water and sawmills that hung about. No place for a musician to spring from. But in some ways it made sense. Jamesburg had been the southern terminus of the Augusta Railroad in Civil War Days, and a planter class had grown fat and lazy there. The town was proud of its culture. Still its most famous citizen was a minor humorist named Thomas Jefferson Bulridge, who had published a slim volume of anecdotes and stories in 1894. He disappeared later in Mexico, an event that made him Romantic, part of local legend. Bulridge made it easier to be an artist in Jamesburg. They have a room dedicated to him at the library, complete with a tempera rendering of what he might have looked like by Miss Jenna Peterson, head for half a century of the Jamesburg Art Society.

On my left, I noted, with sentimental attachment, the road

(still dirt) where Ingrid Halvorssen and I would usually park during our senior year. On cold winter nights, the windows would fog up immediately. We'd take along a roll of paper towels to unfog the windows before we drove back.

Just outside town, the poverty of the countryside starts to give way. No more slat houses or sawmills or poor farms. A few larger houses, then, suddenly, a large white sign, repainted twice a year, proclaiming Jamesburg as a "Georgia City of Honor," some Chamber of Commerce ploy started years before to increase tourism.

The town is perfectly ordered. A central square with a small park and a statue of Brigadier General Erasmus Johnson, leader of the Jamesburg Rifles in the Civil War. He and all his boys were killed at First Manassas, which put the town out of the war in 1861, a fact generally overlooked in military histories. It had been six months since I'd been home to see my parents, a fact Mom regularly berated me with. I drove through town, through the dusty square where nothing is more than two stories, past Dad's store, came down Lumber Street, hung a right at Case, and four houses down on the left was my homeplace.

I still dream about that house. It was built in the 1880s, in the new boom years after the carpetbaggers had left. White clapboard, with a kitchen and two bedrooms added out back. A spacious yard which, in earlier years, my mother kept landscaped. Now it was not so neat, with lilies and ivy sprouting everywhere, bulb plants dead and splayed in the hedges. Dad never cared for cutting grass or hedges. Privet was soaring. A red-tip photinia my father had planted was now twenty feet high and profoundly ugly. The grass needed cutting, and a messy nest of sparrows hung over the front eaves, like an old man's stray beard. I parked out front.

Clarice Clayton came right out, slim and beautiful, wearing a solemn brown dress and a look of urgency. Her usually silent neighbor and best friend, Ula Nickles, came out with her. I turned the car off, and it idled for a moment. I got out, and Mom rushed toward me.

"This is the darkest day of my life," she said. In her youth, she'd been quite beautiful, with rosy cheeks and clean blue eyes. Now she seemed merely healthy beyond belief, fine color, strong arms. As she emoted, I saw my features playing through hers. Everyone always said I looked like Clarice Clayton.

"You said that the day I got a C in drama in high school," I said. "Where is he?"

"He's in the dining room," she said in a strangled whisper, "preaching. I found your father's gun and was going to shoot him, but all the bullets were gone. You and that Linker boy probably stole them. I called your father, but he told me not to worry. He always says that. He won't be home for four more days."

"For God's sake, Mom, you wouldn't have shot your own nephew," I said.

"Like a rabid dog," she said. She had spent years trying to teach me to shed my southern accent, and her success was remarkable. "Dog" came out "dahg," nearly Boston-Irish or at least upper Midwestern. "It's a wonder he didn't strangle me in my bed or," she said, her voice dropping half an octave, "rape me where I lay."

"Mom," I said, "I remember Clarence as being a kind of befuddled little boy. You recall the trial. He didn't even know it was a liquor store, and he didn't have a gun. He just asked the clerk for five dollars."

"Yes, and he said that he thought it was the bank, too," Mom said. "You can't trust a man. The only man I ever really trusted was my father, God rest his soul. And your father, of course."

"Can we go inside and discuss this?" I asked. "Your yard looks like hell. That red tip may reach heaven before it's all over."

She took my arm and jerked me with amazing strength toward the front door.

"You remember my friend Ula," she said.

"Hello, Mrs. Nickles," I said. "Are you helping Mom defend herself against the menace inside?"

"Well, I reckon," she drawled.

I walked behind my mother up the creaking stairs and onto the porch.

"Mom, your last letter had a cryptic reference to Ingrid. What happened to her?" I asked.

She turned to me triumphantly and smiled like Bernadette.

"Goodness," she said, "you haven't heard?"

With that, she left me dangling and walked into the house, where I could hear Clarence bellowing in the dining room.

The essence of the house was unchanged. I felt my childhood wrap around me like comforting arms. Dad sleeps in his chair after supper. You came into the high-ceilinged living room, an old-fashioned parlor with a dusty sofa, throw-covered wing chairs, a few marble-top tables, a wildly out of context Chinese chifferobe Dad had shipped from Hong Kong. The rug was oval, ropes separating. Mom's piano was a baby grand on the far left wall. A bookcase still had all my school pictures, from first through twelfth grade lined up. Just as I was starting to feel at home, Clarence came out of the dining room.

"God be with ye, Ford Clayton!" he thundered. "And with all thy kith and kin!"

I say he thundered. Thundering to Clarence was more of a heavy squeak. Always something of a joke, Clarence had never grown past five-two, weighed probably one-twenty-five, and was a shadowy, pinch-faced version of my uncle. There's a medical term for this condition, but it escapes me just now; still, Clarence was elfin, ears ending in Spockian points, big Adam's apple and huge feet.

All his life, he'd been beaten up, mocked, tricked into awkward situations. As a young man, he was briefly engaged to a foul-mouthed, very obnoxious girl named Olene. I remembered her, shapeless, self-obsessed, chain-smoking, and bitching about every subject that came up at the dinner table. A month before the wedding, she ran off with an old boyfriend and got married in Calhoun Falls, South Carolina. Clarence was disconsolate and drank himself comatose, but after a time, he came out of it.

He was a salesman at the Western Auto store. He became a haberdasher at Markham's Fine Clothes, but he fell asleep in the stock room while smoking and burned up twenty-two pairs of women's pedal pushers. They fired him. Next, Clarence was a cop for a while. He wrecked his car while on duty. After that, he was in charge of a picking crew at the peach orchards, Mexicans mostly, none of them able to speak any English. He told them outrageous lies. The owner of the orchard found that Clarence had basically backed the pickers into servitude, had them cutting his lawn and waxing his car. Out of work again. Clarence had schemes, though. He bought a franchise for plaster Jesuses, but he didn't do very well. He was the first man in southeast Georgia ever to have an Avon franchise, but women found him naturally offensive, and so he flopped at Avon. He got into Amway for a time, got out. Nothing stuck. He'd been drinking heavily and talking about Olene, who'd divorced her husband and remarried a bread salesman, when he knocked over the liquor store in Clancy, a town twenty miles away. My family was aghast. I was already out of the Conservatory and in New York with Camille when it all happened. Clarence had been sentenced to twenty years, and he could have been out in six but for confused and abusive behavior at his parole hearing each year. Everyone was pleased at his continued presence in prison. I'd more or less forgotten about him. But now, here he was in living color, like a diminutive version of the Orson Welles character in the movie they made of *Moby Dick*.

"This place is not the same without Jill and the kids," I said, ignoring Clarence, which wasn't easy.

"Are you divorced yet?" said Mom. She threw the back of her right hand to her forehead.

"No, Mom," I said.

I felt a grapefruit-sized lump in my throat and wanted to be anywhere but home. Ula stared blankly at us.

"I did not escape from prison, actually," said Clarence. "I was released by God himself. This is my holy mission."

"Holy, holy, holy," Mom said, a little hysterically. Taking this as an injunction of some kind, Clarence leaped onto the piano stool and began to preach.

"And Gawwwwddddd delivered me from the bowels of the prison, up onto this land to spread the word of His salvation," chanted Clarence. "And when He cameth to me in the celleth area, He leaneth down and said into my ear that I should...*lo! hark!*"

He screamed the last two syllables with such shattering urgency that Mom jumped a foot and grabbed my arm. She looked at me with a *do something* stare, then we moved toward the den, leaving Clarence on the table harking and loing and screaming in crypto-Elizabethan language about salvation. He kept yelling. Mom closed the door behind us. She had, for some reason, purchased a bean bag chair that dribbled its tiny excelsior all over the rug. Ula, astonishingly, flopped down in it. When Ula hit the chair, tiny styrofoam pellets flew everywhere. Mom ignored her.

"He did that for an hour last night," said Mom. "Did you bring any bullets? I think we could bury him under the chinaberry tree."

"Mom, for God's sake," I said. "How can you think of such a thing?" She paced for dramatic effect.

"Well, maybe we can't actually kill him, but we've got to call the police, at least," she said. "Maybe they'll kill him when they storm the house."

"Can we talk about this calmly?" I said. "I don't want anybody getting shot. Besides, he is my cousin."

"He's a felon," said Mom. "And he's a wretched preacher. If he'd lived in sixteenth century Florence they'd have hung him from the Stinche by now."

"Thank you for putting this event in historical perspective," I said. "Okay, okay. I'll call the cops. Let's just do this gently."

The police chief, Marvin Bolerson, had been a buddy of mine in high school, and he said he'd be down with some handcuffs after he'd made a phone call or two. It took him forever. Marvin always was slow. Clarence quit preaching and took a nap on the sofa in the living room while Mom made us watercress sandwiches (terrible), Kraft Macaroni Dinner (all right), and sweet tea (marvelous). She'd gotten a CD player, and we listened to excerpts from *La Bohème* while we ate. Soon, we heard the car out front. We all crept out. Clarence was still asleep on the sofa, snoring and muttering, so we eased past him and came onto the porch. My mother ran past me and threw herself into Marvin's arms, and he staggered backward and only staved off collapse by throwing one arm around a front-porch column.

"Mrs. Clayton," he gasped, "you're going to make me throw my back out again." Mom stepped back from him.

"Marvin, get in there, quick!" she said.

"Ford, long time no see," he said. We shook hands. "How's Jill and the kids?"

"Fine," I said.

"Why's your gun not out, Marvin?" asked my mother. A brindle dog lying in the street lifted its head as Mom got toward the end of her sentence. Marvin tilted his cap back and leaned on the post and shook his head.

"Miz Clayton, I called the state, and Clarence didn't break out using a bar of soap shaped like a pistol," he said.

"What?" Mom said.

"He was paroled three days ago, Miz Clayton," said Marvin. "He's done his time."

Mom's face drained of its normal rosy color, and she backed up two steps, hand on her chest, mouth slowly dropping open.

"I'll be damned," I said.

"But true," said Marvin. "So I'm afraid he's all yours, Miz Clayton. He's clean and free."

Just then, Clarence appeared inside the screen door, his features softened by the wire mesh. He was smiling and making the sign of the cross.

"Peace be unto thee, Warden," he said in a Pope-like voice.

"Marvin, I'd like for you to have me put to sleep," said Clarice Clayton. No one said anything. The dog got up and ran off down the street.

Clarence wandered away for a time. Mom, instead of being euthanized, went to the VFW to help prepare for the bingo game that would take place the next night. She disapproved, but Dad was a vet, and they had gone to the VFW every Friday night for thirty years. It was an autonomous act on her part.

My young adulthood, my adolescence, my youth, my child-hood, my cribhood — all were safely stored in the attic. My mother kept every scrap I ever wrote, every school picture, everything. She'd said it was for future biographers. What if Beethoven's mother had done this for him, she cried one night after it was clear to me that I'd never amount to much as a composer.

You got to the attic through a half-door in my old room. When I ascended the stairs, I'd found my room unchanged, and a deep calm fell over me, and soon I was in the still, dusty attic, sitting cross-legged and looking over the shards of my past. What clues lurked there? Would I find a message written in baby talk, then first- grader, then regular English, something to explain why I was now wobbling off my life's unmoving pivot?

I found a cache of old letters. Two windows on the front of the house let a faint sunlight smudge the raftered attic, but I had to turn on the light, a single hundred-watt bulb, anyway. I took a rubber band off the first letter and opened it.

Dear Mom,

I am haveing fun at 4-H Camp. I am becomeing quiet a canoe paddler, and I have made a new freind, Arthur Jones from Saveanna. We saw a water mocasin Thursday but it ran away. I hear there are allegators here, but dont you worry, because I am becomeing very brave.

That is all I can tell you for now.

Your son,
Ford Clayton
P.S. Tell Daddy their's a Gallant-Belk not two mile from hear.

I felt there was a certain ignorant charm about the letter, which I did not remember at all, though I did of course remember 4-H camp, which was at Shot Cane Creek, forty miles toward the coast in a swampy, moss-hung camp area that I loved. I opened the next letter.

April 12

My Darling,

I'm writin' you from Granny's place here in Little Rock. It's a dump. I'm so bored I could die. I went out last night after everybody was asleep and walked into town, which must be twelve miles away, and I found the nicest bunch of kids listening to a radio and smoking. And so I fell in with this boy named Louis......

"Arrgghhh!" I yelled, throwing the letter away from me. God, did I remember this one, Ingrid's first "Dear John" letter, in which she even had the temerity to call me her "Darling," though for her that was nothing more than form; she probably mailed in her power bill with that heading. I'd wept when I got it, since it went on to describe in some detail how she and Louis had become inseparable, and she even hinted they'd had carnal knowledge of each other.

I opened the next one. It was from Camille and had been written to me not long after I left her in New York and had come home to reassess my career. I knew that much after reading only two lines.

Monday night
Ford,

Wouldn't it be somewhat dazzling and wonderful to be the next Julie Jeanne Eleonore de Lespinasse and conduct a literary salon? If you were here, I could resurrect their theme, Je ne fais qu'aimer, je ne sais qu'aimer.

Lately I have felt like Omphale, Queen of Lydia, because the booking agency has got the gig for me in Alice Tully Hall and then at Carnegie, and finally three dates around London. It's a crime you aren't here, but you abandoned me, so what can I do about it. Last night I read most of The Pillow Book of Sei Shonagon *in the fairly new Ivan Morris translation, which knocks the shit out of the partial one by Arthur Waley. Sei was a lady in waiting. I would not be a lady in waiting, I'm tired of waiting, tired of everything. Ford, I'm practicing eight hours a day, and I worry I'll destroy my fingers as Schumann did, but it's either practice or drink and smoke pot.*

Last Friday Elaine and I got into a furious argument about Schelling's Von der Weltseele. *You know, nature is a visible spirit and spirit is invisible nature, that shit. Well, Elaine, for nearly fifteen minutes thought we were talking about Schiller rather than Schelling, and when I went into a rave about Weimar classicism being no better than German romanticism, Elaine got up and walked out. It's always the same......*

And so on for another nine pages, furious ramblings through philosophy, psychology, history, music, and intimate personal problems, presented with the clinical disinterest of an aging medical school professor.

I threw it on the pile and opened the next one.

Tuesday, April 8, 1970

Dear son,

The enclosed check should be of some help to you for the remainder of this term at the Conservatory.

We got the first shipment of bell-bottomed trousers into Jamesburg last week. They look like sailor's trousers, and I hear they are becoming popular with the younger set.

Dad

For some reason, the impersonality of it lacerated my heart; I was surprised to find my tears pattering on the sheet as I stared at his handwriting. I closed it up and put it on the stack. I opened another.

Friday the 13th

Dear Ford,

Saw a new production of Lazarus Laughed *in the Village tonight. Putrid. They applauded too long and I walked out.*

What I'm seeking in my music, darling, is this divine pleroma, something like gnosticism, knowledge rather than faith. I applied that to the Scriabin Preludes with mixed results. If I can't bring gnosticism to the piano repertoire, I'd rather die with a silver bullet in the brain like Henri Christophe (he was Toussaint L'Ouverture's lieutenant in the Haitian revolution and not to be confused with Jean Cristophe, pitiful creature of that second-rate Nobel laureate Romain Rolland). Can you believe the arrogance of that shit Nixon?

Oh, Ford, why couldn't you have been the Pururavas to my Urvasi?

Camille de Malone

Reading a letter from Camille was like being one of the segments of a roman candle. When it went off, you exploded with it, not knowing half of what she meant, though the "de" I knew was from her affection at the time for anything French. I opened one more, and as soon as I saw it, my heart collapsed like a failing hot-air balloon.

Hi Sweetheart,

I got home safely Thursday, but already I miss you so badly that I don't know what to do. This summer is going to last forever, and I hope you can come up once if your Daddy will let you off.

Jenny is growing right up and getting pretty. She will be fourteen this fall, and I can hardly believe it! She's singing "Amazing Grace" at church Sunday and is so nervous about it!

I'm going to write you a long, long, long, long, long, letter later today, but now I've got to drop Mama off at the beauty parlor and then go out to my Aunt Alice's to help her put up some beans and stuff.

Here's my hug and kiss to you. I miss you so much.

All my love,
Jill

This was too much. I put all the letters back into the box, turned off the light, and walked back through the half-door into my old room and sat on the bed.

It was in this very room that I'd read the Grout *History of Western Music* and known exactly where my name would come when the book was in its fortieth edition. I even wrote a section on myself to be included, talking about my symphonies (nine, of course), concertos, operas, chamber works. I would sit here on rainy nights smoking a pipe by the window so in case my father came upstairs, he wouldn't smell smoke (he never did), listening to Rachmaninoff's *Second Piano Concerto*. I knew with heaven-sent certainty that I would be someone one day. The mission was holy. I was an avatar, a saint. I was tapped by God for musical divinity. I daydreamed my apotheosis.

I closed my eyes in the silence of the room and saw the

Okalatchee River, the county, Jamesburg and my youth, all my friends from childhood, and back past that, to my parents as laughing youngsters, just starting out with *their* dreams, and I wondered, where did it start or end? Was this the reason for all philosophy, to win the victory of scope over your own life?

I sensed that scope was within my reach, but somehow I'd mucked it up. Jill was part of my scope. Camille de Malone was certainly part of my scope, and I knew in that moment that I had to rescue her from the streets of New York, that without her part of my puzzle I'd be condemned to repeat the failures of my last twenty years. If I could regain my scope, perhaps I could find my soul as well. I wanted my soul.

I felt drowsy, and I lay back on the bed of my boyhood, and when I awoke, it was after five, and for a moment, I thought I was back in high school. When I realized the year, that I had somehow blundered into the solitude of middle age, I stood and uneasily walked downstairs, my heart beating far too rapidly.

The dining room was empty. On the round oak table was a note from my mother saying she'd gone to the store to buy dinner. A P.S. said that the gun was in her top bureau drawer in case I needed it for anything. I heard the sound of two balloons rubbed violently together, and I tiptoed into one of three downstairs bedrooms and saw Clarence lying on his back, snoring. I went outside and walked around the house.

I came back inside, and when I got into the kitchen, I heard the sound of Scripture. Clarence had awakened and was sitting in the living room reading, so help me God, from the Book of Job.

CLARENCE ATE NOISILY, HIS THIN FINGERS ripping the chicken apart with practiced fury. Mom watched him with wide eyes, sure he was some kind of barbarian who'd invaded her gentle home. I wasn't sure if his feet reached the floor. He was country-starved poor, like the kind you saw forty years ago but rarely now.

"Must you eat with such dreadful manners?" Mom said finally.

"The Lord careth noteth how a man taketh his substenance," said Clarence sagely.

"*Sustenance*," Mom corrected, her teeth clenched tightly around the word.

"I saw a cat in your backyard this afternoon," I said, trying to change the subject.

"Verminous beast eats my chickadees," said Mom. "I tried to shoot it once, but I put a hole in the side of Mrs. Garriss' house across the way. Never could shoot a pellet rifle."

"You didn't try to shoot a cat," I said.

"Passeth them potatoes," said Clarence.

"Of course I did," she said. "Cats *are* rodents, after all."

"Mom, I know you went to college, so I'll try not to seem condescending, but cats are mammals, not rodents," I said. "Rats and squirrels are rodentia."

"Cats are definitely rodents," said Mom.

"We had a cat at the work camp in Jefferson," said Clarence. "But it escaped." He let it sink in. I stared at him. Mom was right; his manners were atrocious.

"Was it a prisoner?" asked Mom with heavy sarcasm.

"Well now, that's a thing to thinketh on," he said.

"It's sorta like, well, we're all prisoners of something or another," said Ula, who hadn't left.

"Ula was a philosophy major," said Mom sarcastically. Ula didn't seem to mind.

"I studied history," said Ula. "I used to could play the harp."

"Just like an angel," said Clarence. "The heavenly bandeth of angels, lo, they playeth on they harps. And harmonicas."

We all stared at him. I was startled by his apparent lunacy, but Mom was becoming more wrung out with each of his words. I was going to let it drop. Mom couldn't. It wasn't in her nature.

"What?" she said. "Did you say angels play harmonicas?" Her voice rose a bit near the end of the sentence.

"Sure," said Clarence.

"Where did you discover that theological conceit?" said Mom.

"It ain't conceited, it's true," said Clarence. "The children of Israel took out they timbrels and danced. I read it. I couldn't figure what a timbrel might be, but it's got to be a harmonica because it's small enough to take out from somewhere. And if the children of Israel had 'em, I know angels do."

I've always been able to turn away from ignorance. My mother is not so well blessed, however, and her face turned crimson as she probably thought about Moses playing the harmonica.

"And what did they play on the harmonica?" asked Mom. Her voice was too loud.

"Country music," said Clarence.

"Country music!" yelled Mom.

"Yeah," he went on. "See, most of theseth Israelinos wasn't from the city, they was from the country, so I figure when they made music, it was country music."

"Israelites!" shouted Mom, coming halfway out of her seat. "And they didn't sing country music. Nobody but morons listen to country music!"

"Sorry, Aunt Clarice," said Clarence, genuinely confused at her anger. "I was just trying to be a good conversationer."

"Heavenly days," said Clarice.

"Look, Mom, this is all nice, but I have to be getting back to Asheville," I said. "I've got to go to New York in a couple of days, and I don't know when I'll be back."

"Lots of folks needeth saving in New York," said Clarence dreamily.

"For God's sake, Ford, don't go to New York," said Mom. "It's a dreadful place. Why would you be going there, anyway? Not to stage your opera, by any chance?"

"Mom, my opera will be staged before the Millenium, I promise," I said. "No, an old friend is in trouble, and I need to go see if I can help her."

"Haveth you ever noticed how close apostle is to opossum?" asked Clarence.

"She was a friend in college," I said, "and now she's a street person. I saw her on a documentary about street people. She was once a promising pianist, and now she's wearing combat boots and pushing a grocery cart. You remember, Mom. It's Camille."

"Jesus wept," said my mother. "That weirdo? She spent an entire evening one time trying to talk to me about the Counter Reformation and Lope de Vega."

"That was after her conversion to Catholicism," I said.

"I had a Vega once," said Clarence. "Run it into a bread truck."

"Okay, she was a weirdo," I said. "But she was my friend, Mom."

"Friend?" Mom said. "Weren't you engaged or something?"

"Sort of," I sighed.

"But I don't understand," said Mom. "How on earth will you find her?"

"I don't have a clue," I said.

"We had us a Clue game in Jefferson," said Clarence. He paused a beat. "But that old cat winkied on it."

"Call the paramedics," said Mom, pushing back from the table.

The conversation went like this for a time, strung somewhere between Oscar Wilde, Billy Graham, and Monty Python. Mom shot daggers at Clarence for his oafish table manners. Clarence told us about his struggle to figure out how many slices a loaf of bread had in Jesus's time and what kind of fish he'd served at the Sea of Galilee.

"My money's on catfish," said Clarence.

"Jesus Christ would not eat a catfish," hissed Clarice.

"He made it," said a shocked Clarence. "How come he wouldn't eat it?"

"Because catfish eat garbage," said my mother. "It would be like eating a vulture."

"Did you love her?" asked Ula suddenly.

"Yes, I did," I admitted. "But that was long ago and in another country."

"If you composed as often as you made literary allusions we'd all be rich and famous now," said Mom.

"Quoth the raven, 'Nevermore'," I said darkly.

"Ravens eat garbage," said Clarence.

"The world is full of garbage," said Mom. "Eating it should be no problem for some creatures. I think...I think...."

She stood slowly, and her fork fell to the floor. Her face turned crimson and she grasped at her chest.

"Clarice!" shouted Ula.

"Mom!" I yelled.

I caught her as she started to crumple to the floor, making bizarre choking sounds, her eyeballs fluttering, then turning up in her head. I laid her flat on the floor.

"Ula, call an ambulance!" I commanded. Mom grasped my hand and her eyes came back down.

"No....no...." she said weakly. "Let me die, here and now. Let me see with my own eyes how my son's about to waste his life by leaving a wonderful wife and running away to New York."

"Running away?" said Clarence.

"She's hallucinating," I said.

"Hannndddddd...the Law Gawd unh-made-a the fishes!" yelled Clarence, ready for his first eulogy. Mom sat bolt upright.

"Shut your damned mouth while I die!" she screamed. Unnerved, Clarence backed into a corner, mumbling. Mom lay back down. She coughed a couple of times, and by now I was beginning to doubt that anything really was wrong with her. "Son, if I live through this heart attack, I think you should come back and live with your poor mom and take care of her while she convalesces."

"You don't look all that sick to me," I said.

She coughed a couple of times and looked pitiful.

"I'm not a well woman, Ford," she said.

"Peace be unto ye, whore of Babylon," said Clarence helpfully from the corner.

At this point, a miracle occurred. My mother rose from the dead, began to fume and blow steam and rushed at Clarence, knocking down a chair and nearly toppling Ula, who retreated with her muttering into the next room.

"You dumb little squeaky-voice son of a bitch!" she screamed. She pushed him with amazing strength, and he fell over a chair and landed on his shoulder.

"I was just preaching, Aunt Clarice," he whined from the floor. "How come you did that?"

"You called me the whore of Babylon!" she yelled.

"I thought she was a good woman," he cried, trying to sit up. "Like Glenda in *The Wizard of Oz*."

"Ford," she yelled, turning to me, "go out into the backyard this minute and dig a grave under the chinaberry tree."

"Jesus!" screamed Clarence. He jumped up, brushed past her, went through the living room and out the front door. I ran at his heels, came into the twilight and saw him running off down the street holding a small, battered suitcase. I went back into the dining room, and Mom was eating chicken.

"Is he gone?" she asked.

"What happened to your heart attack?" I asked.

"I heal quickly, dear," she said. "It's a family trait."

I tried to summon something wise, but it wouldn't come. Instead, I ascended the stairs to my old room, went through the half-door into the attic and, in the faint light of the hanging bulb, gathered up the box of letters Mom had saved and brought them out under my arm. I came downstairs, getting out my keys, making sure their clank and jingle was audible.

"Leaving so soon?" asked Mom.

"Mom, you hinted something had happened to Ingrid," I said. "What did you mean by that?"

"Oh, it's nothing," she said. She seemed positively cheerful.

"I really want to know," I said.

"Oh, well, it's just that she's in the calaboose over in South Carolina somewhere for stabbing her third husband with a screwdriver," she said. "Sure you won't stay for more dinner?"

I brooded as I passed over the James River. If healing quickly was a Clayton family trait, you couldn't prove it by me.

"FORD CLAYTON, GET YOUR SORRY ASS OUT HERE!"

I was reading on the bed, going through a book called *Medieval and Renaissance Music*, when I heard her voice. It had been snowing all day, and since half the students lived off campus, all classes had been canceled by mid-afternoon. Ronny was at the desk we shared, furiously working on a piece for violin, viola, and piano.

"You hang out with the classiest chicks," Ronny said.

"Fuck you, Favors," I said with a grin. I got up and opened the frame window. Flakes of paint came off in my hands. Although it was not yet night, a deeply silent darkness had come with the snow. It was mid-January 1969, still our freshman year, and Camille was below me, wearing bell bottoms, a flaming red overcoat and a muffler with black and white checks. Her cheeks were stained from the cold, and her wine-colored lips were even darker than usual. Snowflakes blew into the room, ping-pong ball aggregates of dry flakes.

"Hey, Camille," I said. "How was your Christmas?"

"I'm an atheist," she yelled joyfully. "I don't celebrate myth. Would you celebrate the birthday of the Cyclops?"

"Probably not," I laughed.

"Come on, we're sculpting Mozart and Constanze out of snow over in front of the library," she said. "We need your discerning eye."

"Do you really think I have a discerning eye?" I asked.

"Goddamnit, you're a stubborn boy," she said. "Okay, no, you don't have a particularly discerning eye, but we need help making the piano."

"I'll be right down," I said.

"Well, hurry," she said. "I'm freezing my tits off out here."

"We don't want to throw the campus into mourning," I said.

She smiled, knelt gracefully and formed a snowball, and heaved it up toward me, missing by nearly ten feet. I ducked anyway, to make her feel better, then closed the window.

"Are you really going out there to make a snowman?" asked Ronny.

"You can stay in here and be the miserable artist for the both of us," I said. He shook his head and began making more marks on the music paper, working rapidly. I dressed in my own bell-bottoms, a Navy pea jacket, and a purple stocking cap. I came into the hall, passed a couple of guys who were using a long cardboard tube and a wad of paper as bat and ball. I ran down the flight of stairs into the marble-floored foyer and out the front door into a snowball that hit me square in the jaw. I spit snow for nearly thirty seconds and tried to keep the fluff from sliding down inside my shirt. Camille was leaning against a leafless oak, laughing, arms folded across her chest.

"I'm such a fool," I said. "Did you learn that in New Orleans, the Crossroads of the West?"

"I learned it in Gstaad," she said. "Have you ever been there?"

"I should have known," I said.

She came up to me, brushed the snow from my hat, and threaded her arm through mine, and we walked on the quiet sidewalks across the campus. The snow was nearly a foot deep now, and in truth I'd only seen four snows in my life in Jamesburg, the deepest two inches, and this was magical to me, Hollywood, holy, innocent.

"Don't you think Boulez makes Bernstein look like an idiot when it comes to composition?" she asked. "Don't you just love *Pli selon pli?*" Before I could answer (I didn't have a clue which was better) she had veered away from them completely. "It's like comparing Giotto and Cimabue."

"That was the first thing that came to my mind," I said.

"Oh shit," she said. "I'm behind on my harmony exercises. I might need some help later, Georgia."

"Okay," I said.

"Wasn't Kierkegaard the biggest asshole who ever lived?" she cried.

"I was thinking that just a day or so ago," I said. She stopped, reached inside her coat, and took out a cigarette and lit it, then grinned at me as she exhaled a small cloud.

"Georgia, you're cute," she said. She took off running, and I came up behind her as we rounded the Practice Hall and came in sight of the Library. Wolfgang and Constanze were there, looking more like Mr. and Mrs. Frosty except for some bizarre clothing in which they had been dressed. They were seven feet tall, and funny, and the piano before them, half finished, needed work. Probably ten boys and girls were there, screaming, laughing. When Camille walked up, they seemed to turn toward her for advice, and she gave it liberally, directing them (me included) in how a Steinway Grand really looks. We threw snowballs as we worked, sang Schubert lieder, choruses from opera, Simon and Garfunkel and Joan Baez. A pretty girl named Caroline, who was a fabulous alto, could not stop laughing because her nose was running like an open faucet. Our faces were all shades of pink and red.

"That's it, they're finished," yelled a boy named Burt, who was in my counterpoint class. "Everybody get the fuck out of the way and let's look at them."

"Yeah, get the fuck out of the way!" yelled Camille.

We moved back. We'd been there nearly an hour, and I felt numb with cold. The snow was more intense now, filling every corner of the world, softening shapes. Camille offered me a cigarette, and though my smoking was of the under-the-back-porch variety, I'd smoked often with Ingrid, who ate cigarettes for breakfast. The aroma of burning tobacco was marvelous. We fell silent as we watched.

The streetlamps on campus came on as we watched the Mozarts, and a pale glow was cast over them, and Camille took my hand. In a clear voice, Camille began to sing the "Ave Verum Corpus," and we all joined in. It might have been a freezing Vienna day in December 1791. The feeling that went through me like trembling shock was of deep pity for Mozart, for music, for us, for everything. And the others felt it, too; the place and the time was sacred.

The group became jolly again a minute later, started to scatter as the snow suddenly was so heavy we could barely see through it. I was standing in the gloom, feeling the intimacy of snow when I realized they were all straggling away. I wheeled around, looking for Camille, and saw her leaning against a thick beech tree, face serious, looking right at me.

"Let's go to the Chapel," she said. "I've got to get my hands on a piano." She stepped up to me and pushed my hair back.

"It's probably locked," I said. "Classes have been canceled and all."

"I will be your Iduna, Bragi," she whispered. "Come on." I did not know who Iduna or Bragi might be, but we walked rapidly together, step for step, holding hands, me sniffing from the cold, she humming. By the time we got to the back door of the Chapel, the snow was being whipped by a rising wind, and despite the campus lights, darkness had come to the North Carolina mountains. We tried the door, but it was locked.

"Oh well," I said.

"Screw this," she answered. "We're getting in." She ran ten feet to a small window that went down into the basement, pushed it hard with her foot, and it angled back, opened. She suddenly slid into the building as if it were a monstrous reptile that had swallowed her. I looked around, saw no one, and followed her.

We were in a cold and musty storage room. It was dark, but we could see from a street light near the window the ghostly shadows of music stands, ranks of folding chairs, boxes of decorations for Christmas, a box of conductor's batons.

"Come on," she whispered. She made her way across the room and opened a door. I was right behind her, ascending stairs into an anteroom before the stage. Then, suddenly, that fast, we were on the stage in the silent Chapel, the only sound our feet on the ancient, creaking boards as I walked with her to the piano. She sat, threw off her coat and her gloves, cracked her knuckles, and put her hands on the keys. I walked slowly around so I could see her lovely face, and her eyes were closed.

Her touch on the keyboard was profoundly personal, mannered but unintentionally so. When her emotions rose, she had to play, like a junkie needed a fix, and now, I felt a fatal yearning for her as she played. The sound, at first, barely escaped, as if the piano wanted only Camille to share the luxury of the music, but then it washed over me, and it was Rachmaninoff.

She played the eighteenth variation from the *Variations on a Theme of Paganini*, and I knew at that moment what I had suspected before, that I was mad for her. I would write great concertos for Camille Malone, and we would become legendary, each filling the other's strong needs. It was only after she had played for thirty minutes that I realized how cold the Chapel was and that the wind outside was nearly howling.

She played Chopin's *"Raindrop Prelude,"* and when she finished, she turned on the stool toward me, nearly in silhouette now, arose, came to me, and sat. We reached for each other, held on, face to face, and then she slid forward, pulled me close, and for the first time since I'd met her the September before, Camille kissed me. She was not only a virtuoso on her instrument; she was born for this, too. It lasted for perhaps thirty seconds, seemed like days. I was immediately bursting with passion, sure I would die if I could not enter her whole, but then something entirely unexpected happened, which, I came to know, marked Camille more than anything. When the kiss broke, and we sat on the quiet stage, faces an inch apart, I was ready to make wild professions of love, to pledge my life to her, even though I barely knew her. I was not ready when she began to cry.

"Georgia, I'm so afraid," she said in a choked whisper. "I'm so, so afraid." She put her face on my shoulder and wept. I stroked her hair.

"It's all right," I said. "It was just a kiss."

"Not that," her voice said behind my neck. "I'm afraid of love."

"I think I love you," I blurted. She leaned back as if she'd touched a hot stove.

"No, no, no," she said. "Goddamnit, why'd you have to say that?"

"You're beautiful," I said. "You're wonderful. I need you, Camille."

"Jesus, Ford," she cried, "it's not that easy! Every kiss always has to be de profundis or everybody wants to die. It's just a thing, a moment. Everybody wants a utopia, this damned Erewhon where everything makes sense, only the world doesn't make sense. Viet Nam doesn't make sense, Nixon doesn't make sense, Abbie Hoffman doesn't make sense, Allen Ginsberg doesn't make sense. Everybody thinks in order to know something you have to hold it."

"I'm sorry," I said softly. "Please let me kiss you again."

"What would that prove?" she said. "Now you're trying to hold me. I just wanted to kiss you."

"Camille, you're getting a little hysterical," I said unhappily.

"Hys...Georgia, you've seen too much TV," she said. She rushed at me, fell noisily to the floor, kissed me once more, then jumped up and disappeared off the edge of the stage. I wanted to rush after her or kick myself or mate with anything female and breathing, but I merely sat on the cold stage, somehow thinking she'd return, then finding she clearly wasn't. After fifteen minutes, I softly called her name, and heard nothing but the sound of wind and snowflakes outside.

Shamed, I got up and went back into the basement and found the window open where we'd come in. Snow was blowing in, settling over the dark shadows of music stands. A chair had been pushed in front of the window, and in the center of it was a footprint, steadily disappearing under the snow.

I climbed back out and walked through the deepening white, wondering why she'd run from me. Later, when I got to know her better, got to know both that kiss and the way she made love, I knew why she did not care for anything that could possess her, that she was wind-blown, witchy even, impatient, and always in motion mentally and physically.

Back past the Library, I saw that Mozart and Constanze had already lost their outlines to the snow. The piano was a hump, nothing more. When I got back to the room, Ronny Favors was still working on his trio, and two boys next door had become so drunk they were staggering toward the bathroom. It was not much past seven.

"You look frozen," said Ronny. "What in the hell you been doing, Clayton? Did your thing fall off trying to bop that chick out in the snow?"

"We made a snowman," I said. "Snowmen. Wolfgang and Constanze."

"Well, that's erudite for a Conservatory," he said. "I'd have made Mahler."

"Yeah," I said. I picked up a half-open bag of potato chips from the desk and sat heavily in the chair, my shoes dripping. "Ronny, you ever think about what is life and what is art?"

"Is this the night for a deep discussion?" he said. "It's just as well. I'm done on this for tonight, anyway." He thrust his manuscript into a large brown folder and walked to the window and looked out. "You think it's ever gonna quit this shit?"

"I like it," I said. "Are you going to eat?"

"I already did, while you guys were out freezing your rears off," he said. "The dining hall closed at seven, too. I think you've left yourself only the vending machines in the basement."

"Fuck it, I'm not hungry anyway," I said.

"So did you see your hometown girl at Christmas, or what? You seemed mighty glad to see that girl beneath the window."

"I told you Ingrid and I broke up," I said. "She told me that she wanted a silver pattern and china and crystal and shit like that."

"What did you tell her?"

"I said I wanted to write *Die Meistersinger*," I said. "And she asked me what in the hell that was, and when I told her, she started laughing. She said it was just fat ladies screeching."

"A critic," he said.

I ate a few chips.

"Okay, to answer your question, I'd say Ingrid is life and the girl beneath the window is art. Is that close enough?"

"You're such a shit," I said. "I mean, what do you really want to do with your life, Ronny? When do you find out how good you're going to be? What if there's only one of us in the whole McCandless class of '72 who's supposed to be a great composer? Then what?"

"Clayton, only tight-assed little morons think such thoughts," he said. "We're supposed to be here learning about the mysteries of snatch."

"But wouldn't it kill you if you turned out not to be the one?" I asked seriously. His laughter was deep and genuine.

"You must have a strange family if you worry about whether you'll be a great man," he said. "Look, Clayton, that just happens. Either you have it, or you don't."

The door suddenly burst open, and Charley Barstow and Ed Jacklin, who lived next door, came storming in talking at once, both stir crazy.

"We're going over to Mary Grandville and have a panty raid," said Charley. "Ronny, get your thin ass in gear. Ford, you're dripping all over the floor of ancient and honored Tarmot Hall."

"Yeah!" yelled Ronny, and he slid into his heavy coat and followed them out. I fully intended to follow them, but instead I sat for a long time thinking about Ingrid and Camille, about sex and fame. Who was Kierkegaard and why did Camille think he was an asshole? I was on top of the world in Jamesburg, honored by my high school class, and here I was painfully limited. Should I be grateful for Camille's kiss, or should I rip my flesh apart in hope of another one?

The steam pipes clanked. I walked to the window, saw dozens of boys in a snowbound caravan laughing and heading toward the girls' dorm, falling, throwing snowballs, full of anything but art. Maybe I should have stayed with Ingrid and "practiced" baby-making.

The top floor of Tarmot had a study, and I was sure no one was there, so I got a pencil and notebook and walked up two flights. I was right, of course; no one was studying in a snowstorm. I went inside and sat at a table near the window where the thin arc of a streetlight was cast inside the room. I wrote a poem about my confusion, dreamed that I was like the dying Schubert doomed and world-weary. That was what separated me from them, that was why I would be the single member of our class to approach greatness: the mystery and romance, the ring and the book, the castle and the round table.

Three days later, I came into our room and found Ronny laughing convulsively as he read my poem. To my shame, I said nothing, did nothing but retreat, believing with all my heart that when the single genius from among us was named, I might not be on stage, but I wouldn't be far away.

THE PHONE RANG. I WAS SITTING AT MY DESK, trying to get ready for my musicology class, trying to catch up for a lost day, watching the new genii flow past the McCandless campus beneath my window.

"Ford Clayton," I said. Lately I'd been answering the phone as if I expected a call from the governor rejecting a stay of execution.

"Hi, Ford," a man's voice said. "I tried to call you yesterday, but you were out."

"Oh, hi, Ricardo," I said, relieved it wasn't the governor. "I had to go down to Georgia. There's trouble in Jamesburg."

"Sounds like a Rory Calhoun movie," he said. I could hear him oomphing and puffing on his Latakia. "Nothing serious, I hope."

"It involved my mom," I said.

"Oh," he said. "Look, I was calling about our appointment tomorrow. I don't think I'm going to be able to make it. Luanne and I have been invited to a wine tasting at the Biltmore House."

"Next thing, you'll be dining with the Quayles," I said.

"Are you in crisis or anything?" he said. Before I could answer, he turned away and gave some kind of lengthy instructions to his secretary regarding the proper number of scoops needed for his coffee. "What was that? Are you in crisis?"

"I'm in confusion," I said. "Besides, if I can wrangle it, I may be leaving town for a spell."

"Leaving town for a spell?" he said. "You're being cryptic,

Ford. Does this involve Jill?"

"It involves Camille," I said.

"Hmmmmm," he said. I had told him about her, but he obviously didn't remember. "Hmmmmm" was always one of his delaying tactics. He was probably confusing her with Starr; I didn't seem to care.

"So I'll call you when I get back to town, if I leave," I said. "If I don't leave, I'll call you when you get back from the Biltmore House, unless you decide to go on a tour of Burgundy and other wine-producing areas."

"You have a great deal of hostility," he said truthfully. "I'd be glad to drop by for fifteen minutes on the way to the wine tasting, if that'd help."

"Ricardo, fifteen years would probably not help," I said. "Look, I'll get back to you. Who knows, maybe my opera will be so successful I'll *buy* the Biltmore House."

"Is your opera almost finished?" he asked.

"Give or take a lifetime," I said. "I'll see you soon."

"See you, Ford," he said.

I hung up. My jaws were working, grinding. I had to meet with Edgar Fuller, the head of the Musicology Department, about my trip to New York. Camille could have launched into one of her explosive analogies about Sisyphus if she were here.

The phone rang once more. Miranda Terrell waddled past, leaned in as I watched the ringing phone and winked at me. She lumbered off.

"Yes," I said softly.

"Ford, it's Thom Brackett," he said jauntily.

I put my hand over the receiver and said "shit" in a loud voice, just as a female student known as the Madonna of Musicology among a few of us wandered past. Her real name was Irene, and she was president of Musicologists for Jesus, a small but fervently vocal group on campus. She glanced at me with forgiveness and pity; I wanted to wave my arms over my head at her, say something devilish. But Irene merely disappeared. I knew she'd be praying for me, which I probably needed.

"Hi, Thom," I said, pronouncing it "Tom" instead of "Thom"

as penitence for having sworn in front of the Madonna. "Has Jill decided to leave me the matchbook collection or is that all up in smoke now, too?"

"Ford, your sense of humor is inappropriate to your situation," he said. "A man facing the loss of everything should be more reasonable."

"I ran out of reasonable last week," I said, "and I'm nearly at bottom on pleasant. What can I do for you?"

"You should call Jill in Macon," he said. "She has agreed to give you a month."

"She has?" I said.

"She has," he said sternly. "I must tell you that you should take this as a temporary reprieve, though."

"Like a phone call from the governor?" I asked.

"Really, Ford," Thom said. "The papers are ready to file, and when she gives me the word, they'll be in court the same day. I'd be looking for an apartment if I were you. Something small, with one bedroom and an electric blanket."

"I get the point," I said. "I'll call her today, Thom. Thanks for being such a genuine lawyer about this."

"You shouldn't needle me, Ford," he said. "I tried to convince her to file last week. We have all that info about you and Miss Starr Coventry."

"Thanks once more for your precise information, Thom," I said. I pronounced it "Thom." He snorted slightly, like a petulant bull. "I'll call Jill and get back to you."

"Don't call back tomorrow," he said. "Lainie and I are going to a wine tasting at the Biltmore House."

"Ack," I said.

"I beg your pardon?"

"Nothing," I said. "Thanks, Thom. I'll call Jill. Hope the wine is bold yet restrained."

"Amazing," said Thom.

"Ack," I repeated, but he'd hung up on me, which was proper from his point of view. Thom had once been nothing but an ambulance chaser, hounding morgues and funerals looking for work, but he'd hit the big time a few years back with an out-of-court class action settlement in a wrongful injury suit. When he became rich, he became respectable, joined the country club, and began to hobnob with legitimate blue-stockinged barristers.

But I had no emotions to spare on Thom. Instead, I turned to Jill.

I had met her when I was twenty-six, already back to teach at McCandless after getting my Ph.D. at Columbia. She was a student at Crayton County College, twenty miles away, came to my campus one weekend with a friend. She was a senior, four years behind me in school, and I was struggling through the loss of Camille, whose wanderings had already taken her to Europe for a second time. We started dating almost immediately, and she took me home to Macon to meet her parents and younger sister, Jenny. Her dad was fat. He had a W. C. Fields nose and huge breasts that waved at you when he walked. Her mother was a saint. She was sweet, silent, and patient, which was Jill to a T. Jenny, on the other hand, was wild, unstable, and had already had an abortion. Mr. Maple owned a men's clothing store downtown, and the former governor of Georgia, Eugene Talmadge, bought suits from him. That had been forty years before, but Mr. Maple still talked about "The Gov'ner" as if the man, long dead, were the guiding spirit of the business, which, truthfully, was barely still making money. I saw his stock once or twice, and it was years out of style. I knew something of haberdashery, having worked at Gallant-Belk, so he liked me immediately. Mrs. Maple, Jill's mom, approved of everything. If anybody did anything, there must be a reason, she said. She forgave all manner of madness. She had arranged for Jenny's abortion, was sad about it but nothing more. Mr. Maple, of course, never knew. During our marriage, both finally died, he to a massive heart attack and she to cancer of the uterus which she refused to have treated. She had converted to Christian Science late in life.

I meditated on them as I dialed Jenny's house in Macon. A tiny, elfin voice said hello. It was Jenny's son, Arnie, who was seven.

"Arnie, it's Uncle Ford," I said cheerfully. "Is your Aunt Jill there, please?"

"Yes," he said, not leaving the phone.

"Would you get her please?" I begged.

"Yes," he said. "One moment, please."

Well, at least the kid had phone manners. Camille never had phone manners. You'd pick up the receiver, and she'd start yelling into it without a salutation of any kind. I stared at the large box of letters I'd brought back from Jamesburg as I waited for Jill to come to the phone.

"Hi," Jill's voice said. It was soft.

"Hi, Honey," I said. "How are things in Macon?"

"The same," she said. "I'm starting my new job tomorrow at Macon College. It's been busy."

"I bet," I said. "How are Jenny and Bobby and their kids?"

"Jenny and Bobby aren't doing too swell, but the kids are great," she said.

"What's the problem?"

"Bobby's a jerk," she said.

"What's new about that?" I asked. "This is the same man who still listens to *Frampton Comes Alive!* all the time, isn't it?"

"I gave you the thirty days, Ford," she said. "Were you calling about something else? Can I bring Kathy and Jay up next weekend?"

"No, no," I cried, "you can't do that. I've got to go to New York on business. I'm not sure how long I'm going to be there."

"What's in New York?" she asked.

"Business," I said.

"Hmmmmm," she said.

"You're sounding like Ricardo, for God's sake," I said.

"Well, it's a relief to me," she said. "I didn't want to come up there, anyway. Call me when you get back and tell me how business was."

"Jill, about the thirty days," I said. "You do know that I love you."

"You really hurt me," she said.

"I'm trying to find where I diverged from my true calling in life," I said. "It's the middle of my life, Jill, and I'm very lost now. I'm on this spiritual odyssey."

"Well, your priest was a redhead, darling," she said impatiently. That stung. Jill's barbs were nothing if not accurate.

"I deserved that," I said. "But in thirty days, I'll try to be able to see things straight. Jill, let me ask you something. If I've got it clear, find out where I went wrong, would you take me back? I miss you and the kids."

"You've really hurt me, Ford. I'll never go through this again."

"I understand," I said. "And if in thirty days I can't see this all clearly, I'll call Thom and tell him to file away. I'll move into a cave and eat roots and berries."

"I don't want it all," she said. "I never wanted you to suffer."

"Mankind is made for suffering," I said. "Mom used to tell me that when she was in the throes of Puccini."

"How are your folks doing?" Jill asked. I didn't want to go through the trip to Jamesburg, nor did I want to tell her of the box of letters. I fumbled for a word, instead reached for the box, pulled out the first letter on top and it was from Camille, postmarked 1974. I did not open it.

"Fine, fine," I said. "Look, as soon as I get back from New York, I want Kathy and Jay to come up. Are they at school?"

"Yeah," she said. "Arnie's home with a cold. Just call me."

"And me?" I said.

"I do want you to be happy, Honey, but I'll never go through anything like this again," she said. "Do you understand that?"

"Philosophically, emotionally, religiously, and so forth," I said. "I miss you, darling. I really do."

"I've got to go now," she said. "Hope your trip is successful."

"Bye now," I said, and she said goodbye, and suddenly I was alone once more. I glanced at my watch and it was five after ten, five minutes past my appointment with Edgar Fuller, a man who did not take time lightly. I cursed, threw the letter back into the box and ran into the hall.

Edgar's office was down the hall on the left, past Miranda's. He was only thirty-six, author of seven books, Ph.D. from Yale, and the possessor of a fastidious nature that was irritating and alien to me. Fastidious was an understatement; he actually dressed and acted like a pimp, always in natty suits and shirts, pinned up ties, razor-trimmed hair, shoes so shiny you could shave looking into them. I looked into his office, and his dour secretary, Sigurd Mathias, was glancing at her watch and arching her eyebrows at me.

"One more minute, and I was canceling," she said. Her outer office was filled with her disorganized desk, a computer and, along the walls, rows of dissertations not opened since they were approved. Sigurd was fiftyish, with an astonishing build: a broad, heavy head with streaky gray hair, flat nose and wide-spaced green eyes, a slender, breastless chest atop a torso flaring to hips so ponderous she looked like a moving sea vessel. When she got up and walked to Edgar's door and tapped on it gently, I watched the mismatched ensemble of her body with amazement.

"Dr. Clayton is *finally* here," she said disgustedly. I heard Edgar mumble something, and Sigurd backed away grudgingly. She certainly did protect Edgar. I went in. She lumbered back to her desk. Her hips were the width of Rhode Island. Her neck looked like a comma in a sentence she might be typing. Edgar, on the other hand, looked like a plate from *Vanity Fair*. He was sitting behind his executive-size desk, whose surface was immaculate except for a coffee cup with a picture of Bach on the side.

"Ford," he said. He reached out for my hand without rising, and I struggled around his desk and shook his long fingers. You shook Edgar's fingers; he would give you no more. I sat in the chair next to his desk and glanced once around the room. His bookcases were only half full, the rest given over to his collection of unicorns, which he'd bought all over the world. There were marbled unicorns, Delft unicorns, stone ones, dark wooden ones from Zaire, a zinc one from Greece, an abstract one he'd bought in Paris, unicorns everywhere. Miranda had once confided in me that she thought this collection was a compensation for what was probably an undersized male member on our department head, and though I laughed it off, I'd mentioned it to Ricardo, who only mumbled, but I think he agreed. In addition to the unicorns, the room had a sofa and a table in front of it with a neatly stacked collection of Bach scores. He drank coffee from Tanganyika that he made Sigurd grind fresh each morning. He wore a pinky ring with a large sapphire.

"Edgar," I said.

"Now," he said, "what can I do for you?" His tie looked as if it had been pressed in the past eight minutes or so.

"Edgar, I've got to go to New York," I blurted.

"For the weekend?"

"For as long as it takes to get some business transacted," I said. I thought about Camille, about how it would sound. Jill's departure was the subject of gossip among the faculty, but administrators tended to look at what kind of role model I was, and I knew they didn't think much of me in that regard.

"And what kind of business might that be?" he asked grandly. He cocked his head with phony attentiveness and tented his fingers. No, I couldn't tell him about Camille or about my meditations or soul searching. I decided all this in three seconds, having planned when I came in merely to tell the truth. But truth is overrated. So I lied.

"There's a chance that the New York City Opera might stage *East of Eden*," I said, choking on the lie. The impact of my words was unexpected; they buoyed me, made me feel as if there was a small chance that they *just might be true*. Edgar looked genuinely pleased.

"Well, for God's sake, Ford!" he cried. "That's wonderful! When did you find out?"

"Well, only recently....uh, Tuesday, I think," I said.

"I didn't even know you'd finished it," he said. Finished it? Finished it? Of course I haven't finished it, you sleazy putz, I've never finished anything, never finished my relationship with Camille, never told my father I loved him, never made Jill feel truly loved.

"Just about," I said. "Only have a little work on the overture."

"Well, for God's sake," he said.

"But it's my courses," I said. "Do you think you could...."

"I'll get a grad student to cover," he said. "What do you need three, four days?"

"Well, it could be more like a week," I said.

"We could handle that," he said. "The New York City Opera! Just imagine that, Ford!"

I briefly imagined it. My name in lights, slickly printed on the program, then the adulatory reviews, raves really, comparing me to, say Berg, maybe hinting that this was the finest opera since *Wozzeck*. A standing O. Endless parties. Being lionized. *Interview* magazine with my face on the cover.

....then I was back at fifteen suddenly, staring, if not drooling, into the past, seeing the premieres of my symphonies, chamber works, song cycles, my name famous; then, in hoary old age, my hometown unveiling a statue of my head, and finding a solid twenty-page chunk on me in Grove's and....

"Ford, are you all right?" he asked.

"Sorry," I said, jolted from my youth, from the stage to the realization that the opera was halfway through the first act and only in piano score. "Anyway, how about it?"

"Okay," he said. "But no more than a week."

"Fair enough," I said.

"Are they scheduling it for next season?" he asked. The truth suddenly seemed at hand. But no.

"Probably," I said.

I stumbled back out of his office, and Sigurd was typing like a three-toed sloth, poking suspiciously at the keyboard of her computer as if she were trying to squash ants. I went back into the hall, started to feel an anxiety attack might be imminent. I went into my office and closed the door.

I reached out for a letter from the box I'd brought from Jamesburg, took it from its envelope, started to read, felt the world slowing down around me, my breath coming back.

Friday night

Dear Shithead,

If you had been more like Il Furioso than Clarabelle, you'd be sharing London with me tonight. I went to see 'Tis a Pity She's a Whore' at a small theatre near Covent Garden. Wretched mess. Oh, my Theban seer, why have you left me so bereft?

I began to chuckle at this point, and my attack of nerves eased considerably.

How right Rozanov was! The center of humanity is sexuality, but sex is usually like stomping a butterfly......wait....did you ever read Rudin, by Turgenev, or were you the fool who told me he'd never read the Russians? That's you, a hero without a war or a cause. You can dream but not act. I told you as much in New York.

I was willing to play Countess Guiccioli to your Byron, but you wanted to play Edgar A. Guest to my Abigail Van Buren. All right, all right, perhaps that is too harsh. But not far off.

Camille, you moron. You overeducated moron.

Let me make one thing clear: I am no Cephalus, and you ain't no Procris. Go read "Lycidas" again, Darling, and send me your report. After tomorrow it's on to Lutetia (Marginalia from me: antique name for Paris from Lutetia Parisorum [the mud town of the Parisii, which is what Caesar called it]) where I play for the first time the Prokofiev 'Toccata,' a dumb, empty piece I know the Frogs will adore.

I am going to see Proust's home. You should be so lucky.

Your wife,
Camille von der Malone

My vision was restored. I laughed at her. I wanted to see her, to rescue her like a Byronic hero, come dashing back south with her. I felt strong and happy. I didn't worry about Edgar Fuller.

Suddenly, the door burst open, and someone terribly familiar came strutting in the office, with a grin that told me he was thrilled to be here. I had a heart attack. Maybe this one was real.

"Hallelujah!" yelled my cousin Clarence Clayton. "I once was lost, but now I'm found, was blind, but now I see!"

CAMILLE ESTABLISHED THE MALONE SOCIETY in the early spring of 1969. She wrote a flyer, had it printed at her own expense, asking that anyone interested in a "Philosophico-Musico-Politico Discussion Group" should meet at the Student Center at 8 p.m. on a certain friday night. I was not at all sure I had the barest interest in politics or philosophy, but I felt I could hold my own in the "musico" part, and so I went to the organizational meeting.

They were in the corner, eight of them, Camille standing in front, lecturing. I was late. I'd taken a nap after a brass methods class and didn't get there until nearly eight-thirty. They'd pulled chairs around her, and she was standing there, face flushed from excitement, while the others, the men bearded and long-haired, the women with waterfalls of straight hair parted in the middle, listened appreciatively. I sat down, and they all stared at me unpleasantly. I was clean-shaven, uncool.

"If you're going to meet with us, Georgia, you'll arrive on time," Camille said. She glared at me. I smiled and nodded. I recognized a couple of the kids, but most of them were strangers. They were all intense, on the edge, ready for verbal brawling with each other. Camille was talking about music.

"And I think one of the first orders of the Malone Society is to list which composers are not worthy of our study," she said. "And for beginners, I'd like to nominate that charlatan of the puerile, Fred Chopin." There were a few knowing chuckles and nods. Clearly, this was a group looking for a hero. I loved Chopin, but I wasn't about to argue with her. "And, and, then there's that old fart Haydn, who was, let's face it, nothing but a servant." This was marginally more controversial, but no one said anything. "And then you got, like that political miscreant Dmitri Shostakovitch." A small flicker became a flame inside my musical heart: I'd always loved the *Fifth* and *Seventh* Symphonies.

"What's wrong with him?" I said. They all turned to me, speechless. Camille's face reddened, then she smiled indulgently. She was obviously dealing with a child here, and she wanted to be patient.

"Bobby, tell him what's wrong with the Big S," she said. Bobby, who looked like an uncooked stick of vermicelli with a wispy Ho Chi Minh beard, raised one eyebrow.

"He's a bourgeois functionary," he said. "A toady for conservatism. He's never explored music. While Penderecki was moving into new areas, Dmitri was madly retreading old ground."

"Splendid," said Camille. "Did you get all that, Ford?"

"I got it," I said. "I just think it's horseshit."

The Malone Society was not off to a good start. Once in high school, my friend Waco Putnam and I started a discussion group, and we'd usually head out on a subject like "What is art?" and wind up in a detailed analysis of which girls had the most impressive chests. It takes a dedicated zealot to run an intellectual group named after oneself, and Camille was nothing if not dedicated.

"I am placing you under the restriction of silence," said Camille.

"Right on," said a girl who hadn't smiled since cars had fins.

"The what?" I said.

"As president and founder of the Malone Society, I sentence you to silence for the remainder of this meeting. Is that clear?" she said.

I was dumbfounded. This was like a cell meeting in 1917. My face got hot. The others stared at me. I found later that Camille attracted oddballs like a sock attracts lint, a fact that did little for my own unformed sense of self-esteem. The truth was that after two quarters at McCandless, I was beginning to know how desperately far behind I was.

"Sure," I choked.

"Now, as to who else is not worth our discussion," said Bobby. "Please continue." Bobby clearly adored her. In fact all the girls and boys there adored her.

"Yes," she said. "We will not discuss Nicholas of Cusa, who was a bargain-basement Copernicus. Leibnitz and his freaking Great Chain of Being are out. Rachmaninoff, Scriabin, Aaron Copland, and Verdi are all off limits." One of the girls, a glandular marvel who was nearly six feet tall and weighed well over two hundred, was furiously taking notes. "Robert Traill Spense Lowell, Jr., is hopeless. Not a word about Koster Palamas, unless you feel strongly about O tafos, but certainly not Tragoudia tes patridos mou." No one there knew what she was saying any more than I did, but none of them let on; I alone looked at Bobby and mouthed the word "what?" soundlessly, but he merely looked away from me. The fat girl was nodding vigorously. "We will vomit, as a group, when anyone mentions Carlyle or Sartor Resartus." Chuckles all around. "Pierrot is fine, since Schönberg used him, but anything from bunraku is out. I'm the only gidayu for the Malone Society. Fichte is a god, and will be fine for our discussion, but Kierkegaard was a freaking fool, and he's out. We can discuss Mondrian and Camus, but Gauguin and D'Annunzio are out. Any questions so far?"

Well, yes, Camille. What kind of childhood led you to spend your life becoming an encyclopedia of intellectualism? Where was the hopscotch and tea parties and strolls in the park with your daddy and going to see movies and Roy Rogers and Dale Evans and Rocky and Bullwinkle? I was silent like the rest of them, because she played with nouns and verbs with the same brilliance that she played the keyboard. Years later, I asked Camille what in the world inspired her to form the Malone Society, which, in its time became quite famous, and she merely shrugged and said, completely in character, "I was bored."

She went on. The forbiddens: German romanticism, the I ching, Captain Marryat, Duns Scotus, Buffalo Bill, Jean Arp, Petrarch (a fool because he was obsessed with Laura), William Howard Taft (a tub of blubber and therefore without discipline or spirit), the Waverly novels, Oliver Goldsmith.....she went on for nearly ten minutes, raving and ranting, but looking more and more beautiful, like a preacher in the throes of the spirit. Camille caressed even what she claimed to despise. The areas acceptable for discussion: Bach, Beethoven (except *Fidelio*), Stravinsky, Schönberg (naturally), the Irish Renaissance and Yeats, Swift, Conrad, Franklin Roosevelt, Marcuse, Franz Fanon, Huey Newton and Bobby Seale, Malcolm X but not Martin Luther King (and this was less than a year after he was killed; to Camille, Martin was simply "not interesting"), New Wave cinema and anyone believing in the *auteur* theory, Ezra Pound, John Berryman, Arthurian legend, Voltaire, Strindberg, Ibsen....

I sat, dazzled in the light of her restless and confused mind. Even the fat girl had quit taking notes. No one expected this, that one pretty girl, already gaining fame as the best piano student on campus, could know this much, could with such force lay bare how ignorant the rest of us were. The very idea of having defended Shostakovitch evaporated from me. When she finished her rant, she gave us each a sheet with topics for our weekly discussions. She wanted us to vote, even though the Malone Society was carefully despotic. I still have the list, having saved it as an icon of my college days. It was:

1. *Flood myths and how they affected French literature*
2. *Erasmus and Marcuse*
3. *The Lie of Tchaikovsky's talent*
4. *Symbolism in* The 400 Blows
5. *Structure in* Moses und Aaron
6. *Black Power and the rondel (An exercise in creative thinking)*
7. *A comparison of Chinua Achebe and Eugene O'Neill*
8. *Bonnie and Clyde and Paolo and Francesca*
9. *Hermann Hesse's* Demian *and good and evil*
10. *Nietzsche seen as an explorer of power*

I read the list, and I was afraid. The others looked over it and made knowing comments about the purpose and the intellectual acumen of the Malone Society. We voted to start, on sequential weeks with three, four, and ten, and Camille thanked us and said the order would be seven, nine, and three, which everyone agreed was a far better choice.

Later, when the others were all gone, I hung around in the corner, waiting for her to gather her papers. She was hard not to notice. Her fingers were long and slender, her eyes bright. She glanced up as she was leaving and came toward me with a wave and a smile.

"Hey, Georgia, what did you think?" she asked.

"I was just wondering how your holidays were, if you went to the beach or anything," I said. "I wasn't going to ask about the Great Chain of Being or Shostakovitch."

"Intelligence is command," she said. "You're just too small-town to be believed sometimes, Georgia."

"My name's not Georgia," I said coldly. "And I thought you felt something for me. That night in the snow. That was special to me, and you ran off and left me." I'd seen her around, but we hadn't really talked since then. Now I felt a righteous anger. We walked outside.

Asheville was blossoming into spring, one of the world's loveliest cities that time of year. Because of its altitude, spring comes late, but when it breaks up from the warming soil, the town is all flowering shrubs, bulbs, and aching green. Thomas Wolfe ran away but never really left, and Zelda Fitzgerald came here to go nuts while Scott was writing the "Crack Up" articles for *Esquire*. It was nearly ten and the street lamps illuminated lovers on park benches, hippies throwing Frisbees, early season laughter from the dorms. And, as always, from the hidden corners of the campus, music, as rote as scales, as glorious as Bach.

"Ford," she said softly. "I'm sorry about that night. It was just that snow always makes me revisit the losses I've suffered. Something about purity and childhood. You know, 'Backward, turn backward, O time in your flight, make me a child again, just for tonight.' That kind of thing."

"What's the poem?"

"Something my father used to say," she said quietly.

"Can I carry your stuff?" I said.

"I'm a feminist," she said. "That's an insulting thing for a man to say to a feminist."

"When'd you become a feminist?" I asked.

"I am all things as a woman," she said, as if repeating a line she'd practiced in front of a mirror. We were heading for her dorm.

"But back to that kiss, Camille," I said desperately. "I mean it was something really, uh....I mean it was, uh...."

"Cat got your tongue, Georgia?" she asked with a fruity laugh. "I can give a kiss, can't I?"

"I'd sure like another one sometime!" I heard myself say. I felt like an idiot. She merely laughed again.

"What would I get out of it?" We were nearly to her dorm.

"Memories of having kissed a man who would later be incredibly famous," I said.

"*I'm* going to be famous, Georgia," she said. She turned and came close to me. I could smell her breath, cigarettes and a breath mint.

"What if I promised never to discuss James Fenimore Cooper or something?" I asked. We had stopped out of the light next to a willow tree that danced in the breeze. Fronds dipped at us, moved back and forth like a hula dancer.

"He was an idiot," she said. "Tell me, what makes you want to kiss me again?"

Brother, she was pushing it now, begging me for a compliment, possibly in hopes that I'd weasel along. I was all set to do that, to pay homage to her eyes, her hair, her intelligence, and general beauty. Instead, I did something completely out of character. I took her papers from her forcibly like a Hun or a Visigoth, threw them on the ground, and grabbed her arm, pulled her to me. Our noses were almost touching. I looked at Camille fiercely and saw that she had closed her eyes, was trembling slightly, waiting for my touch. We kissed. Her fingers tangled in my hair, wove invisible patterns. Her lips were soft and wet, her tongue explored me, tasting my own tongue, my teeth, my gums, licking my lips, breaking once to lick the sensitive inside of my ear, then kissing me again powerfully. She began to push me gently backward out of the light, behind a large row of prolific forsythia, through a clump of hyacinths. I caught a pungent whiff of the flowers. We came into a patch of

sweet, gentle grass, and we sat down in it, still kissing. Her breathing was labored. I could not breathe. I gasped. I could not believe
I had leaped upon her or that it had seared her imagination with
such heat. I was a brigand, and this feminist who hated everything
was clearly furious for my touch. She wanted to be carried away,
ravished, watch me swing from mizzenmasts; she did not want me
to talk about Aristotle or Kant. She took off her light jacket and
laid it on the grass, and we lay upon it, and as we kissed once more,
her hands explored my chest, then came around my hips, back
between them as far as she could reach.

I pushed her back slightly and began to unbutton her shirt.
She was willing. As a feminist, of course she wore no bra, and soon
I had divided the light from the darkness, the cloth from the flesh,
pushed the shirt halves back and was staring, with appropriate
adulation and groans, at her small but perfect breasts, each topped
with a plump nipple that rose and fell with her breath. We were on
the sea, rising and falling with our unmatched breathing. I thought
this would be it, that heavy petting would be the end, that in a
moment we would both feel sheepish, but of course I underesti-
mated the fabulous Camille. She pushed me back slightly. She was
making noises from another language, perhaps another species.
She reached down between us, loosened my belt, unzipped my
pants, and then with irresistible strength pulled my jeans and
underwear down. The cool air was shocking, but nothing mattered.
The Good Side of Ford Clayton briefly considered the fact that
being caught might mean expulsion from McCandless, but flesh
instantly won over philosophy when she got to her knees and
repeated the unbuttoning and unzipping. I stared with disbelief in
the shadows at the dark triangle between her legs.

At first, I was discreet. I tried to muffle my animal whines. I
kept thinking, *I can't believe this is happening.* But there was no
doubt. *Camille Malone and I were doing it in the bushes.*

As with all religious experiences, this one did not last long.
Camille was going through her impressive array of oaths, swearing
and breathing into my ear. Her breasts felt hot pressing into my
chest. We were liquid fire. Camille, I apologized, I'm going to....and
then, I did. Luckily, she did as well, though unluckily, she decided

it was all right to scream. We were still moving as she yelled, and I brought one hand up to her mouth, and she bit my hand with her perfect teeth. I gasped, looked down at the plum-colored lips on my pale hand. That image has lingered.

It was not my first love-making, but it might have been. I have never again felt that gasping fear of discovery mixed with ecstasy. Slowly, Camille and I began to feel like humans again, and her teeth relaxed against my palm, and she looked at me with tear-blurred eyes. Two guys walked past just on the other side of the hedge, laughing and talking about nothing in particular. We held each other tight for the silence. They left, and we rolled away, dressed silently, looking around for hidden voyeurs, then we walked, hand in hand, in silence for a time after she had gathered up all the papers of the Malone Society.

I did not make love to Camille for another eighteen months, though much later she referred to our night in the bushes as an experience not of sexuality but of religion and, perhaps, her first glimmer that Catholicism held what she needed as a human.

Still, the memory of that night easily lasted eighteen months, has lasted eighteen years.

I took Camille to her dorm, kissed her deeply that night and wandered back toward Tarmot Hall, renewed as you always are after love. I felt mature, manly, in touch with the spirits of composers past. Ronny was gone, I didn't know where. He drank heavily that spring, had two girlfriends at once. The dorm was quiet. I took out a sheaf of manuscript paper, made a cup of coffee with my single-cup brewer, and wrote the apotheosis in music of my encounter with Venus.

I was a Romanticist, the heir to Mahler, even Rachmaninoff, perhaps, more legitimately, Samuel Barber. So I wrote at the top of the paper *An Adoration for Strings* and subtitled it "For an Angel." In the upper right hand corners I wrote "Ford Clayton, 1950- ."

I stayed up half the night, sketching out the work, which I still have. It sounds suspiciously like Barber's *Adagio for Strings*, though a version written by a high school piano student. The faculty quartet here read through it once about five years ago, though I had discreetly changed the title to *Stringmusic Number One*. They thought it was pleasant, which, of course, translates into weak. Still, hearing it brought Camille back to me, if only for a few minutes.

When I showed it to Camille a few days later, she played through it, transposing from the four parts to piano two-hands.

"Ford, it's a crock," she said. She had acted the next morning as if our lovemaking had never occurred, and I was crushed for days, even more so after her blithe dismissal of the work I wrote for her. "I mean, it's all right, but it reeks of late Mascagni or something."

I lightly defended myself but agreed that the work was overheated and out of tune with the late sixties. After that, our friendship cooled, though Camille was always there. I stayed, incidentally, as a charter member of the Malone Society, which existed for most of my years at McCandless. It was not until the winter of 1970 that Camille and I realized that we were like psychic twins, that, as she said, God meant for us to be together.

In the latter stage of our love, she once played for me a piano work she'd written in my honor. It was incredibly complex and lovely, as much unlike my work as possible.

That night in the bushes, as much as anything, was why I wanted to regain Camille, steal her back from the streets. Because I had decided long before that Camille Malone was the immovable object that diverted me into a cul de sac of my middle age from which I was now trying so laughably to escape.

CLARENCE AND I HAD NEVER BEEN PARTICULARLY close as children, though he was the first cousin closest to my age. While I was daydreaming about sonata form, he spent a lingering adolescence pretending he was Superman or reading the Edgar Rice Burroughs books on Thuvia, Maid of Mars. I read those books, too, but Clarence was still reading them when he graduated from high school.

Clarence and I saw each other around town and at school. I never liked him. My mother sent me to visit at his house one memorable summer day, and Clarence took me boating in the remote edge of a swamp. He'd taunt gators on the bank, call them names, throw rocks at them until they'd scuttle into the water toward us. I was thirteen and not prepared to die.

"You can visit Clarence to see what you should never become," Mom would say. "He's a good example for you, in his own way."

"I know what I don't want to become," I'd say. "I promise I'm not going to be Lee Harvey Oswald."

"Be good about this," Dad would say. "When you come home, I'll have a big surprise." Usually it was something wonderful; my father's love was constant.

Nothing in our past might have prepared me for Clarence getting religion. On the other hand, nothing prepared any of us for his stint in prison. And yet, now, at the single most crucial moment in my life, when I was realizing with some profundity (a state not natural to any of the Claytons) that Camille held the key to my future, here was Clarence Clayton, my idiot cousin, standing in the doorway of my office at McCandless. I had almost forgotten telling an egregious lie to my department head.

"Clarence," I said, not smiling, "what in the hell are you doing here?" I didn't invite him in, but he came anyway.

"Heard you telleth your Mama you lived in Asheville," he said. "The rest of it was, ah, easy."

"Please, for God's sake, don't talk to me in your Bible language," I said. "I'm not in the market for religion."

"Oh, okay," he said. He sat in my guest chair, his feet barely touching the rug. "I hitchhiked. I knew you worked for a music place, and I just asked around. When I was in the can, we had us a singing society."

"You did?" Suddenly, a vision passed in front of me: Bartók had spent years tramping the Hungarian hinterlands collecting folksongs, and maybe I could render a similar service in American prisons, where men were....Jesus. What works the mind can affirm.

"Clarence, I can't help you. I'm leaving tomorrow morning," I said. "Driving over to Greensboro to get the train. Cheaper way to go, and besides, I'm afraid of airplanes."

"If God have meant man to fly, he'd of given him feathers," said Clarence sagely.

"Clarence, I saw my old girlfriend, Camille Malone, in this documentary on street people," I explained patiently. "She was wearing brogans and a threadbare coat and was pushing a grocery cart loaded with rags and cans. It's not exactly like going to my class reunion. Her hair was matted and dirty, and her eyes seemed to be turned away from each other at forty-five degree angles. She could see the entire horizon, like a frog."

"Well, hop to it!," said Clarence with an obnoxious laugh.

"Would you puh-leease leave me alone?" I shouted.

"Oh, is this personal?" he asked. "I lost track of my manners in the big house."

"You weren't in the big house," I said with some heat. "You were at a farm work camp in Jackson County."

"Hey, don't tell me what it was until you've plowed a mile

behind my mule," he said. "I made that up."

"Oh, Christ, please leave me?" I asked.

"But I'm lonely for the company of some people I know," he said. "You mama throwed me out. What was I supposed to do?" For some reason, I remembered what kind of lover Camille said I was.

"You're the goddamn Thomas Dewey of romance," she had screamed at me.

"Camille, what in the hell are you talking about?" I asked.

We were eating lunch in the tweedy comfort of the Algonquin Hotel, and several people glanced our way when she started to lose control.

"You are to romance what H. R. 'Bob' Haldeman is to public service!" she screamed. "The passion in your soul wouldn't fill a thimble, Georgia. You might as well spend your life in some stone cell studying Babylonian warrior gods!"

"Is your mind out to lunch?" asked Clarence.

"Sorry," I said. "I got to daydreaming."

"Well, I've made up my mind," he said. "I'm a-going with you."

"You can't."

"Sure I can," he smiled. "This here's America." Well, who did I have to blame but Ford Clayton?

"I give up," I said. "If you're bound, come hell or high water."

"Hey," said Clarence, "I wrote that, too. How'd you know about that? My lordy, it's gotten all the way to North Carolina!"

We went back to my house when my day was over. The faculty meeting had degenerated into a screaming match. A classicist named Maria Valois said we were teaching more Mahler than Padre Martini.

By the time I had ordered a pizza from Domino's and Clarence had taken time off to pray, I felt a deep sadness and yet an excitement percolating around me. The inanity that Clarence embodied and the fecundity of my Camillian recollections were water and oil. I was not sure which primal element I represented. I could not get off my mind the idea that perhaps the New York City Opera *was* somehow planning to stage the opera I hadn't finished. Maybe that lie was a joke arranged by a jolly god.

After we ate, I tried not to think about anything. Having Clarence around helped that process, and soon I was almost grateful he was there.

"Did you bring any clothes or anything?" I asked.

"Every thing that I got, is just what I got on," he said. "That's from a song by George Strait. You know country music, Cuz?" I remembered his suitcase, but who knew what had happened to it?

"For God's sake don't call me Cuz," I said. We were in my bedroom, closet door open, picking out things to take. "No, I don't know country music. I study real music."

"Country music *is* the only real music," he said. "Jesus was a country music singer."

"That's the dumbest thing I ever heard in my life," I said. I got underwear, socks, and shirts and put them in my large, expensive Samsonite suitcase.

"Well, it's true, Cuz," he said. He tried on a shirt of mine, and it looked like a circus tent on him. "Was this preacher feller in the Big House with me, and he explaineth it all. You got anything with French cuffs?"

"No, I don't have any French cuffs," I said. "And what in the hell was a preacher doing in prison?"

"Well, that was a thing," he said. "Name of Rev. Wilburn Moran. Everybody called him Preacher Moron, though. Said he was in there for loving his flock too well. That's what he said, but I got me this friend in the office, a trusty named Jerue? He looked up Preacher Moron's record and found he'd bought a whole entire professional movie setup with the offering money and was making dirty movies with some of the altar boys."

"And this is a man whose opinion you trust?" I yelled. "We're talking about music here, Clarence. Music is the altar of my life, the place where I worship and work."

"Well, you're getting awful het up," he said. "These pants are way too big, Cuz."

"I don't have anything in a thirty-two weasel," I said.

"You shouldn't orta treat family this way," he said. Absolutely. "Besides, I been gone a long time. I miss the talk of good friends and such. And now I got religion, it's my bounden duty to spreadeth it all over the world, like grass seed and fertilizer."

"Fertilizer's getting pretty close," I said.

"Anyway, Jesus was a folk singer, with a guitar and everything," he said.

"And a harmonica?"

"That's what a timbrel is, sure as I'm standing here," he said, nodding. I tried to picture one of the altos in the *St. Matthew Passion* whipping out a harmonica and playing a recitatif with the full baroque orchestra; it was a ghastly picture to me, the perfect snob.

"I can't have this conversation," I said. "Look, Clarence, I don't know why you're here, and I can't offer you anything. The honest truth is that I never liked you when we were kids."

"Oh, I know," he said. "But I was possessed by hellish fiends. Like that time I tried to get the gator to eat you."

"That scared the shit out of me," I said.

"You was just too much of a mama's boy," he shrugged. "I was trying to turn you into a he-man."

"How does being consumed by a reptile equate with being a he-man?" I asked. I walked into the bathroom and got my toiletries.

"I just thought you orta quit being such a parlor child and see some of the world," he said. "You'd a been better off if somebody'd beat your ass a couple of times real good."

I came out of the bathroom holding my cologne, feeling suddenly ridiculous, angry because he probably had a point.

"Look, you dumb backwoods hick, I could whip your ass in two seconds," I shouted.

"What, you gone after-shave me to death?" he asked. I looked at the bottle in my clenched fist. I started laughing.

"I'm in the middle of the change of life," I said, "and I just can't handle trying to deal with a cousin recently paroled for knocking over a liquor store."

"I ain't asking for money," he said. "Just a few extra clothes and a train ticket. I'll just be like your private preacher or something."

"Preacher Moron," I said as I stowed the toiletries in the

suitcase.

"He's got eight more years," said the very sincere and honest Clarence Clayton.

Clarence collapsed on the sofa after dinner and immediately started snoring terribly. I turned out all the lights and ascended the stairs into the darkness. As I came into the bedroom, I saw, by the door in a neat pile, my suitcases (two of them) and the box of letters I'd brought from Mom's attic. I turned out the light. The window was open. A cool breeze fluted through, across the room. I took off everything but my shorts and got in.

Dreams: I was distant, floating on my back in the blue grotto of Capri, listening to the water whisper against the chalky walls, then something soft, louder, and I realize it is the Veni Creator Spiritus from Mahler's Eighth, and Gustave himself is floating past me on a barge, with choruses, orchestra, and everything, and perhaps they're rehearsing, and I start to dog paddle and shout to him that I love his music so much, but he turns to me scowling, puts a finger to his lips and yells "Ssshhhhh!"

That became the wind, which turned me into another place entirely. I was in a field of wheat. It was nearly harvest time. All around me, I felt girls and boys laughing, playing, then I realized I was in the Merita Bread commercial for "The Lone Ranger." I sat up, and he was standing near me in his mask, and I realized I was young again, just a boy, and not far from him was Zorro, and then Sky King. I was buoyant, thrilled by the feel of youth, and then I heard my name, and it was Joey from "Fury," and I was at the ranch with Jim (still played by Peter Graves) and Pete, where I'd always wanted to grow up instead of Jamesburg.

"Joey, can I ride Fury?" I asked.

"Sure you can," he said. "And Packy'll be over for lunch, and we can have peanut butter sandwiches with that good Merita Bread."

"Is this a commercial or the regular show?" I asked.

Before he could answer, I was in a jungle, pursued by everything in the night that crept, slithered, pounced, or crawled. I was running, falling, crying for someone to help me. I came to a pool of water, and a stunning light came from this cave, and I leaned down to drink and saw my reflection in the pool, and my face was an old man's, full of unpleasant years and wrinkles, hair gone, wispy beard all snow. No, I said, I do not want to be old yet. And up near the cave I saw my father, and he was smiling and waving, pointing into the light, telling me this was where I had to go. Is that death? I asked. It's not ladies' foundations, he said with a wink.

I gasped at the light. I sat up straight in bed and said a single word out loud.

"Jill," I said. The bedclothes around me were damp. I glanced at the clock and saw that it was only twelve thirty-nine. I got out of bed and walked to the window, unhappy with my stomach's middle-age weight, not daring to glance in the mirror where Jill dressed for dreary faculty parties.

I saw my backyard, silent in the moonlight. I saw the moon. It was nearly full, and its chalky craters hung benevolently over the mountains. I saw other houses, lights all out, my neighbors, some of them young, many quite old, every night turning out the lights, wondering what the next day might bring. Once Camille had explained to me that each year we pass the anniversaries of events to happen in the future. Every year of your life, you pass the date on which you will later die, she said, and I found the idea repulsive, but she was philosophically stimulated. Every birth, every death, every good or ill omen, you get a chance to see that day, ahead of its time, but without knowing. "Think," said Camille, "how many December the sixteenths there were before Beethoven was born on the date. All that practice for a genius!"

I crept down the stairs. Clarence had shifted on the couch, head at the other end. Still snoring like a saw on a pine knot. I walked in my underwear, shirtless, into the kitchen. Was I feeling a euphoria? Perhaps. Camille once lectured me on achievements in old age. She went straight for Verdi, of course, but then she veered to *Trilogie der Leidenschaft*, which Goethe wrote at seventy-five.

"Of course, it was tripe," she said, "since he was trying to bargain his way out of dying by then. But he was at least trying to forgive Werther for all the shit he spread around."

I poured a glass of milk and smiled. I got some cookies and sat at the table in the darkness. Cold milk and cookies. A blessing from the gods, one of the thousand miracles. What else? A peppermint candy after surviving the dentist. The smell of magnolia blossoms. The sound of the organ at early Mass on Sunday morning. A woman sitting on the edge of the tub shaving her legs. The silence that falls when the conductor raises his arms. Fresh bread. Snow before dawn. The Great American Plains.

I drank the milk and finished the cookies. I gently opened the door and walked into the backyard. Men had walked on the moon, so I should be able to find Camille. If life is random (Camille, after her conversion to Catholicism, believed all was preordained and inevitable) nothing has a point. We all invent our own gods. Mine was the Great God of Bach, tradition, and family and ancestors. We believe to complete the circle.

An embrace. A hug. A ring. Anything circular is a message from that other world. I lay in the dewdamp grass and stared at the moon, then closed my eyes and inhaled the spring of mountains.

I PULLED THE GLUEY BACON STRIPS APART and lay them in the skillet, sipped my coffee as I waited for the hickory aroma to rise to me. Clarence was still sleeping on the couch. During the night he'd found an afghan Jill had made, and it was spread completely over his mink-thin form like a parti-colored burial shroud. The bacon began to shrink. I took the margarine from the refrigerator and smeared it on six pieces of oat-bran bread and put it in the oven, though I did not turn it on yet. Having two children makes you an adept short-order cook. Except I no longer had two children. They were living in another state, and I was about to begin a journey to a city of nine million to look for a solitary ex-pianist who'd lost the dream. I took five eggs and cracked them into a silvered mixing bowl, added a spoonful of sugar and a healthy splash of milk. I watched the colors swirl as I mixed it thoroughly with the whisk. When I lifted the whisk, ropy strands of eggs and milk drained slowly back into the bowl. By then, the bacon needed turning. I spread a pad of paper towels so I could drain the bacon when it was finished.

Two minutes until six. Outside, it was still dark, but when I looked from the window over the sink, I could see lights starting to come on. I walked back to the stove, lifted the cooked rashers from their bed of oil, laid them on the paper towels.

I poured off most of the bacon grease into an old coffee cup, then dumped the eggs into the pan and watched them solidify, begin to bubble. They rippled. Rich yellow, lovely, and sweet. I scrambled them with a teflon spatula Jill had won as a prize at a wedding shower. She'd been so proud of the spatula, said it was the only thing she'd ever won. Then I turned on the oven, and soon the aroma of toast began to mingle with bacon and eggs.

I took a minute to get the paper. On the front page in huge letters was the legend DEMOCRACY IN USSR? Tom Cruise had his hair shaved off for the new movie he was making. Cooking breakfast, having everything ready at once, was almost like good sex, Camille had said after our first full night together, back in the years when you had to play man and wife. I wasn't sure how Camille might know that. She was without question one of the most wretched cooks since the quest for fire first began. She knew too many things from books, of course. But she also had another level of knowledge somehow. I once accused her of accidental profundity. This was near the end in New York when we were breaking up. We were in the Strand Bookstore in the Village, and she'd made the statement that "Bach wasn't about music; he was about algebra." Did that make sense? Probably not, but it had the ring of possibility.

"You've stumbled once more into the zone of accidental profundity," I said. We were downstairs. High bookshelves hung over us. I was miserable at our impending breakup, but being awash in old books was a kind of glory.

"You'd say that, you Republican weasel," she said. She was waving a copy of *Tertium Organum* at me. She was by then no longer a Roman Catholic.

"I'm not a Republican, Camille," I said, fangs bared.

"Not on the rolls," she said. Her face turned blush, rose. "Not actually registered. But in your heart, you know I'm right." It was a Nixon campaign slogan. "You and John Mitchell are brothers in grime."

"Brothers in grime," I said with a laugh.

The toast was ready. The eggs were steaming, not burned. The bacon had drained and was neither too fatty nor tastelessly lean. The coffee smelled wonderful. I got out two plates (yes, I thought, these were wedding gifts from Jill's sister) and arranged the food neatly. As a secret, I left room for a parsley sprig, which I didn't have, wouldn't have used. Like Hemingway's theory of the iceberg in fiction. You can leave out anything as long as you know it's left out, and the reader will sense the effect. I'd taken the theory from art to life.

"Road crew! Road crew! Count off!" a hoarse voice cried from the other room.

"He thinks he's back in jail," I said out loud. Clarence came into the kitchen, eyes blurry, hair spikily askew.

"Time to eat," I said.

"The blessings of a new day upon this here dwelling," said Clarence. He hadn't put on his shirt. No socks, just his jeans. His ribs looked like a washboard, chest sunken slightly, but his muscles were long, sinewy.

"Well, dig in," I said. I felt a deep satisfaction at having it all ready at the same time, warm and aromatic.

"Ain't we forgetting something?" Clarence asked.

"What?" I asked.

"Returning thanks," he said. I stared at him.

"Make it quick," I said. "We need to get on the road. And I've got to call about the paper and the mail." Clarence clenched his eyes tightly. I merely sat.

"Howdy, Lord," he said. "This is Clarence Clayton, checking back in right before breakfast with a big howdy do." I opened one eye and glanced at him. "We're fixing to start out on a trip of some sort today, but I'm hanged if I know why my cousin Ford is being so good to me. Nobody else was ever good to me as you know, including Mommer, who once spanked me nineteen times with a Bo-Lo paddle." My other eye came open. "So I'd like to thank you for my cousin Ford and for this food, which includes..." he opened his eyes here for an inventory..."eggs and bacon and...."

"Amen," I said.

I unfolded my napkin and began to eat.

"You interrupted the Lord," said Clarence, crestfallen.

"He'll get over it," I said. "He's God, remember?"

"Well, this just beats all," he said.

Hunger, though, overcame his faith, and soon we were both eating. He finished first, like a starved dog that, years after being saved, still ate each meal as if it were his last. He picked up the newspaper, and flipped through it. He didn't seem to notice the space for the missing parsley; that, perhaps was a gesture for the absent Camille, in itself something missing. Perhaps the entire exercise was a metaphor for what I had lost. Then again, you probably don't miss parsley when you're eating out of garbage cans.

"Tom Cruise's got to get his hair cut for a movie," said Clarence Clayton.

I washed dishes while Clarence showered downstairs. I walked slowly through my house, down my hall. All the school pictures of Kathy and Jay were out here. I went by them slowly. *Your father is a liar*, I said to their impassive but smiling faces. Jay looked like me, everybody said. Kathy had the best features of us both, a lovely, even beautiful girl. Oh, Ford, they'd say, she's going to break some hearts when she grows up. They'd said it in the hospital the night she was born. I was too cowardly to be in the delivery room, and when they called and told me to come see Jill and the baby, I asked, "What is it?" and the doctor on the phone (I was in the lobby) said, "I'll let her tell you." So I went up. She was already in a private room. I got there and kissed her. Lips cracked, her color gone, but the most glorious smile this side of a Florentine madonna. "What is it?" I said looking at the small, wiggling body beside her on the sheets. She lifted the cover, and I saw Kathy's innocence, her plump pink, sweet body, and I was ecstatic with my daughter. I leaned down and kissed her bald head. I could see her heartbeat in the top of her skull. A nurse was behind me. "She's going to break some hearts when she grows up," the nurse said. *Now, your father is both an adulterer and a liar*. Jay was much the same. Head full of hair. Laughing boy. Beloved of Kathy, who played with him like a baby doll, never jealous. Halloween costumes. She was a ghost. Made Jay up like a big pumpkin. Jill made the costumes.

I could not take the sentimental remorse, so I went upstairs. I reached down into the box of letters next to my suitcase, took one out and sat on the bed. It was from Camille, of course.

Postmarked in April 1975. From Oslo, Norway. Stamp might be worth something, green, some queen. Christiana? Christine?

Christian?

Thursday night

Dear Pyramus,
The horror. The horror. Last night in the middle of some Chopin
waltzes on stage, I went blank. I kept playing, but I drifted outside my
body and saw a dazzling emptiness about it all. The sound was plinky,
hollow. I had to quit. Management was incensed. The audience puzzled.
I have cried all night long. It's all blágue, my Chevalier. I need you, my
Manitou. This is going to sound like the general stupidity of Theognis,
but I need you and everything about you. The personal God again, the
shallowness, willingness to accept small victories and forget the truths of
the ages. I'm in a John Fucking Cheever short story and I can't find the
page where it begins or ends. I will be awaiting you at the Swan Hotel
in Oslo. Look for the big black swan. Birds of a feather flock together.

Your frantic,
Thisbe

I'd been back in Asheville by then, a new assistant prof of
musicology at the alma mater. I remember sitting in my office,
slitting the envelope, feeling sorry for her, a mild warmth at her
failure since she'd tried so hard to push me into becoming her
manager. Now, I felt only sorry. I refolded the missive, crammed it
back into the envelope, threw the whole thing back in the letter
box.

Back downstairs, I went outside to check on the ancient
encrusted station wagon we'd have to take. I had not turned it on
in six months since we bought the Volvo for Jill. I kept driving the
MG. The station wagon was a Ford. There is something perverse
about driving a vehicle with your name on the side. The house,
naturally, had a large two-car garage, that symbol of mythic Beaver
Cleaver America; Camille used to rave about "Two-Car-Garage
America" when she was deep into the philosophies of poverty or
race. The air was redolent with grass and boxwood, new sun and
earth. I opened the front door of the garage, letting its weight pull

my arm back. Garage doors have a life of their own. The bay on the left was empty but for Jay's old Big Wheel and seven sacks of clothes I'd never taken to the Salvation Army. "Camille would die for some of these clothes now," I said. I thought briefly of taking a bag, but that would be condescending. She hated condescension. The lumbering Ford was still there, patient and long-suffering as an arthritic family pet. I opened the door, which screamed for oil, got in, and took the key from the sunflap, turned it on.

The car groaned against the gas flowing into the carburetor. It seemed happy at rest, was surprised and indignant at being turned on again. I glanced at the gauges, saw it was full of gas. When it finally caught, a bilious cloud of black smoke exploded from the tailpipe, and I backed it out of the garage into the morning air. Was this the great adventure? Perhaps. My next door neighbor, John Hobbs, was standing in his own driveway, twin to mine, putting his briefcase in a sleek new 280-Z, black, like something from a thousand years hence or past. I got out. He grinned at the specter of the Ford.

"Getting rid of the moose?" he asked.

"Going on a trip," I said. "I should have told you, John. Could you and Etta keep an eye on the place?"

"Where you going?"

"New York," I said. "An old friend's in trouble."

"Gone long?"

"Don't know."

"Oh. Sure. We'll take a peek at the place."

"Still got your key?"

"Yeah."

"Well, eat anything you can find," I said.

"Heard from Jill?" he asked.

"Yes," I said. "Hey, look. It still runs. That must mean something."

"I'm sure of it," he said. He got into the Z and backed down the driveway, was gone. I never liked John. I went back into the house and finished packing, including my letters. Clarence came walking out with an old suitcase of Kathy's with pictures on the side of The Partridge Family. He seemed excited. He held on to his much-abused old Bible in his right hand.

"And lo, the heathens cringed when Preacher Clayton arriveth," he said.

"You're not a preacher," I said with some irritation. "You're an ex-convict sponging off a cousin without the good sense to tell you to get lost."

"Come on, Fordy," he said. "Don't be a Pharisee."

"Look," I said, "you load this crap in the car. I've got to call the paper and the mailman."

"Don't look now, but some poor soul's done rode up into your yard looking for a handout," he said.

"That's *my* station wagon," I said. "There's nothing wrong with it. You're welcome to walk back to Georgia."

"Hostile not thyself towardeth me," he said.

"Clarence, I *am* hostile toward you," I said. "I'm hostile toward you for the mere fact of your existence, much less the fact that I find, to my great surprise, that blood is thicker than water."

"Huh?" he said.

I called the paper and the post office. The paper lady was very nice. The person at the post office seemed irritated; this was something of an imposition to them. I then went through the house, shutting everything down, turning off the hot water heater, upstairs to make sure everything was unplugged.

The phone rang. Loud. I was back in the kitchen, and I glanced at the clock on the oven, saw that it was four minutes after eight o'clock. It was the office secretary, Sigurd. She was not pleased to be speaking with me.

"Dr. Clayton, I knew you were going to be out for a time," she said, "but there's a message that you got late yesterday I thought you should have."

"Really? It isn't from Publisher's Clearinghouse or anything?" I asked.

"It's from the Homeless Hotline in New York City," she said. I suddenly noticed everything, each separate tick and sigh of the house. I waited. "Dr. Clayton, are you there?"

"Yeah," I said.

"Anyway this Homeless Hotline called, and it was a message

from someone named Juliet, who said she was coming to Myrtle Beach to meet you." Sigurd sounded disgusted.

"*Myrtle Beach?*" I said. My voice sounded strangled.

"That's what the message says, Dr. Clayton," she said. "I believe, if I repeat it, it shall say very close to the same thing."

"Thanks for calling," I said. She hung up without saying goodbye. I sat at the kitchen table. I could hear, outside, the gastric rumblings of the station wagon and the voice of Clarence, rising with the spirit. What in God's name did this mean? Was it some symbolic act? I was Romeo, of course, she Juliet, but....

My God! I had told her I'd be waiting for her beneath the *Circle Beech* on Campus when I'd called. Mistranslation! Wars had been started out of such confusion. Now, believing I would save her, she was on her way to a South Carolina beach town. I wasn't going to New York. I was going to the Coney Island of the Coast. I locked the back door and stumbled into the sun.

"Fordo, you look all white," said Clarence. He came over toward me. "If you's to eat brown eggs, your skin would cleareth up."

"I, uh," I said, but I couldn't seem to manage anymore. "I think I need to make one more phone call before we head out for the beach."

"Did you sayeth the beach?" cried Clarence. "Lo! I am afraid of the deep water and, unh! the big fishes because, unh! I cannoteth swim!"

I walked inside without bothering to explain yet, took the phone from the wall in the kitchen and dialed Jamesburg. It rang four times before she answered it.

"Clayton residence," she said in a mock-British voice, something Jeevesian, a house servant.

"Mom, you're starting to sound like Little Dorrit," I said with a sigh.

"Ford? Is that you?" she asked, her voice still in Britface.

"Mom, this is embarrassing," I said. "Why are you talking that way?"

"I don't want people to know I have no servants," she said. "My goodness, have you run out of people to talk to, Son?"

"Please don't needle me," I said. "And before you start insulting me about my social skills, speaking in Dorrit doesn't exactly make you seem like an opera diva."

"That's true," she said. "I'm just trying to keep up appearances, though. Are you coming home again in the next decade, or are you still planning to get maced half to death in the New York City subway system? Your father thought the Clarence thing was funny. I'm bereft."

"That's why I'm calling," I said. "I just wanted somebody to know that my plans have changed. I'm going to Myrtle Beach instead. And in case you wondered, Clarence is here with me. He hitched up here. I'm thinking of killing him."

"Dear, you are more intelligent than I could have guessed," Mom said thoughtfully. "Could you push him off a pier or something, darling? He's a blot on the family name, though, God wot, it's the Clayton name and not my own."

"Mom, you've been a Clayton for forty-four years," I said.

"On paper," she said. "Why the change of plans?"

"It's too long and sordid a story," I said.

"Just tell me it doesn't involve drugs or anyone underage, and I'll be able to go to my grave," she said. "I'll go unhappy, of course, but at least not devastated."

"God, in one breath you want me to drown my first cousin off a pier, and in the next breath you're worried about contributing to the delinquency of a minor," I said. "Look, I've got to go. The car's running in the driveway."

"Ford, listen to me for once. I do love you, dear," she said. "I'm merely worried for your future. You should be doing great things. I'm only trying to see that you fulfill your potential."

"Well, I hear the New York City Opera's considering staging *East of Eden*," I growled. "I'll make sure you get loge seats, Mom. Thanks for all your help."

"Call me if you get into trouble, son," she said. "And I'd prefer tickets in the fifth-row center instead of a loge."

"I'll call," I said. "Take care."

Suddenly it all seemed perfectly clear. If Homer had written about me, *The Odyssey* wouldn't have made it through a single canto.

CAMILLE WASN'T ENTIRELY OFF BASE in thinking I'd summoned her to Myrtle Beach. We took a romantic holiday there as seniors at McCandless. I daydreamed of being beloved by everyone as an old man: works performed all over the globe, a healing force, name in the history books, named *Time* Man of the Year. Camille, on the other hand, saw old age as the inevitable rot of promise. All her stock was in the youth movement of the sixties, and she never adjusted. I accused her of trying to stay an adolescent. She said I was prematurely senile. I didn't see it clearly, but in a way, she was right. Camille was a performer, and they make most of their fame in extreme youth; I wanted something else, the slow fame of creation, a steady curve of accomplishment toward some distant death. Perhaps the only time she was not the high-strung pianist and I was not the brooding solitary dreamer was our week at Myrtle Beach. We ate seafood. I took her deep sea fishing. We made love unhurriedly, at night, in the daylight, with care and planning and with sudden passion. She had great fears, and when they'd sweep over her, she would suddenly begin to cry, cling to me, undress me. I let her. It was exciting, of course, but frightening somehow, too, and Jill's steady-eyed love was its powerful antidote.

I explained to Clarence why we were going to Myrtle Beach instead of New York.

"Well, this don't make you look very good," said Clarence.

"I flee, therefore I am," I said.

"A bird in the hand is worth two in the bush," Clarence said.

"I wrote that." We were heading south, toward the Piedmont and then the flatlands. "It got all the way up here, too. Huh."

"Christ," I said. "Clarence, you didn't write that. It's an old saying."

"It's only three years old," he protested. "It's in the *Golden Book of Clarence Clayton*. Words to helpeth in each and every day. That's what it says on the title page."

"The *Golden Book of Clarence Clayton*?" I said. It wasn't an opera, but at least it sounded finished. Maybe creativity was more genetic than environmental.

"Unh huh," he said. "I wrote it, and my friend José in the office typed it up for me. It's knowed of in a foreign country already."

"What?" I said.

"Well, it is," he said. "José's Mexican. He was in for bringing a truckload of mary jane over the border and across the South into Georgia. He wrote his mama about my *Golden Book*. So I know it's knowed in Mexico." I glanced at him. He seemed very pleased with himself. "So, it's knowed in a foreign country."

"What else is in this book?" I asked.

"Well, mostly, it's advice on how to liveth your life," said Clarence.

"You mean with advice on knocking over liquor stores?" I asked.

"You have to give a man a chance," said Clarence. "Jesus done giveth me a chance, so why can't you?" He gave a little cry. "Hey, that could be a Country and Western song."

The countryside laved me, honeydew-ripe, reflective. Everything was full of rainwater, swelling with green, incongruous with my nasty mood.

"Nope, that was a dumb idea for a Country and Western song," said Clarence. "I can't get nothing to rhyme with 'forgive.' So I reckon I'll just read us some of these letters from this box to keep us entertained."

"Hey, that's private property," I said. I turned and tried to grab the box, but he just moved across the seat while I swerved to stay on the road.

"Nobody ever got hurt by reading something," he said. "You

know who sayeth that?"

"Thoreau," I said angrily.

"No, José," he said. "That's why he typeth my *Golden Book*. Here's one." He began to read:

Dear Ford,

Now that the funeral is over, I want to tell you in brief what your grandfather was really like.

I remembered *that* letter, my mother's confessions, an endless, rambling missive.

It was an intimate inheritance, the story of my grandfather, my mother, of the context of Ford Clayton, even through the oblique vision of Clarice. It was none of Clarence's goddamned business. I pulled to the edge of the road, and we teetered on the rim of a gorge.

"You're about to falleth off!' yelled Clarence.

"This will only take a minute," I said. "I'm going throw you off the cliff."

"Hey," said Clarence. I got out and opened the back on the side facing the road. Cars were pouring around me. Clarence scooted across the seat, still holding the letter, then he opened his door and got out. I came around the back of the car, saw him standing eight inches from a shelf that flew down toward a river a hundred feet below. A nasty fall.

"I'm going to kill you now," I said. I felt like Humphrey Bogart. *A scene: me making a speech in court, trying to explain why I'd killed my cousin, not actually defending it, but, well, explaining the philosophical underpinnings of such an act. Fichte? No. Nietzsche? Possibly.*

"For reading a letter?" he said. He still held it, now to his chest.

"You deserveth to die," I said. I came on around the station wagon. "Those aren't letters. They're clues. They're blood and bone and sinew."

"And then God createth the fishes!" Clarence yelled.

"They're my birthright, my inheritance, my road not taken!" I shouted. I was making a speech. "And you have no right to read them."

"You can haveth it back!" he cried. "Touch me, and I'll jump!" screamed Clarence. We both stopped. He was standing on the rim of the gorge like a high diver ready for the plunge. Now this was a dilemma for me. My cousin was prepared to throw himself from a precipice to keep me from killing him. Not the stuff of epic poetry. Sibelius probably would've written a tone poem about it, but zilch from anybody else. No Wagner opera.

"Wait," I said. "*You* are going to jump if I touch you?"

"That's right," he said. A wind arose. Clouds covered the face of the sun, and all the greens dulled. The face of the deep was filled with Clarence ruffling the pages.

"I know what I'm doing," I said calmly. "I'm going to fling a weasel from this great height."

I debated silently. In my mind I'd already somehow slain the diminutive Clarence, an act not wholly worthy of a man whose work might be staged by the New York City Opera. We were tightroping along mortality; one slip for either of us, and death would be there in the rocky debris far below.

"You're right," I said. "Clarence, you drive. I'll sit in the back and try to calm down and not be a burden to you."

This was an important step for me. Unfortunately, Clarence took advantage of my eloquence and did it one better.

He fell off the mountain.

Clarence's right foot had crumbled the friable earth, and he'd gone down as if through a trap door. Foot tangled in a vine, he stood suspended in a green stirrup long enough for me to grab one hand, then the other. He weighed perhaps one-thirty, and I pulled him up like a child. He had dropped the sheets of my mother's letter, and they were fluttering down the gorge, getting smaller each second, looking finally like tickertape.

"You all right?" I asked him. We were leaning hard against the station wagon. He was genuinely afraid.

"I am," he said. "It just give way under me. I thought I was dead." We both looked at the pages. A single sheet caught the hawk's thermal and rose and rose and rose. Goodbye, Mom. Goodbye, Grandpa, goodbye funeral, goodbye to all that.

"I've got you now," I said.

"Look at them pages," said Clarence. "I didn't mean to do that. I was just trying to be funny. Onliest thing I had in jail was being funny, until I got me religion."

"Let's get out of here," I let go of Clarence's arm, and the imprint of my fingers lingered.

And so he did drive, despite the fact he had no license. And he drove rather well. He talked about movies. His favorite was *The Sound of Music*.

"I like that go-kart song," he said. I was trying to tune him out, looking at the mountains, smaller every minute as we descended. "You know, 'High on the hill, stood the lonely go-kart.'"

Mom would have blown a gasket right about here.

"Yeah, I liked that one," I said.

"You get to yodel in that one," he said. Given the chance, even if he gave it himself, my cousin could not resist yodeling. And so he did. It was terrifying, ear shattering, unmelodious, yet somehow hypermusical, like Placido Domingo in electroshock therapy. I said nothing. Ignore them, and they'll go away. Rain, rain go away, come again some other day. The lonely go-kart. Oh-de-lay-de-hoo.

I dug toward the bottom of the box and pulled out a letter that was obviously Camille's. She always put stamps on sideways, saying it had theological intent, though to whom never was clear. Clarence was listening to a call-in show from Greenville, South Carolina, and three consecutive phoners agreed that anyone who burned the flag should be electrocuted.

I opened the letter and read.

Sunday morning, early

Ford,
In die solemnitatis vestrae, dicit Dominus, inducam vos in terram fluentem lac et mel, alleluia.

Ah, early post-conversion, and I silently translated: In the day of your solemnity, saith the Lord, I will bring you into a land that floweth with milk and honey, alleluia.

Good morning, darling, and God's rich blessing upon you. That offertory is from Exodus, of course, which you probably knew from your Methodist upbringing. Today, I have so much longing for Christ, for His mysteries, that I wish you were not home on Easter vacation so I could explain to you my feelings.

My mother, a confirmed Presbyterian, has taken my conversion with some confusion, though she believes any religion is a good religion. Can you believe that? It's like saying any political party is a good party. No, I believe only in the mysteriousness of the Roman Church now, Ford, in its symmetrical splendors. If I were innocent, I might consider orders.

I took a long walk this morning down Esplanade all the way to the Cathedral, not far from Pirate's Walk, and the house where Faulkner wrote his first novel. A group of Creole singers was in Jackson Square, and their melodies were so dark and inspired. I carried my Missal with me and sat on a park bench among the flutter and coo of the pigeons and read of Jesus with all my heart.

Do you think symmetry exists, darling?

I looked out the window at the mountains. I want to believe it, Camille. I have strong desires for the Godhead in this creeping middle age. I doubt it, but I will prostrate myself before it. Life surely is in the sonata form; fast, slow, fast, and at the end, getting faster and lighter, brass coming in, we shall all rejoice.

I think symmetry is the body of Christ in our lives. I believe in the Pope and his apostles. Oh, Ford, all my life I've searched for something to believe in. I worshipped at Music, sacred Music, and it nourished me and bled me and gave me strength and fear and honor and peace and shadows. Darling, I have lived in the shadows so long.

And now, Camille? Bereft on the streets of Gotham? Hitching south to some beachfront to meet the man who failed not only you but Music herself? How steep are the shadows now?

But enough of theology. As a Protestant, you must find the world a disorderly place, where symmetry is belief and not knowledge. But when you feel the losses of protesting against the True Church, remember I will not abandon you. Read Psalm 138, where it says, "Thy friends, O God, are made exceedingly honorable; their power is become very great."

Now, they are coming into the square, the lost men and women of this town, and I ache for the pity of their lives. The bookmarkers from my Missal flutter in the wind, and I am dumb to tell you how sweet my reverie, how much I miss you.

> *Yours in Christ,*
> *Camille*

I folded the letter and put it back in the envelope. But I was already tired, and in the afternoon, we hit Columbia. Just find a motel and crash. When we hit the city limits, my cousin was so wound up he invited me to climb every mountain with him.

"I'm trying," I said. Boy, was I trying.

I READ ABOUT INGRID'S ENGAGEMENT in *The Jamesburg Times*.
Mom bought me a subscription, kept it coming to Asheville during
my years there. Spring quarter of my freshman year had come, and
I was mad for Camille after we'd made love in the bushes weeks
earlier. She, on the other hand, felt it was no more significant than,
say, a hiccup or a nice walk. Still, seeing Ingrid's glazed grin in the
Times was a shock, and the boy she was marrying was even more
shocking, a mad-eyed, dark-faced boy from Savannah named
Westfall or Westall or something like that. He was in the commercial fishing business. That was what the engagement announcement said.

"He's a fucking shrimper," I said with disdain. Ronny Favors
and I were sitting on the roof of Tarmot Hall. From here, the view
was splendid. The weather was clear, sharply cool. The day was
nearly over, but I had a meeting of the Malone Society later that
evening to plan what would become the first anti-war rally in the
history of McCandless. "She had the future Gustav Mahler, and
she's going to marry a man who smells like Saturday night on the
wharf."

"Love," said Ronny. He toasted the sentiment with a Dixie
cup full of red wine. I joined him. The trees were full of birds,
cardinals cheeping quarternotes, mockingbirds in endless arching
melodies. Faint wisps of music drifted up toward the first stars.
Mandatory spring quarter recitals would begin soon, and everyone
was practicing frantically. Camille was to perform a Beethoven

sonata, and she had, the weekend before, practiced one section for five hours. One five-bar section. "Who knows why women do things?"

"That's a sexist comment," I said. I tried very hard to toe the party line: anti-war, pro-women's rights, pro-decriminalization of marijuana, pro-Allen Ginsberg. I didn't believe much of it, but that didn't matter. Ronny, on the other hand, was a philosophical conservative. His god was William F. Buckley. He belonged to the Young Americans for Freedom and had short hair. But we were good friends by then, and we gently chided each other on politics and spent most of our time talking about girls and music.

"I don't care," he said. He raised his cup. "Here's to the girls in their gingham dresses." I raised my cup aloft in the wind.

"Here's to the girls in their bell-bottoms and tie-dyed T-shirts," I said. We laughed and drank. The wine warmed my stomach. "And to Ingrid Halvorssen, the dumb whore."

"That's sexist," he said. We both laughed. "Why don't you admit the truth?"

"Which is?"

"She was just too much woman for you," he said.

She was that. Camille was too much woman for the Western World, however, and I had gone straight from Ingrid to her.

"She's too much woman for anybody," I said. "Last time I was home, I saw her and she'd gained twenty pounds working in a fudge shop over Christmas."

"Besides, what about Camille de Malone?" he said cheerily. The door to the roof opened, and a pretty girl named Jeanine, who had flowing dark hair, gray eyes, and full lips came out. She saw Ronny and smiled sweetly. They'd been going together for a few weeks, and she clearly adored him.

"Hi there," he said. "I was just quizzing Ford here. He is to girls what *The Titanic* is to seaworthiness." Jeanine laughed too brightly, and I stood gallantly, aware that I was a sexist pig, that courtesy was as clearly my inheritance as was the Clayton capacity for boredom.

"Hi, Ford," she said. We'd had a reeds class together, and she was eager but not very talented, though still beyond me in virtually every aspect of a musical career. "I thought you and that Malone girl were a thing."

"We're just good friends," I said, unhappy at the conversation. Their hands clasped.

"Oh my God," Ronny said. "Lovers should never be good friends."

"Honey, don't say that," said Jeanine softly. My cue to leave. I excused myself, left them embracing above the heights of Mc-Candless with a view down the mountains toward the city. So she thought me and the Malone girl were a thing. We weren't even half a thing. What did that make us, I wondered, half a thing? A th? I said it out loud:

"We're a th," I said.

I got to the second floor and went into our room and swept a sheaf of materials from Camille off my study table, took them with me for the meeting, which was being held outside beneath the Circle Beech. I came down the stairs two at a time, outside under the chestnut trees, thinking vile thoughts about Ingrid, who'd had the temerity to get engaged just because I'd broken things off with her. Imagine her not pining for me, forever, but waiting only a few weeks to find a new guy. Mythology would have never survived Ingrid.

The circle at the massive beech tree was really a shallow semicircle, a Greek theatre. McCandless had a tradition of presenting Sophocles in the original there each spring, and it was considered an honor to be named as a performer. All the students came, pretended to understand, and then felt self-important. It's still done, too. As a professor, I have to attend and remark on the beauty and stateliness of the words. That night, the only goddess in the amphitheatre was Camille.

I was late again. My watch, a non-waterproof Timex Mom had given me at Christmas the year before, was seriously on the fritz, and as soon as I saw Camille standing up front, the other eleven in the seats, I knew I was in for a scalding. We were twelve, the clan of Camille Malone. Lights ringed the Circle Beech; you could sit there talking or dramatizing all night. The one really fine performance I ever saw there was *Long Day's Journey into Night* which shattered me. But that was later on, my senior year, another time in the indistinct future; just then, they all turned to me, humorless. Camille glared at me as I took my seat on the second row.

"Georgia, you can ask us to wait, but can you ask Viet Nam to wait?" yelled Camille. A few of the others mumbled "right on." I was suitably chastised.

"Sorry, my watch stopped," I said. I pointed at the offending instrument. They weren't impressed.

"Well, the war didn't," said Camille. "I am not running the Malone Society for the benefit of undisciplined morons. Now stand up and make your confession to the group."

This was a ritual she'd worked out, oddly enough, two years in advance of her Roman conversion. Anytime you pissed her off, the penalty was some inner confession, ripping the teeth from your soul, so to speak. A fat girl named Billie had to confess at one meeting because she'd defended Lord Dunsany during an argument. Billie had begun to weep and admitted that her father had abused her. Even Camille was touched, but I was furious, and I walked Billie back to her dorm afterward. She was tight-lipped and embarrassed by then, but I felt awful for her.

"I confess that I like being a gentleman," I said, rising from my seat. Scoffs. Long-haired boys saying "Jesus" and shaking their heads. The girls glared at me, except for Billie, who was amused.

"A gentleman, Georgia?" said Camille. "That makes me want to puke. You mean like holding a chair for a *lady?*" She spit out the word "lady" as if it were a mouth of wormy apple. Chuckles all around. I said nothing. "Sit down, Georgia." I did.

Camille shuffled some papers before us. Up the hill, a violin was practicing Vivaldi, getting it wrong at the same spot every time, starting again. Over and over. Birds sang. The evening was sweet, and I was hot-faced at being a gentleman. I'd just get up and tell them all off, screw this Malone Society and you, too, Camille, you bunch of sycophants and babies and damaged infants crying for each other's love, you....I did nothing, of course.

"Now Che Gibson has a song for us," she said. I'd always thought his name was Buddy, a tall, thin guy with a wispy beard and bad teeth. I met him years later. He'd filled out, cut his hair, fixed his teeth, and was a band director in Virginia. Then, he was a rabid leftist. He might have been a communist if he'd known what one was. Che? Party line. I couldn't say anything. I'd already had to confess.

"Che" got up with his guitar and sang "Blowin' in the Wind." We sang the chorus with him and swayed back and forth. We bathed in the thick luxury of sanctimony. Che finished, and we applauded. Camille stood. She was worked up. She looked through her papers dramatically, then tossed them in disgust on the ground. Her face was twisted and confused.

"I was going to make this speech about the corrupt nature of the military-industrial complex," she began, "but I see now that the issue is larger than that. This war is nothing but a Gothic travesty. Right? Heraclitus was right when he said 'It is not possible to step twice in the same river.' Elaine, give us another one from Heraclitus."

Elaine was stork awkward, tall as a basketball player, all elbows and knees. A hell of a flutist, though.

"Men do not understand how what is at conflict is at harmony with itself," she said softly.

"Excellent," said Camille, "except you get a fucking reprimand for using 'men' rather than 'people.'"

"Sorry," said Elaine.

"So what does this mean?" cried Camille. Two guys up the hill were throwing a Frisbee and laughing. I wished I were there, but then again I'd had carnal knowledge of Camille, and I would do damn near anything to achieve it again.

"That this war is evil and cannot go on," said Joe Carnes. Joe lived in Tarmot Hall, a little twit who had a talent for rebelling against authority and brown-nosing the faculty at the same time.

"Not exactly," said Camille. "Do you remember Candide? *Il faut cultiver notre jardin.* That's the philosophical axis here, friends. If we are ever to regain that metaphorical Garden, we must suffer pains of the flesh. Therefore, I see the war in Viet Nam not as a historical event but as a stairstep in the purification of the species, an inevitability. Now, who wants to argue with me?"

Nobody said a word. I sure wasn't going to after she'd ripped me up for defending Shostakovitch. But you want my opinion, Camille? I seriously believe you're cracked, darling, that you are so lost in the world of words and music that you wouldn't know the real reasons if they nibbled on your sweet kneecap. She fumed because we wouldn't fight with her.

"Anybody?" she yelled. "Does anybody here have the courage of her convictions?"

"Or his," I muttered. Shit. She came for me.

"Or hers," she said unhappily. "In your case, which is it, Georgia?" Everybody was relieved to be off the hook; they laughed at me with superior disdain. Something swelled in me, but I hesitated. I was torn because I knew that intellectual confrontation was an aphrodisiac to her.

"I was wondering that about you," I said.

"What?" she cried. "Are you starting to absorb crap from that freaking Republican roommate of yours?" I said nothing. "Are you going to tell us next your idol is Richard Millstone Nixon?" Chuckles. Relief. "Or maybe even Bare-Ass Goldwater? Come on, Georgia, are you a spy in the Malone Society?"

"You're pretty when you're mad," I said, as if none of the others were there. Nothing could have raised her fury more; I could have accused her of actually *planning* the Viet Nam War and received less hostility. She could not bear my personal interjection in her screaming diatribe. And so she fired me.

"You're out of the group!" she shouted.

"I thought we had to take a vote," I said, looking at the others.

"All in favor of kicking Georgia out of the group raise your hands!" she commanded. Each hand shot up in a Roman salute. All good party members. I got up and walked up the amphitheatre steps, as their silent hostility followed me. Camille waited until I was gone before she started shouting again.

I never wanted to see her again, and, in fact, I didn't speak to her until the following fall. The Malone Society's anti-war rally fizzled into fifteen students waving signs made on poster board with Magic Markers. It was near the end of the quarter, so most of the students were studying for finals, practicing for recitals.

In my composition class, I had met a gentle girl named Nancy

McLeish, and the night I got canned from the Malone Society, I found her sitting on a bench in the lovely grounds of McCandless, writing in a small notebook. Her class project was a piano sonata, which made eminent good sense. On the other hand, I was writing a Mass for unaccompanied voices, a task I was wildly unprepared to carry out.

Nancy was Camille's polar opposite. Flaxen hair, an easy grace, quiet as a nun, steady gaze, a girlish laugh like a brook over stones. She had hip-length hair and wore old-fashioned long dresses. She was from Virginia. I didn't know much more about her. She wore no makeup, and her features were plain until she smiled, and then something about her was angelic. I was walking in great angry strides when I found myself ten feet away. She was looking at the dying light over the pond that held its glassy surface for two acres in the center of campus.

"Hi, Ford," she said. "Whatcha doing, taking a walk?" She looked pleasant, then she smiled.

"Hey, Nancy," I replied. "You out gathering musical ideas from nature? Next thing you know, you'll be writing a new *Pastoral Symphony*."

"Oh, no, I was just, you know," she said. She closed the small book. I sat down next to her.

"Just what?" I asked.

"Writing some stuff," she said shyly. "Just thoughts and stuff. Trying to sort things out. It's nothing. I'm embarrassed." Embarrassed? By God, Nancy *was* embarrassed. Nothing would so daunt Camille de Malone.

"What kind of thoughts do you have?" I asked. She laughed.

"It's nothing," she said. "You know, like poetry." Ah, a lovely girl who wrote poetry, blushed over it.

"Did you ever read *Candide?*" I asked.

"No," she said. "I know Bernstein's music, though. I'm sorry."

"Sorry?" I said. "I'm *crazy* about anyone who hasn't read *Candide*. Just reading a lot of books doesn't make you a genius, you know."

"I'm not a genius," she said.

We talked on, about her sister Ann, whom she adored, her

dead parents, killed in a commercial air disaster in California, her dream of being a choral director in a small college in the mountains. I heard the collective shout of the Malone Society in antiphonal recitation with their Great Leader. I sneered at them.

"Would you like to walk around the lake?" I asked. It was dark by then. A cluster of ducks hugged the edge of the land, clucking softly.

"I was going to go practice my Bach," she said. "I'm not much of a pianist. I can't seem to make myself practice."

"Me, either," I said. Well, I *was*, but it wasn't showing. That's what Mom told me, anyway. "Come on. Let's stretch our legs." And so we did.

The well-worn path around the lake cradled us, the stars came down in her hair. The moon was heavy, chalk and cheese, and we moved slowly, talking about Keats and the music of Frederick Delius, her favorite. All was languid, and a mild spark hummed between us. I know she felt it from the way she moved back and forth, toward me, then away from me. Nancy was not courted, never taken to a prom in high school, plain as pudding. Her parents were dead, and she was steady but unloved. I ached for her. On the far side of the lake, we sat on a park bench. The only light was from the moon and the corona of the campus half a mile away. We could not hear the music now, only the messages of nature, whispering and benevolent.

"The whole world looks like a poem from here," I said moronically. "Look, you can see the stars and moon in the lake."

"Oh, look at that!" she said. She raised her thin arm and with her finger connected the dots on the water as if it were a puzzle. "The whole world's upside down."

She lowered her arm, hugged herself and began to cry softly. She was disoriented over her parents' death a year before.

"What's wrong?" I asked.

"I'm sorry," she said. She tried to stop. "You think I'm a nut."

"No, I don't," I said.

"I'm just so...." she said. She stopped, holding it back like a child. Then she cried, and she was surprised (as was I) when I swept her into my arms on the park bench and simply held her. She wept on my chest. She trembled, while I stroked her hair and told her to hush, that everything was going to be all right. I could see her fingers digging into the flesh of my arm. Such long, narrow fingers. She pulled back, her face heavy with grief, but the tears had stopped.

"You're just so what?" I asked.

"Alone," she whispered.

"No," I said.

In moonlight, she was lovely. I was strong, her dream God with a strong shoulder. I was a God. I felt like a God. It seemed immoral. But it was also wonderful, strengthening, and erotic beyond belief. I wanted to kiss her worse than anything on this earth. Tears came down in silver drops along both cheeks and curled into the corners of her mouth.

"I want to believe the world is a good place," she said, "but my parents died, and my sister's marriage is no good. And there's this war, and black people in the South, and...."

"This isn't the best of all possible worlds, Nancy," I said, "but it's the only one we have, the only life we have."

Yes. That look in her eyes, desperate for love, for me, for Ford Clayton, for my touch. It felt sexual, but it was not. It was a powerful innocence, a friendship suddenly there beneath the endless night. I thought briefly with anger and disdain of Camille and her stupid society. Let them rot. Let Ingrid Halvorssen rot. The tears of one lovely girl in moonlight was worth a thousand Camilles and her close reading of Sartre.

"I should be going to practice my Bach," she said.

If I had let it go then, simply nodded, we might have never fallen in love, which we certainly did. But I was dancing in the house of poetry. I was kissing the rim of a Grecian urn. Confused, but poetic.

"Bach's been here for three hundred years," I said. "You won't always have the stars in your hair."

Not bad. Our faces came close. A mockingbird arrived for us, landed in a nearby tree, sang wildly of love and innocent sacrifice, of fatal love and truth. God sent it. I knew that. I did not close my eyes, but Nancy did, and she was begging for my tender lips.

I kissed her softly. Tears came out easily from her gentle closed eyes like droplets on a rainy pane. Her mouth tasted good, faintly like cinnamon or gum, and I put my hand behind her head to hold us together. It was shocking, now kissing a girl I'd barely known an hour before, a sudden rush toward intimacy. She came into my arms, and we necked for an hour, not getting closer toward sex, not farther away toward shock at our closeness. We merely sat under the canopy of mountain stars and kissed and kissed and kissed. She was ardent but unskilled, a lovely combination, trying to please but afraid of being wrong.

Finally, reluctantly, we rose from our seat, not talking, afraid of words now, and came back around the lake, my arm around her shoulder, her arm around my waist, and as I walked her back to her dorm, the Malone Society came storming past in lock-step cadence, shouting "Hell no, we won't go!" They were getting ready for the fight to come. I was getting ready for a summer back home in Jamesburg and a stream of letters from a girl who had no love but my own.

THE ANTI-WAR RALLY WAS SOMETHING OF A FLOP, before its
time. Exactly a year later, after Kent State, after Cambodia, the
campus had to close for three days because of day and night
marches and speeches. But in the spring of 1969, Camille merely
led the ragtag clot of Malone Society Protestors around campus
with ill-calligraphed signs. We made fun of them. They shouted
and sang. Billie did a few Joan Baez songs when they lit in front of
Jumper Hall, but her voice sounded more like Wayne Newton.

I had not forgotten the ubiquitous Camille, but I was mad for
Nancy MacLeish, though we'd done no more than hold hands and
kiss a few times before spring quarter ended and I was back home
in Jamesburg. Dad couldn't understand my mooning around the
house. Mom, on the other hand, encouraged it.

"Ah, Fordy, all great loves begin with a single walk in the
moonlight," she said. "Look at *La Bohème*. Look at *Madame
Butterfly*."

"Look at *Madame Bovary*," I said sourly. We were sitting in the
backyard beneath a canopy of thin stars, drinking sweet tea. Our
metal lawn chairs, painted white, bounced when we did.

"You are a strange child," she said.

"I'm no child," I said. "Would you mind if I smoked?"

"Ford!" she cried. "How dare you smoke here!"

"I don't smoke, Mom," I said. "I just wanted to see what you'd
say. I smoked a Winston once and nearly met God."

"A charming man could, conceivably, smoke a pipe," she said.

"Never a cigarette. Darling, if you're serious about this Nancy thing, then you simply must attend to your habits."

"Don't be condescending about her," I said. "She's the sweetest girl I've ever met in my life."

"Sweet is for a Whitman Sampler," she said, reaching over to touch my arm. "Does she know the works of Keats and Shelley?"

"Don't be absurd," I said. "That's obvious." Well, not so....in fact, I'd seen a copy of *Listen to the Warm* by Rod McKuen on her desk in the dorm, though I said nothing about it. But it was disconcerting, like a close friend showing up for a funeral in a black suit and brown shoes. "Your attention to my girlfriends is so patently reductive, Mom." A shock. The words came straight from Camille von der Malone. But I was through with her. Wasn't I?

"Then you must bring this charming child home," Mom said. "By the way, what is her favorite opera?"

"*Cavalleria Rusticana*," I lied, knowing Mom loved it.

"Well, perhaps her taste in music after all equals her taste in men," she said. She smiled at me and nodded, having been both loving and clever.

"Thanks," I mumbled, embarrassed.

She would do that to me. Once when Ronny Favors came home for a weekend, she came rushing out to the car, wearing a green dress, a handkerchief sticking from the sleeve, and hugged me, whirled me around, giggling, laughing. If I had not been an only child, she might have lavished some of her gifts upon someone else. Ronny laughed, but my face was pulsing, red.

I got the first letter from Nancy just after I'd started to work for the summer with Dad at Gallant-Belk. He was extremely worried at the time because some money was missing.

"Ford, I don't know who to suspect," he said in the office from which he'd thrown nothing away for thirty years. "But nearly four hundred is missing, and I'm starting to look seriously at Norma as a suspect."

"Norma?" I half shouted. He squinted his face and shushed me hastily. "Dad, she's nearly seventy years old. She told me once that her first shoes had buttons, for God's sake."

"I know what I know," he said darkly. "You just help me keep an eye on her."

And so I became a junior G-man, giving Dad regular weekly reports on Norma's activities, including the fact that she was apparently becoming quite senile: she was taking stacks of men's trousers and putting them in ladies' foundations for no apparent reason. She would clock out at odd hours. The rest of the staff had been quietly taking care of her, it turned out, for some months. Dad, the good manager, refused to vary from his thesis about her guilt, though, so I kept an eye on Norma for most of that hot summer.

The building had an unused second floor where Dad would put pre-ordered Christmas season stock. I went up there once when I was nine and found a flaming red bicycle with fluttery streamers sprouting from the handles. Later, it showed up beneath our Christmas tree, and I knew with certainty then that Santa was my father. In the corner was a stack of old, unsold stock Dad periodically culled to give to the church for indigents, bagged in croaker sacks. I'd sneak to the attic, take out one of Nancy's letters from Virginia, where she lived with her sister Ann.

She said lovely things, told me how the trees bent in the wind, about her dark moods. She would wait from darkness until first light to see dew in a spider web. I sighed for the poetry of her interest in me. Yet something was missing, and I knew it even then. She signed all her letters "Cheerio, Nancy" with a big dot over the i in "Cheerio."

Also, Ingrid's marriage was not going well. She came into the store one day and backed me into women's underwear.

"You could be Mr. Ingrid Halvorssen now instead of Burr," she said. "But no, you had to go off to that bigshot music college." She turned "music" into two very long syllables with molasses gooiness.

"Burr?" I said. "You married a man named Burr?"

"He's strong as an ox and has a tongue like a rattlesnake," she said proudly. Heads turned our direction. Norma was stacking boys' shirts in a display of percale sheets for our June white sale.

"For God's sake, be quiet," I said. "Somebody'll hear you."

"Everybody hears me," she said even louder. "I just wanted you to know that I was the biggest fish that ever got away from Ford

Clayton."

"I'm truly crushed," I said sarcastically. "Why'd you wait so long to get married?"

"It's your own fault," she said gaily. She walked toward the lingerie, and I followed, hoping to shush her somehow. Dad had asked Miss Elma Watts, who'd worked for him for ten years, to order a line of romantic lingerie, and so she had, filmy, blatantly sexual garments that embarrassed my father but sold quite well. Ingrid picked up a lacy brassiere with half cups and held it to her chest. "Is this my size? Could you measure me to make sure?" A few giggles could be heard around the store. Dad was in the office working with the adding machine, something he did several times a day. He was always worried that things just didn't add up.

"I'll get Miss Elma," I choked. I know your size, I thought. But then again, so does Burr. She was prancing around now, taunting me, waving the bra like Miss Liberty on the barricades of the French Revolution, leading the citizens on.

"You could do it, Ford," she said. She stomped her foot. "I want you to measure me, now!"

"Why are you doing this?" I whispered. I know now that it was because she was hurt by my rejection — or was she merely loaded and aiming destructively at any man in her path?

"Doing what?" she yelled. "I just want my chest measured so I can buy a bra to impress Burr, my husband." Miss Norma came over. She had a sweet face. She's long gone now, dead of a stroke the year I graduated from college, but then she was in the first sweet and terrible stages of senility.

"You have a darling figure," said Norma. "I believe a thirty-four C would probably give you the support you need."

"Thirty-six, D!" yelled Ingrid. "They've grown since me and Burr got married." Oh, great. I looked around, smiling squeamishly. Everybody knew we'd gone together, of course, even customers; they also knew she'd married that spring.

"Is there some problem here?" Dad's voice. Christ almighty. I turned and threw to him a look of innocent terror, and he knew at once what had happened, rescued me.

"Your son won't measure me for a new garment," said Ingrid.

She took tiny dance steps around the black-and-white tile floor.

"He can't," said my father decisively. "One of the ladies can help you, Ingrid, but you know Ford can't measure a woman."

"Why not?" she demanded. All pretense of work or shopping had stopped. She regarded me with violence. Might she have been packing a screwdriver, even then, in her deranged pocketbook, waiting for the right moment to stuff it between my ribs?

"Because I own this store, and I say he can't," Dad said. "Now if you persist in this, I'll call your husband at the sawmill."

"He's only working at the sawmill till his boat's out of hock," she said. She backed up a step, quit dancing, hung the bra back up.

"You're not going to come in here and try to lure my son into trouble. We can see what's happening here. Norma's a witness."

"I've not witnessed since the church retreat in 1948," Norma said distractedly. Dad ignored her. I began to giggle without tact or restraint.

"I was just window shopping, anyway," said Ingrid, starting toward the front of the store. "And I don't see a thing in here a sow would wear."

"That's very true," said Dad. "You should go over to Savannah. *They* have stores for sows."

"What?" cried Ingrid. Her face was pulsing. "I'm never coming back to your store, Mr. Clayton. Do you hear that? Never!"

"I'll call a press conference," my father said laconically. Ingrid stormed out, and Dad turned and went back to his adding machine without saying anything else to me. Norma took a stack of bras and hung them on hangers in the section with raincoats. Miss Elma moved them all back. I went to the office.

"Thanks for that," I mumbled. "I didn't know what to do next."

"Nothing meaner than a mean woman," he said.

"Mom always says that," I said, grinning.

"She's a big one for truth," he said. "Now, I have to balance these figures, son, if you'll excuse me."

And so I excused him, spent the early part of that summer working in the store, reading poetry and novels on the clothes bags upstairs. Each night, after dinner, in the silence and memories of my upstairs room, I worked on a massive composition, my *Symphony Number One for Large Orchestra, Double Chorus and Separate Brass Band*. I'd fallen more than ever under the spell of Mahler, and I wanted to leave a monument, something no one could ignore, even if they did not like it. Of course, I was seventy years out of date by then, and by August I understood painfully that the piece was far beyond my grasp, but I was nothing if not dogged. I played parts for Mom, who lied generously. The words were from Whitman, and she approved mightily of that, though Dad never made much of the body electric.

It was in the middle of this summer, my days like slowly melting tar from the roadside, that from nowhere, and with a zeal that surprised even me, I received a letter from Camille Malone. She was distracted and blunt.

Dear Georgia,

All summer, I have just been goddamn raging against the freaking Father of Waters down here at Jackson Square. I have a job as a juggler's assistant, dressed in a feather boa to gather crowds. Tights. It's humiliating, of course, except in the nihilistic sense, but I could find nothing else save clerking in some cheesy clothes store. So like Demosthenes, I speak with my mouth full of the pebbles of anger against the river here.

This war is the great tragedy of your generation, Georgia, and you didn't even come to our rally. Even though you were ejected (quite rightfully) from the Malone Society, you could have shown your mind was in the right sphere. Ah, southern boy, you are no free thinker.

My mother thinks she has cancer. She, in fact, has hysteria. So does my grandmother, who lives in Baton Rouge. Hysteria is the pendant that dangles from my neck. My Gift from the Magi. Did you ever read Heine's poem "Atta Troll" about the death of a trained bear? That's me.

Cordially,
Camille Malone

Huh? I kept the letter along with the poetic missives from

Nancy, found myself reading, re-reading it, trying to fathom her hysteria, why she considered herself both a trained bear and one who rages like Demosthenes against the Mississippi. Wait...*a juggler's assistant?* I wrote her back cautiously, but I got no answer. Nancy, on the other hand, wrote doggedly, even when she had nothing to say. In July, she began to send homemade envelopes constructed from the Sunday funnies, colorful, maybe avant garde if done by Camille, but, from Nancy, childish. Her letters were all the same. She talked about Ann, her parents, occasionally about music, mostly about everyday nothings like her job in a sewing shop. She was not a juggler's assistant.

I began to wait until I had five letters from Nancy before answering them. She scolded me. I shrugged. She wrote less, and so did I, and finally, toward the middle of August, we were corresponding only once a week, and the "i" in "cheerio" no longer had a circle for a dot.

But I had greater problems than Norma's senility, Camille's tights, or Ingrid's public need for a brassiere. That summer, I thought that I was going mad.

Toward dusk each day, when I took a walk in the cemetery not far from my house or sat brooding over a sonata by Schumann (who threw himself into the Rhine, Camille was to remind me later), I felt my brain disassociating. I had deep night terrors. I could not sleep for more than an hour at a time, so I was at my desk writing reams of anguished poetry. My weight fell off, dark circles appeared beneath my eyes, and I became profoundly nervous. I worried why Camille did not write back. Nancy became a millstone; all summer she'd demonstrated that her intellect and her emotional breadth were painfully shallow. She wrote that she'd never heard the *St. Matthew Passion.* Camille knew it virtually by heart. I tried to start a discussion of Kerouac (it was 1969, after all), but she thought he was an actor from the Kraft Playhouse on TV. Still, that was merely an irritating distraction compared to the deep, unshakable melancholy that descended over me, something full-born from early eighteenth-century *Sturm und Drang.* I went raving into a thunderstorm one night with my penknife clutched convulsively in my hand, as if I might slit my wrist, that fragile bracelet which holds us into this life. I planned nothing of the sort. Looking back now, I see it as acting, a fantasy of the wronged suitor, of Vienna long before electric lights brought the end of Romanticism. True Romantics, Camille had explained to the society, lost their *modus operandi* when electric lights began to brighten the spooky candle-lit corners of rooms. She hated the Romantics, of course, though after her conversion she was charitable toward them (and everyone, more or less). She came to love Keats, for example. That summer, I would write music all night, then fall weeping on my bed. Tears, idle tears, I told my mother when she asked, and she was quite pleased by my passionate fevers, tried to buoy me but not too much. She always held that great art came from great suffering, though Camille thought great art came from great planning. And so I turned my upstairs room there in Jamesburg into a crypt, full of slowly melting candles and dusty fears. Camille wasn't the only person with hysteria. I began to become silent and brooding at work, and Dad worried about me; even Norma patted me on the back one day, called me Frank, which was her own son's name, and told me that I should always keep on the sunny side. I was touched, but not enough to shed my familiar sadness. I read a book about Emily Dickinson. I could do *that*. I'd sit in the window of my house for the next thirty years, doing nothing, watching the world moult and change around me, writing, writing, and when they smelled the foul corpse, came to haul me out and clean the terrible debris of my life, they'd find Nine Symphonies, chamber works, five masses, concertos for piano and violin and cello....and my name would be known by all as the New York Philharmonic prepared the cycle of my works.

In the midst of this, Dad announced to us one day that the Clayton side of the family was having a family reunion late in August at Edward Bigelow State Park, thirty miles from Jamesburg. Mom thought it might be good for me to go, since I seemed to be slipping beyond Romanticism into sloth.

It had to be on a Sunday, of course, since Dad couldn't miss a Saturday at Gallant-Belk. I groused, but we all fell into the car and headed early one morning in that endless, heat-struck month to the park. We passed watermelon stands with ripe, thunky fruit piled high beneath canvas awnings, fields of cotton or soybeans, deep river bottoms where black water moved like treacle in the bug-thick shade. I saw poor black men in fields, manual laborers whose poverty was heartbreaking but largely ignored, families of white children, out of school for summer, hanging around some sinking unpainted front porch doing nothing, dragging toes slowly through the sand while sitting on a swing. A horse stood motionless in a nearly grassless field. But even then, my corner of the state was changing, not being made safe for opera but for the newly rich, for swimming pools and ranch-style brick homes in the middle of fields. Farming was losing its grip of two centuries, and nothing would ever bring it back.

Edward Bigelow State Park was fondly called "The Okefenokee of Gilmore County." Actually, the Gilmore County Chamber of Commerce was the only group calling it that, but they were very proud. Black water, turgid, crisscrossing waters, cypress knobs, alligators, billions of undifferentiated insects — and a large picnic area on a swollen elbow of land overlooking the Lokatchakee River. By the time Dad parked, much of his family was already there, and I saw them, aunts and uncles, cousins, my grandparents (his parents) who lived in Casey, halfway between the park and Jamesburg. They'd come from all over the state, even from South Carolina and Alabama. I saw remnants of families not quite mine, my grandfather's brother's people, including a cousin of sorts who had convinced himself that he was really a Creek Indian and went about wearing a Cheyenne medicine bonnet as proof.

"There's Odelle," said Mom. "And she's not even pregnant. She must have been in jail."

"Clarice," said my father with sweet warnings. He adored her, never raised his voice to her, but he'd gently chide her when she irritated him. Odelle was my first cousin. She was twenty-five, had borne four children out of wedlock, and given them all up for adoption. Everyone liked her, forgave her, merely shrugged at her sexual indiscretions.

We got out, and Dad and I got the picnic basket of chicken and sandwiches Mom had made. Its fragrant delights had chased me all the way from Jamesburg. Hello, Aunt Jane, hi Uncle Bob,

Jimbo, you've lost weight....we met and mingled, and I began to watch my Dad, saw his bright face, full of joy here with his family, and I felt, with reluctance, that my drama was crumbling. At that moment, as Dad laughed and joked, danced around with shuddering, hand-clapping joy, Clarence Clayton came up.

This was several years before he knocked over the liquor store. His hair was short and clogged with Vitalis. He wore a two-pocket shirt, baggy shorts, and black shoes with mid-calf blue socks.

"Hi, Ford," he said through his nose. He was a head shorter than me, even though he was twenty, and I was only nineteen. "You working for your daddy this summer?"

"Clarence," I said drearily. "Yeah. What are you doing?"

"Pig chaser," he nodded, smiling, as if he'd announced the recent arrival of a Guggenheim.

"Pig chaser?" I said. I was an aesthete that summer, dreaming of castles and gravestones; pig chasing smacked of peasant revolts and mucky filth. "What in the hell is a pig chaser?"

"Chase pigs to catch 'em before they slaughter 'em," he said. "I'se lucky to get the job. Reese Bunyan nearbout got it, but we had a chaseoff."

"A what?"

"Chaseoff," he said. "Each of us got to catch five pigs. Man's got hisself a stopwatch. I beat by thirty-two seconds. Got me a job as a pig chaser."

"Lord," I said.

"Thanks," said Clarence. "I'm proud to have it, too. Reese stepped in a snake hole and twisted his ankle. Then this sow took a bite out a his leg big as a apple. You tried my momma's vinegar and banana casserole yet?"

"No," I said. "I haven't tried it. Wait, Elsie's calling me. See you, Clarence."

Elsie wasn't calling me, but I pretended, and Clarence didn't catch on. I drifted to one side, into the deep shade of Spanish-moss-hung trees and watched my father. I got a plate, ate, then went back to my tree. Dad was light as a water strider, all backslapping and laughter; I could never remember having seen anyone so happy. What, I wondered was the composition of his pleasure? Family?

Perhaps. Being the center of attention? Undoubtedly. He was not an unhappy man, nor were any of the Claytons; even Clarence was bouncing from one group to the next, probably telling about pig chasing, bringing with him good cheer and the aroma of Vitalis. Already, I was wrestling with the philosophies that later drew me back to Camille, especially when she Saw the Light, even though it was Catholic and not Protestant. She would hold my hand near the Circle Beech, and instead of ranting and rating every illness of humanity would say: *Haec dies, quam fecit Dominus: exsultemus, et laetemur in ea.* This is the day which the Lord hath made: let us rejoice and be glad in it.

And so, against my Romantic will, as I watched Dad that day, I rejoiced and was glad for his happiness, his communion with the saints as we blessed the food, with his family, through the still, aromatic Sunday at Edward Bigelow State Park.

And so, as we drove home, having parried another visit from Clarence, having talked to Odelle, who told me without guilt or apparent concern that she had missed two periods, having discussed the aesthetics of swamps with Mom and how they could be a fine setting for a folk opera — as we drove home, I silently swept away cobwebs that had accumulated that summer.

I was not a doomed, Romantic artist. I wanted to live forever and be loved by the world for the power of my genius. I wanted adults to respect, admire, and covet me. Neither was I attracted to Nancy, who was lovely and bright and hopelessly shallow. No, the woman whose face kept swimming back into my cloudy tank was Camille Malone, who at that very minute was probably cursing her lot as a juggler's assistant on a New Orleans street. I was in her power, hopelessly full of magic spells and speeches that only she could engineer.

I stopped answering Nancy's letters. I began to write a piano sonata in A major, forgetting (for the time at least) about my gargantuan Romantic symphony. I bought a two-hundred-watt bulb for the lamp in my room and banished the candles. I took long walks in the countryside around Jamesburg and wrote pastoral poetry. I exercised in the backyard with a set of barbells from Sears in Savannah. I devoted myself to health and vigor just as President

Kennedy had asked when I was a mere boy.

Without complaint, I cut the grass, trimmed hedges, went to church with my mother, and appeared to enjoy the sermons. I would be good. Perhaps a saint in my own way, a godly man.

Two events, however, changed my sunny servility.

One afternoon in mid-August, when the streets were thrumming with heat and silence and no one had been near the store for hours, Miss Elma Watts, whose gray demeanor was rarely ruffled, went into my father's office and closed the door. All morning, she had been agitated and red-eyed, stopping as if rehearsing a speech, then failing to deliver it. I was on the sales floor doing absolutely nothing. When the store was quiet like this, I withdrew a secreted volume from beneath a storage shelf in the shoe department and read. That summer, it was perversely enough, *East of Eden*, and I remember the exact words I was reading when the small drama's climax came in ringing words from the office. The beginning of Chapter Thirteen: "Sometimes a kind of glory lights up the mind of a man." I read the line, looked up briefly and heard my father's very loud and disgusted voice. Five others worked there, three high school girls, Miss Norma, and an ancient black man named Curly who did not seem to move more than twice a day. He was gone. The others stopped and stared at the office and listened, Dad's voice resounding, rising louder and louder. (One of the high school girls, Liddy Lalouche, had a crush on me, but I didn't care for her, though I kept a watchful eye on her compact and tantalizing rear. Everyone called her by that lilting, euphonious but ultimately impossible-to-pronounce entire name.)

No one breathed, least of all the boss's kid. In a moment, the door opened, and Miss Elma came out, crushed, walking on infirm knees. Dad stormed out behind her.

"And don't ever set foot in this store again!" he screamed. Fists were clenched. Miss Elma skittered toward the front door, dropping a nail file and a crumpled tissue from her purse. She wept. The silence was thick as plaster. I walked toward Dad, wondering what had happened, but knowing only too well.

"What's wrong?" I asked. He speared me with angry eyes. His face was twisted, like the sudden appearance not of my father but of his *double*, a concept of German Romanticism. When you saw your double, your own death was claimed to be very near.

"Ten years!" he boomed in a voice I scarcely recognized. "Ten years she works for me!" He went back into the office and slammed the door, and I knew all, as everyone else did. They went back to work, their zeal redoubled, feather dusting, straightening, sweeping, even though no one was in the store. I remember that the sky outside began to take on a hazy cast, then grew heavy and dark almost instantly as a summer storm swept toward town. Nothing was unusual about that in the least, but that day, it seemed an omen.

I read no more of Steinbeck. I straightened all the shoes, even though they were as rigidly correct as a drill line at the Citadel. An hour passed, and with it a, storm broke over Jamesburg with stunning fury, making the front plate glass tremble and sway in and out with updrafts and downdrafts.

The rain was torrential. I went upstairs for my usual midafternoon break and sat on the bags of clothing and re-read for the fiftieth time the letter from Camille, trying to divine some code in it. Entirely possible, I thought. Could "juggler's assistant" have meant something clandestinely philosophical? I watched the rain over the rooftops of the businesses in the well-ordered square in downtown Jamesburg.

When I came downstairs, the second event that changed my summer took place before my stunned eyes. The door from the office burst open, and Dad came staggering out, grasping at his collar, pleading with his eyes for help.

I have since tried to summon the sequence of events. Nothing comes back. The surfaces of my brain have conspired to eliminate it from that point until later when Mom and I were in the waiting room at the hospital. I recall no ambulance, no screaming employees, no end to the storm.

I do remember holding Mom's hand, remember Dr. Elwin Essex coming from the emergency room's double doors of the James County Hospital and looking relaxed and cheerful. Mom was trembling but brave.

"Is he still alive?" she cried.

"Clarice, he's just fine," he said. "His heart rate is fine, there's been no apparent coronary. We have him sedated mildly now. His vital signs are all fine. Sometimes these things just happen. I think he might spend the night here, but he should be able to go home tomorrow."

"God is good," said Mom, crying. I cried, too.

He did come home, and his silent and somber state lasted but a day. After that, I never saw Dad angry again. What little anger he possessed had been exorcised. He became cheerful, hardly raised his voice. He, like Mom, was worthy of my worship.

In early September, three weeks before school started for fall quarter, I got a postcard from Nancy which informed me she was leaving McCandless to become a missionary for the Southern Baptist Convention. She blessed me and wished for me the best, that God would guide my steps.

I took that as a sign to become morose once more, and soon I was full-blown into candles and stormy night walks in swamps and cemeteries. By the time school began, I was completely ripe for Camille Malone.

CLARENCE HAD NOT SEEN THE OCEAN IN YEARS, so by the time we got to Conway, after spending the night in Columbia, he was bouncing all over the back seat of the car.

"Well, he-magine a thang like that!" he cried with joy. "Naming a town after a Country and Western singer! Jesus hisself must be smiling up in Heaven."

"They didn't name the town after Conway Twitty," I said. "It's just a name."

"Oh," he said, disappointed. "Names are like easy women. Once you give 'em money, they'll perform anything for you. I wrote that. Anywho, I got to prepare myself for the heathenry at this beach," he said. "After all, I been washed in the blood of the Lamb."

He mumbled incantations for the half hour's drive to the beach, crying at the strayed ocean birds, the flat black water, the dark sand, even the string of screaming real estate offices, each trying to outbid the other for attention from tourists. Still early spring, the traffic was light. Later, in June, cars would be strung day and night from Conway to Myrtle like baubles on a necklace, Mommy and Daddy and Chip and Katerina, bikes on top, plenty of dough, kids seeking tiny swimsuits and summer loves, Daddy the nearest restaurant.

I'd last been to Myrtle with Jill and the kids three years before, and though it had some of the gaudy toppings of a tourist trap, the Grand Strand beaches were lovely, and by now, high rises had invaded, Hiltons and Ramadas and everything else.

"There!" screamed Clarence, jumping up and down, shaking the car. "I see the promised water!" My eyes followed his skinny finger and saw a swimming pool behind a cheap and decaying miniature golf course, whose windmills and tunnels bore huge flakes of old paint.

"That's a swimming pool," I said. "Do you care where we stay?"

"Somewhere near the Philly Stones," said Clarence breathlessly.

I knew I could pay for pleasant surroundings, fine restaurants, a pool. I settled for The Gordon House, an incredibly rundown two-story motel in the heart of the video game and rubber-shark district. I parked out front. Clarence saw, between a sign for Live Sharks and half-price T-shirts, the wide green expanse of the Atlantic Ocean.

"Over there's a bigger pool," he said. "Let's us stay there."

"That's the ocean," I said.

We got out, and two teenagers strolled past, one a boy at least six and a half feet tall, the other a girl a foot shorter; both had blue-black hair of an identical shade; both had tattoos of writhing snakes on their arms; both were emaciated beyond belief.

"Heal thyself, druggie scum!" screamed Clarence holding his Bible high.

The black-haired duo turned toward Clarence, laughed him off, kept moving. Clarence seemed delighted with it all, went dashing off across the street toward the Live Shark tank.

"Come on," I said. "Let's get a room." He reluctantly came back across the street.

We walked up the steps, which sagged and groaned beneath our weight. There were two porches, one downstairs, one directly above it. From the second floor, guests must once have been able to see the ocean; now they saw the roof of a towel shop. A man with a startling, hairless stomach sat in a rocking chair, making the runners creak beneath his immense weight. Next to him was a foul-looking old woman who had gone nearly bald and was concealing it poorly with a hair net.

"The foodth okay, but the sheeth hath stainth," the man said in a eunuch-high lisp. His face was also hairless.

"The food is not okay," growled the old woman. "It is full of messages from the Evil One. They grind them up and put them in the salt shakers, and when you season their vile food, you're eating the words. They invade you that way. Everyone here wants to invade you." She was whispering, leaning over.

"Oh, Mommy," the man said. In full view of her, he put a fat finger to his temple and made a circular motion. She leaned back and rocked. Undaunted, I opened the front screen door, which was held by a fiercely tight spring to the frame. Something stubborn and probably directly descended from my father's conservatism drove me toward the front desk. I was bound for it.

A man with a huge head and tiny shoulders was behind the desk. Hanging on the wall behind him was a stuffed fish, so heavily coated with dust it might have appeared on a platter, as if immersed in a daring and much-coveted sauce. The man smiled at me. In a chair across the small lobby, a young man was sweating terribly, smoking a cigarette down to his dirty fingernails. The counter man was smiling now, revealing, like a broken zipper, twin rows of crazily positioned teeth.

"Welcummme to the Gordon House," he said. He took his hands from below the counter; they were huge, almost cruel. His voice was deep, lost in a barrel. "Would you like a ruummme?"

"Yes," I said.

"Yes, yes, yes, you absolutely must stay," he said.

"We will," I said. "Two adults. Sort of."

"Oh my," he said with a smile. I did not notice that the TV-watching smoker had drifted toward us, was now standing a few inches from Clarence.

"You got a cigarette?" he asked. His eyes were wandering without focus around the room. Clarence did not have far to go. Camille von der Malone could be about; I felt her in the fearful voltage of the room.

"We don't smoke," I said. I gave him a dollar. He seemed indifferent, left the place, screen door slamming on its fanatically tight spring.

"Dimmy has bad manners," the desk man said. "Let me get you that key." With that, he took a step and disappeared up to his nose behind the counter — what was this, going downstairs? No. He walked slowly to the key slots on the side wall took a step and was tall again.

"Hey," I whispered to Clarence, "he's a dwarf." He got a key and came scuttling out from around the counter and told us to follow him upstairs. He was about three and a half feet tall, simian arms, but humming a cheery tune....I could collect *Dwarfs' Tunes*, weave them into a symphony, something original and, and....Halfway up the creaky stairs I realized the tune was "I Feel Pretty." The hall upstairs was undusted. Rooms on either side. Window at the stairhead, crusty lace curtains long since gone sienna that waved to us in the steady breeze. He opened a door, and we looked inside: sagging bed with a weakly threaded chenille spread, two chairs with huge scoops where your butt would rest. A bureau made of plywood, streaked mirror over it, a ceiling fan that was whirring slowly, and hanging from the cord, a crucifix that moved around the fan's circumference, Jesus not seeming to enjoy the ride.

"Onliest thing I request you do not molest is the Swinging Jesus," he said. "We're knowed in the *Guinness Book* for that. I'm proud of that."

"Lordy," said Clarence.

"Catholic?" I asked.

"Umhuh," he said. "Raised in Charleston, moved up here. Worked a circus for years. I like this a whole shitload...scuse me, better. Room's thirty-eight a night or two hundred a week."

"Why have you got a Jesus on the fan?" asked Clarence.

"Way I figure it, the whole joint's always being blessed that way," he said.

"It's perfect," I said. "We'll take it. By the way, does the name Camille Malone mean anything to you?"

"Camille Malone," he said. "Can't say it does. You can pay me when you leave." I came back out into the hall and saw the door leading to the upstairs porch. I went out into the hot shade and sat in a rocker. The porch was leaning forward at ten degrees, to shed water, I supposed, but it gave the eerie sensation of falling, a giddy, almost erotic feeling; two choices, jump or fall, it seemed to be saying. Jump or fall. From the balcony I could see the tourists streaming along the streets. Where had Camille and I stayed those years before? I remembered how it looked, but the name was lost in the miasma of distance and loss.

Was it time to ask what I was doing here? Was it time to ask what I was doing *anywhere*, if Camille was indeed the key to things? Was it time to approach the sea and ask it the repeated imponderables of our limited appearance on this quaking globe? It was.

Clarence wandered off, and I walked down to the beach. The afternoon waned, but the sun hung high, a dull sightless eye of molten wax, dripping heat on the sunbathers. I quickly categorized them all: posers, strutters, those who are embarrassed, and those who are indifferent. At my age, I was indifferent. Teen-age girls with swimsuits that boasted but did not conceal strutted past, all points and folds. I tried unsuccessfully not to leer.

This was like a pilgrimage or a quest or something. Maybe I'd have to joust for Camille's honor or enter the archery contest on the Grand Strand to prove myself. The truth was that I really missed Jill. All my guilt rallied through the indifference and lust for strutting women, told me how much I missed her, that she would be crazy at the end of thirty days to even mildly consider a reconciliation. I knew with the ponderous power of the ocean that I did not deserve Jill.

On the other hand, neither did I deserve Clarence, and at that moment, I saw him up the beach, standing on stacked chunks of broken styrofoam, waving his arms and preaching.

"Oh God," I said out loud and with a groan. "My cousin's up there preachifying." From where did *that* non-word spring?

"H-annnnd I say unto you, unh, that this is a den!" he shouted, "a den of ininkyties!" The passersby looked amused or confused. (*Iniquities,* I translated.) Four or five people, superior and amused, had stopped to listen. I glanced over them, saw they were educated adults, superior, escalating income, no need for religion. Faith was for the have-nots of the earth, not someone who drove a BMW and watched the ocean loll against the sand from a twenty-story penthouse. "H-annnd that you should repent of yore sins! For hath not Jesus hisself taken one fish and tu-hurrnned it into a thousand to feed the crowd at that, uh, what was it, uh, football game. Yeah! A football game that the Savory fed 'em all with one fish and a loaf of, hunhhh!, bread! Repent of yore sins as I haveth, and find the light at the end of the eternal!"

They were laughing at him. I cringed. What kind of grammar did John the Baptist possess, anyway? Wasn't he a voice crying in the wilderness, "Prepare ye the way of the Lord"? The four listeners drifted off down the beach, and no one took their places, and finally, the only ones in the neighborhood were Ford Clayton and Clarence, whose voice was whining against the waves. He stopped, breathing hard, looking out to sea. A strong, salty wind was moving his hair. His Adam's apple was going up and down, and he looked down with sadness and failure at his black shoes on the white styrofoam.

What was the price we paid for our Fools? I spun through the kind of association game Camille foisted on the Malone Society, leaping from one image to another, building a rich fugue: seeing Clarence in Harlequin's stripes, medieval tubs barely afloat on the swelling seas, signs of the cross, True Belief in talismans (talismen?), cold castles, and Clarence dancing, singing dumb songs for the visitors from Mantua; then shifting seasons, and seeing a blazing hearth and the jerking gaiety of sackbutts and viols, heaped platters of rich food, gouty young men watching half-naked Nubians shake finger cymbals, then here comes Clarence in his Fool costume, and the Beautiful People in Florence all watching him, even hook-nosed old Lorenzo De Medici, who wouldn't have a twentieth-story penthouse; he'd have the whole Grand Strand, piano-playing chickens, Live Shark Shows and all.

The vision cleared. Camille smiled somewhere. I walked without speaking toward Clarence, who stepped away from the spot, forgot he was on the styrofoam and fell flat on his angular face in the sand. I rushed to his side to help him up.

"Are you hurt?" I asked. "This probably isn't the place to set up shop." He didn't bother dusting the sand from his trousers. He was smiling benignly.

"Ford, look at that," he said, nodding at the ocean. "If you went straight across there, you'd come out in Australia! Just think on that!"

I thought on it, decided not to correct him. His face was suffused with peace and joy.

"Now," he said, "when do we start to find this pore child of God what's missing from you?" He smiled at me. People drifting past stared at him; he was dressed for a street corner in Eufala, Alabama, not for the beach. He was oblivious to everything, as an animal is oblivious to its death; just as we must grieve for our pets since they can't do it for themselves, I grieved for Clarence's mad innocence.

"Tomorrow," I said. "I'm exhausted tonight."

"Bet yore bottom dollar it's tomorrow!" said Clarence. "I made that up."

He went dancing down the beach. I burst into easy laughter. What was it about Clarence that was so infuriating and yet so easy to take? He was simply operating on AM in an FM world, I thought; no, that was stupid. He was a Fool in the Court of the World. Better. I'd have to ask Camille for an analogy.

I ate early, went alone to our room in the midst of a rising and ferocious thunderstorm. I sat on the edge of the bed. The downdraft blew the old curtains straight out, then the updraft sucked them into the screens. Darkness never came. Neon from the strip glared sullenly through the window, off and on, like a Mickey Spillane novel. Laughter came from outside, but not much, since rain was coming straight down over the wet neon. I got up and sat in a chair next to the window. I could see across the porch to the wet streets. Down the way, a store named The Gay Dolphin seemed busy. Everyone was happy. A ferris wheel, empty in the storm, kept turning anyway not far away. My hand trailed off the chair arm, brushed the box of letters I'd obsessively brought. 'Twas a time for deep digging. The Schliemann of old letters.

I pulled one out, knew from the envelope that it was from Camille, this one from New Orleans during Christmas break of our senior year — this leaping forward a year in my narrative of her life to myself.

"Devout," I said out loud. A car playing loud rock stopped at a light, throbbing, then moved on, changing from music to a mere heartbeat. I opened the letter, turned it toward the neon.

Friday evening

Dearest Ford,

Dilectio Dei honorabilis sapientia! I'll translate, since I know you have little Latin: The love of God is honorable wisdom. The beginning of the words of St. Joseph of Cupertino. From the Missal: A humble Franciscan Friar who never possessed the earthly sciences, was favored by his crucified God with a marvelous grace of contemplation, with the spiritual privileges of priesthood and with the remarkable power of miracles.

Pray with me, darling. God grant us the serenity to understand this world and the wisdom to ignore it. Amen.

I wish you could have been with me this morning. You know how much I hate Christmas break, how difficult it is here in New Orleans with my parents. I knelt on the banks of the River just beyond Jackson Square, and I lifted the Father of Waters with my fingers and blessed myself and all the wretched unhappy peoples of this world, and something came into me, a healing, darling. Do you know the ecstasy of a healing? Like a deep wound that closes sweetly before your eyes, from angry red to clean pure skin.

Tonight I know the ecstasy of a healing and long for your hand on the keyboard of my soul. When you enter The Church with me, our future will be clear.

A small parish in The Netherlands? Perhaps.

All I know is that this part of my heart is with you back there, that the light of God is the light of our lives, and that all music is ultimately an exaltation, and that is why it is the fabric of our lives.

Yours in Christ,
Camille

I'd forgotten. She wanted us to be Christian missionaries to the Dutch, an idea she later used to *prove* that her entire Catholic phase was simply a twist on her manic-depressive illness. In truth, when she came back from that break our senior year, she came back the old Camille, unsure about anything, and shortly after we graduated and moved to New York, she decided that God was an illusion meant to deflect her from Life.

I put the letter back in the box. Above me, Jesus kept on spinning. Why was I smiling?

Jubilate Deo, omnis terra.

THE SLIM SHADOW OF NANCY DRIFTED AROUND ME that delicious autumn at McCandless, but it was driven away quickly by Camille. The intense summer in Jamesburg left me eager for the healing winds of Asheville, and when I got back late that September, heard music already coming from every crack and direction, I filled with a joy I could barely contain. To this day, I associate my greatest joy at McCandless with the lovely renewal of Fall Quarter, the resurrection of old friendships and loves, the sweet second chance for affairs of the head and heart.

Ronny Favors was in fine fettle. We stayed roommates, and he shouted when we saw each other in the dim lobby of Tarmot Hall.

"Clayton!" he yelled, "What's the good word, buddy?"

"Hey, Ronny," I said with a broad grin. "How'd you stay out of jail for a whole summer?" Whereupon he grabbed my arm, and I followed him with swift acceleration through one of the girls' dorms, where we saw a beautiful girl half naked, whooped, ran, once more avoided trouble. I was in top form, and we laughed, made new friends, stayed up half that first night, smoked too many cigarettes, drank too much illegal Scotch, solved too many wars, trashed too many composers. I told them about my huge Mahlerian symphony, and they, all Twelve-Tonists and somewhat fervent Bergians, derided me mercilessly. I was a silly anachronism, but I didn't particularly care. We sang the traditional McCandless songs, used guitars to veer into the day's folk junk, became serious about The War, then talked of the summer's love conquests. I lied, as they all did.

Though I thought about her, I did not run into Camille until two days later. A robin's-shell blue sky arched over us, cool and sharp, and the beech and dogwood trees were climbing into their gold and crimson profusion. Classes had begun, and I was no longer upset to be merely a journeyman in the world of music, lost among the brilliance of composers and performers. I had this brief sense of the fullness of life, a state that we all so desperately try to relive later in our years.

I was carrying an armful of books when I heard that voice come toward me on the sparkling air.

"Hey, Georgia, how in the hell was your summer?" she cried.

I turned to my left, and she was standing on the sidewalk in front of Jumper Hall. Her long brown hair was shining in that peculiar mountain light late in the sunny season, and she wore bell-bottoms, a ratty football jersey with the number "13," and a smile broad as the limbs of the Circle Beech.

"Camille!" I cried. "I wondered where you were. How was your summer?" Dumb.

"Not worth a fuck," she said. "I don't lie about stuff like that anymore. Don't you hate it when somebody lies just to pass the time? I find it intellectually dishonest. What did you accomplish during the heat-stroke season?"

"I got your letter," I said. "Were you really a juggler's assistant wearing a feather boa?" She laughed brightly, face coloring.

"Actually, I clerked at a Woolworth's, but that's an awful thing to admit," she said. "I did, however, work hard on my reading, writing, and composing. I did Dostoyevsky, Houseman, Klopstock, Heine, and Murger. Also wrote me a little novel, an updating of certain scenes from *Julie, ou la Nouvelle Héloise*. And I wrote a piano sonata that takes nearly two hours to perform, if any attention at all is given to my metronome markings. I practiced nothing but Bach all summer. He would have been a fascinating man to seduce, I think."

"Not to me," I said. She laughed.

"What did you do, Georgia?" she asked.

"I worked in my father's store and tried to write some on a

symphony," I said.

"The symphony as a viable art form has been dead for at least sixty years, Georgia," she said with some pity. "Besides, it's just jerking off. Write me a piece for piano, and we'll both get famous. By the way, the Malone Society kicks back off next Thursday night. You coming?"

"You kicked me out," I said.

"I hereby kick you back in," she said. "I'm starting to look at things from a.....oh, I don't know. Oh, what happened to the twinkie you were flirting with last spring?"

"She transferred to Julliard," I lied.

"Well, it's not like you were in love with her or anything," she said.

The first meeting of the Malone Society was uneventful. Camille welcomed new members. Billie, the fat girl with the mustache, was back, even fatter, hairier, and meaner than ever. The new kids had heard of Camille, and some were clearly afraid of her. But they came anyway, about fifteen now, ready to listen to her monologue. She spent nearly twenty minutes yelling about how we'd lost the clear goals of the minnesingers, that somebody named Heinrich von Ofterdingen, the court poet, was a real genius we should emulate. Just remember the function and forget the court, she said. Knowing laughter. Hegel and historical process held the floor for a time, then the rupture between humanism and Evangelism following the publication of Calvin's Institutes in 1541. We had listened to her virtuoso lecturing for nearly forty minutes before she got to Republicans, saying we should be in the streets against the war in Vietnam, that it was corrupt and immoral, that American boys were dying for no reason at all. Whereupon she flung herself into a foaming tirade against Henry Luce, who had died a couple of years before. Except for the veterans, none of them had ever seen anything like it.

I paid no attention to what she said, of course. Her face caught fire; her hair flamed, fanned when she turned. I kept my mouth shut, didn't point out that she held sway because those of us who never lost control somehow admired those who nearly always did.

We stood publicly foursquare against such things of course, for order and process. Even our presence at the Malone Society meetings testified to that. But with Camille, it was more: Beauty and its attendant halo.

In short, I had fallen in love.

The textures of that autumn were rich and friendly. Ronny and I became inseparable, even more than our freshman year, spilling our guts over trivial but deeply felt matters of school and heart. We talked often, far into the night, about music and how it made us feel, associating colors with keys, laughing at the over-rated, praising those who died too soon for their full virtues to flower.

One night in early November, when I was having a terrible time with a harmony class (Ronny never had a problem with any academic class), I threw my pencil across the dorm room in disgust and walked to the window. From our second-story perch in Tarmot Hall, we could see the green expanse of McCandless. (An aside: sometimes now, between quarters when the dorms are being cleaned, I'll sneak up to room 202, stand wistfully in that same window, pretend I feel the same as I did then. Different, of course, but not far removed from the memory of a favorite blanket.)

"What's your problem?" asked Ronny.

"I'm just....I don't know," I said. "I have trouble with modulations. It's just bullshit. And I know Carpenter's going to give me a C anyway. Who remembers what Beethoven made in harmony?"

"He studied with Haydn," said Ronny, looking down at his own note paper, which he easily filled. "Probably made an A."

"Besides," I said, "I'm, it's that...."

"You're crazy in love," he said. He grinned. "My God, Clayton, you're the most lovestruck youth it's ever been my misfortune to witness."

"Let me ask you something," I said. I turned a chair around, straddled it and faced him. "She sort of scares me. How can you be in love with someone who sort of scares you?" Ronny began to tremble with laughter, not spilling it at first, then gloriously exploding in a shower of mirth.

"Love is supposed to scare you, asshole," he said. "Where have you been, Ford? Love is the ritual of the mating imperative."

"You sound like Camille," I said.

"Look, if you need myth and mystery, be my guest," he said. "Throw in religion and sentiment and maybe even Elizabeth Barrett Browning. Next thing you know, you'll be talking about romance."

"I *am* talking about romance!" I cried. "Would somebody please tell me what's wrong with romance?"

I was facing the window, being dramatic, so I was unaware that four other boys had been standing in the door, watching my performance, Charley Barstow from next door, two freshmen and a guy named Huddleston who was well-liked but horribly disfigured from a fire when he was a child.

"I'll tell him," said Charley. They all came spilling into the room, bringing with them the rank odor of tobacco and cheap wine, which they were drinking in Dixie cups.

"Oh, shit," I said. "Damnit, Ronny." He laughed at me, leaned back and watched.

"Romance is fine if you've had all your shots," said Charley, striding back and forth, showing off for the freshmen. "It's fine if the object of your desire is someone who has the same goals as you, Ford, though preferably not of the same sex."

"Fuck you, Barstow," I said unhappily. They all roared.

"I'd steer clear of Italian girls, though," he said, "since they tend to grow beards later in life. You might want to look for someone from Norway. But then that might bring up Ingrid, the girl from back home who waited ten minutes after you left for college to get married."

"Eat shit," I said.

"Hell, he's talking about that crazy Malone chick anyway," said one of the freshmen. He was a tall, heavy boy with hard, drunken eyes and close-cropped blond hair. He seemed out of place at a music conservatory.

"What did you say?" I said. "What's your name anyway, asshole?"

The room grew quiet.

"Come on, Ford," said Ronny, standing and coming around

the desk.

"If you want romance, I'd pick up some fag hereabouts rather than touch that Malone girl," the boy continued. His voice had the pronounced drawl we'd all tried hard to lose. He seemed proud of it. "Besides, I heard she spent last summer as a whore down there in New Orleans." He said it like "N'Arlins."

I felt blood rush into my face, and I knew that something was going to happen. The other freshman disappeared. Charley talked to my enemy, said calming words I did not hear. In fact, I heard nothing, only the rushing of my blood and what he'd said about her summer. A juggler's assistant? A feather boa?

I waited for two seconds, put my hands slowly on the back of a metal desk chair, picked it up and threw it at the freshman. He ducked, but one leg caught him hard on the chin, and blood blossomed there. He staggered, touched his bloodied chin, let out a bull-howl of rage and came for me. Charley and Ronny got out of the way.

He swung suddenly, hitting my temple with his fist, and I went down on my rear, stars and cartoon birds whirling up and down in a syncopated rush. My head cleared almost immediately, and as he glowered above me, I rose like a great whale breaching the sea surface, *slam!*, right under his chin. He stumbled backward into the hall, and I rushed after him.

"You son of a bitch!" I screamed. "Take back what you said!" *Take back what you said?* What was this, fourth grade? We wrestled furiously in the hall, and I soon realized that he was mostly bluff, that I was, in fact, stronger, more directed. After all, insulting your woman was traditional cause for murders in the hills of North Carolina.

"Whore," he choked, "whore." His blood was flying all over both of us now, and just when I thought he was going to give up, he hunched over slightly then rose with an elbow that hit my nose squarely. I fell again, bleeding from both nostrils. "Whore." I rose slowly, as if in supplication. My right hand moved in the dim hall light, and I saw a dozen boys yelling for us to stop, a dozen urging us on for no particular reason.

I hit the right side of his face just beneath the eye. He went down like a heavyweight. Didn't move. A couple of guys turned him over, slapped at his face and he groaned and came around.

"Jesus, Clayton," said Ronny. "Are you all right?" I felt nothing but rage for the world. What if he was right? What if my beloved had been giving blow jobs on a stained mattress in some dive on Bourbon Street?

"Leave me alone," I muttered. My head throbbed terribly. I walked past them, coatless, and went downstairs, out the front door, and into the lamplit stillness of the campus. When the cool, nearly frosted air came into my face, the pain was indescribable. I began to cry. I bled, wept, my nose ran. My right hand throbbed with pain from the winning blow I'd struck. Did I have to know? Once and for all? I did.

Mary Grandville was up a slope on the other side of Jumper, and I staggered toward it, the Madman of McCandless. Men were not allowed in the women's dorms after nine, so the moment I went through the front door into the lobby, I was breaking rules. The rules went all to hell when I ascended the stairs to the second floor, where she lived. I heard a guitar. Someone was singing Peter, Paul, and Mary songs. Hers was the fourth door on the left, but in my haste and disease, I knocked with tremendous fury on the third door, and when it opened, when a girl wearing a T-shirt and panties and an expression of high terror so pure that even I shivered, all hell, relatively speaking, broke loose.

She screamed. Let me clarify this. *Scream* is too delicate; try *went into deep-seated audible hysterics.* The doors all opened, and girls started yelling, screaming, slamming doors. Camille's door remained closed.

"It's all right," I tried to say. "I was looking for Camille Malone." My wounds distorted the words. I sounded like a punch-drunk pug from some grunting cheap club in south Chicago. The girl in front of me kept screaming, backing up. Her roommate, also wearing only a shirt and panties, joined her soprano with a rich alto, and soon their duet resounded through the dorm: "Camille! Camille!"

Her door opened, and suddenly she was there, yawning. She wore a tie-dyed T-shirt, bell bottoms and a shocked expression that seemed out of context on her pretty face. All other doors closed against me. I was monstrous, bloodied, swollen. No one could have been uglier or more miserable. I realized I was crying as well.

"Oh my God," said Camille. She took my arm and pulled me into her room, a place that somehow I'd never been. Her roommate, a girl named Lois, had recently gone home with mono, so the cubicle was hers alone. I took its contents in briefly: huge poster of James Dean, poster against the war, books in various stages of reading jacked open on every surface, the warm smell of cigarette smoke (illegal in rooms, of course,) and the chill from an open window, record player softly playing Joan Baez. Two beds, two bureaus, and Camille making me sit in a straight chair.

"I'm all right," I sniffed.

"Georgia, for God's sake, what happened?" she gasped.

"I just killed a man in cold blood," I said. Her eyes went wide, and for the first time, I saw in her an innocence, a childlike awe and pain.

"What?" she cried.

"I'm just kidding," I said. My breathing started to return to normal. "I was just in a fight. And you...you..." I couldn't ask a thing. There was a shouting in the hall.

"Get in the closet," she said. I obeyed. When I climbed in, I found myself in the drapery of female clothing, and the mere idea, the sheer femaleness of the place, gave me an unexpected thrill. Just as Camille closed the closet, her room door opened, and I heard deep male voices, several of them, and my excitement faded. My head drummed, concussion, maybe, or loss of blood, and I felt weakly faint. The closet was full of galaxies; the giggly mad idea of charting all of them sprang full-grown into my skull.

"Not in here," Camille said. Male voices in gauze. Urgent. Unpleasant. "I saw him, though. He's just a student here. He'd been in a fight, he said." Muffled voices. "No, I don't know his name. Trent something or other."

"Are you sure?" This male voice I heard clearly, understood the implicit authority; Camille was hiding me now, breaking rules right and left. I assumed they would ignore her smoking. The door closed. I leaned back and inhaled the fragrance of clothes.

The closet door opened, and Camille reached down, cursed, took my arms, and helped me up.

"Trent something or other?" I said.

"Ssshhhhhh!" she said. "They'll hear you! Come on over to the edge of the bed." I sat with her, thrilled suddenly with the knowledge that she lay here every night. Then, in my galaxial whirr, I noticed that she looked deeply worried about me. "I'm going to the bathroom to get a wet paper towel. Don't move."

She was gone, and I sat there, holding my hands in my lap like a pitiful spinster, and slowly the idiocy of the situation blossomed around me. Why had I run to her: for answers or for succor.

"Succor," I said out loud, laughing slightly. My left eye was disappearing in a mass of swollen soft tissue, but my teeth were all still firmly planted in the gums; I tested their strength with my tongue. I waited patiently, looking with longing and restless lust at her slightly rumpled sheets. Joan Baez was still singing, telling me how hurt she was that the world was full of pain. She just couldn't believe it.

Camille squeezed back through the door and sat next to me, holding a dripping clot of paper towels. She dabbed at my face, cleaned the blood from around my mouth and eyes.

"Georgia, what in the hell did you do?" she asked. She was disgusted with me, but affectionate, too.

"I got into a fight," I said.

"I can see that," she said. She finished cleaning my face, looked at her work, was satisfied with it, but still unhappy with the angry misshapen lump of my face. "About what?"

"Oh, nothing," I said blithely.

"God, the male of the species is a sad thing," she said. "No wonder black widows eat them after mating."

"You're just saying that because you like me," I said. She laughed, and it hit me: No one knew I was there. I could stay. The possibilities suddenly stretched before me like a Bierstadt painting.

"You want a cigarette?" she asked.

"Sure," I said.

We smoked in silence, and when Joan was through complaining, Camille put on a Bob Dylan record. Bob was miserable, too.

None of the singers seemed very happy in those days. Camille moved with a hidden grace; she tried to mask it with a heavy intellect, but in her body was the chemistry of willows in spring breezes. She talked about music for a while, since she'd been studying for a musicology class (ironically, the one I teach now at McCandless), berating the loss of baroque ornamentation.

"The Church knew that splendor was the entranceway to nobility," she said knowingly.

"Huh?"

"Look at it this way, Georgia," she said, "Homophonic music is chordal, a reversion to pre-Baroque conventions, and it changed the way the ear listened. We were on the verge of hearing independent lines, of gaining an even more complicated music. Hell, if the Baroque had lasted another forty years, Schönberg would have been hatched in, like 1880 or something."

She nodded, blew smoke from her precious nostrils, having talked it out, convinced herself, and assuredly, me, too. I needed no convincing. I was watching her braless breasts sway as she walked around the room. My hidden gray matter rose long enough to make this moronic enjoinder:

"But Camille, the Church is nothing but a dictatorial clutch of thieves in league with the military-industrial complex," I said. "That's what you told us at the Malone Society last year."

"Please stop quoting me," she said. "It's rude, in the first place, and, besides, I could be in big trouble having you in here."

"Dames like you live for trouble," I blurted in a gangster voice. Unaccountably, she giggled and shook her head. Then someone knocked on the door and called her name. Female. Young.

"Get back in the closet," she hissed. I got up, not very dizzy any more but having a fine time, and got back in the closet, leaving it cracked an inch. Female voice. Can I come in? Through the crack I saw her, a tall, handsome girl wearing a gown top and white cotton underwear, worn so badly that even in the dim light I could see through them the sweet cleft of a small, rounded ass.

"Violet, what's the problem?" asked Camille.

Violet? Jesus, I knew her! I'd had two classes with her, admired her long legs. Turn around, damnit. Turn around! I said it out loud like a sacred chant. Then she did, and the thick thatch of dark hair was clearly visible, forming a triangle. Hair sneaked out around the front of her panties. She was hairy. I trembled with excitement. This was great! I was having the night of my life! Violet explained the problem, but I missed it.

"Not tonight, darling," said Camille. "I have a splitting headache. I'll help you with it in the morning before class, okay?"

"I'd really appreciate it," said Violet. "I'm already so lost in there."

"Sure," said Camille.

So lost. I thought of Asheville's dead claim to fame, Thomas Wolfe: O lost, and by the wind grieved ghost, come back again. I felt Wolfe in the closet with me, slipped from carnality to literary allusions as Camille opened the door and found me grinning.

She laughed. "Did you see Violet's underpants?"

"I must confess I did," I said.

"Look, I'm tired," she said. "You can sleep on the other bed if you want to sneak out after everybody's gone to sleep, but the lights are going out."

"Thanks," I said. "I'll make it up to you somehow."

"No you won't" she said. "You could never make up to me what I've meant to you." She was right there, and I knew it then, have known it all the years since.

She released Bob Dylan from his troubles, turned out the light. I saw, from the ambient glow of the streetlight outside, Camille slipping from her jeans, saw her long legs and panties for the briefest moment. She turned to the wall facing away from me. I shrugged, took off my pants and climbed into her roommate's bed, thinking I'd get at least a couple of hours' sleep before I had to sneak back into the night. I humored myself by thinking that Ronny was worried about me. Were the police this very minute looking for me? I'd tell them I walked alone in the night, dreaming of vindications and poetry, that the cool caress of the night only calmed my killing temperament. No, I thought of Camille, watched her shoulders in the soft light, rising and falling, rising and falling.

I slept. No dreams. Some sound awakened me, and I opened my eyes and saw a vision, something that will never leave me, that will be inscribed on the back of my eyelids when my casket goes thump against the vault: Venus.

My first thought was of the Botticelli painting *The Birth of Venus*. The window was open, and a cool breeze was gentling the room. Camille stood in a pool of light in front of the window, long hair drifting with the currents, naked as the day of her birth, looking straight at me.

She had shaved her vulva clean. Her legs were slightly apart. Radical females in those days shaved nothing, so her step toward shaving *everything* was even more radical. I was suddenly, immediately, hard. I wanted to say something, fully aware in half-waking that this was extraordinary, a moment I might never again achieve. Soundlessly, I lifted the covers for her, and she moved toward me on small, gliding steps, easily, slowly, taking forever. Her breasts were perfect, tipped with swollen buds, and I turned completely into the boy in the bushes for her.

"Come to me," she said. I stood, staggered from faintness, caught myself. "Take your clothes off." I stripped, embarrassed at the profusion of my lust, but Camille merely glanced at it once, then looked back into my eyes. She moved toward me. I could not breathe. Her eyes were inside mine, our bodies touching now, my crotch against her warm stomach as she leaned to me for a kiss. I opened my mouth, realized blood had dried at its corner, fell away in small flakes when we kissed. Her hand drifted down my chest, grasped me, pulled me down, then up between her legs, resting on the smooth skin of her damp folds.

"I'm in love with you," I croaked, trying to sanctify it, still influenced by the stuffy ethic of Jamesburg.

"Yes," was all Camille Malone said. Did that mean she loved me or that she was glad I loved her or that she merely recognized the sentiment? As in all things, she cultivated ambiguity even in these most private moments.

We began to move, kissing. I tried to think of the trouble I was in, of car wrecks and football games, of the time I'd wasted during the summer, but nothing worked; my body was racing far ahead of hers, and when she saw the panic in my eyes, knew that I was irretrievably lost, she swiftly spread her legs, reached down, and pulled me up. I knelt slightly and entered her standing up. I came back to my full height, and our union was so tight that I groaned, and she smiled and placed her thin fingers to my lips. When her finger touched my lips, a sheer bolt of flame descended from my cheeks down my belly and into the center of our sex. I cried aloud, and she knew that I was coming, and she kissed me, held me as I trembled, then she began to move faster and faster, having found a softer angle, and then she was looking into my eyes with joy and pleasure.

We stood that way, legs aching, unmoving for two minutes, until she stepped back and pulled herself free from me.

"Come on to my bed," I said.

"Good night, Ford," she said. She climbed into her bed and faced the wall, and I walked to the edge of it and stood there until it was clear that she was through with me. She left her shoulders bare above the covers, and as I lay in her roommate's bed, I watched her breathing change into the nightshirt of sleep.

I slept. I awoke and saw by her clock that it was nearly four, so I slipped into my pants and shirt, looked into the hall, saw nothing, and easily escaped Mary Grandville without being seen. I walked slowly under the still-dark chestnut trees, feeling the rich satisfaction of Camille lingering in my crotch and in my arms. What had it meant that I defended her honor and then wound up in her body's safe harbor? Or was it safe at all? She was both more and less than everything in this world. She was Venus arising from the foam; a reckless intellectual who believed everything she read; a brilliant pianist for whom perfection was never enough; even a gifted composer with the fiery temperament of the True Believer.

But if I strutted from her intimacy, it was because she desired me.

I got back to the dorm just before dawn. Ronny was already up, sitting at his desk working on a quartet he'd started a couple of weeks before.

"Where in the fuck have you been?" he asked. "That kid's in some deep shit and so are you. The campus cops were all over this place looking for you. I'm supposed to tell you to report to the dean of men if you show up this morning."

"I've showed up," I said.

Ronny grinned.

"You look like shit, Clayton," he said. "But you really kicked that guy's ass. Where you been? Not someplace illegal, I hope?" What would Camille have said, I wondered? What was the most subversive act possible?

"I've been walking in my dreams," I said. He laughed out loud.

"You're something, Clayton, old pal!" he said. "I can smell it on you a mile away. Jesus, what happened to that studious boy from Jamesburg who wanted to be the next Mozart?"

"Favors, you ask the brightest questions for such a dumb fuck," I said. His laughter rolled around the room.

My punishment was minor, a stern lecture from the dean of men. The other kid quit school the next weekend and disappeared from my life.

Camille had one more surprise, however. She told me the next day that our lovemaking had dazzled her, taken her to jeweled kingdoms she never dreamed (her words). But she also said that she simply did not have time for a relationship now, and that she hoped I'd understand. Then she patted me on the cheek and headed off for a harmony class. I stood under a drizzly sky, torn as usual between anger and untrained affection, then stormed back to Tarmot Hall, seething, lusty, confused.

For Camille, those qualities might have been the Holy Trinity.

THE SIRENS. THEY ARE MOANING FOR ME to swim to their clashing rocks in the sea, but I resist. They will consume me, and I laugh, keep paddling past them, then realize they are drawing me in, the magnetic center of the universe, that I have no choice in this matter at all.

I awakened, found that I was not hearing sirens, but a man's voice. I was staring into the fat face of the Giant, the hairless man I'd seen on the front porch of the Gordon House the day before.

"Mithter Jothiah thaid to tell you breakfatht wath ready now," he squeaked. His round shoulders were immense, bullock-like, but in the eyes was an innocence, a hint of retardation that startled me into uneasy wakefulness.

At that point, he took two steps back and was smacked in the back of the head by our Swinging Jesus, which then ascended into the fan and began to crack and beat terribly with each rotation. He looked up at the sight and told us what was obvious:

"You Jethuth ith thutk in the fan," he said.

The Giant was making mewling sounds and playing with his fingers like Curly of the Three Stooges.

"Would you mind getting out of here?" I said. I thought he would cry. He turned and escaped through the door. I was still half in the lure of dream sirens, but there I was at the Gordon House, hot, flat sunlight coming through the window, and alone. Clarence must have slept somewhere else the night before.

"You Jethuth ith thutk in the fan," I said. The door opened

again. We saw the Giant's mother scowling at the doorway. My eyes went up to the stuck Jesus, which was whapping the fan blade with a terrific noise, threatening to break apart.

"The food is filled with demons!" she said. "Twelve demons will dance in your head. Do you understand? DO YOU UNDER-STAND?"

"I underthtand," I said solemnly. Mama disappeared, having delivered the message. I disentangled the Jesus. It seemed only right.

We didn't eat at the Gordon House. Clarence met me at the front door as I was leaving. I didn't ask where he'd spent the night. We ate at a Waffle House, and Clarence's manners were appalling, but what can you do with a man who was released from prison and washed in the Blood of the Lamb at the same time? After that, I went back to the room.

Clarence wandered off to save souls. I wandered off to find Camille Malone. I walked up and down the main street of Myrtle Beach, watching Paw in his stupid shorts that Maw had bought just before the vacation he couldn't stand. He was looking for a phone to call the office. The kids were poking at each other, and Sister was whining because she wanted to be on the beach, not drifting in and out of towel shops. Maw wanted to try on every T-shirt on the strip.

After a fruitless hour of this, I drove to the county welfare office, which was in a brick building back away from the beach, out of sight of pleasure, as it were. Wilmington's National Public Radio station came in with sharp strength, and in my car, sun-spangled, I listened to Mozart as I pulled into the parking lot, all asphalt, poverty, and boredom. Inside, I found myself standing before a counter, staring at an overworked woman with hard gray eyes and a yellow pencil thrust from behind each ear.

"Hi," I said.

"What can I do for you?" she asked. "Food stamps, third door on the left."

"I don't need food stamps," I said. "I'm looking for a lady."

"You and Humphrey Bogart," she said, then she emitted this thundery, raucous laugh that had barely a trace of genuine mirth in it. I must have looked blank. "It's a line from *Casablanca*. Who's the lady? Sorry. I'm crazy. Everybody here tells me I'm crazy."

"You should be staying at the Gordon House," I muttered.

"Huh?"

"Never mind. Look, I'm trying to find a friend who came down here from New York to meet me. She's a poor, homeless person." It sounded wrong.

"You know how many homeless people come here?" she said. "Go look on the beach, mister. If a tenth of 'em have come by here, I'd be surprised. Where you ought to go look is the beach at night, not the Welfare Office in the daytime. You say this is a homeless lady who's meeting you at Myrtle Beach from New York?" She took one of the pencils out and scratched her cheek with the eraser.

"Sounds odd, I know."

"Downright bizarre."

The police? No. I sat in the car, Bach harpsichord music tinkling on the radio, thinking how much Camille loved that instrument. The Jumper family had donated a fine one our junior year, and Camille could not get enough of its rich plinking. I was driving away, without direction or aim, when sentiment surprised me. Of course! She would be going to the motel where we spent those nights the spring of our senior year at McCandless! But what was its name, where was it now? Did it even exist?

I drove, but nothing looked familiar from that trip. Indeed, 1972 seemed the filmy fabric of some dream. I saw Jungle Golf and nine trillion seafood restaurants, shopping centers, high-rise hotels that sprawled over the beach. What did it look like? Okay, it was...it had....Shit. All I remembered was Camille's tender confusion, the wobbling axis of Catholicism, music, and creeping nuttiness, reading aloud in Latin from her Missal on the beach every morning.

Fool. I was a fool. Jill was right. Even Clarence was right. What was I, Ford Clayton, at this point in my life? I took inventory. Professionally, I had generated sufficient heat for academia, with the appropriate lack of light. Personally, I had driven away a gentle sweet wife and two loving children. My ex-girlfriend from two decades before was wandering (perhaps?) around this seaside burg looking for me. Was she now kind and calm and merely down on her luck and looking for a hand back into the old life? What could I do for her? Or was she supposed to do something for me?

What is the course record at Jungle Golf?

I was developing a theory. In primitive societies, the male dances and shouts and commits wars to stave off the fear of weakness and failure. In late twentieth-century America, the male struts and crows to hide his essential failure to understand the female of his species.

Maybe I was on to something here. If I could only find Camille and discuss this with her. The geometry of my relationships with women, back to Ingrid, told me that I was never in control, not for one moment, that I had given them a stick, begged for a good beating and then complained when I got it. Of course. All men did the same thing. Then women despised the men for their insensitivity and weakness, carried on as they could, growing while their men steadily regressed toward the cradle.

I drove back to the Gordon House, got into my bathing suit, and drifted sadly down to the beach. On my way out the door, Mister Josiah came waddling over to me and tugged at my kneecap with his leathery fingers.

"Sorry about this morning," he said. "I told that moron to knock on your door. You orta try my wife's cooking, though."

"Your wife?" I said. I had a flash of a picture, like a scene from *The Terror of Tiny Town.*

"Beularice," he nodded. "She makes incredible goulash. She's a gypsy, you know."

"A gypsy?"

"She'd be glad to do a private reading for you or anything," he said. "She don't do it like most of 'em. I mean, she don't read a crystal ball or tea leaves or nothing."

"How does she do it?" I asked.

"I'd let Beularice tell you," he said. He waddled off.

Oho! I recognized that — a technique to intrigue me, get me to shell out twenty bucks for this shysteress. Well, I wasn't that easy. This was the new Ford Clayton with whom he was dealing, a man on the quest for the Holy Self.

I came onto the porch, flip-flops clapping, feeling a little stupid in my swim trunks and T-shirt. I wasn't stupid enough to preen and get sunburned. I came down the steps and the Giant eunuchoid was sitting in the sandy yard digging at a hole with a bright red plastic shovel.

"Thorry about you Jethuth," he said.

"It's refreshed my attitude toward theology," I said. He merely smiled sweetly, and I passed him, crossed the main drag, came behind the buildings into a smelly alley where a large tabby cat was gnawing a fishhead and water was pouring from a crusty three-inch iron pipe down a strip of asphalt toward the beach. I ascended a mild slope of sea oats and, like stout Cortez (Camille would point out the historical stupidity in the poem, of course) discovered the ocean. It was then I caught a glimpse to my left: a woman wearing the wrong clothes.

Beach etiquette is obvious. I always thought Richard Nixon's problems could be summed up by his wearing of black wingtips to walk on the beach. You don't wear black shoes on the beach. Nor do you wear a long dress, a funky hat, and boots. She was moving away from me, the clothing ratty, perhaps even tattered, though she was moving at a slow jog. Could it be Camille von der Malone?

I began to run after the figure. My flip-flops slapped stupidly at my heels. Maybe Nixon wasn't so wrong, after all. Should I call her? A beached whale that was once a female human being rolled over to show me her sunblazed legs and chest. All Grumbacher red, straight out of the tube. A Frisbee came floating by my head, and a lanky kid with a deep tan and a G-string lilted past, caught it, tossed it back to someone I could not see. A sextet of pelicans came low over the water in a V, looking into the surf for fish rising to sparkle in the sharp sun. The woman in the dress turned left and disappeared off the beach. I'd never find her. She was too far away. Couldn't be Camille anyway. Camille was probably still in New York cadging quarters from unwary tourists, maybe playing the accordion on a street corner, singing arias outside Lincoln Center as fine ladies bathed in fur came out for intermission. Or was she?

I walked slowly back down the beach, saw a row of beautiful women in minimal bathing suits. After a brief time, I refined my philosophy regarding the strutters, the posers, the indifferent, and the embarrassed. Most people knew their category, but a few were hapless, lost, strutting when they should have been embarrassed, like a fortyish man wearing a toupee and sticking his chest four inches past where nature had most lately left it. Two teenage girls strutted past me, knowing they were beautiful, exulting in the fact. A male with no body hair and an ethereal look posed at the edge of the water, flexing his back muscles and Appearing Sensitive by looking out to sea. Could I be a poser? No. Certainly not a strutter. My body was not too bad, so I was not embarrassed, but I was hardly indifferent. I could be something entirely new. A dreamer. Could I be a dreamer?

By late afternoon, I was bereft, realizing that I didn't know where I was or why. I walked back to the Gordon House as low as I'd ever felt. This was not the symmetrical extension of life that I was told about. This was not even in sonata form, that musical trivet that allegedly mimics life: fast-slow-fast. It was a wayward vivace in a some gloomy minor key, speeding up until the music made no sense, never recapitulated, developed no themes, somehow never managed an exposition at all. Merely a first movement with slight variations, played without stopping for threescore and ten years.

Mister Josiah was working over the sofa in the lobby with a Dustbuster when I got back. He poked and prodded at the unravelling beast as if it were an animal and he were trying to get it to open its mouth. He waved cheerily at me. I waved back and slowly ascended the stairs.

I opened the door, ready for some kind of monologue. I was going to Create a Scene, perhaps weep and wail and then wait until dark and dash madly into the sea dunes. My Schumannesque madness would be evidence that I was an artist; even my detour to Myrtle Beach from New York would make clear that my art was too great a burden. Great art, great burden, great madness. Only that wasn't true. That was Romantic bullshit. I closed the door behind me and stared with unexpected mirth at my whirling Jesus before I looked down and saw that I was standing on a small, dirty card. I knelt and picked it up.

On the front was a cartoon drawing of a drunk with bottles hanging from his pocket, stumbling leeringly down the beach. The caption said "I raised hell at Myrtle Beach!" I turned it over. I read:

Ford,
Well, my goodness. You were a pain to find. Let's have a game, shall we? Please remember it's all in the Book of Kings. Don't try to contact me. I'll contact you, and then we can talk. Tonight somewhere?

Gaspar

Camille! No one else! She had found me, *had found me* and was as loquacious and orderly as a fruit bat. I sat on the bed and read the card over and over, looking for hidden messages. What I saw was disturbing enough. Gaspar—I remembered him. In her Catholic phase she identified with him, one of the three Magi who brought frankincense. But he later became something of a joke in medieval nativity scenes and became a comic servant in the puppet shows. Faust used him. Camille loved poor Gaspar because she insisted there was something broadly comic about even the most appalling human conditions. She called it.....yes. She referred to it as *sweet crudity*.

I ran downstairs, just missing my Jesus (what allusions might Camille make of that?) and grabbed Mister Josiah by the arm just as he was finishing with the Dustbuster.

"Somebody put a card under my door," I said breathlessly. "Did you see anybody suspicious around here today?" The question, hanging between us in the air, suddenly brought forth a surprise giggle from yours truly.

"I don't never see nobody," he said. His arm felt like a metal rod. I let it go. "It's a good habit not to see nothing."

"Then your wife, maybe?"

"You'd have to ask her," he said. "Go straight back through by the stairs to our suite. Knock three times on the door."

"Three times on the door," I repeated.

"Three times on the door," he said. An extremely tall and apparently deaf old man with no teeth wandered past us whistling in music from another sphere. The Gordon House was hurting for business, but it was still early in the season. I held the card and crept past the stairs, found the closed door with "Manager" on it and knocked gently three times. Nothing happened. I waited a moment. Then I knocked three times again.

"Just a minute," a muffled voice said. I waited. Then the door opened and a woman four feet wide stood before me, wearing a veil across her face that looked like a section of curtain from a motel even cheaper than the Gordon House.

"Hi, I was wondering if...."

"Enter, enter," she said in a deep voice. "The future is told here."

"I...the future is told here?" I said.

"Enter, enter," she said, backing away.

She wasn't a dwarf, but she was short, a face so laden with blubber the features were uncertain. I went inside. Their apartment was spacious and ugly. The furniture was from Unclaimed Freight, covered with clear slipcovers, as if the place had been attacked by giant prophylactics in the night. Something like voodoo music was coming from a hidden stereo, all pounding, the room's headache or toothache. I was stunned into silence. I saw another room off to one side, the kitchen, and on the visible edge of a counter was a stack of nasty dishes in sad need of attention. An open one-pound sack of Ruffles was on the sofa, and shards of its contents were scattered over it, the floor and the coffee table, on which a copy of a tabloid was folded back. The headline was about a woman who was pregnant by a space alien.

"Come into the room of the future," she said.

"Okay," I said. Camille's spirit of adventure was increasing in torque; if this was spirit, then flesh was not only weak, it had no will.

The room of the future was behind a beaded curtain, whose individual globules had been overheated at some time and felt sticky, dust-bunny coated, as I swept through it. The small room had the obligatory round table, two chairs, but no crystal ball. What was she going to read, the graying hair on my temples? She sat in one of the chairs, and it cried out in shock, creaking against the weight, straining at its screws. I sat as well.

"Somebody put this card under my door today," I said. I held it up to her. "Did you happen to see who it might be?"

She read the card carefully.

"This is from a woman," she said, arching one eyebrow.

"I believe so," I said. "I just wanted to know if you'd seen anybody who might have delivered this card."

"I see many things," she said inscrutably. She threw the card back to me, and I rolled my eyes as I put it in my shirt pocket. "But what I see most is what is in the hand. Please give me your hand, and I will tell if your trouble with women can be worked out."

Perhaps she did see everything. Already she knew I had trouble with women. Or, more properly, they had trouble with me. Well, what the hell. I stuck my right hand out, and she grabbed my wrist and nearly jerked me across to her.

"Ow," I complained. "That hurts."

"Love hurts," she breathed.

"Well, it's not supposed to," I said. "My mother always told me that love was like a red, red, rose."

"Yes," she said, "but make sure you don't get pricked!" She was delighted with the metaphor, so delighted that she chuckled, and the waves of excess on her face undulated seismically. "Now as for this palm...." She studied it. Her own hands were surprisingly soft, thick fat fingers touching my palm in what could have pleased, erotically, had Beaularice weighed a hundred pounds less.

"What does it say?" I asked. "Does it say if you saw who brought this card?"

"Sshhhhh!" she scolded. Her finger followed the lines on my palm as if she was lost and retracing some obscure route on a road map. "I can see clearly that you're no businessman."

"Correct," I said.

"And that you are greatly confused," she continued.

"Oh, whoopee, you're a genius," I said. She shot me a curt glance.

"But there's more," she said. "You are wondering about many things, about love and women and your career, such as it is."

"Has that spread even this far?" I said, closing my eyes. "Look, this is humiliating. Do you see anything good in there?"

"Yes," she said. "You will not be drafted into the armed services."

"How do you know that?" I said sourly. She pointed to something in my hand.

"Short chow line," she said. I felt as if bats were banking and swarming in my head. "I invented that."

"This has been a major event in my life," I said, taking my hand back, "but I have to be going now. I just wanted to know if you saw anybody." I got up, passed through the clacking curtain and headed for the door.

"I never see anything that happens here," she shrugged.

"Neither does Mister Josiah," I said. "By the way, where's your swinging Jesus?"

"Never had one," she said. "I have to take Dramamine when I get on an escalator."

I let myself out. Back upstairs and in my sordid room, I felt the weight of it all sink upon my shoulders. What is man, I said out loud, that thou art mindful of him? I took the box of letters from the chair and dumped them all out on the bed, then sat there, picked up one. I could read my past as well as my hostess could read my future. This was the letter I picked up:

Tuesday nite

Dear Momma,
The Scouts has finished our first week at Rainey Mountain, and it is fun like you would not beleive. I learned how to make a square not, but instead I mostly made grannie nots. Then I did it right.

We had a hiking expideton to see a waterfall. It was fun. Tom Blancerd fall off a clift but he sufferd only a broken color bone, which is nothing, they say. He will be just like new soon.

Feed Spark and tell Daddy I am doing fine except for this wrash, which is from the water or heat. Some thing even Scotmaisters dont know.

Your loveing son,
Ford Clayton

Were there sirens beneath that waterfall? My whirling Jesus gave no clue. Outside, the daily afternoon thundershower began.

IN THE SPRING OF 1970, THE NATIONAL GUARD killed some students at Kent State. Even at a music conservatory, with its unshakable devotion to routine, scales, and theory, we were afraid, and we tried to decide what to do.

"If you swine had listened to me last year, this might not have happened!" screamed field marshal Camille von der Malone. Her pitiful anti-war demonstration now seemed prophetic, and the sad cluster of the Malone Society had swollen into sixty long-haired girls and boys. We were at the Circle Beech the night of the Massacre, early May of 1970.

All that fall and winter, I had trailed around Camille like a slipped shadow that never quite held her swift pace. We dated, and I believed she loved me, though she never admitted it. We did not make love again.

I began to discover, to my surprise, that I had a genuine gift for musicology. I read on my own for hours of the lives of those great composers, of Beethoven and his ear trumpets; of the structure of Mendelssohn's string symphonies; of Schönberg's revolutionary use of all twelve tones of the scale. My composition also grew in me, and a string quartet made a strong impression when friends performed it in a student recital that winter.

I remember the deep, silky snow and the sweet musical softness of walks through it. Music still seemed to leak from every surface of McCandless.

The night of Kent State that May, groups met all over campus.

No one was smiling. If students at a small school in Ohio could be shot dead for protesting the war, what might happen next? The Army at McCandless?

All the instruments of music went silent. The student government, which Camille thought a joke, called for a three-day boycott of classes in memory of our fallen fellows at Kent State. As a student of history and musicology, I saw it all in the context of the great upheavals in nineteenth-century Europe. The students had always been the intellectual vanguard. Wagner fleeing to Zurich. Revolution. Barricades in the streets. The right wing immediately branded student protestors as communists, and now, more than two decades later, I sometimes laugh at that. We were hardly Reds; we were driven by a much simpler philosophy: fear.

Camille wasn't even a communist. She was, by that spring, a force on campus. And though the Malone Society was held in her fiery sway that night, I watched her performance with amazement and horror.

"And now what has happened?" she screamed. Darkness seemed to wait for her to gather strength, hung in the trees which had only lately found their leaves. "The war has moved to these shores." Polite applause. I stood far in the back. "This is the beginning of the Malthusian decline of our age! Population increases in a geometric ratio, the means of subsistence increases in an arithmetic ratio. And what slows it? You know what slows it? Vice. Disease. Crime. Moral Restraint. And what? And what? War! That's right, War!"

A shiver ran through the crowd, something you could almost see. She had them completely in her spell.

"What is this like? Is this like Marcus Annaeus Lucanus who hated the Caesars and joined Pico's conspiracy against Nero?" she yelled. "Is it?" Her face was red, and those lovely plum-colored lips were wine-dark. "Yes! And Lucan had the foresight to commit suicide at age twenty-five. If you had lived in the Middle Ages, you would have loved Lucan! Go read *On the Eve* by Turgenev and tell me if you could play Insarov to my Elena! My friends, I tell you tonight that it is time that we threw ourselves, like Empedocles, into the center of Mount Etna." Wild applause. Camille was in full rage.

"When Burke delivered *On American Taxation*, was he talking about your fucking tea?" she screamed waving her arms. "No! He was talking about freedom! Say it with me, freedom!"

"Freedom!" screamed the Malone Society. I said it softly.

"When Emile Zola wrote *Germinal* was he talking about workers in the goddamn mines, or was he talking about freedom?" she shouted hoarsely.

"Freedom!"

"I tell you, America is the Laocoön of the Twentieth Century!" she said. "We are being strangled by the serpents of the military-industrial complex, wrapped in the bleeding failures of capitalism which have helped to create the ultimate war, one based not on an enemy's threat nor the feared collapse of world order! It is based on simple, easily understood greed!"

The crowd was on its feet now, in frenzy. They surged forward toward Camille.

"It's...it's...it's like the *Laxdale Saga*!" she said, arms waving like a spider dashing up a wet web. "This country has become Gudrun, and it is trying to cast its dark love on the Kjartan of Southeast Asia." Lots of applause, blank looks and shrugs. "The ooze Dick Nixon leaves makes me sick!" Screaming, laughing, applause, whistles. Other students drifted up, and suddenly a hundred were there, then fifty more, then fifty more. Camille saw them, waved them on. As the crowd swelled toward her, I drifted away, still crazy for everything about her, not understanding half of what she said.

"What did Victor Hugo say?" she cried, striding back and forth. "He said 'The success of a war is gauged by the amount of damage it does.' Then, by that standard, this war must be successful because it did a great deal of damage to our brothers and sisters at Kent State University! Burke said war begets poverty and poverty begets war!" She asked the crowd to bring all their friends and meet the following morning at ten for a march on the administration building to ask that McCandless be closed for three days in sympathy with the dead in Ohio. The energy level was close to violence.

Then something extraordinary happened, the single act in her speech that probably sealed the success of the protest. Camille raised her arms for silence, and the crowd fell quiet. She was the Toscanini of demonstrations. For nearly thirty seconds, she held her arms aloft in the silence and waited until the only sound was the wind in the new leaves.

"Albert Einstein said years ago that the next world war will be fought with rocks," she whispered. "For the sake of this world, we can't let that happen." A chill of acknowledgment swept through us. "Ten a.m."

And then she was gone. Like a water sprite or vision from a Weber opera, she simply dissolved into the mist, and the crowd, boisterous once again, broke into small groups, angry, determined, afraid. I crept through them until I came to the wooded area behind the Circle Beech and walked through it quietly, came out on the other side, saw Camille standing on the edge of the pond where Nancy and I had briefly thought we were in love the year before.

She was alone. I came up to her and she turned, saw me, looked through me, turned back. She was crying, sobbing, heaving. I stood beside her and looked at the moon floating on the surface of the still water.

"Ford," she choked, "we're all going to die. Everything's going to die."

"Everything dies," I said. "No way around that. You were wonderful back there, Camille."

"I don't want everything to die," she sobbed. "I want to live and live and live and live and live, and I want every tree and flower to live and everybody who was ever born to live. Why does God let things die?"

"I thought you were an atheist," I said gently.

"I am," she said, suddenly defensive, but she softened. "Only there has to be some meaning, some philosophy that....and if I call it God, that doesn't mean that it's the one in the Bible. Oh, Ford, you look into the pond and see the moon, and people have walked on it now, and we don't know a fucking thing more than we ever did. We're still killing each other over nothing at all. Where's the consolation? How can you bear to live in a world like this?" She turned to me, and I saw her face, genuinely wanting an answer I did not have.

I shrugged. "I'd rather be alive in this world than dead in another one."

"I feel dead in this one," she said.

"The crowd didn't think you were dead," I said. "Why are you so depressed, Camille? You're a brilliant pianist with a tremendous future ahead of you. Isn't that enough?"

"No!" she said loudly. She walked ten paces and then turned toward me. "It's not enough. I want to see the world whole, to see where I'm supposed to fit into things. I don't feel like I fit, and I never have. I'm a catalyst, not the chemicals themselves."

"You're the melody," I said, trying to turn things back to familiar ground, "not the symphony. Why isn't that enough?"

"Nothing's enough," she whispered. "Nothing's ever enough."

She backed up two steps and then turned and disappeared into the moonlight. I did not follow her. I felt lost and alone as well. The world was falling to pieces. They were shooting college students. The war was going to kill all of us. Why go to school at all? Why learn the rules of harmony to be shot in Viet Nam?

They were awake all night. I slept fitfully. Unaccountably, Ronny, who had been in the crowd, was suddenly feeling liberal, and he wanted to rage, but I was exhausted and told him to do it in another room. When morning spilled over the sills, the world was full of electricity.

We marched. Camille was the drum major of McCandless. She gave wild speeches to wild applause. I was invisible, not participating but watching all the same. No one attended classes. Our faculty, almost uniformly liberal, came with us, and the President, a wizened old man named Knight (who had once been a fine tenor, I heard) bowed to the heat of the moment and the pragmatism of the crowd and declared McCandless Conservatory closed for a three-day mourning period.

Ecstasy. The crowd, reverting to its normal posture, immediately forgot the war and sang, organized parties, and got drunk. I was not involved. I did not feel triumphant. I hated the war, but I could think only of Camille. I went to her dorm, but her roommate said she'd hardly been there, and by the third day we were closed, which bled into the weekend, I was worried about her. I looked all over campus, finally found her in the balcony of the chapel (yet another gift from the Morris Jumper family).

The balcony was small, cramped, mainly an access to the console for the pipe organ, one of the best in the state.

It was late Saturday afternoon. I was downstairs looking around when I saw Camille upstairs.

"I've been looking all over for you," I said.

"Leave me alone," she croaked.

I went back to the lobby and up the staircase to the balcony, ascending slowly through the silence of Saturday. My footsteps were hollow on the steps. The stairs turned twice, rose into darkness and then through a small door and into the light. She was ten feet away, and she did not acknowledge me at all. I came around in front of her. She sat, childlike in her seat, hands folded in her lap, eyes staring ahead.

"I've been worried about you," I said.

She said nothing. I sat on the floor in front of her. I could see her cheeks were thin, that she had not been eating, that her eyes burned with some mad fire.

"I said I've been worried about you." Nothing. "Camille, please, don't shut me out. I love you."

She turned toward me. Her mouth line wobbled.

"Don't say that," she begged in a breaking voice. "Please don't say that."

"I mean it," I said.

"I can't love anybody," she said. Her voice was thick, wraith-like, more spirit than body. "I'm death." A deep chill shot through me. "I'm death."

"You're a pianist from New Orleans," I said. "Death's a lot taller than you." She didn't smile or laugh.

"I'm meant for nothing but death," she said. "The world will die, the music will die, the breath of every woman and man will die. It's too terrible! Terrible!"

"We're supposed to stay too busy to notice that," I said.

"Besides, it's bad form to be pointing it out."

"Leave me alone," she said.

"I'm not going to leave you alone, Camille," I said. "I love you. I have to take care of you even if you're crazy. That's part of the deal."

"Am I crazy?" she asked.

"No," I said, but thinking just the opposite. "Just come and let me buy you something to eat."

"Food is evil," she said. "The world is evil. Everything is evil." She stood and leaned dangerously over the balcony rail. "Jesus is following me. He won't leave me alone, Ford. Why won't he leave me alone?" She turned for an answer I didn't have, but instead she suddenly folded down, collapsed, fell back from the edge.

I rushed to her, lifted her in my arms, shook her, begged, and she came briefly back to, raving about Kent State and demons and Jesus and various writers and philosophers. I was looking into the face of death, all right. At least death as I imagined it, the lost center of my world, ravings, fear of everything, no way to tell if it were holy or profane.

And that was how, late in the spring of 1970, I came to escort Camille Malone to New Orleans. She spent three days in the campus infirmary, sedated, counseled. When she came out, she was full of silence, which was eerie for someone as talkative as Camille. We finished the quarter, and when Camille, in tears, asked if I'd take the bus with her back home, I accepted quickly. Dad didn't mind me missing work.

The breakdown changed her, propelled us into the mythic countryside in silence. She stared out the windows, pale, mouth turned down at the corners.

"Do you believe that there is an order in the world?" she asked me somewhere in Alabama.

"An order?" I said, stalling.

"A reason that we are put here in our time on this planet," she whispered. "I've always assumed there was no reason for anything but what we placed upon it. Free will. Objects acted upon."

"Who knows?" I said. "You want a Mr. Goodbar?"

"Ford, I'm serious," she said, turning in the seat. She took both my hands in hers and looked into my eyes. She was begging for answers now. "Do you think it's possible that a baby born in Bethlehem two thousand years ago might have been the ultimate example of self-contained logic?"

"Camille, a lot of people who major in music are religious," I said. "You always made fun of them. All the way back to the Middle Ages. Bach was pious."

"That's it," she exclaimed. "Piety is what attracts me. I have always been in thrall to excess, and now I feel as if messages from some other world were dancing in my head."

A fat woman sitting across the aisle eyed us warily as she wrapped her thick lips around a piece of chicken. Camille's eyes were child-wide. The look of someone placing her entire trust in the saving grace of something immortal, invisible.

"Camille, what use would you have for piety?" I asked.

"I'm not interested in piety per se, any more than Bach was interested in the quarter note," she said. "I'm interested in truth, Ford. When I was in the infirmary, my head was filled with this glorious light, and the light was like a liquid flowing along the radiating spokes of the sun. And I was inside the light."

"Maybe it was a headache," I suggested stupidly. She smiled and shook her head.

"God," she choked. "It was God. Not an old bearded face stained with omnipotence and laws. Just this liquid light that was warm but not hot, sweet but not sticky."

I realized then for the first time how closely religion is related to sex, and I wanted to be her priest, her brother in the monastery cell, praying on our knees, denying ourselves all but each other's arms.

I cradled her in my arms after that, and we spoke little the rest of the way to New Orleans.

Her house was a huge, century-old structure on Rue D'Anjou, not far from the French Quarter. She had an attic room, choked with books. Her mother was intense, dark, and literary, while her father was a gynecologist, often gone. I planned to stay for a week, so I moved into a small room downstairs which connected with the parents' bedroom. He was Winslow and she was Dora.

Dr. Winslow Malone was short, wide, and dark, with the narrow nose of a man who had once had looks but lost them early. His family was from Houma, and Camille spoke with fear and awe of *his* mother, who ruled her brood with a wicked tongue. Her mother, however, was an enchantress, a filmy image of Camille, quiet and pleasant, happy that I'd brought her daughter safely back from Asheville.

The air was laden with breezes that never quite began. Salty. Thick. Camille took me to see the French Quarter, and I was swept away by its attractive decadence. We held hands as we walked. The cathedral on Jackson Square seemed to sway over us. Ships lumbered past in the endlessly wide Mississippi.

"Your mother is nice," I said. We were sitting on a park bench early in the morning. I had tossed the entire evening before, wanting to creep to Camille's room.

"I'm drowning here," she said. "Do you think this could be a test from God?"

"Camille, how come you're talking about God so much?" I asked. "Why don't we go get a cold beer and talk about music?"

"This is serious," she said. "Aren't you afraid of the journey to the next world without knowing all the answers in this one?"

"It never occurred to me that I'd know any answers," I said. "I'm still trying to figure out how to tie a Windsor knot."

"Silly," she said, laughing. Silly? In months past she would have called Berlioz a Romantic pig who should have been drowned by his nursemaid in the Seine shortly after birth. "I think the people who most understand this world are the ones who spend their lives in quiet contemplation. Like nuns and saints and priests."

"Nuns and saints and priests, oh my!" I said. For a moment, something flared in her eyes, the old fury, but it died in a soft puddle of forgiveness.

"I have a lot to think on," she said. "A lot indeed."

"What about thinking of us," I mumbled.

"I *do* think of us," she said. "I want to know why you came into my life, Ford. What force aligned our axes so that we'd meet, so that without fail we would be sitting here today on this bench in this park?"

"Maybe it was just chance," I said. "I'm more concerned if I'll ever get to hold you in my arms again."

"Silly," she said. She slid to me, and oblivious to three nearby street painters, a singer ripping up a blues song, and a long-haired boy singing a bad version of something from Woodstock, we embraced, kissed.

If this was her religion, it had my vote.

Four days later, not having had the courage to creep to her room in the night, already dreading the summer back home, I spent my last evening at dinner with Camille and her parents in the house on Rue d'Anjou. Camille had showered and put on a pretty dress. A *dress*? Yes, a dress, long and feminine; it even had a flirtatious ruffle around the hem. Winslow was unhappy for some undisclosed reason, and he kept gritting his teeth and muttering while Camille and her Mother scuttled back and forth, bringing food, making traditional women's small talk. Winslow finally brought his mutterings to the surface.

"I mean, today you have to be a hawk or a dove," he said. His dark face was explosive. Camille's only legacy from him was his dark lips. "So, Mr. Clayton, that's what I was wondering, are you a hawk or a dove?"

I felt a chill, even though the room was still and hot. The honest answer was that I was a chicken, but I could not imagine giving that answer, so I lied.

"Oh, I'm a hawk," I whispered. Camille was in the kitchen.

"Damn right," he said. "Nobody but a fool would be against this war. Those fools at Kent State probably got what they deserved."

"What?" I said.

"You heard me," he said. "I figured with that hippie hair, you'd probably be on the side of the commies. I'm glad you're a hawk. You should see a barber, though."

Camille and her mother came back in. The dining room was crisply formal, with silver and china in a mahogany buffet. We weren't eating off the good stuff. The table was expensive, and the chairs elaborately carved. Evening was settling over New Orleans, and I wanted desperately to be home, back in Jamesburg. I could not breathe. Camille seemed like a stranger. I wanted something familiar, some gauge of Ford Clayton, topography, history, even Camille screaming through the history of philosophy. I wanted music. The Malone house had no music. Winslow detested everything but military marches, Camille had told me, and those only on national holidays.

"So, how is that corn?" asked her mother with a broad smile.

"With all due respect," I said, staring at the centerpiece of fresh daisies and zinnias, "I was just thinking what a complete asshole Dr. Malone is."

The silence lasted five seconds, and in it, the world throbbed. I felt my head swell with pride for two of those seconds, abject terror for the next three.

"I'll be goddamned," he said, rising from his chair.

"Daddy!" cried Camille.

He wanted to kill me, and I didn't blame him. I stood and backed into the corner.

"He said the Kent State students deserved to get shot," I said.

"Does that really matter?" her mother said, wringing her hands. "Let's sit back down and try the squash casserole. I heard that it might rain by tomorrow, wash some of this heat away."

Camille stared at her father and tears began to flow from the corners of her eyes.

"You goddamned dove!" Winslow thundered. "I knew you were a dove the minute I laid eyes on you. You come down here with my daughter, and you don't work or anything, and you're a goddamned dove. I ought to kick your ass, but instead I'll just ask you to get out of this house right now."

He began muttering again, this time about Germans and Japs and the Battle of the Bulge and the Berlin Wall and making the world safe for democracy. I fled the room while Camille's mother sat primly, having slid into some wifely shell from which, I imagined, she would not soon emerge.

Camille came with me to my room and stood crying in the doorway while I packed my suitcases.

"He hates anybody who tries to love me," she said, choking

out the words. "And he hates anything I try to love. I wanted to talk to him about the Church, and he just laughed. He told me that all women loved Jesus so they wouldn't have to love their husbands."

"Camille, I provoked him," I said. "It's time for me to get out of here anyway. If you can drive me to the bus station, I'd appreciate it."

"But Ford, I'm close to being able to love you," she said. She did not try to stop the tears. I went to her, took her in my arms and held her against the darkness of her upbringing, confused, angry, wondering what in hell I was doing there.

"Sshhhh," I said. "You're going to be all right. And even if you can't quite love me, I'll always love you."

"Will you?" she asked desperately. "I want to believe that wherever I am you will be the one who will always love me. When nobody else will, I can know that you will be there for me."

"Me and Jesus," I said.

She poured her soul into the tears, shuddered. She hiccupped for a moment, clung to me, and I felt nothing but a trembling pity for her.

We escaped through the back door. Through the archway into the dining room, I saw that Winslow was stuffing his face with food and his wife was motionless, staring straight ahead with a chilling reserve that might have been practiced madness. Camille drove me the mile to the bus station, and I got a ticket for one leaving in three hours.

"I'll stay with you," she said.

"Camille, your mother probably needs you," I said. "I didn't mean to cause problems for you."

"Ford, I wish I could cast my burdens upon the Lord," she said in a small, frightened voice.

"You sound like you're asking for permission," I said. "I thought the great Camille Malone never asked permission for anything."

"I need permission," she said. "I need to feel like you need me. That somebody needs me. Do you understand?"

"Yes," I said.

"Then give me your blessing," she said.

I blessed her, hugged her, told her that if the Church attracted her she did not need to fear anyone's opinion. Religion is a matter of faith, I said, and therefore no one can be right or wrong. It's like love.

"Oh, Ford," she said.

The three hours fled, and we kissed deeply, and I climbed aboard the bus in darkness, heading across the South, toward some restless future. The ride to Jamesburg took two days, and when I stumbled unshaven, pale, half-blind from the bus, and called Dad, he came and picked me up and did not complain about how I looked.

I was nearly asleep when I realized Mom had put Puccini on the stereo and was singing along.

I AWOKE TO THE SOUND OF BREATHING next to me in the bed. I turned sharply to see my cousin, Clarence Clayton, lying next to me, gulping snores and twitching like a dog in front of a winter fire. I climbed out of bed in disgust, awakening him in the process.

"Praise the Lord," he said weakly, fighting to re-enter some dream.

"God almighty," I said. "Where in the hell have you been, Clarence?" He sat up, hair Alfalfa-ed; he wore a Myrtle Beach T-shirt, and a goofy grin turned his face lopsided.

"It was this big electrical storm just after midnight, and I come to sleep with you," he said.

"It's only five to seven," I said looking at my watch. The information didn't seem to mean much to him. "Where were you yesterday?"

"I was a missionary," he said. He smiled at the thought. "I was a missionary to the Philly Stones."

"Which Philly Stones?" I asked.

"The ones in Rudy's Bar," he said. "Lord, my head hurts."

"Did you spend all day drinking in some bar?" I cried. "Clarence, missionaries don't get drunk with the people they're saving."

"I was only saving Fonda," he said. He got out of bed, revealing two skinny stork legs that descended from a pair of boxer shorts that might have fit King Kong.

"Fonda?"

"Ain't that a sweet name," he said. "I think I may have saved her. Or she saved me. I disremember at this junction." He walked to the window and looked out at the rising sun. "That was her name. Fonda. Fonda Peters."

"Fonda Peters," I groaned. "Clarence did you get drunk with a whore?"

He fell to his knees beneath our whirling Jesus.

"Forgive me, Lord!" he said, but a grin spread across his face, and I couldn't help smiling myself. It was about that time I noticed on the floor behind him, another postcard that had been thrust under the door. I got it while he was asking Jesus to help Fonda to get over her sins and to charge less as a new Christian.

The card was of the Grand Strand beaches, with no words on the front. I turned it over. In pencil, crude, it said this:

Fordus,
Portas coeli aperuit Dominus et pluit illis manna, et ederent:
panem coeli dedit eis: panem Angelorum manducavit homo, alleluia.

Babette

Well. This was Camille all right, and she had changed into a combination of Father Divine and The Phantom. I knew a bit of Latin, so I translated: *The Lord opened the doors of heaven and rained down manna upon them to eat; He gave them the bread of heaven: man ate the bread of Angels, alleluia.*

"Clarence, look at this," I said, wanting to share my news with anyone. I handed him the card and he scanned it briefly as he stood before me. If he'd moved a few inches, the feet of the Jesus would have whapped him in the head.

"It's wrote in Hindoo," he said gravely. "I'd say it's a warnin' that the heathenry's up to no good."

"That's Latin," I said. "It's about the bread of heaven. Camille wrote it and put it under the door. She's here, and she knows I'm here."

"How did she know where at to find you?" he asked. Clarence had explained that he was trying to speak correct English, since you saved more souls that way. His approach to the language, however, was more sadistic than etymological.

"She must have seen me on the strip here and followed me," I said. "But she's afraid of seeing me or something. This is just stuff from the Missal about the bread of life."

"Hey, that's from the Good Book!" Clarence said too loud. "The nerve of them Hindoos stealing a line like that. No wonder God's blowing up Lebanon."

It was clear that being with Clarence was going to require linguistic nimbleness. It was equally clear that seeing Camille had something to do with bread. She was a great one for symbols.

We ate with Mister Josiah and the handful of others staying at the Gordon House. The fat eunuchoid slurped his food horribly while his mother muttered and stared with suspicion at the salt shaker. The tall, toothless deaf man attacked his food as if he held it personally responsible for his problems. I did not eat much or well.

Clarence and I got in the asthmatic station wagon and began to cruise the strip. Warm, sunny day. Families already looking for ways to blow their American Express Travelers Cheques. We went into the Gay Dolphin, which was a multi-floored gift shop. Clarence was amazed by a collection of rubber snakes and an entire wall of kids' bicycle license plates. They were out of "Clarence," however, and he took that as a sign.

I drove back out of the tourist area to Highway 17 and had not gone down it a mile when the fresh aroma of baking bread came lilting into my nostrils.

"Don't that smell good," said Clarence. "I'd get to bake bread at Jefferson sometimes. You know new-baked bread smells like a woman. That's why they sayeth it rises."

"What does rising have to do with....." Wait a minute. Fresh bread? I started looking around, saw on the next corner a large industrial size building, and over it, a loaf of plastic bread whirling around. I pulled into the parking lot. In addition to the baking plant, they had a day-old bread store. The company was called Stranded Loaves. Pretty clever.

I parked and got out, saw at one glance that the window of Stranded Loaves was littered with notes and handbills, for the greater Horry County Fair, for helicopter rides over the ocean, fifteen minutes for twenty-five bucks, for babysitting services, for a guy trying to sell a 1962 Bel Air Like New One Owner. Crammed between a flyer for a rock band named Idylwild and another for someone named Horace trying to sell a washer/dryer was a fluttering piece of scrap paper in pencil. This one was not even in Latin:

> Hi, Ford,
> You're just as clever as I remember. How's the game so far? I'm having a blast. So much to tell you. I'm ready for the new religion; are you? So go to the phone outside the Sandstorm Motel, this evening, 1830 hours. I am starved for the music of your tears.
> Clara Schumann

"My God," I said.

"God's got awful handwriting," said Clarence, peering over my shoulder.

"It's from Camille," I sighed. "I've found her. Or, rather, she's found me. I've got to be at a phone booth at the Sandstorm Motel tonight at 6:30, and she'll call."

"Like James Bond," he said. I handed him the note, and he read it, handed it back, made no comment. We drove back to the Gordon House, and all the time I was replaying Camille's eccentricities: when did a tic become a madness? Was she, in some perverse and perfect way, a metaphor for my generation, willful, overbred, sensitive, taking everything in every country in the world as a personal affront? I wanted to ask the girl who sang "Ave Verum Corpus" when we were freshmen if she knew who I was. Camille, darling, what was that elixir we all drank, the potion that left us, two decades later, crying in our mead, men without armor, women without a language of their own?

Clarence went off on his own, no doubt to Rudy's bar, where he would probably be talking about the pagan origins of Ash Wednesday with Fonda or something. I walked upon the beach.

Starr-less, Jill-less, with the heaving ocean mocking me, I walked for miles. I inhaled the salt air, tried to clear my head. Would Edgar Fuller have called the New York City Opera by now to check on me? My own tangled web was wrapping me in its fatal coils. My skin was white. I watched young women already tanned this early in the season, staring hopefully out to sea, as if their dream man might arise at any moment. They saw romance and ecstasy, awakening to champagne and strawberries; they saw picnics and courtship, a sylvan setting, everything a Zeffirelli picture. Adam and Maiden. Romeo and Juliet. I saw the midden of the ages.

By the time I got back to the Gordon House, it was nearly two, and I lay beneath my Jesus, whom I'd begun to call Bubba for some perverse reason, and I slept. I dreamed that I was coming from backstage to direct the Metropolitan Opera Orchestra in the world premiere of my opera, *East of Eden*. Crowd on its feet. Thunderous applause. Was I already famous? I was. I turned around and, with Bernsteinish élan, gave the downbeat, only to find that my opera's overture sounded suspiciously like music from some other opera.

I felt panicked. Would anyone notice that I was something of a fraud? The curtains parted grandly — I realized I was in the old Met, the one long since torn down, the one whose curtain they cut up into tiny swatches and sold on memorial album sets. I glanced up at the stage as I beat time, and sure enough, the set was stolen directly from *La Bohème*, and the first aria, which seemed to have started already, was note-for-note from the Puccini opera, and I turned and glanced at the crowd, and they were muttering, like, Hey, wait a minute, this is nothing but rank plagiarism.

I kept beating, and suddenly a flourish of trumpets offstage announced something, then the orchestra, blowing hard, began to play the grand triumphal march from *Aida*, and suddenly, captured Nubians were bringing trunks of gold, shields with hair fringe, and a live elephant onstage with Mimi, who had appeared and was coughing badly.

The audience was in an uproar by now, but I could not stop conducting. I heard them leaving behind me. I turned, and only a couple of people were left, obviously critics, taking notes with devilish delight, and when I turned back to the stage, Camille was front and center dressed as Carmen and launching into the "Habanera." Then I saw headlines from the *Times* whirling cinematically at me, MAJOR FRAUD IN NEW OPERA, then FORD CLAYTON

ARRESTED FOR BEING A DUMBASS and finally, my picture on a magazine cover with the headline: FAMILIAR NOTES: SCANDAL AT THE METROPOLITAN OPERA.

I awoke. A thunderstorm was in progress. My watch dutifully reported the time as 4:18, and I lay on my damp, tangled sheets and listened to the rain. Ah, a dream I truly deserved. The Great Plagiarism dream, scourge of every creative person. At least it wasn't the Drowning in a Tidal Wave Dream or the Killing Someone You Know Dream or the Having Some Dark and Terrible Secret That You Suddenly Realize Everyone Knows Dream. I could handle the Great Plagiarism Dream; it was one of the standards in the repertoire of the Night World of Ford Clayton.

I got up and sat in the rocker, looked out the window. If I could have seen over the towel shops, would I have seen a storm-tossed sea? If I was lost on the sea in some board-creaking sloop, would Jesus stick his finger in the brine and calm it just for me?

There is an age we thinking humans reach when a single answer is not enough. We want, simultaneously, to know why we still kill each other in the Middle East, why some men go down with aneurysms at thirty while others go down with kidney failure at ninety; why books paint love as one thing and life paints it as another; why the music of this world will always remain a solitary statement to one person and that is its strength; why men who want passionately to be artists often only stand and wait.

I told Ricardo last year that if this was midlife, I didn't care for any, thank you.

"But Ford, we never have a choice," he said, puffing on his pipe, Latakia smoke clouding the room. If enough smoke gathered, would smoky rain fall upon my chair? "We aren't asked to choose in life, only to survive what is given."

"Who's that from, Edgar A. Guest?" I asked.

"Then I'll be more blunt," he said. "We're all going to die, and there's nothing we can do about it, not one damned thing. The only thing that separates a great man from an inconsequential one is how well he loves."

"How about how many operas he writes?" I said idly. "Or how many patents he registers or how many leper colonies he founds?"

"Ah," said Ricardo. He set the pipe in an ashtray so crowded with matchsticks it looked like the equipment room after a hockey game.

"Ah?" I said. "Meaning what?"

"Meaning you always confuse what you do with who you are," he said. "Women, in particular, can't understand that about men."

"How do you know?" I asked unhappily. "Were you once a woman, Ricardo?"

"It's in the literature," he said, glancing at his watch, the signal that I had already gathered too much wisdom that day.

I watched the rain. Get a letter from the box, and let it be your seer and guide to the universe, Ford. That's stupid. What am I doing here, just pack up, go drag Clarence out of that dive and forget Camille. But she's already this close, she'll get to Asheville from here and cause problems. The compassion thing, too. You can't leave a suffering fellow human being. Also there's the where-did-I-take-the-wrong-road angle. Get a letter from the box, and let it be your seer and guide to the universe.

So I did. I dug deeply, sat back in the rocker. Forked tongues of lightning licked the sea somewhere past Big John's Towel Paradise. I opened the envelope.

November 9, 1968

Dear Son,

I am sitting here in the backyard early in the morning, a cup of coffee on the arm of the chair, the sound of Haydn coming from the record player. So far this morning I have seen wrens, chickadees, cardinals, titmouses, crows, starlings, sparrows, cowbirds, and, circling high overhead, a Cooper's hawk.

Is school going all right? I hope you have made many new friends. I remember when I took you to the first grade, you cried and cried and clung to my skirts, and I was flattered and upset at the same time. A child is supposed to miss its mother. Only you are no longer a child.

And I am no longer a young mother. That's life! The trees are just changing here, but I bet the leaves are already gone in Asheville....

I could not read any more. The passing of that time, from now — where in the hell had it gone? We lose years like car keys. Let's see, I had a great time in 1978, but I was away for 1980 through 1985. No, I don't know where I was or what I was doing, probably in a coma or visiting another planet.

I had more immediate problems than sad nostalgia; I had Her Madness, Camille Malone, waiting in some dank dive to call me.

So I got the phone book, looked up the Sandstorm Motel, found it was twenty blocks away. I showered and went down to the lobby, where Mister Josiah was sitting on a sofa reading a copy of *Hoard's Dairyman*.

"My wife's making Lodger Pie for supper," he said. "Can we set a place for you?"

"Lodger Pie?" I said with a shiver. "What's that?"

"Oh, it's a secret," he said. "It's got three meats and four vegetables, and then there's that other thing."

"Other thing?" I said with a secret sinking thrill.

"Don't axe me," he said. "I don't even know."

"Sorry, but I've got to meet a lady," I said. "When my cousin comes back, tell him I'll see him in the morning or something."

"We'll save you some Lodger Pie for breakfast," he said. He went back to the magazine. "They've got a new treatment for mastitis, by the way."

"It's about time," I said.

The Sandstorm Motel had been abandoned, boarded up. A plastic sign out front had been pummeled with vandals' rocks so often that it was barely readable. I was half an hour early, so I parked near the phone booth, which seemed fine, locked the station wagon and wandered around the building; signs blossomed all over it, warning against illegal entry. Great clumps of seagrass sprouted around it. Paint came off in table-sized sheets. The windows had sheets of plywood nailed over them.

Around the side, I saw the swimming pool, which had a few inches of nasty, still water; bugs and trash mingled on the patina. A sign said another Hilton Hotel would be opening in a year. They'd come in and wipe the Sandstorm Motel away, leave no trace. Nothing but some postcard that Aunt Jo and Uncle Bub got from the family for spring break in 1961. On the end was the old bar and restaurant. I walked past it, came over a dune clogged with sea oats, saw a few older women in modest swimsuits and silly hats walking down the beach, looking for shells in the wrack or glancing out past the breakers toward Africa: thinking of their husbands now gone or maybe Daddy, *do you remember how Daddy came home from the store every Friday night with penny candy in his pockets and.....*no, it's too sad. Just look at the sea and its eternal immensity, plan to work on the qualities of hope.

It was six twenty-five. The tide of my blood was coming in. Soon it would be full, as far as the water ever rose to the land. I walked back past the Sandstorm Motel's empty rooms: love once transpired here, honeymoons and marriages trying not to fall apart. Where were those lovers now, I wondered. In their quiet houses, thinking of what had robbed them of the years, with memories that got shorter each season.

Six twenty-seven. By the phone; I'll have a heart attack if it rings. The sky reflected in the puddles of the old parking lot.

A car full of black women came past. No one in the car was talking. Was that an.... *BRNNNGGGGGGGGGGGGGGGG!!!!!!!!!!!!!!!*

The sound of the phone was unearthly, luminous. Melodic, a cathedral in the heartlands of France. A summons to the rector's study. I stepped up to the phone, lifted it off its cradle, and in a voice that Alan Ladd never used in the movies, I croaked, "Hello?" A silence then. The silence of old tombs, uncut book pages in the Ashmolean Museum in Oxford. Of fields before storm, just before.

"Camille?" I nearly whispered.

"Hi, Ford!" a female voice said. It *did* sound like her. Where had all the years gone? Fumblings in the background, a striking match, exhalation from a lit cigarette. "How do you like the game so far?"

"Camille, for God's sake, don't turn this into a joke," I said. "Where are you? I've been worried about you, I saw you on that TV program about the homeless, and I thought, my God what...."

"...Build thee more stately mansions, O my soul," quoth she.

"Where are you?" I nearly shouted. "I want to help. I...I can help, Camille. It's crazy, but I'm a professor at McCandless now, teaching musicology, and, and...."

"We've got to be careful about this, Adelbert," she said with a laugh.

"My name's not Adelbert!" I said. "I'm sick of your allusions. I never knew what we were talking about before you ran off to Europe. It's Ford! Ford Clayton!"

"Weren't you the one who asked me to come?" she said. "And any educated person should know of Adelbert von Chamisso. Remember now...he wrote *Peter Schlemihl's Wundersame Geschichte*. This is a real kick, talking to you again. "

"Where are you?" I asked.

"I'm around," she said. "I just wasn't sure you really wanted to see me or if you'd just had a fit of nostalgia or something."

"I saw you on that special about the homeless," I cried. "I wanted to help. What went wrong, Camille?" She began to laugh.

"So that's it," she said. "This is great."

"What are you talking about?" I asked. "Why are you playing games?"

"Just do things my way," she said. "There's a small bar in the Ramada on Sixty-Second Street. I'll wait." She paused. Was this the truth? I did hear some buzzing around in the background.

Click. I had known that all the time, that my choice of women was tempered by some desire for the uncontrollable, the outrageous, the irrational. Except for Jill, she of the marriageable background, the sweet cheer, the darling girl of every family's heart. I adored Jill. I loved the kids. I wanted our house back, the regular, clock-ticking stuff, getting up in the morning, eating bad things, watching stupid sitcoms, taping Johnny, having coffee, and watching "Sunday Morning" on CBS when you might see great musicians stop by....And yet I'd nearly destroyed it all by flirting with Starr, by calling Camille, by everything. I should have been named Adelbert. Would serve me right.

I drove along the Coast Highway, seeing cookouts. Folks laughing, working over burgers, drinking beer. Three grown women on a deck playing guitars, singing, and laughing. A child taking a first wobbly roll on a two-wheeler. The air was turning blue, dusk-hazy, and sweetly reeking of salt marshes and sea sand. The Ramada was easy to spot, more than twenty stories. I did not know the etymology of Ramada; Camille might settle for Ramayana, the Indian epic poem, monkey dances and all. Or *Ramona*, by Helen Hunt Jackson, one of those romances I read in high school, but which Charley Barstow denigrated with all the works of E. P. Roe and Hallie Ermine Rives. Already I was slipping back into Camille mode. I parked next to the Ramada.

A pretty blond woman behind the front desk told me the bar-restaurant was on the seventh floor. I rode up. The elevator opened, and I saw a bulbously fat man and a bored, disgusted woman who must have been his spouse. His stomach was seeking lower floors, a toothpick dangled from his greasy lips; she was birdy-thin, pursed lips, eyes waiting for revenge. I shuddered as they silently passed me. I walked down the hall, hung a left, and saw a glass door that was held against the wall. Sounds of tinkling glasses and soft jazz spilled into the hall.

A couple was leaving as I went in. The man had a deep tan and white clothes. His girl was hanging close, chin against his sleeve. They looked perfect, but the world wasn't perfect. I wondered if he had ever lied to his boss. Sure, but discreetly and for the right business reasons, with calculation. The woman was not his wife.

The bar was on the left. Fifteen-foot-high windows faced the sea. The ambiance was quite pleasing, and the easy sound of group laughter came toward me. My heart was mad. Mouth gone dry. A phrase kept lilting through my head: *Nobody ever forgets Camille Malone.*

A waiter with a slightly foppish air came toward me, smiling broadly.

"One for dinner?" he said.

"I'm meeting a lady in the bar," I said.

"Of course, sir," he said, and he turned to lead me to that promised land. Then he stopped in mid-glide, turned and eyed me.

"Something wrong?" I asked.

"You name wouldn't happen to be...." he said, pulling a small piece of paper from his very neat apron. "Ah, you wouldn't happen to be a Charles Bovary, would you?"

"What?" I said.

"Are you Charles Bovary?" he said. "If you are, a lady left this message for you."

"*Je suis Sharle Bovary*," I said darkly. I looked past him into the small bar, saw no familiar faces. He handed me the note and I opened it, turned it toward the light.

The handwriting was the same as that on the postcards.

Charles,

I'm having such a good time here! Don't be angry with me, Ford. You can call me timid, saying anything you like. I'm just not quite ready to see you face to face. Are you busy tomorrow? I'll find you.

Emma

"Son of a bitch!" I shouted. Loud. I realized as I looked up that the room had gone silent and was staring at me.

"What's wrong?" asked the waiter.

"Sorry," I muttered. I smiled apologetically, but my apologies were not accepted by the crowd. I had disrupted their dinner. All evening, perhaps for years, they'd wonder about me, about the note, knowing no doubt that it was from a woman.

When I got back to the Gordon House, I was deeply upset, exhausted, and in no mood to find that my cousin Clarence Clayton had organized a rummy game in the lobby or that Mister Josiah had all the luck on his side.

THE ROOMS AT THE GORDON HOUSE DID HAVE PHONES, and after dinner, when Clarence was shuffling cards again downstairs, I called Jill.

The night was warm. A fluid breeze brought the pleasant sounds of streets and entertainments. I'd turned my fan off, and Jesus hung sadly down from the fan, no longer eligible for the *Book of Records*. I didn't plan to call, but my fingers moved around the old dial phone like a blind man reading some cylindrical text from Babylon. I didn't expect Jill's sister, Jenny, to answer the phone. Jenny had never liked me.

"Jenny, it's Ford," I said.

"Oh, hi," she said. Cold. I heard her turn away from the phone and repeat my name, I guessed to Jill.

"How are you and Bobby doing? The weather okay in Macon?"

"Fine and fine," she said.

"Great," I said. "Can I speak to Jill, please?"

"What about?"

"Did she ask you to ask that?"

"Why do you ask that?"

"I just asked," I sighed. "Jenny, this is starting to sound like a Three Stooges routine. I just need to talk to her. Tell her it's a matter of life or death."

"Is it?"

"Does it matter?" I said hotly. "Maybe AT&T is enjoying this banter, but I'm not. Please put Jill on the phone." She said nothing. I heard female giggling in the background. Villains! It cut through my male-bonded heart to hear long-distance sport made of me.

"Hi, Ford," said Jill. "How are you?"

"The convivial lie would be that I'm fine, that the world is still round, and that in the past few days I've achieved the first steps toward Nirvana," I said. "The truth is that I have never been more miserable in my life."

"Really?" she said happily. "No kidding."

"Really," I said. "Are the kids okay?"

"Other than missing their daddy, they're fine," she said. "You sound kind of desperate."

"I am desperate," I said honestly.

"Your cookie lose the key to the bedroom?" she asked acidly.

"I deserved that," I said grimly. "Every word of it. But I told you the truth. It only lasted two weeks. She's in Asheville."

"Asheville?" said my wife. "And where might you be, Ford?"

"I'm in Myrtle Beach," I said. "It's about Camille, Jill. She came here looking for me. I talked to her on the phone tonight. But she's acting like we're part of some chess game. I think she may be wacko."

"You're attracting an interesting crowd of girls these days," she said. "One is about fourteen years old and plays a harp, and the other sounds like the linen girl at the Bates Motel."

"Is this the chapter labelled *Wife's Just Revenge* or something?" I asked.

"Was there a reason you called, Ford?" she asked.

I went silent for a moment. Why had I called? For that familiar, steadying voice, her gaze in my imagination, the memory of her tenderly holding the kids as babies, nursing Jay, my own Madonna, Jill Clayton, teacher of remedial mathematics.

"It's a long story," I said.

"Well, I'd just love to be an audience, but I'm doing my nails," she said. "Are you closer to resolving things? I talked to my lawyer today, and the clock's ticking, you know."

"How is Thom?" I asked, pronouncing it wrong.

"Better, apparently, than you are," she said. "Then again, it seems like everybody's better off than you these days. Are you staying in a penthouse at the beach?"

"I'm staying in a dump run by a dwarf and a fortune teller," I said, close to tears, "and there's a Jesus hooked to my ceiling fan. He whirls. You can look it up in the *Guinness Book of World Records*."

"All this and theology, too," she said. I heard her voice grin. She was having a great time.

"Anyway, Jill, I'm working things out," I said. "I'm beginning to see the light at the end of the tunnel."

"You and Henry Kissinger," she said with a yawn.

"Just be patient with me for a few more days," I said. "I think I'm beginning to see what's wrong with me. And believe me, this isn't easy to admit. As you so eloquently put it, I'm a miserable fool who's throwing my life away, but now I think I'm finding my way back through the thicket of my past."

"Oh," said Jill gaily, "like finding out the diamond you bought was really a zircon?"

"A painfully accurate and rather mean-spirited analogy," I said.

"Mean-spirited?" she chuckled. "Are you hinting that I should have pleasant views about your scattered, and I mean that in so many ways, girls?"

"I mean that I do love you, Jill," I said, "and when next you hear from me, I may know the secrets of the ages. Then I will settle into pleasant middle and old age, fulfill the promise I showed in my early life, and never stray again from the path of righteousness."

"I'm not trying to be nasty," she said. Was her voice softening? "But I really do have to do my nails. The kids are in bed, or I'd let you say hello. Kathy had to do a drawing today, and you know what she did? A crankshaft. Isn't that the cutest thing you ever heard?"

"Aaagghhhh," I groaned. "Look, be good. I'll call in no more than two weeks, Jill."

"Bye, Ford," she said.

"Don't you have any wifely advice?"

"Don't eat anything raw, and keep an eye out in the rear-view mirror for pawns and rooks," she said.

"Jesus," I said, and the next sound I heard was her brief "Bye, now" and the dead wire.

I lifted the phone and dialed frantically. Another human voice to wake me. She answered on the second ring.

"Hi, Mom," I said. "It's me, your only son, Ford Clayton."

"Dear, I'm glad you rang me up," she said, using a vernacular she'd learned from some Agatha Christie play or something. No one but my mother ever said "rang me up" in the history of Jamesburg. "I cannot for the life of me understand why Jack Klugman has to spend each and every episode of 'Quincy' screaming at the top of his lungs. What kind of Thespian apprenticeship would have prepared him for such a thing?"

Sweat began to form on my temples.

"I'm doing fine, too," I said. "How are you?"

"Oh, pooh, son," she said, "don't be so wounded. I was going to inquire about your health. Have you and Jill made up yet?"

"Not yet," I said. "I just talked to her. I'm at Myrtle Beach."

"Well," she said.

"The only person here with me is Clarence Clayton," I said, "my recently paroled cousin." A silence.

"You and Clarence took a vacation at the beach?" she asked with great confusion.

"I'll explain it when I'm home for a fortnight," I said. "Look, Mom, can I ask you a question, and I want you to give me an honest answer."

"Yes?"

"Was there a time when you knew that I was...well, shall we say, diverging from the rest of my high school crowd?" I asked. She laughed. And laughed and laughed. "God, Mom, you're savaging me. Please stop this mirth. I'm nearly forty. I can't handle mirth."

"I knew you were different in utero," she nearly sang.

"Please, that's revolting," I said, cringing.

"When you were five years old, I found you on the sofa, not moving, when *Verdi* was on the record player," she said. "Most of your friends were learning about Babar or something, and you were listening to Verdi. You were always a sensitive little boy, but other than that, just normal as pie."

"Do you have any idea why I'd have a weakness for women who are unusual?"

"Like that Ingrid thing?"

"Look, I'm sorry I asked," I said. "I've got to be going anyway. Uh, maybe Jack Klugman yells because he wants to be heard or something. Or so people will think he's full of passion."

"There's more passion in a whisper than a shout," she said wisely.

"Well, when you get your own TV show, you can whisper," I said.

"Oh, these are just reruns," she said. "All these shouts are years old. As much history now as Demosthenes."

"Bye, Mom," I said. "What's Dad doing?"

"He's attacking on old chair with a saw in the basement. Take care, son," she said, "and come to see me soon. I love you."

"Love you, too."

Pick a letter, any letter. Sudden laughter and shouting from downstairs. Clarence probably just won again. I suspected him of cheating, something he learned in the Big House. Scattered over the bed, pick any letter. I thrust my hand into the pile, took one out, didn't look at the return address, opened it. And couldn't read it. I threw it down, left the room, went downstairs, past the jolly cardplayers, out the door and into the salt-smelling streets of Myrtle Beach. I needed to Create a Scene, dramatize myself into some sense. I went straight across the main drag, between two buildings, past the drainage from SEE LIVE SHARK, over a swelling of sand and sea oats (ILLEGAL TO PICK SEA OATS). I saw the dark wet ribbon of sand. Jill had revealed the sad truth that these were merely mud flats, she who'd grown up going to Panama City each summer.

I stopped walking. The surf was the same Homer had heard, the same Demosthenes had shouted against, the same they'd used to ride into Anzio. The same, the same, the same, the same.

"The same!" I shouted. "It's all the same!"

"It's all the same to me, too," a voice behind me said.

I turned sharply, surprised, embarrassed. A woman. She wore jogging shorts, a top of cornflower blue. Nikes. She was flushed and breathing a bit from jogging, I guessed. Short blonde hair, lovely clear eyes.

"I'm sorry," I said. "I didn't know anybody was near me. I was just musing on the fate of the century."

"And you decided it's all the same?" she said. There was something of teasing in her voice. Why was she talking to a strange man in a spot lit well enough to see but too poorly for security? I could be a sorcerer ready to turn her into a pig.

"It's that time in my life," I said, laughing. "I got lost a few years back, and this is my feeble attempt to put things right and quit hurting people."

"Particularly the ones you love," she said. I stared at her. Something was familiar. The accent or her near-smile? She walked, slowing down from running. I walked along with her, not knowing where we were going.

"Yes," I said. "How'd you know that?"

"You always hurt the ones you love," she sang. Her voice wasn't bad. It wasn't good, either. I laughed. I realized that she had long, muscular legs, a clean stride, that I was powerfully attracted to her and that she knew it.

"I've noticed that, too," I said. "Do you mind if I ask you something?"

"Shoot."

"Aren't you worried talking to a strange man on the beach?" I asked. "I could be really deranged." She laughed.

"You don't look deranged," she said. "You look a little lost, maybe, but not deranged."

"Lost, I am," I admitted. "But it just seems risky for a beautiful woman like you to...." God! What was I doing?

"....Do you really think I'm beautiful?" she asked. She stopped, almost did a modeling turn so I could check her out. She was close to my age but in superb condition. "That's sooooooo sweet." She danced along the sand lightly. "That's sooooo sweet."

"Well, I, uh....."

"Because they all say you look nice on the outside, and then...." She suddenly looked dark. The smile faded. A tic developed at the corner of her mouth. "Then all they want is to fuck you. All they want is to drill a hole in your soul until all the fluids and bones leak out on the sheets and washed with socks and, and, and then they have you by your pretty NECK." She was glaring at me now. My blood congealed. I took a step back. She smiled sweetly. "But not you. You're sooooo sweet. Sooooosweet."

"Sirens," I choked.

She turned her head to hear what I heard. But all she could have heard was her own voice. Which was enough. I turned and took a step, a quick step. Then I ran. She was laughing at me, her deep laughter speeding me on. My chest ached, and I ran and ran, past the wash from LIVE SHARK, across the street, past the rummy game, that was, happily, still in progress, up the stairs and into my room. I closed the door and turned on the fan.

I knelt before the altar of letters. I opened a succession of them, reading only the first page:

Hello, Darling,

It's Wednesday but it seems like the weekend will never arrive! I have spent the whole week thinking about our wedding, about how unbelievable it is that I found you out of all the men in this world. When you think about it, there's no way to understand how two people who love each other, who spend their lives together, ever meet. I only know that I adore you and that in the moment I say "I do," I will mean it more than

Tears welled up in my eyes. My throat closed from grief and joy.

Dear son,

Enclosed is a money order for $50, which your Mom and I decided to send you as sort of a surprise. I know that you could use it for extra clothes and so forth.

Did you get any snow out of that system last week? We got a dusting even down here, and I understand the mountains got a bunch.

I'm selling ponchos now. First time anybody in Jamesburg ever saw them, but I've already sold seven or eight and they're so ugly.

I remembered the ponchos, paisley, hideous, perfect for those times.

Dearest Ford,

I've spent this week thinking about Bernadette. I saw that movie with Jennifer Jones, and darling, that's what I wish I could be. Somehow a martyr to something, suffering silently for some terrible pain or sin. I admire the missionary life so much....

All Nancy could get on one page, big loopy handwriting.

Well, Jesus H. Christ, Fordy,

How come you ain't wrote me over the holidays? What am I, the Arimaspasians and you a Gryphon? I hope the Fagin of McCandless has had a nice time for this Easter season. By the by, if Jesus rose from the dead, what did the Easter bunny do?

Can you barely conceive what a tragic, stupid moron Muzio Clementi was? I just listened to some of his keyboard crap, and a greater piece of trash never obscured musical truth. It isn't even sickening enough to be an emetic, for God's sake.

Camille, Camille. Who are you now? The naked and shaved Venus beside my bed in a pool of light? A red-faced girl who would practice scales for hours and hours? Beatrice or a Siren on the Rocks?

I put all the letters back into the box and set it next to the rocker. The room had no TV, no radio, nothing but the Whirling Jesus. Raucous laughter from downstairs.

I stripped, lay down on the sheet, dreamed *The Divine Comedy of Ford Clayton*. Endless hoops of fire, me jumping through them, women all begging me, then mocking me, sweet tortures, naked women, legs spread, inviting me, then falling over to deny me; Camille on this flame throne, Queen of the Damned, and music, the *Requiem Mass* of Giuseppi Verdi, the great mass for the dead, of which I was one, having never solved life and been sentenced eternally to repeat my same indecisions, same moronic behavior in all things. And I called, like the aged Ulysses for my children (or was it Old King Cole for his pipe and his bowl?) and told them I was setting out on this voyage, because memories of my trip to Circe and Nausicaa were too bold to let me sleep, that I would be pushing off soon, they were to guard fair Penelope (Jill) while I went to hell itself in search of my mortality.

Then I saw myself as this old man shuffling through the Biltmore House, which I apparently owned, soft slippers sliding on the marble floor. And silence. No tourists. Just me, fires on the hearths, completely alone....and I go to the front door, but it is closed, stuck, and I realize then that the price for this life is that I'll never escape, that no one ever escapes, that all lovely women and career-dreaming little boys and crazy cousins and fortune tellers and dwarfs and dumb administrators....that all of us are on this side of the mirror, and that the other side awaits us all.

And this is what middle age means, running through the Biltmore House in a silk robe and slippers, even owning the goddamn thing, and knowing, finally understanding once and for all, that it doesn't matter who owns anything, that the only thing we take from school to beach, from home to adulthood, from sweet lover to sweet lover, is the occasional glance from another's equally frightened eyes.

I awoke suddenly, sat up. My watch said it was nearly four. The day when Camille would find me. I fell back against the pillow. I would give her this day. No more. Then I would go back to Asheville, call Jill home to me.

The mad dog's breath in the silent room belonged to Ford Clayton.

I SAT IN MY APARTMENT IN TOWN, recopying parts for *The Song of Ruth*, and Camille Malone, in a modest dress, legs tucked under her hips, sat in a chair across from me, reading her Missal.

Winter, 1971. We had moved into separate rooms in the Dorchester Arms two miles from the McCandless Campus. Juniors had that privilege. Camille had come back from New Orleans the previous fall quiet, studious, deeply religious, more amazing than ever.

The change in Camille was, I decided, a metaphor for changes in the campus, in our world. The war was definitely starting to change focus. Our world retracted once more to harmony and counterpoint, to what we all loved best: music. At Christmas, Camille even completed her conducting class by leading the McCandless Symphony in a stirring version of the Franck *D Minor Symphony*. Ronny Favors was still my best friend, after Camille, but I was not long just friends with her; we loved, held each other close. We wrapped ourselves in each other's world.

She turned the Malone Society into a religious group, discussing the Virgin Birth, encyclicals, Lives of the Saints. Membership changed, was respectful, finally fell apart, until, at the first meeting after Christmas, in early 1971, only two people came—Ford Clayton and Camille Malone.

The Song of Ruth was my magnum opus, Ruth as a contralto, Boaz a tenor of course, small chorus and orchestra. It was pretty in an anachronistic way, but I believed in it, trusted that I had finally achieved the life for which I'd always dreamed: Robert and Clara.

That day is crystal to me, etched, immovable, yet beyond that image, nearly irretrievable. I remember Camille reading: *May the Lord enkindle within us the fire of His love.* I glanced up at her amazed face; she was surprised by the consolation of religion. Yet often she was silent and brooding, speaking with open admiration of the clergy and the sisterhood of nuns.

Another snowy day on campus: Camille walking with me, not quite lunch, but no classes for a time. Flakes the size of Communion cups, freshmen shouting and building a grand piano of the icy fall. Not a sigh of wind. She wore a simple blue coat and rust-colored muffler, boots, girlish mittens, ear muffs. I was wearing blue jeans and mackinaw, a New York Yankees cap. We had ditched our books in the Chapel and walked arm in arm, listening to the shards of music from the practice halls, from other rooms, all kinds of music, jazz improvisation, rock, folk, Renaissance, Gregorian chants, plucked guitars. All instruments in their faint scales. I thought I could never tire of it, and I was right. Camille's cheeks were pinked with the cold.

"They look so young," she said.

A clutch of kids built a snowman. They whooped and yelled, not able to believe their good fortune at being away from home, independent for the first time, realizing they'd live forever without any responsibilities. I already felt old enough to be a parent.

"I wonder what they fear."

"Why don't you wonder what they love?" I asked.

"Because a person's strength is in mastering what he fears," she said softly. Only a few months before, she would have screamed at anyone using "he" as an indefinite pronoun. I marveled at the politics of grammar, said nothing. "No one ever became great by making the most of his good points alone. David said in Psalm 77: 'In the day of my trouble I sought the Lord: my sore ran in the night and ceased not: my soul refused to be comforted.' But then God came into David's heart, and he wasn't afraid anymore."

We walked for a while. She held to me.

"I'm not afraid since I met you," I said with reasonably excusable sentimentality. "I feel like I can do anything. Do you feel that?"

"I can do all things through the Lord Jesus Christ," she whispered. She crossed herself.

"How about through Ford Clayton," I said.

"You mustn't joke," she said without smiling. "You mustn't blaspheme."

That day we drove back to the Dorchester with the daylight giving up early, roads terrible with snow, but getting back safely. Going to my apartment, she to hers, then I met her at seven. She was cooking spaghetti and wore a teal dress of simple lines. The windows were steamed, dripping. Her place. Her small radio, and on it, the *Nutcracker*, perfect snow weather. Her movements in the kitchenette, pouring red wine, setting the table, playing house, pretending benign glories of the world, amen.

We sat, and Camille folded her hands under her chin. So did I.

"God, grant us the peace of thy salvation and the glory of thy light as we eat this food for the nourishment of our dear bodies," she said, "and guide and protect us, particularly Ford, whom I love. *Recordare mei, Domine, omni potentatui dominam, amen.*"

"Amen, " I said.

A wind arose as we ate. The weather howled. The apartment building was cold, and we laughed and shivered with cold wine and the spaghetti, which was slightly undercooked but marvelous all the same. I helped her clear away the dishes, and we sat in the embrace of a single table lamp, listening to a Mozart symphony.

"Do you ever think about dying?" she asked.

"Not if I can help it," I said.

"But you must," she begged. "Without that constant plaint, there could be no obedience to the Church."

"I don't see brooding about it does much good," I said.

"But it can come with the swiftness of a sword," she said.

"Maybe two thousand years ago," I said. "Swordplay has noticeably declined in North Carolina in the past two centuries."

"There's no need to make fun of me," she said.

"I'm just trying to change the subject," I said. "Why are you even bringing this up?"

"Because tonight I must offer you my complete confession," she whispered.

"I'd rather get drunk and fool around," I choked.

"Ford, this is the gift you must offer me," she said. "Full attention to the darkest details of my past." I felt hot and uncomfortable.

"I read in *Reader's Digest* that it's best not to tell about your past to a new love," I said.

"I must have your absolution," she said.

"Camille, I'm not God," I said. "Not even close."

"Ford!" she shouted. A brief flash of the old Camille von der Malone. I was impressed. I sat back and waited.

"When I was a little girl and Daddy was going to school, we lived in an apartment in a seedy section of New Orleans," she said. "My mother and father never fought, not once, but things were wrong between them. They simply did not love. Perhaps I did not understand that, or perhaps I did. Anyway, I cried all the time, Ford, for days and days. I would cry my eyes out, wanting to be the daughter of different parents. And when I cried and cried, my parents could not stand it. They looked at each other like animals trapped, doomed to slow, unpleasant deaths.

"And so they began to use this big walk-in closet. My father emptied it and put a big chair and a lamp and a set of Britannicas he'd bought at a used book store in it for me. And a complete set of Bulfinch's *Mythology*. The first few times, they locked me in there. They'd yell through the door, 'Camille, honey bear, we're going out for dinner,' and they'd escape from me, and I'd pretend I did not hear them. And I'd sit and read the Brittanica for hours and hours, finally falling asleep in my big chair. And this went on until the tears stopped, but I could not escape the room. Each day when I came home from school, I would go into the closet, with its lamp and, in the warm months, a small fan, and I'd read and read. I became Penelope. I was Florence Nightingale. Then I was Franz Liszt. Then I was Beethoven. Music began to thrill me as nothing else could.

"I asked Daddy for a piano, and desperate for anything, he bought an old spinet, and I took lessons from a series of teachers, each of whom I surpassed in short order. Music made me happy. I realized about then that my parents were in no way unusual, that they loved each other the best they could. But by then I was living an interior life. I did not fit in at school. They left me alone, but I had one friend, Johnny Gateau. Like me, he loved music. I thought I was falling in love with him.

"But then T. D. Malone came along."

"Who's T. D. Malone?" I asked. The wind outside was howling.

"My father's younger brother," she said. "He was working on an offshore oil rig, and he came to spend a weekend with us when I was fifteen. I was fascinated with him. He told stories. He was dark and good-looking, but something violent played about him, and he drank without stopping.

"On that Saturday night that he was there, I had practiced for an hour and read from James Joyce, turned out the lights. My room was upstairs. I did not hear him come into the room. When I awoke, he was sitting on the edge of the bed."

"Please don't tell me about this," I said. I got up and walked to the window. Darkness was over the face of the earth. Snow blew in the lamplight.

"You must hear my confessions," she said. I could not sit. "He was on the edge of the bed, and he was stroking my hair, and I said 'T. D., don't do that.' I sat up. I could smell bourbon all over him. And he only said one thing, but he kept saying it over and over, 'You're just a sweetheart, Camille. You're just a sweetheart.' And I was paralyzed. He pulled the covers slowly off me, and I could not move or make a sound. Was it a dream? No. I was only wearing a short gown, and he looked at me when the covers were off, and I was breathing so hard. I wanted to scream. I was so afraid."

"I understand," I said. "Please stop, Camille."

"And he leaned over me, taking off his shirt, and he was a Catholic, though my father had no religion, and T. D. said *'Diffusa est gratia in labiis tuis: proptera benedixit te Deus in aeternum, et in saeculum saeculi'*, which means Grace is poured in thy lips; therefore hath God blessed thee forever. Then he started saying again that I was a sweetheart. He took off his pants. The room's light was from the moon, full and heavy. Then his undershorts, and I felt a terror I'd never felt in all my life."

I sat in one of her chairs across the room, shaking with anger and fear.

Her voice became hoarse. Her eyes were glazed, frightened all over again. She stood and walked around the room in steps as slow as a minuet.

"And he raped me," she said. "The pain was beyond belief. He stank of whiskey. I cried silently and beat my small fists on his back, but he would not get off. Then he softened, and though I was a virgin, I knew what had happened, and I was terror-struck. I could not breathe. He went to sleep on top of me. I pushed hard, and he rolled off and hit the floor, and when he did, he got up and put on his clothes and left the room."

I wept. If he had been in Asheville, I would have killed him. Camille saw my tears, looked at me with pity.

"The next morning, he was there at Sunday breakfast, acting as if nothing had happened," she said. "And I sat there, staring at my food, and Mama kept saying I was scrawny as a bird, and that the boys would never pay attention to me if I didn't eat. T. D. was joking with Daddy about something. I was terrified that I was pregnant, could barely move, ashamed, but not knowing what to do.

"Then I saw the long bread knife on the table. Mama baked delicious bread, and she'd bought a long sharp knife to cut it. And I saw this picture in my head of T. D."

I stood, shaking. Camille had changed from a minuet to a crazy waltz, moving around the room from table to chair. I thought back to our few lovemaking sessions and felt profoundly ashamed.

"And so," she said, "I came out of my chair, grabbed the knife and stabbed him in the back. The blade was like a putty knife going into something soft and yielding. Everyone began to scream. Blood flowed out around the wound. T. D. could not reach the knife to pull it out, and so my father did, and my uncle fell to the floor, blood everywhere. The ambulance came, and so did the police. T. D. lost a lot of blood, but he lived. I never saw him again. I was released to my parents' custody, but I could not tell my father what had happened in my room that Saturday night.

"I found ways to keep that night from coming back, Ford. I drank and used drugs. I read every volume of Britannica several times. I practiced the piano for nine hours without stopping. My parents were so afraid of me, afraid, too, that I'd be put in an institution."

I wanted to throw up. I backed toward the door, unsure of where I was anymore. A romantic evening with wine and spaghetti had turned into a nightmare from which I was unsure I might awaken.

"I can't stand this," I admitted. She said nothing. She seemed frozen, unable to say a thing or speak. "I said I can't stand this, Camille. Why did you tell me all this? Why?"

She said nothing, like the Tar Baby. Immutable, a fact of nature. Two minutes passed.

"Father forgive me," she whispered, "for I have sinned." Dry husks, autumn fields, the sound of dry wind on dry dirt roads. I fled out of her apartment to my own, hands shaking so badly I could scarcely open the lock on the door. I got my coat and hat and muffler and went for a walk in the blizzard.

The snow came sideways now. It filled my eyes, my mouth, stung my cheeks softly. I had harbored this secret: that Camille was a virgin when, as freshmen we made love in the bushes, that my passion had overcome her goodness. Now I realized that her passion had overcome my inexperience, despite Ingrid. It was a horror. I couldn't imagine such a thing. A boy named Otis Marsh, who was a few years older than I, had beaten his new bride to death with an electric space heater when I was a senior. I once drove up on a wreck in which a little girl had been killed instantly, saw her grieving mother screaming in the arms of a state patrolman. I saw the pictures of Viet Nam every day. Riots in the ghettos, suppression in communist countries. The world seemed mad. A man named T. D., some damned oil driller raping Camille and then getting stabbed in the back at breakfast. I recalled Camille sitting in the balcony of the Chapel, crying that everything was useless. All revolved back to that night; all she wanted from the world, all she'd ever asked was to be left alone.

Music left you alone. A Haydn symphony filled your spirit. A Schubert quartet in a minor key: medicine for all ills. Lost in Mahler's *Eighth*: the way of all flesh. Was that the bond of music that held all of us at McCandless, that holds me there still? A sweet hatch from this world into another, one where uncles don't rape you? Where wars made sense and consolation was always at hand? Music healed your spirit like aspirin lowered a fever.

I walked alone in our neighborhood, which was not very good nor very bad. It didn't matter then. No one was out. Street lights flickered, went out. I turned: power all gone now, all lights out. The light from the snow arose. I saw a traffic light swaying back and forth as if it were guided by a giant's idle foot.

All was whiteness. Trees trembled in their glacial coating. None of the houses seemed familiar. I slipped and fell hard on my left elbow, immediately worrying that I might not be able to play the piano. I cursed God. I screamed and cursed T. D. Malone.

I followed a street, it went nowhere. I retraced my quickly filling footprints, went down another street, was more lost still. I leaned against a brick wall, breathing hard, starting to realize with un-Romantic clarity that I could, in fact, *actually die* out here. And so I ran. Blind. Snowblind. I fell and slid into the middle of a deserted intersection that during the day in spring would be clogged with cars. The traffic light above me swayed and swung, and I scrambled up and ran again.

I came around a corner, found myself in front of our apartment building. Oh God, I thought, thank you, Lord. I let myself into the dry lobby, went up the creaking wooden stairs to my apartment. I shed the coat and muffler, trembled, ran my hands under hot water. My feet were numb. I walked around in my bare feet until feeling prickled back into them. I'd probably used all the hot water left; the power was off here, too. I sat in a chair in the small living room, wondering how I'd gotten there, what I should do next. I'd wind up as a choir director in Alabama or something. I'd never be a famous composer. Who the hell were the famous composers now, anyway? Better to die young like Schubert or Keats. Leave nothing but a few cryptic clues to....a knock on the door. I did not move, said nothing. Again.

"Yeah?" I said weakly.

"Ford?" Camille's voice said. I opened the door.

"Hi," I said.

"You have to hear the rest of my confessions," she said.

"No, goddamnit, I don't," I nearly shouted. "I don't have to do this, Camille. I'm not your father or your priest. I'm not the one to bear your guilt. I'm a nobody, a small-town kid from Georgia who will never amount to anything. I'll live and die and be bored and make other people bored. I don't want to live where you live, either in religion or rape or music or drugs or anything. All I want is to fit in quietly. I just nearly got killed in a blizzard. I ran around and howled like a crazy man. You have no idea what this does to me."

"You had to hear it," she said stubbornly. "You can't love what's only gossamer. I'm flesh and blood, Ford. You believe that the world is good, that art is noble, and that happiness is everlasting."

"What was I supposed to believe?" I said. "My mother told me it was that way. She said beauty is truth, truth is beauty."

"Then my confessions are truth and so must be beauty," she whispered.

"Then find someone who values truth more than I do," I said. "I think it's an overrated virtue. What matters most in the world is the sweet illusion of eternal life, and wherever you get it is fine with me. You're getting it through religion, and I'm getting it through music. To live forever in love without suffering. That's beauty, Camille, not truth."

Even in the bare light of the room, I saw a brief smile. She stepped into the room and closed the door behind her. Came into my arms. Her lips were just under mine, and my teeth were locked in back, defiant, yet ready to fall.

"You are so gentle," she said. "My gentle man." Her words smelled like Italian food and wine. I could almost taste the word "man."

"I need you," I said, choking. "I need to pretend you're what I need. Is that so bad?"

"No," she said. "No more confessions. Just now."

My bedroom was small. She steered us toward it, and I felt the most profound confusion of my life, wanting her body with a temple-pounding urgency yet feeling a glory in the possibility of refusing to make love if she wanted.

"What do you want?" I asked.

"To spend the night in your arms," she whispered in winy words. "No more than that."

We kissed once in the cool room. That night of the storm in the winter of 1971, no other man or woman lived on the surface of this earth.

We slept in our clothes. And in the morning, when the storm had quelled and the mountains were temples of ice, we drank hot tea (I had a gas stove) in the cold room, smoked a cigarette, and talked.

Neither of us was particularly happy when she left later that morning to find that the power was back on and that cars were struggling down the streets.

I was ecstatic and repulsed by it all, wishing she'd told me none of her confessions yet believing that we'd be together for life, that we'd marry, that we would not have secrets.

Which proved how little I understood life. Which proved how little I understood Camille Malone.

"THAT'S THE PROBLEM," SAID CLARENCE CLAYTON as he forked a steaming glob of grits into his mouth, "Religion's just not no fun." We were at the Waffle House, and I was looking around us for The Phantom, wondering if she'd turn up in disguise.

On the way over from the Gordon House, Clarence told me about his monster headache, about going back to see Fonda after the rummy game the night before, of gin and tonic and guys and dolls. He had decided being a preacher wasn't his true calling after all.

"But Clarence," I said, "you spent the last three years in the Big House planning to be a preacher. What about all that time you put in? What about converting the Philly Stones?"

"I reckon I got it wrong," he shrugged. He slurped his coffee from the saucer, making a raucous gurgle, like a gate opening on Hoover Dam. "I think I'm gone get me into another line of work."

"Like what?" I asked.

"I'm going to Hollywood and be a movie actor," he said calmly. Stars danced in his eyes. My tiny prophetical cousin, slick hair and all.

"They'd like the part about your checkered past," I admitted. "Every time you starred in a movie, they'd call you the ex-con movie star."

"Uh huh," he said. "I sorta want to be in, like, you know, Lassie movies or something."

"Lassie movies?" I said. A fat woman with thick, dirty glasses leaned over from a booth near us.

"Dog was male," she said in a husky voice. "All them years they told us it was a female." She clucked and shook her head. She wore something brown that was too shapeless for a dress and too large for a pup tent. "Lied. Movies always lie, that's why folks likes 'em, but they orta told us she was male." She nodded her head sharply to put a period on the sentence.

Camille? I studied her. No. This woman was fiftyish, mustache, cigarette smoldering in an ashtray, fat fingers that never played a scale. But what would my ex-darling look like, and how could I tell her that I was leaving that night whether she showed up or not?

"I coulda saveth her," Clarence said, gesturing toward the woman, who heard him but was indifferent. "But anyway, I could do Lassie pictures or superhero things." I choked on my coffee but said nothing. In a booth at the other end of the Waffle House, a man and woman were arguing about who was going to clean their bathrooms, him or her. They were going through gruesome details about it, which we all were trying to ignore. I craned around. Nah. Camille never was a black woman. About the only thing she never was.

"Clarence, what are you going to do, I mean, really?" I asked. "You don't have any money, and like I told you, I'm leaving tonight to go back to Asheville."

"You wouldn't be needing a house boy?" he asked. "Just until I made enough to goeth to Hollywood?"

"No," I said. "My life's confused enough right now. I made some serious mistakes, and I'm trying to correct them now."

"I done that," he said without guile.

"That's what I'm asking, then," I said. "What are you going to do, now that you've given preaching a try and found out it's no fun? I mean, before you become a superhero?"

"Well, I got me a crim'nal record, Cuz," he said, lighting a cigarette. I waved the smoke away, but it came back. "I thought I'd be a preacher, but I can't do that if I don't believe, can I?"

What? What? You can do anything if you don't believe, Clarence. It's only when you become a true believer that you can

do nothing, that failure is inevitable: take our last year at McCandless. He saw me sideslip into another time, and he opened his
copy of the Charlotte paper and read quietly. The fat woman who
knew about Lassie started to leave and then ordered another
plateful of hashbrowns.

Fall of 1971, Ronny gets busted for possession of pot. Things
speeding up here. He gets a suspended sentence, but it scares the
everloving bejesus out of him. Camille comes back from summer
vacation a lapsed Catholic, though still somewhat religious, now
leaning toward Buddhism, Hinduism, Zoroastrianism but with a
dash of Saints and Nuns and the Pope. Her piano technique takes
a leap forward over that summer, while my compositional skills fall
largely apart. Malone Society reconstituted as a kick-ass club to
infiltrate the wormy apple of the Republic (a direct phrase from
Camille's first speech that fall), and she and I find that God is
replaced by dogma (anagram for God Ma, she finds out with delight), and she writes, in three weeks, a complete opera based on
Nathan the Wise by Gotthold Ephraim Lessing, set in Jerusalem
during the Crusades. It's a Muslim-Christian thing, she shrugs,
walking off with the composition prize for the fall. She also wins
the piano prize, playing obscure piano works by Arthur Honegger.
I try to write a piano concerto for her, fail miserably. Ronny
rehabilitated. Runs through women's dorm, doesn't get caught this
time, either. Camille and I living in separate rooms, still in the
Dorchester Arms, sex minimal, friendship skewed, my world lopsided at best. Camille wanting me to be her manager when she
leaves on a world tour if she can go to New York, have a successful
debut, and get bookings. Me applying to graduate school in musicology at Columbia. This dumb newsreel of that senior year, when
the black and whites all turned gray, and I began to realize that this
world was not my oyster and that Camille might never get out of
this thing alive.

In fact, as I looked out the window of the Waffle House, heard
the black couple arguing about cleaning out the garage and the
short-order cook screaming for a waffle, I found myself in a stupor
or trance (how close are they? Camille can tell), seeing the one
indelible scene, which was that spring of 1972, not a month from

graduation.

We're meeting, the Malone Society, at the Circle Beech, and I'm hanging back. The air is lavender, late of a day, gentle and calm, and Camille is trying to find her successor at the helm of the now-legendary society. So, she says, who's gonna take up his crux and foller me, y'all? Who's the one who's gonna take over the Malone Society and deal with the likes of H. R. Bob Haldeman, and, and, make clear to these upgrading undergrad cretinettes that, um, Lucretius was all awhack in writing didactic baloney like *De rerum natura* 'cause the only flipping things really didactic are things that don't propose to teach a thing? And they mumble, the few members of the Malone Society. Poor Billie, gone from fat, when we were freshmen, to cabin-sized; some others, too, lovely girl named Iona for whom I had a secret attachment, though she lets us all know she's a radical feminist, and I approve out loud, which in her eyes *proves* I'm a crypto-macho sexist boar, and trying to do the right thing, I admit that it's probably impossible for a man *not* to be an odious oinker. (Oddly, when I told Jill this story years later, she rather agreed with that about men.)

Anyway, Camille is standing there, whipped up and pretty, when this freshman, male, I've only slightly met, stands up, about to pop. He's tall and intense, wears chinos, plain nerdy double-pocket shirt, glasses thick enough to shield defendants at a Mafia trial. And he raises his hand in a Roman gesture and at the top of his lungs screams, "Whore!"

I've heard this before, and I feel blood flood my face. By now I know about Camille's uncle, about her dramatically fouled-up sexual life. But just hearing that word from this mole from the Young Americans for Freedom, or whatever, brings it all back — the fight with the kid in the dorm, that night with Camille in her room.

He yells it again. Then Camille yells one word at the top of her lovely lungs, a charm against this political intrusion. She doesn't yell "Liar!" or "Fool!" or even "Asshole!" No, she yells the first thing that comes into her mind, which happens to be:

"Georgia!"

And I'm in the air, flying like the Caped Crusader down three rows of the amphitheatre at the Circle Beech, and I grab him by the neck, tumble down, whap him with a good left in the nose. Bloody mess. He whimpers like a pup, scrambles up, and runs off. I feel for three seconds like Odysseus, for three days after, like a fascist idiot.

Then to my finals: God, I know it all. Just ask me. The *exact nature* of Brahms' relationship with Clara Schumann; the use of pedal points in the organ works of Franck; Lutheran theology in Bach's cantatas; Schönberg both pre- and post-dodecaphony; Jewishness in Ernest Bloch's stuff; that flute-playing monarch gadfly Frederick the Great's compositions (new species, Camille tells me); Shostakovitch's *Fifth* and how he said it was a Soviet artist's reply to just criticism, but it wasn't that at all, really, uh....

Fogs. Hazes. Smokes. Small scenes with Camille. *The Joy of Sex.* Screaming arguments. Acceptance to Columbia. Mother happy. Future not something to dwell upon. Senior year at McCandless. Graduation, all black gowns and stuff, and Camille won't wear hers as a protest, and nobody cares, which pisses her off mightily.

"A comet's gone hit the earth in four million years," said Clarence.

I looked up. The arguing black couple was gone. The fat woman who'd been eating hashbrowns and revealing the truth about Lassie was gone. A sullen family had taken her place. Obvious newlyweds sat where the black couple had been. They fawned and cooed.

"Only newlyweds fawn and coo," I said stupidly.

"What's that?" asked Clarence. "Sounds like a answer on 'Jeopardy'."

"It is," I noted. "The question is: What's the Title of Wallace Stevens's last poem?"

"I knowed Wallace," he said with a nod. "He was a trustee, till he stole some greens from the kitchen on Thanksgiving."

I smiled.

All day long, we wandered. We went to the Gay Dolphin, and Clarence bought a fossil shark's tooth necklace that he immediately put on. We ate club sandwiches at a grill called the She Gull, where the waitresses all had to wear pirate garb made of crepe paper and put together with staples. Was that piratess Camille? No. Camille was never, so far as I remembered, from Puerto Rico.

By midafternoon, I didn't *want* to see Camille, was counting down the time when we could check out and leave, or rather, I could. Clarence had already said he thought he'd give Myrtle Beach a go as a businessman. I didn't ask what that meant. He hit me up for $200, which I promised to get with my American Express before the day was out. In my mind, I was on the road, heading for Asheville. I missed my kids and my wife. I missed not thinking about Life and Death and such. Bored with it all, Clarence left me at exactly 3 p.m. and headed for the Ripley's Believe It or Not Museum, where they had a castle made of toothpicks or something. Said he'd meet me at the Gordon House at five before I hit the old road. I felt a new affection for him. Why? Who knows. I watched him bounce off. He was just damn glad to be here. I wanted to feel that way.

It was therefore quite appropriate that when I turned around to saunter the other way that I saw, across the street in front of a towel shop, tanned and relaxed, white shorts and a T-shirt, smiling and waving at me the Penelope of this Odyssey, Camille Who-Didn't-Look-Homeless-at-All Malone. Her hair was shorter, but otherwise she was the same, waving, waving, a siren.

I walked into traffic. Car horns went off, but I ignored them. Maybe millions of people walk by, but Camille, I only have eyes for you. On the front of her T-shirt was a silk-screened Mozart, and he looked like hell. What should I say? Where should I begin to cover the past twenty years, and did she need "saving" — and could I save her? Would there be any tenderness left? I walked right up to her and found out with some relief that she took care of that.

"How'n the hell you been, Abélard?" quoth Camille Malone. Tears came to my eyes.

"I've fared lo these years with some mediocrity, Thisbe," I said.

"Jesus, if you're Abélard, I'm Héloise," she laughed. "I'm Thisbe only if you're Pyramus. Come on, let's talk business."

Talk business?

She took my arm and pulled me down the sidewalk, and then we turned down a narrow, garbage-littered alleyway and moved across the dunes onto the beach. Seagulls cried. A V of pelicans soared a foot off the water, looking down. My heart was beating all mad. I wanted, like Molly Bloom, to say *yes yes yes* to Camille Malone. She stopped as we got into the mud flats, turned to me.

"*What's this about?*" I cried. We faced each other, and not waiting for her answer, swept away by joy and confusion (a metaphor for life?) I grabbed her, pulled her thin body to mine, and kissed her with a passion I could no more control than I could reverse the loony-tune tides of Myrtle Beach. Her breath was cigarettes, beer, and Camille; I remembered all three. As we kissed, all things fell away: building Wolfie and Stanze in the snow, the night in her dorm room, going nuts in the organ loft.

"Ford, for God's sake," she said. Her eyes were filled with mirth.

"I'm sorry, Camille, I'm crazy," I said.

"I gathered as much," she said. I looked at her. "Isn't that why you sent for me?"

"What?"

"This is the New Zone we're in now, Fordy," she said with a pleasant smile. "New Zone of the Millenium. We knew it was coming. You and I always knew it was coming. And that's why you sent for me. It proves it. We are the keepers. That First Myth. That's us."

"Camille, you're not making sense," I said. "God, where has Time gone? What happened to you, love? I saw you on that program about the homeless, and I couldn't believe that...."

"....what's a home but a turtle shell," she sang, "a cling of doom, a map to hell?"

"A home's a place where you can survive this world," I said. "It's the only thing that makes this world endurable."

"Zowie," she laughed. "When do we start?"

"Start what?" I asked. "How are you eating? Where are you staying? I didn't even mean to call you here. I said I'd be waiting for you at the *Circle Beech*, not at Myrtle Beach. And that was just in a fit of sentimentality. God, Camille, you were going to be the next Horowitz, the next Wanda Landowska. What happened to you?"

"Well, well, well. And what happened to you?" she asked, backing away. "Are you still member number one, or what?"

"Member of what?"

"The Malone Society!" she cried. "*Gloriosa dicta sunt de te, Camellia.*"

"Please don't talk Latin at me," I said. "Can't we go somewhere for a beer or something and bring each other up to date?"

"On what?" she said happily. "That's not a wedding ring on your finger, is it?"

"Yes," I said. "Her name is Jill. We have two kids, a boy and a girl."

"Arf," said Camille Malone. "That's truly amazing. I didn't believe you'd be so normal. What do you do for a living then. I guess you have a *job*."

"I'm a professor of musicology at McCandless," I said defensively. I wanted to add, W*ant to make something of it?* This was sliding out of control already. She began to laugh. Oh, Lord. What was I doing, trying to exhume that other life. Pandora stood before me, giggling.

"Well, well, well," she said. "The Class of Seventy-Two Becomes the Middle Class. You could write an opera."

"And you?" I said. "What do you do for a living, Camille? What happened to your music? What happened to your parents? What happened to Catholicism? What happened to the girl I used to love more than anything on this earth? Is this what *you've* become, avoiding invented conspiracies, sponging off others' good graces?"

"All in good time," she cackled.

"Jesus Christ, have you become the Wicked Witch of the West? *All in good time?*"

"Cigarette?" She had taken a pack of Winstons from her waistband and was lighting one. I shook my head. "What else have you given up, Ford? Booze, sex, and piano practice?"

"I think I'm getting a sunstroke," I said. "Can we please go somewhere else and discuss this?"

We went to a small bar called The Sloop a couple hundred yards down the beach. Clarence said he was spending time there, and I could understand why. Not yet four, the place was mostly deserted. I bought us each a beer. We sat in a dark booth. My hand shook as I sipped my beer. She smoked again.

"How'd you get here?" I asked. "Is it hard to hitch?"

"Oh, I flew to Hilton Head and rented a car," she said.

"What?" I said. "Camille, you're homeless. I saw you on that documentary. You push a shopping cart and wear combat boots and a heavy coat in hot weather. You pee in the gutters and eat garbage. I saw what I saw."

She laughed brightly, an Old Camille laugh, and for one pulse-stopping moment I was back in school, walking with her, nearly hearing the sounds of all the instruments from open windows.

"Ah, Mr. Manichaean Universe," she said. "You limit yourself, Georgia. You always have."

"Then tell me how to live a full life!" I said. The bartender glanced at me and then back at 'The $100,000 Pyramid' on his small TV. "Tell me the secrets of the universe." Her smile faded, and intensity replaced it.

"I'm not crazy, Ford," she said. "I've just tried to spend my life being different. Life's too short not to be weird. My flock understands this."

"Your flock?" I said. "Are you a TV evangelist now?"

"I am the patron saint of what never could be," she said. "I preach to those without the clues of universal spirit. I spread all religions in the name of Nogod."

"Nogod?" I said with a shudder. "What in the hell is that?"

"Nogod is the absence of a benevolent universe," she said. "No St. Francis, no goblins, no walking on the water, junk like that. No *Iliad*, no *Odyssey*. The inner journey to knowledge through the keyholes of the soul."

"I don't want to know about keyholes to the soul," I admitted. "I want to know what you've done for the past twenty years, Camille. Are you happy? Do you have friends and lovers? Do you still play the piano? What happened to the uncle you stabbed?" A blurt. A life pouring up and out, but I couldn't hold it back.

"T. D. Malone?" she said. "Long, long dead. Drowned when he got drunk and fell off an oil rig in a storm. My parents are long dead, too. Dad had a stroke, Mom got cancer." I winced. She shrugged and blew smoke. "Sometimes now I sneak into churches and play. It's not important." But was it? "I have been a great lover. Lived with a guy for nine years, love of my life."

"I'm glad," I said.

"Well, he's gone now," she sighed.

"Where?"

"To the numbers," she said. "The numbers of the lost, the dispossessed, the married, the dead, the food stamp recipients, the attendees at the Super Bowl; to the numbers of zeppelin riders, drowned off oil rigs, played concertos, won the lottery. We've all gone to the numbers. So you? You been a winner at old McCandless?"

"I have not been a great lover," I said. "I've been a damned fool. My wife left me and took the kids. I was having an affair with a woman half my age. I don't like being crazy like you do."

"Disorder is the only order," she said with a grin.

"Then I want to pretend!" I nearly shouted. "I want to pretend God's in his heaven and all's right with the world. I want to pretend in the pre-ordained clockwork of the stars, Camille. I'm one of those men who can't go too far into the mind without getting lost for good."

"'Tis a pity, life's a whore," she smiled.

"I don't want to be a whore," I said. "I want you back the way you were when we were freshmen. I want you to be young and beautiful, and I want to be young, too, with possibilities before me. I want to start over with a light heart and an easy step, Camille. I want to believe in faith, hope, and charity."

"Awfully worked up," she said. "Well, all that's over now, and you might as well get used to it. Every day I'm closer and closer."

"To what?"

"The meaning of life," she said. "Why else would we be brought into this realm of such terrors?"

"I was hoping you'd tell me that," I said. "Aren't you the saint and the prophetess?"

"Of Nogod," she said. "I can bless the nothingness of your non-immortal nonsoul if you like."

"I feel like I'm in Act I of *Waiting for Godot*," I said. Then I arrived, without warning, at what my soul really wanted but what I feared more than anything on this earth. "Would you like to go back to my motel room?"

"For what?"

"Sex?"

"Sex?" she laughed. "Haven't seen each other for two decades and you immediately want to play hide the sausage?"

"God, that's a sickening image," I said. "I'm sorry. I don't even want to. I just had to ask."

"Forget it, that's just biology anyway, right?" she shrugged.

"Oh my God," I said. "I've lived for years off the glory of our first two sexual encounters, and you say they're just biology?"

"What were they?" she asked. "I don't remember that."

"In the bushes, and then standing up in your dorm room after I'd gotten my face busted in a fight defending you."

"Can't remember either one," she said. "Proust was full of crap, you know. Memory isn't the homeplace of life or art. It's only the moment of the act. The moment of the act. But if those two times were important you, I'm glad. To each her own epiphanies."

"Or his," I said.

"Whatever," she said. "I'm essentially nonsexual now. I haven't participated in four years, haven't missed it a lick, so to speak." She laughed. I didn't. "So you're taking me back to Asheville now, or what?"

The pure giddy tingle of her question might have sent me into a downward spiral of fear had not the door to The Sloop opened at that very moment and my cousin, Clarence Clayton, come in laughing with a woman on his arm. She wore a semi-transparent halter top and shorts that rode an inch into her crotch, outlining it with pleasing clarity. Clarence saw me, came over, weaving slightly. Drunk, I thought, wincing. The moment of the act.

"I'll be dadburneth!" said Clarence. "You must be the Camellia!" Camille's face fell slightly, eyes dazed with Clarence's cheerful ignorance.

"And *you* must be Fonda Peters," I said to Clarence's "date." She grinned and nodded, showing a quarter-inch gap between her middle teeth on top. She had freckles. I hadn't seen a woman with freckles in a long time, I mused. But her hair was brittle from repeated dyeings.

"And *you* must be Ford," she said. "He's done told me all about you, and..."

"Uh, Fonda...." said Clarence.

"....and let me tell you this is the first time I ever met a true to real life inventor!" She shook my hand proudly. Clarence looked squeamish. "Imagine, having been the one to invent the moon rocket!"

"Oh ho," said Camille. "I'm in the presence of nothingness. No doubt about it."

"Huh?" said Clarence.

"This is my cousin, Clarence Clayton," I said. "This is the famous Camille Malone."

"Fonda, your shorts are halfway to your uterus, in case you care," said Camille. Fonda smiled and squinted her eyes at Camille.

"What are yours halfway to, Honey?" asked Fonda. "Guate-mala?"

"Lord," I said, "Let's not. Clarence, why don't you and Fonda join us? I'll buy us a nice pitcher of cold beer." I stood and slid in next to Camille, and they sat opposite us. Camille and Fonda eyed each other knowingly. Clarence was very proud of his "date." Our waitress was tired, wore no wedding ring and was obviously pregnant. Her eyes were not Circean. She had bitten her nails nearly to the moons. She brought us a pitcher of Bud Light, frosted mugs for Fonda and Clarence. A jolly little tea party. Come, jolly playmates, come out and play with me....some song from early childhood?

"So what else you invented?" Fonda asked me.

"He's the creator of our collective soul," said Camille. "The James Fenimore Cooper of twentieth-century crypto-realism." Fonda looked at Camille with confusion.

"Naw, I meant like, you know, rocket engines, or stuff like

that," she said. "I'm so proud of Clarence and what he done invented. He's gone be a rich man."

"What did you invent, Clarence?" asked Camille.

"The player accordion," said Fonda with a gummy grin. "He's gone be rich as Uncle Scrooge."

Whoops. The thrill of moronity catching up with me; player accordions, dwarfs, *East of Eden,* rocket engines, and Camille and....

"The player accordion!" screamed Camille. "The perfect invention for the twentieth century! Not only completely useless but painfully unlistenable."

"Well, I didn't say that exactly I was, uh, you know," mumbled Clarence.

"Don't you just love it when he's bashful?" asked Fonda with admiration. "Just like that skunk in *Bambi,* was it?"

Others started straggling into The Spinnaker: clutch of women smokers with deep voices; old couple, time running out; couple that might have been newlyweds. Hello, young lovers, I hope your troubles are few. Clarence began to talk about things he knew nothing about: inventions, current events, the world of the past few years that he'd seen only through newspapers. Camille put her hand on my shoulder and listened with obvious pleasure, but she kept a wary eye on everyone coming in. Was that woman with the paisley muumuu a potential convert? Well, why the fuck not? I'd leaked through a Crack in Time. I wanted back. Like Rod Taylor in *The Time Machine,* not able to get away from the Morlocks. Everybody around me looked like a Morlocks. Would the Morlocks make a good subject for an opera? How about *Adam Trask Meets the Morlocks?* The sun was yawning, getting tired of his job for the day. Poor Apollo. At least he knew what his job was.

"So you were an advisor to President Carter?" asked Camille with a twinkle of her darting eyes. Clarence smiled helplessly at me.

"Yeah, on, uh, matters of religion," he said. "I was a preacher for uh, well."

"You never told me you used to be no preacher man!" said Fonda. "This old world's a crazy place!"

"Religion?" asked Camille, interest peaked. "Let me ask you something then. Do you think there's a reason, historical or theological, why the Armenian monks should keep attending the olive trees at Gethsemane? Is that act protective or provocative?"

"That's where Jesus done went to pray and where Judas betrayed him," said Clarence. The word "betrayed" came out in a fearful, dusty whisper. "Matthew and Mark both talk about that."

"Hmmm," said Camille.

"Bible stuff's okay," said Fonda. "Y'all know anybody's got any good pot?"

"Good God," cried Clarence, "I don't want to do no more time."

Whoops. Cat out of another bag.

"Do time?" asked Fonda politely.

"We're all doing time," said Camille. "One way or another. And the sentence is for life, and the crime is being born."

"Well, your rhetoric has gotten sophisticated since last we met," I said.

"Don't pretend you're Gideon," said Camille. "Nobody's listening."

"That's in Judges, Chapter Seven," said Clarence. "When they blew the trumpets and broke up all their pots. Gideon delivered his people from the Giddy Knights."

"Gideonites, but I'm impressed," said Camille.

"I'm horny," said Fonda hopefully.

"We're all part of Abraham's bosom," said Clarence.

"What about my bosoms?" cried Fonda.

"Lazarus begged at the doors of Dives," said Camille. She leaned forward and stared at Clarence.

"The other Lazarus was the one from John who was the brother of, uh, who was it, uh, Martha and uh...."

"Mary of Bethany," said Camille. Clarence beamed and nodded.

"Right," said Clarence. "When Jesus saw their faith, he said unto the sick of the palsy...."

"....Son, thy sins be forgiven unto thee," whispered Camille Malone.

"I'll be damned," said Clarence, leaning back with undistilled delight.

"I'll be paid," said Fonda unhappily, looking at Clarence.

"I'll be leaving," I blurted. I'd already given Clarence $200. Now I gave him my VISA card.

"What?" asked Camille. "We've only just met."

Fonda took one of the fifties from the table and stood and stuffed it in her pocket with difficulty.

"Camille, this was a mistake," I said. "I've not been well. I thought you were starving up there in New York, homeless and destitute. I took pity on you, but you didn't need pity."

"Wow, a VISA card," said Clarence. "Do I just sign your name, or what? I might go back to jail. Oops."

"Jail?" said Fonda angrily. "I'll be goddamned. Another fucking convict. When am I gonna learn not to mix business with pleasure?"

"I thought your business *was* pleasure," said Camille. I smiled. Fonda stomped out the door of The Sloop. Clarence watched her ass as she left, but he didn't seem too broken up about it. "Jail, huh? What for?"

"I sort of robbed a liquor store," said Clarence. He picked up the credit card and regarded it with wonder.

"My," said Camille Malone.

"You're right," I said. "They'd think you stole the card. Tell me where to send money. As soon as I get back to Asheville, I'll send it. The Gordon House?"

"Did you pay that dwarf?" asked Clarence.

"I saw him," said Camille. "He's cute, in an ugly kind of way. I don't trust him. He could be a spy."

"He's not a spy," I said. "He's a dwarf."

"Anyway, I got a VISA card," said Camille.

Well, why the hell not? She probably had a money market fund and a condo in the Bahamas, too. Being homeless was a state of being for Camille; money was a state of mind. I began to laugh. What else?

"Hallelujah," said Clarence with approval.

"Coitus, ergo sum," said Camille, now leering openly at the

diminutive Clarence Clayton.

"Hindoo again!" yelled Clarence. "It's a sign, Ford! God's done give me a sign!"

They were talking about the Miracle of the Fishes when I backed away, went out the door and stumbled toward the Gordon House to get my stuff. What prophecies would Beaularice cast upon me now? And how far was it to Asheville?

THAT WAS IT, THEN. I COULD JUST WALK RIGHT OUT on Camille Malone after our first meeting in twenty years, leave her without having a clue about how she'd come this far. I could live without knowing the denouement. I could just go back to the Gordon House (I did), pack my box of letters and suitcase (no problem) and pay Mr. Josiah what we owed so far (he was happy), and tip my imaginary hat goodbye to my Personal Whirling Jesus (*Quam admirabile est nomen tuum in universa terra!*).

I could just drive back to Asheville, go back to work. Forget Camille Malone. I got, in fact, as far as Conway before I turned around and drove back, muttering darkly the mantra I'd suddenly remembered from 1968: *Nobody ever forgets Camille Malone.* Being the perfect middle class gent that I am, I postponed my new search and possible epiphany to take a room at the Ramada Inn. They had an indoor pool, a sauna, a gym, video games. No dwarfs. Nothing for *The Guinness Book of Records.* The room was large, cool and quiet. Proper. A peppermint on the pillow, with someone's compliments. I liked it. I wasn't suited for Adventures in Moteling. By the time I showered, took a few minutes to look with disgust and dismay at my reflection in the mirror and then hope I was still attractive to women from sixteen to eighty, I drove back to The Sloop, parked next to a Mazda Miata, which I wanted. The station wagon was pitiful. I didn't see the police car until I got around front.

Unlike its afternoon lull, The Sloop was hopping, lots of men with tattoos, painted women, regulars, irregulars, dense smoke and that fearful edge of possibility that older single people so desperately chase. Something of an uproar. Two tables were turned over, beer was splattered around. Bar brawl. Nothing to lose your way over. I glanced around, saw nothing of Camille or Clarence. An old couple with thick glasses and shapeless clothes sat without expression at a table. They looked foreign somehow. The cop was writing with the stub of a pencil into a notebook.

"What's going on?" I asked the old man.

"You don't hardly want to know," said the woman. The man started to open his mouth. "Because you ain't never seen nothing like that, trust me."

"Like what?" I asked.

"Like these preachers screaming and then getting into a fight," she said again. The man looked wan. He wanted to say something, but he knew he'd lost that fight years ago. I felt ill, thrilled.

"Preachers?" I asked. "What kind of preachers?"

"This hag and a skinny man," she said, lighting a long, unfiltered cigarette.

"She was a goddess," said the man with deliberate defiance. He stared at the old woman, eyes bulging out, weak chin thrust.

"Christ, Horace, don't be an ass," she said. "You bring a foolish old man to the beach, and what happens? Does he get rest and sunshine, or does he leer at the trash? I'm asking you?"

"Oh God," I said. "What were they preaching about?"

"She wasn't making no sense whatever," said the old woman.

"Perfect sense!" the old man blurted. He tapped a loose fist on the tablecloth for emphasis. "She told us that in any other dimension we'd be vegetables, but here we're all trapped. We're all delegates for the essential boredom of something or other."

"Hogwash!" the woman cried. "The man told us we was all going to spend eternity burnin' in hell unless we did something, but he was just as stupid as the hag. Neither one of them made no sense."

"Goddess!" cried the old man. He thumped his hand.

"Hag!" the woman said. "Sea hag!" Then, overcome by her

own joke, she began to laugh, coughing out smoke, then just coughing. The man was more wan than ever, became silent again.

"How long have they been gone?" I asked.

"Sixteen minutes," said a fat man at the next table. He had a watch with dials, formulae, compass, etc. "Must have been a team. Left right after the shrimpers attacked 'em."

"Shrimpers?" I said.

"Arms like Popeye, every one of 'em," said a young woman sitting by herself at a booth. Her legs were crossed at the crotch, and she was swinging one foot faster than an NFL kicker, pumping away but not appearing to get anywhere.

"Shrimpers with arms like Popeye got into a fight with the preachers?" I asked.

"They work hard all day, don't want to hear that crap here," said the fat man.

"Lots of crap around here," said the old man, looking straight at his wife.

"Oh, it's *awake*," she said acidly.

"Then they called the cops," said the young woman. "You got a cigarette? Come 'ere and buy me a beer, honey."

"Did anybody see which way they went?" I asked.

"South on foot," said the fat man. "He walked like a grasshopper. She moved like she wore ice skates."

"Graceful goddess," said the old man, eyes huge. He leaned across the table. The cop was finishing up. Waitress started delivering beers again. Music back on the jukebox. Hank Williams, Jr., said all his rowdy friends had settled down, and he wasn't happy about it.

"Cheap whorey sea hag!" the old woman cried.

"Jesus," said the young woman.

"I got a cigarette," said the fat man wistfully. She looked him over and shrugged.

"Bring it on," she said with great sorrow. The fat man got up and slid into the booth with the young woman. The old man and old woman had engaged in a wordless staring match.

I went back outside. Up on the main drag, the lights flashed with endless encouragement: play basketball with this scrofulous chicken; buy a towel that says you did it in Myrtle Beach; tour the spook house; play miniature golf; drag the kids around and remember you can't get this, wherever you come from.

Nor could you get Camille and Clarence, no matter which world they inhabited. I felt like Ray Milland in his lost weekend, stumbling from store to store, ashamed that I'd run out on Camille, ashamed of Clarence, ashamed I'd lied to my boss, ashamed Jill had left me.

An hour passed, then two, and I seemed to be getting nowhere, walking back and forth, feeling the familiar tug of hunger, not particularly wanting to see Camille, not able to stop looking. I felt a need for music swell in me: for some reason, I wanted to hear a Schubert Mass or perhaps even the Mozart *Requiem*. All I got were car radios at max volume, blamming the bass notes of rock as they passed in the streets.

Another hour. I was going nowhere. A thunderstorm was in the offing, and I watched as it built, and I even wandered past the Gordon House but didn't go inside. I found my car down by The Sloop and drove back to the Ramada Inn, got parked and into the lobby just as the storm elbowed up the beach and squatted angrily over the hotel. If I walked, mad, on the beach in the storm, what were the chances I'd be dramatically swept off this earth by a sudden bolt of lightning? Would later poets write sonnets about me, the Wandering Musician, who was lost at sea?

You'd be a minor statistic on one day of one year, both of which are soon forgotten, Ford. I went to my room. This, then, was the end of the story, the end of me. I'd lost. Camille was crazy, could tell me nothing; Thom, Jill's lawyer, could call to tell me that the clock was ticking. My opera *East of Eden* was not going to be performed by the New York City Opera, principally because it had never been written.

The phone rang. I answered it.

"Lordy, hallelujah!" said Clarence Clayton. I'd never been so glad to hear a friendly human voice in my life. "You all right, Cuz? We called half of the motels in Myrtle Beach. Camillia said she saw you wandering around on the street tonight."

"I'm glad to hear your voice, I guess," I said. "I was just

thinking how we're born into this world alone and go out alone, and no matter what comes in between, we can't ever get it quite right." I let go and bawled.

"Good grief," said Camille into the phone. "If you're going to do this, then maybe we ought to wait until morning to give you the announcement."

"What announcement?" I sniffed. "Camille, where are you? Did you and Clarence get into a fight at The Sloop with a bunch of shrimpers with arms like Popeye?"

"*Dulce et decorum est pro patria mori!*" she said happily. I felt buoyed, elated. "The swine. Clarence and I are true inheritors of the Dukhobors, Fordello, my Fordello. The shrimpers were delegates. We told them of their eventual fate and the current slop of their lives."

"Yes!" I cried. "You did! And they were still talking about it — you were almost legendary! Are you at the Gordon House?"

"My place," she said. "The Sand Crab on South Beach, and let me tell you, a couple more nights here, and we'll *all* have the crabs. They haven't changed the sheets here since the Reformation."

Love, love, love! Her madness was infectious! I was ecstatic to be alive!

"Your place!" I said. "What announcement is Clarence talking about? Are the cops looking for you?"

"Did Holderlin look over his shoulder for Hegel?" she asked. "Did the hoof of Pegasus create the Hippocrene?"

"I reckon," I said.

"Georgia, listen to me," she said patiently. "It's epic and saga, religion and lack of it. It's kismet and the Kit-Kat Club. It's the *Laxdale Saga* and Miss Jane Marple. Clarence and I are the Guides, and you are the True Delegate."

"Is this so excitin' you could just puke?" said Clarence, grappling with her for the phone. She called him a little shit and took the phone back.

"Georgia?"

"I've never been a delegate," I said. "I don't have a clue what you're talking about, Camille."

PERFECT ♦ TIMING   235

"Of course you don't," she said. "But you will. The world will. This is your spawn, Ford, the meeting of East and West, or, more properly, northern Germany and southern Georgia. Clarence and I discovered the keys while drinking one of several pitchers of margaritas at a soon-to-be-famous hangout called The Burger Shack. In years to come, it will be known as the founding place of the one religion that was finally useful to everyone. Pragmatics and mystery in one handy, convenient package."

"I'm about to bust a gut," said Clarence. She called him a nitwit and grabbed the phone back.

"You and my cousin are founding a new religion?" I said. "Based on what?"

"Based on the *Volksung Saga* and the *Baptist Hymnal*, principally," said Camille. "Are you washed in the blood of the dragon?"

"How would I know?" I asked.

"No one knows until they take the *Text and the Test*, pardon my moronic pronoun antecedent error," she said. "It'll all be there in the *Text and the Test*. This won't be a religion *anybody* can join, Fordy — what good is a religion *everybody* claims to understand? With the *Text* and with the *Test*, we will make sure that all members have the mental capacity to grow."

"What if somebody fails the test?" I asked.

"A question I'd expect out of you," she said. "What is it, did your father grapple with Failure like Leda with the Swan, and you were its spawn? You've always sounded positively nostalgic about failure."

"You didn't answer me," I said.

"Then there'd be something like a condemnation," she said.

"I got that all worked out," said Clarence.

At this point, a cursing and slapping ensued at the other end of the line, followed by Clarence's high-pitched, apologetic voice. She called him a few more names and told him to get to work on the *Text* and quit acting like Julia Damn Ward Howe, for God's sake.

"Don't worry about it," she said, coming back on the phone. I said nothing for a moment, and she'd temporarily run out of steam. I stood at the window, watching lightning bolts bang into the sea, feeling calm now, wondering if, in a world such as ours, the Burger Shack might actually be seen one day as the Munich Beer Hall of Camellianism. "Are you still there?"

"Camille, I got to ask you something," I said. "Were you ever really homeless?"

"Who really ever has a home?" she asked.

"Stop the sophomoric bullshit," I said. "I came back because I couldn't leave you tonight. You know?"

"Of course."

"Well?"

"No, I've never lived in the streets or eaten trash," she said. "I was, in fact, doing research on the homeless for a magazine article I was going to sell to *The New Yorker*, the pigs. I regret to say they advised me my talent lay in other areas."

"That's dishonest," I said. "You wouldn't really know how they felt. People are starving in the streets all over America."

"Here's where you say, 'Just like my soul has been starving for something meaningful ever since I walked out on you in the Big Apple,'" she said. "Admit it, Ford. You've never gotten over the fact that I'm living the life of Esmerelda, and you're Claude Frollo while you want to be Quasimodo, hump and all. You want the world to be the receptacle for Romance and your nuttish ideas that come straight from the nineteenth century and pulp fiction."

I thought about Charley Barstow slamming me for reading Hallie Ermine Rives and Gene Stratton Porter.

"You want the world to be this Citadel of Light, and you're frustrated because you can see it's nothing but a Palace of Darkness. In the New Religion, we recognize that Darkness. We embrace it. It is nothing bad. It simply is. No hell, no devil, no heaven, no Pope, no TV swindlers. Pretend that your precious sweet idea of the world is the *Lusitania* and I've got the U-Boat and I've got the torpedoes. Getting clearer, Hon?"

"Pretending to be homeless is dishonest," I said. "Look, can't we discuss this in person?"

"Not tonight," she said. "Anyway, I do volunteer work for the Homeless Hotline. That's how I got your call. We have to get ready for a press conference day in the near future. This is the most fun I've had in ages!"

"Please don't involve my cousin in your bizarre schemes," I begged. "He's innocent enough."

"You take an assistant where you can find one," she said.

"Is that all I was to you, Camille?" I said.

"Georgia, you're trying to put the pieces of the puzzle together again," she said. "Listen to me: *no pieces, no puzzle*. Clarence, write that down. *No pieces, no puzzle*. Almost as short as 'Jesus wept', too."

"Jesus wept," I said sincerely. "But Camille, I loved you. You were the great love of my life. What about loving each other in that cold apartment and whispering about our future? What about your music? What about that lovely girl I met in the Chapel when we were freshmen? I want her back. That's what this is all about."

"No, no, no, no," she said. "This is all about *Le Lutrin*, Fordorino."

"Please explain," I shouted. "I never understand your damned learned allusions."

"Then you'll never pass the test," she said. "Mock epic by Nicolas Boileau-Despréaux. Argument in Sainte-Chapelle between the choirmaster and the treasurer over the position of a lectern. That's what religion is."

"Your life is....is, uh, as crazy as if, uh...." I spluttered. "I mean, hell, you might as well have stabbed *me* with a Phillips screwdriver as, uh...."

"You sound like you could use a Darvocet," said Camille von der Malone sweetly. "Get some sleep, and meet us tomorrow morning at the Waffle House over on 17. Then I will give you your assignment."

I slumped against the wall, defeated, wondering suddenly what she was wearing. I wondered if Clarence were spending the night with her.

"My assignment?" I said.

"Like Lycaon, you wish to test the divinity of the Gods," she said, her voice tripping with laughter. "Very well. Your eyes shall be opened. And your ears unstopped. Happy?"

"Happiness," I said, thinking somewhere of generations of

severe Clayton women, "is not for this world."

Therefore, it made perfect sense that Camille and I laughed together at that point, and that I hung up and slept like a dead man ready to voyage through the Underworld and take the *Test*.

CAMILLE CAME FLYING INTO THE WAFFLE HOUSE like a careening car, talking as if her face were on fire and her words were water. Clarence was behind her, scribbling on a yellow legal pad with the blunt end of what appeared to be a Putt-Putt pencil. Neither seemed to have slept.

"Ford?" said Camille out loud. I cringed. She waited until everybody looked at her. Everybody but me. She and Clarence swept over and sat in the booth across from me while the morning murmuring over eggs and toast resumed. Before either could say a thing, a waitress came over. Camille told her to bring them coffee and eggs. Clarence shrugged; he was too busy writing.

"Have either of you slept?" I asked. Camille's eyes had the shellacked look of saints and madwomen.

"What is sleep but, a, uh....." said Clarence. He tapped his upper teeth with the pencil. "What is sleep but a leap frog into your whatnot?" He hooted and leaned over the pad and wrote. "I'm the only single man who'll have ever wrote his own Bible, Ford. Camille thinks I'm a genius."

"She does?" I asked. I looked at her for confirmation. The waitress brought them coffee, refilled my cup.

"I think that this place," said Camille, looking around disgustedly, "is a metaphor for what we're up against. It's like the battle of the Lapithae and the Centaurs. The former had invited the latter to wedding ceremonies, and the Centaurs got drunk and tried to make off with all the Lapith women, including the bride. We've never changed since the Battle of the Centaurs. It's swirling the cape of reality in front of the bull of human arrogance." Clarence made a little cry and wrote furiously. "It's not even a metaphor. It's a mataphor. New word for comparisons of the taurean mode."

Sitting on a counter stool not four feet away, a thin old man smoking a cigarette and reading *USA Today* seemed upset by a chart of some kind. He kept muttering and shaking his head. Camille was wearing a T-shirt with repeated pictures of Bach. She smelled of soap and some light cologne. She was not a street person. She was, perhaps, the Eternal Madwoman, roaming out of control, drawing in the earth and its inanities, but she was not homeless. She was right: her home was the blue dome of the sky, this land, this earth. Somehow, I was the waiting one, her Penelope, and she had adventured in the world of her mind with as much courage as Odysseus had ever shown.

"I see," I said.

"Tell him about the decision," said Clarence.

"Ah," she said.

"What decision?" I asked.

"We have confirmed that this new direction for the earth's wretched ones cannot be unveiled in this backwash of Coppertone and teenybopper bun heaven." She was talking very loud and people stared at her.

"Camille, people are looking at you," I whispered.

"I know," she grinned. "Anyway, this morning I was thinking on Lucina, the Roman goddess of childbirth, and I realized that a mountain is where all new religions are born. Olympus. Mount Sinai. Asheville."

"Asheville!" I shouted. People looked at me now.

"Listen to this," said Clarence. "The tone of the bone is not neither copper nor tone. How's that?"

"Elusive," said Camille.

"Thanks," said Clarence proudly.

"Not Asheville," I begged. "Camille, that's my home. You can't come back there and start—" I wanted to say running amuck, but that seemed indelicate.

"....running amuck?" she said. My jaw fell slightly. "It's where

we'll announce the *Test and the Text*. Start letting people line up
to read the *Text*, take the *Test*."

The waitress brought their eggs. They ate hungrily. I felt hot.
The man on the stool noted with an alarmed whisper that fifty-
eight percent of the people in Idaho were in favor of something.

"I forbid you to do this in Asheville," I said.

"You what?" smiled Camille. "Forbid? What are you, the
keeper of the keys?"

"Oh boy," said my cousin. He grabbed his pencil and wrote
and wrote.

"I'm serious," I said, leaning over. "I can't have this happening there. I mean it's harmless enough here, but not where people
know me!"

"Abélard, you're forgetting that this isn't about you," said
Camille. "You seem to think that everything that happens in the
world is about you."

"Everything that happens among you and me and Clarence in
Asheville *is* about me," I said, trying to whisper.

"Tell him where it's gone be," said Clarence.

"An eager man is a useful man," said Camille.

"Whoopee!" said Clarence, redoubling his writing. "I'm
getting more for the *Text* than I ever thought I would in a Waffle
House."

"Where is it going to be?" I asked.

"The Circle Beech," she said with delight. "That is where the
Malone Society ended, by the way. And even in today's climate
of business and uninvolvement, they won't be able to resist the call
to join a religion so new it's barely hatched from its gilded shell."

"I beg of you, don't do this at McCandless," I said. I put my
hand over my eyes. My head hurt.

"It's done already," she said. "Can't be helped. You yourself
must surely believe in the symmetry of life, if not its mysteries."

"Lord love a duck!" cried Clarence Clayton.

"Camille, this is getting out of hand," I said.

"The genie's out of the bottle, Georgia," she said. "Don't try
to stuff her back in again."

"Then, I'll have no part in it," I said. I tried to sound like

Gregory Peck.

"That coffee okay, hon?" asked the waitress on her way past the table. I nodded.

"I don't remember anybody inviting you," she said, "although it makes sense. You were sort of the first member of the Malone Society."

"I can't do this," I said. "I'm getting out of here. That's it. I can't do it. I'm going to leave you both here to sort this out."

"Don't mean squat to me," shrugged Clarence. "I've got my work and my Camellia. I'm the handservant of the cause. That's what she said last night."

"I had been drinking," said Camille.

"Anyway, she's got a credit card and money and a rent-a-car, and I got to write the *Test* afore my natural wisdoms start to leave me," he said.

"I'm serious," I said. I was halfway out of the booth.

"Wrong," said Camille. "*We're* serious. *You're* the house god of the middle class."

And so I was. I fled back to the Ramada Inn, got the new mint the maid had left on the pillow, paid my bill, and fled. I turned on the radio and listened to Bach on the harpsichord as I drove to Conway and, this time, did not stop. The hot road seemed like a line of ice: I was imprisoned in life just like Satan was stuck in that lake of ice in the last circle of hell. *The house god of the middle class!* The anger made me feel upright again.

I took it for granted that they'd go bonkers for a few days, not sleep, drink too much, and then Camille would disappear back north while Clarence wound up scraping grease off the grill of The Spinnaker. I felt ill. That was their purpose. For her, sowing chaos was not just a job: it was an adventure.

I got to Columbia, and instead of turning north toward Asheville, I veered south, heading across the lowlands toward Jamesburg. Spring was blowing up full now. Farmers bounced on old tractors breaking the land, and as the miles piled up, I sensed the renewal of life, my cup filling again.

The trip was a visual feast: old black women making cane

chairs on the porch; fat kids pumping Big Wheels around a ratty trailer; waving winter wheat, tawny and top-heavy, nodding gracefully to the passing wind; merry streams and shaky bridges, hawks and buzzards and crows; the aroma of the land and the air. The season was in its full sea change. I did not want a new religion, nor did I need Camille to tell me what path I had irretrievably taken those decades before.

I crossed the Savannah River and was into Georgia. I approached ecstasy. Symphonies — grand adventures I could write for winds and strings and brass — danced in my head. By late afternoon, when the sun was tired but I was certainly not, I pulled into Jamesburg, drove through the cemetery, stopped by my grandfather's grave.

I didn't get out of the car, but as I sat there looking at the stone, I realized how much I'd grown like my father and his father before him. And I realized that a life of moderate accomplishments and genuine joy was fine with me. And for the first time in days, I understood Jill.

I drove through town and turned on our street, and the weight of time unburdened, then burdened me. I was fifteen again, coming home from some late meeting at school, ready to dash upstairs to my room, listen to Mahler, work on my latest composition, burn candles before the muse, go into a Romantic swivet over poetry and novels and opera and sculpture. For a time I even became a painter, whipping out a series of honest, uninspired still lifes, usually with vases and cloths in some voluptuous arrangement. Every art flowered within me. Each discovery staggered me: Redon's *Cyclops*, Schönberg's *Gurrelieder*, the *Art of the Fugue* and the *Anthology of New York Poets*. I remembered the day I read Hemingway's "Big Two-Hearted River" for the first time; when I realized what Michelangelo had achieved; Plutarch and Dante and Bruckner; Plato and Kenneth Patchen and *Beowulf*; Mickey Mantle and Willie Mays and Eddie LeBaron and the Washington Redskins and....I had been sitting for some time in the driveway. The front porch light came on, as it was nearly dark now.

"Hi, Mom," I said cheerily as I got out. She peered myopically into the gloom.

"Ford?" she said. "What are you doing here? Is something wrong?"

"No, everything's fine," I said. "In fact, everything's better than fine." I came up the steps and hugged my mother. She embraced me for a moment and then pushed me back and looked at me skeptically. Dad came on out. He was reading a book about the Civil War.

"Better than fine?" she said. "That's news."

"And not only that," I said, "I'm on my way to Macon to see Jill and the kids."

"I'm glad for that, son," said Dad.

"Have you eaten?" asked Clarice.

"No."

"Come on in," she said. "I'm cooking pole beans and fried okra."

We walked through the house, saying nothing until we got back to the kitchen, fragrant with the smell of southern cooking. I sat in a kitchen chair and the small, familiar table while she cooked. Dad and I chatted. Business was fine. He was taking Mom on a tour of battlefields. It sounded like fun, but somehow I felt as if I'd already been there. A small radio picked up National Public Radio. The news was on. A woman went on and on about some internal political dispute on Cyprus. I wondered who cared.

"It's been an unusual week," I said, suddenly tired.

"Did you find the Camille person at the beach, son?" she asked. "And has your cousin been readmitted to prison yet? I'm sure he's overdue. Surely he must have had ample time to rob a liquor store at the beach."

"Hey, Clarence is okay," I said. "And yes, I did find Camille. Or rather she found me."

"And?"

"It wasn't like it was supposed to be."

"Never is," said my father.

"She's not homeless, after all," I said. "She was doing research for a story that never got printed. She has a credit card and a rental car."

"My, my," clucked Clarice Clayton.

"You don't have to sound so happy," I said. "It can't be a pretty thing for your own son to be spending his life in total confusion."

"Well, confusion isn't as bad as some things," she whispered. She put some of the crisply fried okra on a pad of paper towels to dry.

Mom took a hunk of ham from the fridge, and we ate pole beans, ham, okra, buttered bread, and iced tea. The profile on Cyprus shifted to a piece on warring groups in Sri Lanka, along with lots of sound effects. Finally, the news was over, and Mozart came on. To my surprise, I was very hungry.

"So what happened with this Camille person to drive you away from the beach and back home to your rapidly aging mother?" she asked.

"If guilt were thread, you'd be weaving a tapestry," I said. She giggled. Actually giggled.

"That was clever," she said. "Malicious and petty, but clever nonetheless. I think my grievances are fair."

"I'm sorry," I said. "You're right, of course. Everyone's grievances against me are right. Jill, the kids, you. I've been a fool."

"Um," Dad said.

"What happened with Camille is that she and your nephew Clarence got together and have decided that the world needs a new religion," I said. "They're formulating plans to unburden mankind of its mysteries through something called *The Test and the Text*."

"Just what the world needs, another religion," she said. "We can't figure out what to do with half the ones we have. America professes to embrace apple piety, and then we shoot each other in the streets."

"Apple piety?" I said with delight.

"Oh, I make up things when I'm truly bored," she said. "You should try it sometime."

"I am going to start composing again, Mom," I said. "I feel it coming on."

"You're sure it's not the grippe or something?" Dad asked.

"*Miserere nobis*," I said. And once again, Clarice Clayton giggled like a girl.

I spent the night. In my old room, at midnight, I listened to the years unfold, read a few more of the letters from the box, which I was ready to take back into the attic. My old record player still worked, and I heard my scratchy first love: *Symphony Number Five* by Anton Bruckner. The air was delicious, pulsing through the windows. I was not fifteen, but I felt buoyed on the wings of possibility. That was what made fifteen attractive anyway. Only it didn't end there.

Wednesday

Hi, Honey,
I miss you so much! Mama is feeling much better after the surgery. I hope I never have to have my gall bladder out, but I guess I will if I live long enough.
I've been thinking a lot about us, Ford. And I realize that we were meant to be with each other. It's not algebra. I don't know what it is, but there's a certainty about it, like an equation that simply works out. Why is that? I only know that I love you.
I went to the Women's Rights march Sunday in the park. It was special to me, Ford. Women are oppressed just like blacks, and I know you know it's true. White men rule this world, and that's not to blame you. But when a white man decides, despite the power of his position, to be the poet, the artist, he shares something with women or woman, I guess. And with blacks. Not too much, but something. It's almost an abdication. And that's what I love about you, darling. It's that you value the beauty of the soul more than the beauty of a bank account.
All for now. I love you, my darling.
Jill

July, 1957

Dear Mama,
I think that I sawe a bear last night near the bildeng where my friend Bob lives. He was black and scrablding (the bear, not Bob), and he climbd a tree. I yelled and yelled, and Coach Patkin came to the window and did not see the bear, but said they have been bers in these woods since time imorial. If I am eat by this bear (ha ha) then you can get Daddy to

come get me with a shoebox (ha ha). Tomorrow we are haveing more woodcraft. I have learnt to make a lanyard out of plactic strips. They made us write these noats.

Your son,
Ford Clayton

I laughed and laughed. I tried to summon the ghost of that black bear, but nothing came forth. No matter. He was still there somewhere. Perhaps there was a place for a bear scene in *East of Eden*.

I stuffed all the letters in the box, went up into the attic, crammed it behind an old artificial Christmas tree that had lain there in parts for two decades. I nearly felt a metaphor rearing its ugly head, but I chased it away. Back downstairs, the past retreating, I thought of compositions. I thought of Jill and the kids.

And so I slept in my childhood bed. I dreamed my favorite childhood dream: me conducting a symphony orchestra in a work of my own, then the standing ovation, reviews already out in the papers before the clapping stopped. And on the review page, there was this portrait of Ford Clayton, and next to it....Jesus Christ! A copy of the *Test and the Text*.

I awoke, still in darkness, to the weak singing of a mourning dove. Music, however. I took it as some kind of sign.

SATURDAY. I'D LEFT EARLY FROM JAMESBURG, driven upstate toward Macon, arrived at Jenny's house full of regret and incipient joy. She and Bobby and their kids lived in a pleasant neighborhood full of paved driveways, two-story houses and boxwoods that varied no more than a few inches from house to house.

I parked in the driveway. Bobby's truck was gone, and I knew he'd be at the store until probably nine that night, which suited Jenny fine. A young black boy was cutting her grass. The sound of lawn mowers growled over the breadth of the neighborhood. I went, as always to the backdoor, knocked softly, called Jill's name, heard nothing. Hell, I was family, so I let myself inside. Jay lay on the floor watching "GI Joe," fiddling with a football that was half-deflated. I looked through a window and saw Jenny's kids in the yard.

"Hey there, hotshot," I said. He sat bolt upright, turned to me and turned bright-eyed.

"Daddy!" he cried.

His ten-year-old legs pedaled over to me, and I lifted him off the floor and into my arms. I buried my face in his neck, smelled his unwashed hair, breath like Captain Crunch, thin limbs holding mine.

"Are you bringing us home now?"

"Where's your sister?" I asked. I kissed him on the cheek and he didn't seem to mind.

"Still asleep, I guess," he said with disgust. "Mom and Aunt

Jenny are downstairs in the laundry room. Cobra Commander has got the Joes in a lot of trouble." He pointed at the TV. "When are you going to bring us home?"

I set him on the floor. He seemed to have grown inches since I'd seen him.

"I'm not sure," I said. "I'm going to see Pumpkin."

"Just don't call her that," said Jay. "Mom does, and she hates it. She's got a zit and she's gaining weight. Don't call her the Pumpkin name if you don't want her to yell at you."

"Okay," I said. "Where is she?"

"Upstairs," he said.

I ascended the stairs, peeked in the first bedroom, and there she was, fair hair slipping over the pillow, one leg outside the sheet. I stood in the door for a moment before I realized Kathy was awake. She looked over her shoulder at the slight sounds I made. She sat up straight in bed and smiled at me.

"Daddy," she said softly. "What are you doing here?"

"Came to visit," I said.

"I miss you," she said.

I sat on the edge of the bed and swept her into my arms, smelled her hair. My little Pumpkin. She'd been jolly and round-faced as a baby, in love with everything I did; such worship was unhealthy and irresistible.

"I miss you, too, Kath," I said. "Are you okay, Pumpkin?"

"Are you and Mama going to get back together?" she asked, cutting through all the formalities.

"I don't know, Honey," I said. "The world's a strange place sometimes."

Just as she was about to say something else, I heard heavy, adult steps ascending the stairs, and I let Kathy go and turned, still sitting on the edge of the bed. Jenny appeared in the doorway hauling a large pile of towels, another sacrificial burden of marriage. She hadn't heard my car, and Jay hadn't told her I was there. She did what came natural for her: she gasped.

"Jenny, it's me," I said, standing. She dropped the towels.

"Ford!" she said, the fear starting to fade, replaced by a healthy anger. "What in the hell are you doing here?"

"I came to see my family, Jen," I said. "And how are you doing this fine Saturday?"

Jay came flying up the stairs and stood behind Jenny and looked into the room. He seemed pleased with the scene-in-progress.

"Your family," she said with jewel-encrusted sarcasm. "Well, well."

"Daddy!" cried Jay, happy again to see me. He knocked Jenny out of the way and came and sat beside me. Kathy rolled her eyes with sisterly disgust, slid over, and put her arms around my shoulders. "Let's go out in the backyard and throw the baseball."

"Okay, Tack," I said, using one of the dozen nicknames we'd given him over the years. "But I've got some stuff to do first."

"Like explaining," said Jenny.

"Jenny, didn't you leave your broom double-parked or something?" I asked.

Kathy and Jay both squealed in delight. Jenny picked up the towels, stashed them in Kathy's closet, and stomped with harsh glares past us and back downstairs. She'd be telling Jill I was there.

"Broom," said Jay. "She's a witch sometimes. Uncle Bobby calls her Panda, and she calls him Panda."

"Is that enough to make you gag or what?" asked Kathy.

"I got to go see the Joes," said Jay, vaulting off the bed, and dashing down the steps.

"I got to get up, Daddy," said Kathy. "You have to leave."

"I know," I said. "Go get pretty. That won't take much."

She smiled beautifully, hugged me again, and I got up and started down the stairs, only to see Jill halfway up.

My wife wore ratty blue jeans, a soft sweatshirt I'd bought her on a trip to Bermuda, and Reeboks. Her long hair was pulled back and tied with a ribbon. She wore no makeup.

"You could have called," Jill said. "Jenny said you scared her to death."

"I also called her a witch," I admitted. Kathy came behind me, said *gmrnin Mama*, and disappeared into the upstairs bathroom. Soon, loud rock and roll came past us with the rush of shower water.

"Let's go into my bedroom," said Jill.

She walked past me, and we moved in silence down the upstairs hall. What memories those hips spoke to me: those sweet early days of love, the wonder of pregnancy and childbirth, naked and not caring as we sailed in the secluded coves of freshwater lakes. Of smiles and parties and lying close in bed and reliving agonies of the day. Growing up, all married, her pride over the china pattern, mine over our first piano.

Now Jill sat on the bed. The room was spare and neat. Bed made up. Perfect for a woman sleeping alone. I sat in a chair. Jill waited.

"I guess you're wondering what I'm doing here," I said with a brief, demented laugh.

"Crossed my mind," she said. Her eyes were not angry. "I guess calling ahead was out of the question."

"Jill, I was in Jamesburg," I said. "I wasn't sure what I was going to do until I was pointed this direction."

"Your folks okay?"

"Fine," I said.

"How's your girlfriend?" she asked. Now her eyes were angry.

"I haven't seen her for weeks," I sighed. "Look, Jill, I have something to say to you. This isn't easy."

"I bet."

"Let me be serious while I'm giving my speech, please?" I begged.

"Just don't say the problems of three people don't amount to a hill of beans in this crazy world," she said. She now had a maliciously happy glint in her eye. I realized I had stopped breathing, tried to inhale, found it hard.

"I'm here for forgiveness," I said.

"Well, well," she said.

"No, Jill," I choked, "it's more than that. I'm here for absolution. I want you to take me into your arms and forgive me and come back to Asheville with the kids. In return, I promise you I will be faithful, strong, and happy for the remainder of my life."

She waited, staring at me.

"That's the whole speech?" she asked. "I thought you were supposed to have introduction, exposition, and recapitulation.

The old sonata form. That was only recapitulation."

"Oh, Lord," I said.

"Ford, look, you have an incredibly warped view of the world, you know?" she said. She stood and walked to the window, then snapped back toward me. "You think you can treat me like pure dirt, run around with that tramp, break up our marriage and our family then come back here and say 'Whoops! I was wrong!'?"

"Jill, you're shouting," I said with a wince.

"Shouting!" she shouted. "Why shouldn't I be shouting? I've just gotten my equilibrium back, and sure as God, here you are, out of the blue, trying to knock me down again. And you have the *gall* to come in here and tell me you want to get back together based on the fact that you've decided not to cheat on me and you'll be glad to have me back?"

"I didn't mean it like that," I mumbled.

"That's what you said!" she shouted. "Surely in all the time it took to drive up here from Jamesburg you were mentally working on your speech, if not out loud, knowing you."

"Jesus."

"Anyway, I deserve to scream at you!" she yelled. "I deserve to kick you in your restless balls, Ford Clayton. Sometimes I think Jenny's right about all men thinking with their dicks."

"God, now she's agreeing with Jenny," I said.

"What's wrong with my sister?" she said with icy fury.

"Jill, I'm sorry I implied there was anything wrong with her," I said.

"No you're not," she said. "You're not sorry about anything. So, did you find your old girlfriend Camille? How'd that turn out?"

"I found her," I said. "She's not a street person, and she's not crazy. But she and my cousin Clarence are in Myrtle Beach inventing a new religion."

"Jesus Christ," she said.

"*He's* already working for another religion," I said. A brief smile twitched at the corner of her mouth and then died. "Jill, I may have become an inarticulate moron, but I'm sorry, and I still love you."

"It's not that easy!" she said. I exploded.

"Damnit, do you just want me to crawl?" I shouted. "Okay, then I'll crawl!"

I got down on all fours and came at her. She looked disgusted but then started laughing and running away from me. I began to growl like a dog. She jumped up on the bed, and I grabbed her ankle and tried to gnaw on it. She was kicking and laughing, and I was growling and making unearthly noises.

She stopped laughing.

I stopped growling.

Jenny was standing in the doorway.

"I am going to puke," Jenny said. Jill looked at me as if she'd just realized I was there. She kicked me in the forehead with her tennis shoe. I tumbled backward, rolled over. "I just came to tell you that your clothes are dry and need folding."

"And leave me alone!" shouted Jill at me. Jenny left. Muttering. Jill stood in the doorway. "Next time, call me."

"Am I being sent away?" I asked.

"It's not that poetic," she said. "I just want you out of here. I'm not through being mad at you. And the clock is ticking on filing the divorce papers, Ford."

"Just like that?" I asked.

"Next time, start with the exposition," she said.

She swept down the hall. I lay on the bed, looking at the ceiling, trying to dream the world back ten years. I just wanted this thing to end on key. Hardy har. Musical jokes. I glanced up and saw lovely Kathy standing in the doorway, wearing soft jeans and a T-shirt. She came to me this time and sat on the bed.

"You and mama were screaming again," she said.

"I know," I said. "It was all my fault, Kath. All of this has been my fault. Don't ever blame your mother."

"Oh, I haven't," she said obligingly. "I know all about mid-life crises. I read about it in *Redbook*. Mama said men go crazy when they get as old as you are."

"She should teach psychology instead of math," I said. I sat up. "Darling, I have to go now. Mama kicked me out."

"I figured," she said. "When can Jay and I come up and visit? I miss all my friends, and so does he. I hate Macon. I want to come home."

"I know, Honey," I said. "Mama's just not yet ready to believe me."

"Well, you can't blame her," said wise Kathy.

"No," I said. "You're more and more like your dear mother every day."

"She wasn't the one who went crazy, Daddy," said Kathy.

"That is, without question, true," I said.

She followed me downstairs, and I told Kathy and Jay goodbye, promised to send them a few things from the house they'd left. Jenny came through the room briefly and glared at me. I did not glare back. A deliberate step toward non-craziness. I was going downstairs to say goodbye to Jill, but I realized there was no reason. She'd given her speech. I'd given mine, such as it was.

Ten minutes later, I was heading north, fighting traffic, cursing myself, my luck, my lot, my stupidity. Instead of a fine family with kids who loved me, I had an empty house.

I got to Asheville late in the afternoon. My house was still there. Penelope was not waiting after my adventures, fighting off suitors. No need for me to arrive in a cloak and disguise. No need for brave Odysseus to slay the swarms of men with swift arrows. No goddamn wine-dark sea. The day we bought it. Quite a steal. Couple was getting divorce, wanted to sell quick and cheap. The day we moved in. Kids very small then. I parked the car and went inside. The kitchen table was nearly sagging from mail that my neighbor had brought in for me. The smell of home. No Homer near to write down my lament. Could I write my lament? I laid my suitcase on the kitchen floor. Walked through the house. Cried some. I deserve this! Late sorrows are the ugliest breed.

Sat at the piano. Played Bach. The house got dark, and I quit playing, sat there until I was sleepy, couldn't go up to our room this time.

If I'd known what Camille and Clarence were doing at the beach, I might have stayed in the attic of my old homeplace.

I GOT TO MY OFFICE EARLY ON THE LOVELY, new green campus of McCandless, scene of all my gains and losses, a stage I couldn't seem to leave. I stood in front of my window looking over the emerald quad. I softly quoted a line or two from *Look Homeward, Angel.*

"Well, who the hell are you, Rossini in New York or Tommy Wolfe in Asheville?" said Miranda Terrell. She seemed to have gained weight in the past week, and she smoked a long cigarette.

"That wasn't meant for public ears," I said. Students began to appear behind her in the halls of academia.

"I only have ears for you," she said, then she laughed and segued into a coughing fit.

I sat down and sipped my black coffee, wondering how I'd ever slipped into such a labyrinth. I studied Miranda for bull horns or strung thread, saw nothing but her shapeless pants, bleary eyes.

"That would be a great song," I said.

"Come on, Ford," she said in her near-male voice. "Spill the beans. God, what a revolting figure of speech. Where did that come from? Greasers, no doubt."

"I am overwhelmed by your sensitivity," I said.

"What gives?" she asked. "You didn't really go to the Big Apple to work on your opera did you? You told me three weeks ago that you'd never finish it. That it was practically unbegun. In fact, your exact words were, quote, 'The egg of my opera is there, but I fear I'm not the man to inseminate it,' end quote."

"You have a stronger memory than a sense of tact," I said, wincing. She was accurate, entirely. I had uttered those moronic words when a few of us were discussing our careers.

"Whoops!" said Miranda, "We've touched a little nerve, haven't we?" She ground her cigarette out in the candy dish Jill had brought back from a math teachers convention in Las Vegas.

"In view that the matter is under adjudication, I'll have no further comment at this time," I blurted.

"Huh?"

"It's a line from *All the President's Men*," I said, not wanting to add plagiarism to my other assorted and increasing sins.

"What's under adjudication?" she asked.

"Nothing," I said. "Nada."

"Maybe wobbled off the deep end *is* a precise description," she said. "Sheesh."

She left before I could think of anything else to say. I was sitting, stunned, when Sigurd appeared with a triumphant, malicious smile on her pale lips.

"Dr. Fuller wants to see you in his office immediately," she said. She was absolutely giddy. She knew something bad was going to happen to me. I nodded. She let her victorious glare sink in for two more seconds before she pirouetted and headed back down the hall. No point delaying it.

I came into the hall, feeling lightheaded and ghostly, wind-grieved, having come home again, and screw you, Tommy Wolfe. Straight into Dr. Fuller's outer office where Sigurd was sitting behind her desk, struggling with an adding machine ribbon and baring her fangs.

"I'm sorry I took so long," I said. "I was having a personal crisis of faith in which I was trying to decide if, in the end, God or man or Nada will prevail."

"Really," she said. "Please go right in, Dr. Nada."

Ouch. I was considering using *Dr. Nada* as the title of my autobiography when I walked into Dr. Fuller's office. He was sitting behind his desk, immaculately dressed and groomed. His nails were smashing. His white shirt had been starched and pressed, but not too much, and the red-and-gray striped tie was suitably muted. His hair was razor cut and stylish. He asked me to close the door behind me and sit down.

"Ford," he said, looking extremely disappointed in me, "what in the world is going on with you?"

"What do you mean, Edgar?"

"Let's not play these bullshit games," he said. "Did you go to New York, or didn't you?" He leaned forward on the desk, slid his chair up. This meant he was authoritative, serious. Where do they learn stuff like that, I wondered?

"No," I said firmly.

"And you never had a shred of interest from the New York City Opera in performing your opera, did you?" he asked. One eyebrow was cocked, a sign, I believed of inevitable triumph, like Perry Mason just before the *coup de grâce*.

"No," I sighed. Sighs were bad.

"Ford, are you having a nervous breakdown or a mid-life crisis or something?" he said, suddenly doctorly, my friend and comforter, but it was another bullshit tactic, and I knew it. I waited thirty seconds, trying to find anything worth saying.

"What were the choices again?" I asked. He slid his chair in a rush back to the wall.

"To think that I was so happy and excited for you," he said, shaking his head. "And I told the President. This is going to make me look like an idiot."

"How?" I asked, nettled. "This is my life, not yours."

"The part of your life that works here is mine," he said, rounding each word carefully.

Ah! No man's life is his own! My father often told me that as a spur to become more practical in my thinking, back in the days when I only wanted to live in a garret and create High Art. I'd told him I'd rather spend my entire life in a cell writing the *Mass in B Minor* than saving all the starving children of India. This was at supper one night, and we were listening to Bach.

"Lord, son, that's nonsense," he'd said, shocked. "If you're able to feed a body, you should do that before trying to feed a soul."

"Balderdash," said Clarice Clayton.

"May be, but you give your best gift, don't you?" I asked. "Isn't that what Preacher Johnson said?"

"Sometimes we don't even know our own best gifts," Dad said.

"Piffle," said Mom.

"My best gift is music," I said. "If I could write that (gesturing here toward the stereo) I'd slay all the infidels in Asia Minor."

"Bravo!" said artistic Clarice.

"Good grief," said Dad with a shrug, but he was merely amazed, not unloving. Nothing could make him love us less. That was his gift.

"No part of my life is yours, Edgar," I said carefully.

"Oh yeah?" he said. He was ready for a fight.

"I mean, I'm going to work hard to make up for this and all," I said. "Maybe it is a mid-lifer or something. I don't know myself. Have you had a mid-life crisis yet, Edgar?"

"I don't have time for one," he said. "Look, Ford, why didn't you just tell me the truth in the first place? It might have saved everybody a lot of embarrassment."

"The truth is not that I was going to the beach. I thought I was going to New York to save an old friend. Turned out the old friend didn't need saving. I'd called the Homeless Hotline in New York and left a message....look, it doesn't matter. I screwed up, and I'm back."

Edgar got up and walked unhappily around the room, trying to make me feel like the small boy sent to the principal's office.

"What do you think I should do as department head?" he asked. Sure. Give me the whip, and ask me to hit myself a few times.

"Well, you could order me hanged on a public gibbet and left to rot, where the birds of the air can feed on my miserable carcass and serve as a warning to anyone else who dares to fib about his whereabouts."

He stopped dead. Jesus. I didn't mean to say that. Why couldn't I keep my stupid mouth shut?

"What?" he said.

"I'm sorry," I said. "You should probably assert your authority and punish me somehow. I deserve it." He sat back down and tented his perfect fingers and stared at me for a moment, thinking.

"I can only think of one way that will keep everybody off my case and yours about this mess," he said. "You have to finish the opera."

Fin...God of Israel! My judgment at the dinner table was coming back to flay me into submission. Well, what had my life's work been thus far? As a teacher, I gave myself high marks; I loved teaching musicology and the students liked me, a few rekindling each quarter that old blind adoration of music I'd felt as a boy. But if life is a circle, and my Muse was to be Fear of Retribution rather than High Art, why should I complain? A sudden passion seized me. The words came out just before my vocal cords seemed to throttle themselves.

"Would you accept a mass?" said Ford Clayton. Choirs sang in my head. Muse, *adoremus te.* Tumblers clicked, locks turned, angels sang in my heart; Camille the Catholic, Dad the Rotarian, new religions, salvations, and all the et ceteras.

"A mass?" said Edgar. "Ford, I didn't know you were a Catholic."

"I'm not," I admitted. "Though I dabbled in it. Could you wait a moment?" My throat closed completely. I swallowed. All of it was coming together now, the motifs, entire accents, sections, tympani and this, this long, uh, viola solo in the dies irae, something urgent, fearful yet somehow tranquil. "Okay." My throat was opening back up now.

"How does one dabble in Catholicism?" he asked.

"Bach was a Lutheran, and he wrote the greatest mass ever written," I said. Mom, Dad. Preacher Johnson. Camille. "This is a sign. I have to write this mass, Edgar."

"Is this a religious epiphany now?" he asked.

"It's the music," I said. "I could go right now and sketch it out. My ideas....my classes."

"I could tell the President you're working on something different," he said. "Could we have the premiere in the fall?"

"Schedule it now," I said. I rose. "I'm all right now."

"And *East of Eden?*" he asked.

"I never could picture Okies singing," I shrugged.

He picked at a tooth with one perfect fingernail and shook his head. I let myself out, and Sigurd looked at me with bitter triumph, but I gave it back to her. Only when I got into the hall did the enormity of my promise settle around my shoulders.

On the night of the third day, I sat at home in the dark, contemplating suicide. The actual, razored intent was not serious; I could never do myself in. But the drama of seriously considering it heightened my already nervous state beyond reason. A cold front swung through the state and stalled, bringing noisy thunderstorms. The Bach *Mass in B Minor* wasn't suitable; I listened to the *Symphonie Fantastique* and felt the grotesque, twisted world of the grave reach out for me. All the dead I knew paraded past me: grandparents, Rich Harper, a kid who'd run out in front of a car when we were eight, others. Lightning threw wild shadows around the Jill-less room. I had never meant to hurt her or anyone else; I merely sought new paths for my small life and became lost. No thread now to get back, though, and no way to know which corridor led to my future. Which future did I need for a happy life? How could I love those who loved me? Was gravity a perpetual and inevitable law? Did I need to read *The Four Doctrines* of Sweden-borg in my lifetime, or could I let that slide?

Suddenly, a thrill of the razor's slice overwhelmed me: I found myself stumbling into the kitchen, thinking, maybe, uh, maybe I should actually, really, honest-to-God-no-bullshit, kill myself and relieve everybody of the whatchamacallit, er, burden, of dealing with Ford Clayton.

On the other hand, probably not.

In my book *Rachmaninoff and the End of Romance*, I'd written that the romantic is prelude to civil unrest, the turning axis of a bored world. It is the sweet edge of anarchy in a world that has become too ordered to be borne. When pieces of this sad, exalted puzzle fit too well, we rip them apart, make them fit in the wrong places.

Where had my music gone? Where was the original beating of this unfaithful and justly abused heart? Then it came to me as I lay in darkness on the sofa: music forgives. Without judging, without consignments to hell, music says you are merely the latest weak link in a long chain of mammal flesh: do your best and keep turning toward the light.

The light played along the mountains of North Carolina. Trees of fire. I prayed to all gods. I blessed Bach's Lutheran soul.

But behind it all, Camile Malone still poked me with her pitchfork. I had not yet let her go, and somehow, she knew it.

AND SO, WITH MY PLEDGE OF FAITHFULNESS, my vow of regret, I began to talk with Jill, convinced her that my world was different now. Green days spun past on silken chords. In private, I said awkward sentimental things to my aging shade in the mirror: *to dig and love your home; these are the true aims of philosophy.* But I was no once or future king. I had merely appeared in this orchestral rehearsal for Nothingness, well fit for harmonies, but a sorry concertmaster. Well, I could live with that. Better to be a small actor in a great play than the star of a flop.

And so, that spring when the wildflowers dazzled the roadsides with their profusion, Jill believed me, quit her new job, talked her way back into the old one, and moved back to Asheville with Kathy and Jay. The homecoming was my wildest joy. We'd met a couple of times in the interim, once in Athens, once in Franklin, North Carolina, and she'd laid out ground rules I found both expected and not unlike the Treaty of Versailles. It was clear I'd have no right to a standing army for some years.

I welcomed them with rich love. We grilled steaks, drank whiskies, went to PTA meetings, bought a Siamese cat that Jay named Herschel Walker. Jill and I took evening walks and reminisced about when we'd first met, and she agreed to abide by my one request: no interrogations about my wayward affair with Starr. By then, I saw Starr occasionally on campus, and she had begun to see a boy her own age of whom I was immediately jealous; yet that envy was also an envoy. Go with the last young love of the aged Ford Clayton, young man. God, I was sounding to myself in still moments like Mister Chips.

In this calm center of my rebuilt life, I began not a Mass but a setting of Yeats's poem "The Lake Isle of Innisfree." That masterful, somehow sorrowful yet hopeful poem exactly fitted my chastened state. The scoring was for full orchestra, chorus and soloist, and within a week of starting it, my impulse as a composer came back. I told Edgar about what I was doing, and he was exasperated but at least grateful I was writing; they scheduled the premiere for fall.

By the end of April, we had resettled into our lives. I knew that the wages of philosophy are confusion. Not geared to live with eternal confusion but wanting, instead, small quantifiable bits of life, I decided that if this was midlife, I'd as soon be adolescent again. All was calm, all was bright.

Then I saw the first poster.

It was a yellow typewriter sheet on a bulletin board near Jumper Hall with a single word in block letters:

TEST

For a moment, I felt a giddy sense of fearful recognition. I forgot it. The next day, when I was walking past, the sheet was red, and on it was another single word:

TEXT

This time, a dull thrill shot through my bones. I walked toward it, stood and examined it.

"What is this *Test* and *Text* stuff, Dr. Clayton?" said Bob Jacobs, a student of mine. Bob was from a small town in Tennessee, majoring in performance on trumpet. He wanted to play with the New York Philharmonic. "It's all over the damn campus. These notes are in the dorms and everything, and nobody's seen who's putting them up."

"Probably some crank," I said nervously.

"Everybody's wondering if some standardized test or something is coming up," he said. "It'd be just like this place to throw us a test, right when spring recitals are here. Jesus."

Jesus indeed. *Kyrie eleison*. That night, troubled and anxious, I sat with Jill and the kids at the dining room table, eating a broccoli casserole she'd made even though she was tired after work. I was not being communicative.

"We're studying the human body at school," said ten-year-old Jay. "Vaginas are really gross."

"Mama!" yelled Kathy. "Jay Clayton, you shut your mouth." A wry grin inadvertently creased my lips.

"What's so funny?" Jill asked.

"Nothing," I said. "Jay, this is no place to talk about that. I'll discuss it with you later, man-to-man."

"You're awful quiet tonight," said Jill suspiciously.

"Huh?" I said, hoping for time.

"They *are* gross," said Jay. "It's not my fault. They bleed, too."

"Shut your mouth!" yelled Kathy. "I'd rather have a vagina any day than a stupid little penis."

"Stop it now!" commanded Jill. She shot them a stern glance.

"*You* signed the paper so I could take sex," shrugged Jay. He was entirely right; I had.

"I didn't know about this," said Jill.

"I forgot to tell you," I said. "It was right before school last Friday."

"What else have you not told me?" she said.

"Whuh huh," said Jay with a grin.

"You wouldn't have the *guts* to be female," pretty Kathy said to her brother.

"What kind of guts does it take to look like somebody hit your crotch with a hatchet?" asked Jay.

In the ensuing confusion, I untangled Kathy's hand from her brother's shirt collar, raised my fatherly voice and gave a fatherly speech, spoke with less wisdom than authority and sent them off to do homework with a stern warning. I hate stern warnings, but the scene almost brought me a familiar comfort. Jill and I stayed at the table, were quiet for a time.

"You've got something on your mind, Ford," she said finally.

What should I tell her? Would any words about Camille help upset the muddled balance of our life, or should I simply let her lie? Clearly, either she or Clarence or both had, against my expectations, shown up here, still dabbling in religion.

"It's, uh....."

"A look of distance in your eyes."

"I'm sorry, Honey," I said, smiling. "I'm spending too much time on the *Lake Isle of Innisfree*. I'm putting a lot into the piece. It sort of means a lot to my career. Wait. That's not right. It means a lot to my life."

"I'm glad you're composing," she said. "You need an outlet. All men your age need an outlet." I felt like a small boy caught about to put his finger in a socket.

"Come again?"

"Oh, you know, Ford," she said, waving the air with her fork, "It's well documented. You guys sit around and start looking at the fact that life's going to end, you're halfway through it, and you don't feel like you've measured up. That's why guys your age drop dead from heart attacks playing sandlot football, trying to impress a woman half their age who could care less. It's all in books."

"God, that's depressing," I said. "What about women your age? What happens to them?"

"They learn patience," she said. "And begin to practice living alone."

"I'm cheered up," I said.

Jill laughed brightly, sweetly. "But then again, I have a vagina. What do I know?"

"I'm beginning to see that the uterus is the seat of the known universe," I said.

"We've known it all along," said Jill.

The next day I sat in my office, watching the world swirl past me on the quad, nostalgic as always in the spring. My radio was on, and Bruno Walter was leading the Vienna Philharmonic in Brahms' *Academic Festival Overture*. Perfect. I was between my classes, and the piano score of *The Lake Isle of Innisfree* was on top of the desk, where I studied each note, somehow looking for a feral passage that had intruded its wildness into the perfect order of my new-pledged world.

"This is for you," said Miranda Terrell. She blubbered her way into the room and handed me a manila envelope. "Was left outside my office when I got here this morning. Somebody must have confused our numbers."

"Thanks," I said. She trundled off after shrugging to show me that she didn't care. The outside had only two words, FORD CLAYTON, in large letters; the whole thing stank of fresh Magic Marker. The end had been licked shut. I opened it and pulled out a sheaf of papers half an inch think. They'd been velobound neatly. I was looking at the back, so I turned it over and saw the front page:

THE TEXT
BEING A GLIMPSE INTO WORLDLY WISDOM
AND SORT OF A GUIDE TO THE NEW ORDER
THAT'S COMING REAL SOON.

"Jesus Christ," I said. I jumped up and stared out the window, wondering if I'd see her, see Clarence. What in the hell was I going to do now? My idiot cousin and ex-girlfriend were back in Asheville. God help us all. And so I did then what they intended me to do. I read.

THE BOOK OF NUMBERS

Chapter One

1 *In the beginning was three, indisputridable unholy trinity that excludes the sacredness of the two-backed beast.*

2 *It takes one to know one.*

3 *The first step of Baly was the earth, the second was heaven and third came the regions of all hells, if you believe in such shit.*

4 *A mockingbird don't know no song because he's done stole all the others, so he's no better than a thief.*

5 *Dionysus, Eros, Hades, Cronus, Persephone, Bacchus, Cupid, Pluto, Saturn, Proserpina: a fun bunch of guys who never existed because we invent that which whips up holes in the sacred water; rends*

a tattered edge in the sacred cloth.

6 It would of been more miracleable if Jesus had of fed one person with a thousand fishes, if you ask me. That means something big.

7 Peri hypsous. Opera comique. Athos, Porthos, and satygraha. Sturm und drang: make all that rhyme and you've got what religion passes for.

8 Sticks and stone may break my bones, but worms will never crawl me. (I made that up.)

9 Let's name the five regions of hell: the Styx (Nile), Acheron (New York), Cocytus (Paris), Phlegethon (Myrtle Beach) and Lethe (I forget).

10 Christmas is a comin and the geese are gettin fat. I sang this in the fourth grade, but the rest is gone away. Where do lost songs go? That's a good one!

Oh, no. This document was clearly the calling card of the twin threats to Western Civilization, Camille and Clarence. I held the volume, smiling, then grimacing. Was this any more fantastic than great whales swallowing men then spitting them out whole, than the water of a sea parting, than turning water into wine? Yes. I could see them, drunk and high on the ecstasy of their own created faith, alternating verses. Surely they didn't keep it up for the whole book. I shuffled forward to the next section:

THE BOOK OF GINGER

Chapter One

1 Here, Ginger, good girl. Roll over, play dead, bounce back up, and grab the ball. Do ye likewise.

2 I had me this dog named Ginger at the camp, but I think Elmo Santerino ate her. I ain't sure of that.

3 Ginger was blacklisted in Hollywood, Ginger was a troubadour who was received by Eleanor of Aquitaine, Ginger and Trophonius built the Temple of Apollo at Delphi, Ginger was a golem, Ginger went out after the fleece to return it to Ioleus, but fleeced herself. Poetic justice.

4 A penny saved is worth a penny even a lot later when you take

it out and look at it. If I didn't make that up, I ought to have.

    5 Ginger sat under the piano of Beethoven with a chamber pot, lay before the roaring fire with the hacking Chopin; Ginger lived in Axel's Castle, had the run of the place; Ginger chased the damned Calydonian boar, nipped his ass off.

I read on, heart reaching multiple furlongs per second: *The Book of Places, The Book of Mister James Durante, The Book of Angels, Devils and Natty Bumppo, The Book of Earthly Delights, the Book of Baseball Statistics, the Book of Refusals.* I read from the *Book of Refusals:*

    25 We refuse to believe in the actual existence of Richard Milhouse Nixon and all the goddamned president's men.
    26 We don't have a clue when the White Sox are gone win another World Series.
    27 We refuse to believe in bucolics, dialects, or georgics. Vergil was a candy ass. Tour guide.
    28 I was gone say something, but I forgot it.

I went straight to the end, laughing, madness creeping up my spine like some giant insect. The final section was called

THE BOOK OF ANSWERS

    1 Love is the three-part mirror where you try on the clothes of life, distorted, expensive, coming from a sales rack.
    2 If you wanta be happy for the rest of yore life, never make a pretty woman yore wife.
    3 Wars are fought for one reason: excessive testosterone and a lack of willing twatissimas. If you don't believe me, ask the Accademia della Crusca.
    4 And it came to pass in those days that a scream went out that all the people should be axed. (That means a lot.)
    5 Time is what is left when you are through thinking about time, which doesn't exist in time.

My hands were visibly shaking. I threw *The Text* on my desk, left the office and walked around the campus under a new drizzle, trying to clear my head.

At McCandless, the faith was music: epiphanies of bar score and clef, voice and instruments, charms to soothe the savage manias in us all. The soggy air carried pieces of melody, dark sawings on a viola somewhere. Not far from the Chapel, the place where I'd first met Camille back in 1968, I saw a colleague standing before a bulletin board.

Robin Josephs had once sung in Carnegie Hall, a lieder recital over which the critics raved. She dazzled them with "Gretchen Am Spinnerade." Her voice had, they said, "the lyric intimacy that hints at greatness." At the peak of her rush toward that fame, though, Robin had suffered a terrifying attack of nerves that left her paralyzed, forced her to cancel a much-publicized recital at Town Hall, then a national tour, and finally a European tour. She taught for a time at a conservatory in New England before coming to McCandless, five years ago; now, she taught soprano, sometimes presented faculty recitals. Her manner was shy and winning, and her voice was still dazzling. She stood before the bulletin board, holding a sheaf of sheet music, a red umbrella curved over her head. She was just over five feet tall.

"Hi, Robin," I said. "What are you doing out here?"

"I've got a...." she started. She was staring at the bulletin board. "Hi, Ford. You seen this stuff?" She pointed at a large sheet of construction paper on which someone had written:

TAKE THE TEST
OR BE LIKE
ALL THE REST

"Son of a bitch!" I said. She stared at me with surprise and waited for an explanation of my outburst. How could I tell her about the *Book of Mister James Durante*? About Camille von der Malone and the Malone Society, about new religions? "Sorry. I just get tired of all this cryptic crap that goes up this time of year."

"Uh huh," she said, not sure about me. "This stuff's all over the place, and nobody's seen where it's coming from. I heard from Jeanine Lewis, a student of mine, that late last night her roommate looked out their dorm window and saw what appeared to be a dwarf putting signs up on bulletin boards."

"A dwarf?" I choked. "You can't be serious."

"Why would I make something like that up?" she asked. "Are you all right? You look pale."

"I think I'm coming down with something," I said. "Whatever's been going around."

"But I guess they're only putting it up at night," said Robin. "There's rumors going around about some big meeting or something. All the students are worried about this test thing. Whoever's doing this is working late at night. Lots of trouble for something like this. I'm late."

"Me, too," I said.

"Where you headed?" she asked.

"God only knows," I said. She stared at me for a moment longer, shrugged and moved beneath the red mushroom toward the Chapel.

I was rinsing the dishes, and Jill sat on a stool and pushed her hair out of her eyes. Kathy was doing her homework. Jay had gone upstairs, ostensibly for a shower, but I was sure he was doing anything but showering. He was devious in the usual way of aspiring preadolescents. I expected this deceit, though, worked around it, tried to congratulate myself on my forbearance.

"I don't understand why you've got to go back to work," said Jill unhappily. "Why couldn't you have just brought it home?"

"You know how it is with the kids here," I said. "I've got to plan the final for my musicology class."

"You've been giving that final exam for years," she said. Right. Absolutely. I needed deceit lessons from my son.

"Honey, I just need to get ahead on it," I said. "You know how I get this time of year. Also, I, uh, need to think through the rest of the Yeats poem. It's giving me some trouble."

"When will you be home?" she asked quietly. Dignified restraint.

"Not late," I said. "I hope."

"You hope."

"Don't make it sound so deceitful, Jill," I said. I put the last glass in the dishwasher. The kitchen still smelled sweetly of broiled fish and hushpuppies.

"Ford, deceit is why I left," she said. "I don't like this."

"What do you think, Jill?" I cried. My voice fell to a conspiratorial whisper. "You think I'm going to see *her* after all I went through to get you back up here? That'd be crazy."

"You've been crazy a good deal lately," she said.

"I told you, that's all over," I said. "Honey, it's nothing. You've just got to trust me." Why couldn't I just tell her what was happening? It seemed safer to try and rout Camille early, leave Jill out of it entirely. Somehow I felt Jill would blame me for Camille's presence in town.

"Okay," she sighed. "But I don't like this."

"It's just the end of the quarter," I said. I dried my hands, walked to Jill and took her hand, motioned for her to stand. She did, came into my arms, looked down, then up, close, into my eyes.

"Don't ever hurt me again, Ford," she said.

"Darling, I'm a fool," I said. "You're my only light now."

The lamplight on campus seemed ghostly in the dripping fog. The dies irae from the *Symphonie Fantastique* played only in my mind. Music filled the air like mosquitoes on a summer night. Stereos from open windows, stray notes from the Chapel, other secret places. The practice rooms were soundproofed, of course, but many students chose to escape to work on a difficult passage, in some secret, silent corner of McCandless.

I stood under the Circle Beech in a black London Fog raincoat, cinched tight, rain hat over my eyes, deep in shadow, looking like a pervert. I could be FBI, spying on the campus radicals, if we'd had any. At this very spot, half a lifetime before, Camille had launched the Malone Society at a time when we wanted to believe anything. Screw it, we said: we're tired of propping up corrupt right-wing military dictatorships; tired of dumping chemicals in the waters of the earth, of destroying the soil; we're tired of a handful of old white men deciding the fate of it all, morons of capitalism and communism. Youth power! We could run this world right! Well, we'd grown up, and we had merely slipped on the mantles of our elder goons.

I was daydreaming about Ronny Favors and all my losses from those years before when I was shocked to see a very short man scuttling down the sidewalk two hundred yards away. In the light of the streetlamps beneath the chestnut tree shade, he glanced warily right and left. Some small animal looking for food, wary for a predator. He wore a New York Yankees windbreaker and a fedora. He came nearer, and the perspective changed, his arms now looking enormous, too long, his body dwarf-sized. He was forty yards away, ripping one of the signs off the bulletin board. He threw it on the ground and took another sign from a stash under his arm, pushed it as high as he could reach and banged it a few times with a staple gun in his other hand.

My feet were moving before I knew what I'd say. Should I quote from *The Book of Angels, Devils, and Natty Bumppo*? He heard my footsteps just before I reached him, turned in shock, pointed his staple gun at me.

I was not surprised to see that it was Mister Josiah.

"I wadn't doing nothing," he said. "Password!" He looked around. "Password?" He said it weakly, not sure why he was doing it.

"Mister Josiah," I said. "How in the hell did you let them rope you into this?"

He acted as if he was going to plug me with the staple gun, realized how foolish it looked, lowered it. His massive features looked silly, embarrassed.

"Password," he said.

"Remember me?" I asked. I took off my hat. He stepped forward, turning his head to catch the light. He recognized me, seemed enormously relieved.

"Oh, Mr. Clayton!" he said. "You're one of us, too! I should of knowed that!"

"Us?"

"The New Order," he whispered.

"Sounds like a new branch of national Socialism," I said. "And what's this password crap?"

"Oh, that's just the Leader's charge," he said. "You know. Aren't you one of us?"

"Sure," I said. "But I've been away. What's the new password?"

"Green light at the end of the dock," whispered Mister Josiah. "Here, you need to help put these up." He handed me a few of his posters. I turned the top one lightwise and read:

FIRST READINGS IN THE TEXT
FRIDAY AFTERNOON, 5 P.M.
THE CIRCLE BEECH
IF YOU WANT TO TAKE THE TEST
YOU MUST PLAN TO ATTEND

"Mister Josiah," I said in a friendly way, "could you tell me where Camille and Clarence might be?"

"Whoa no," he said, backing up as if I had a cattle prod. "Nobody's getting that out of me, not even a fellow member. Rule number one: If you squeal, you're not no longer part of the deal."

"Sounds like something Clarence said," I muttered.

"It's in *The Text*," he said. "Go look it up."

"I could look it up," I said angrily. "I've got a copy of that piece of tripe on my desk. Did you leave me that?"

"I can't handle *The Text*," he said in horror. "Only She Who Plays with Fire can handle *The Text*."

"She Who Plays with Fire?" I said. I laughed out loud.

"Don't make fun of her or she'll do a exercism," he said.

"Exorcism," I corrected.

"No, it's a exercism." he said. "She called it that. Makes you dance out the devils. Makes you listen to these singing Chipmunks. Happened to me one night. Horrible. I had to beg my way back in."

"But why are you doing this at all?" I said. "What about your motel?"

"I'm doing it because I want answers," said Mister Josiah. "She

Who Plays with Fire says it best: 'The secrets of the universe are not secrets. There is no universe. There is nothing but a dog under the window begging for scraps.'"

"That must be from *The Book of Ginger*," I said.

"You *are* one of us!" he cried. I was tired of playing games.

"Look, get out of this!" I cried. "Camille is deranged, and Clarence has been in the slammer too long. He's very confused about religion and women and his place in a hostile world." Mister Josiah looked at his watch.

"The time!" he said. "The time!" He started walking off with his heavy, short steps.

"They're going to arrest you all," I said. "You can't do something like this. This is a private conservatory. It's a school of music, for God's sake."

Mister Josiah stopped in the light of the next sidewalk lamp and turned back to me, lifted his fat finger to his lips and shushed me.

"For *Ginger's* sake," he said.

He took off running down the sidewalk, and I did not follow him. Not then. I'd wait until he circled back to the parking area. He'd be easy enough to spot. I just hoped that he'd lead me to the co-conspirators themselves.

And I hoped that Jill wasn't calling my office number.

I SAT IN MY CAR AND WAITED FOR FORTY-FIVE MINUTES until I saw Mister Josiah come strutting back through the lot — the only large public lot on campus. Something definitely simian played about him, swinging arms, purpose, large head. The rain had vaporized into a fine mist. He got in a choking old Chevy pickup, drove away in a clatter, much faster than I expected. I drove after him.

Rain began to bounce off the hood in drops the size of half notes. We drove down the turning roads toward Asheville, faster and faster, until I was cursing his rush. What if Peter and Paul had been such terrible drivers? Who would have known of their Text then? Whose mass would we celebrate? What if Hinduism had won out? Mister Josiah was driving too hard for philosophy. I merely kept up as well as I could.

Which was not well. In a compulsive jerk, I reached out and turned on the radio, and a woman was talking to a radio psychiatrist. Mister Josiah came to a red light, slowed slightly then gunned right through it.

"Shit!" I exclaimed. I did the same.

"Now, Connie from Des Moines," said the psychiatrist, "what makes you think that nobody loves you?"

"Well, Tom, I'm forty-four years old, I'm a virgin, and I can't even get a date," she said sadly. "I feel like the world has passed me by completely. I might as well be a nun."

"Let's talk about it for a moment, Connie," he said in a voice that laved over my upholstery like honey.

Mister Josiah made a wicked right, nearly went into a ditch. He was driving crazily, his big head not more than an inch over the steering wheel. Here came the rain. Heavy. I cursed again. Tom was telling Connie that maybe something she was doing turned men off. He asked her to describe herself. She was a typical, normal, nice woman who'd worked at the same job at the phone company for twenty years. She was stable, a Christian, a volunteer for the Humane Society. Describe yourself physically, Connie, said Tom. Well, I have blue eyes, and brown hair and a nice smile. I'm a little sensitive about my weight.

Mister Josiah hung a right. Flying now, down a strip of fast-food places, blurred in the rain, damn my sorry windshield wipers, hitting gutters, fountains of spray flying out like a horizontal geyser. Let's go with that for a minute, Connie, about your weight. How much do you weigh? Is that important? It could be. Well, Tom, I'm two hundred and twelve pounds, but it's my glands.

"Where in the hell are you going?" I cried.

Now Mister Josiah was taking another right, and I'd never been in this part of town, run-down, slummy, a place where eating was much more important than worrying about Mozart's ternary composition patterns. A fine hand of lightning pointed at the mountains, illuminating us all. Thunder pounded us. Rain loves the mountains, good for the artistic temperament. Connie, your weight may be a symptom rather than just a result, Tom was saying. How tall are you, by the way? Is that important, Tom? It could be. I'm six-two. And you're a virgin, Connie, right? Right, Tom.

I punched a button and found that Vaughn Williams was on National Public Radio. Good stuff for a rain-soaked city. By now, Mister Josiah had come into dregsville, but I could not tell if he knew I was following. I could only think of Camille by now, and my heart and head turned back to that autumn day when I'd first stumbled upon her cursing and playing in the Chapel and how I'd been swept away by her intensity. I thought of the night in her dorm room when we'd made love standing in a puddle of moonlight.

He pulled to a stop in front of a ramshackle house. I eased on past, looking as if, fat chance, I belonged in the neighborhood. On a corner, under an umbrella, a skinny, white man with a cigarette hanging from his lips, was transacting business with an equally skinny black woman. The booming backbeat of speaker with a broken cone half-drowned the lyrical effusions of England on my radio. I drove around the neighborhood, came back and parked across the street. I wondered if Tom had made Connie feel any better. Probably not.

The house was narrow and badly kept. Lights were on all over the place inside. A lone man leaned against a power pole half a block away. He seemed to be dancing some secret step every four or five seconds. A gunshot came from half a mile away. I got out. *Hi, Tom, I'm a, uh, professional man from North Carolina, named, uh, Roger. Hi, Roger. I'm in a mean area of town right now, and I don't know what I'm doing here or why I'm trying to find Camille.* What is it about her? Why had she come back to Asheville to try and establish a new religion with my crazy cousin? *Well, Roger, maybe it's that she's always needed the reassurance that she can't get from love or life or religion. Maybe she's the ugly mirror image of your own disease, and that's why you were attracted to her back in 1968. Hey, I never told you about that.*

I crossed the street, stepped in a pothole, went up to my calf. Cursed. I got behind Mister Josiah's car and peeked around it. Sounds from inside. Music. Er, sounds like, sounds like....oh, joy! Beethoven! A piano sonata! No one crazy could love Beethoven! *Of course, Roger, wasn't Beethoven rather like Camille or vice versa, rather crazy and intense?* Tom, get out of my head, you dumb son of a bitch.

Christ! I ran up the sidewalk, crept onto the porch. Dripping rain off the roof pattered and puddled, ran off down the streets. Inside, a female voice shouting. I stood on the edge of the porch, and its unseen but rotted boarding gave way, broke like a graham cracker soaked in milk. I fell backward into the dripline. For a moment, I merely lay there, up to my nose in pebbled water. I got to my knees and crept onto the porch, cursing. Had I become mad yet? Nearly so.

The music inside ended, and I waited for another record to

take its place. Instead, all the lights began to go out, one by one. Enough of this shit. I banged on the door, spraying water around like a wet dog.

"Camille!" I screamed. "Open this goddamned door!"

The last visible light went out. Silence, darkness, rain. I banged some more, nothing happened. "Green light at the end of the fucking dock!"

I tried the door, but it was locked. I walked into the rain, around the right side of the house. Garbage was overflowing from nasty-smelling cans. The house next door was enveloped in a slow funk; I saw drowsy forms in an open window where rain didn't go in. Smelled the burning rush of marijuana, heavy. I got around back just as I heard a car start, ran back down the muddy side yard to the front in time to see Mister Josiah's car drive off. "Camille!"

Damn her soul to hell. Then I wondered: was this how it was for the Early Christians? Well, there was nothing to do but go back to the office, dry off, check in with Jill and then slink home. I started to cross the street and saw that the world was moving: the street, telephone poles, guttered water, frantic sidewalks clinging to the filthy earth. No; only the object of my stare was moving: my car. It was rolling. A man was behind the wheel. The engine caught.

"Stop, thief!" I actually cried.

A skinny white man was behind the wheel. He looked up at me in time to grin, showing only a few darkened, poorly held teeth. His hair was long and rain-plastered to his face. The car grunted, coughed, disappeared down the street. "Stop, thief." I said it weakly. Laughed.

I slogged toward nowhere. I didn't know this part of Asheville at all. I was fast becoming a victim of natural selection. What I need, Mom, is a Bible verse. She'd ply me with one when I looked down and out as a boy. One threw itself before my feet, from the inner workings of my soaked head:

And when they cried unto the Lord, he put darkness between you and the Egyptians, and brought the sea upon them, and covered them; and your eyes have seen what I have done in Egypt: and ye dwelt in the wilderness a long season.

Thank you, Mom. Thank you, Book of Joshua. As I half-ran down the wet, cracked asphalt, I thought what an odd word "dwelt" was. I realized I was probably the only human on earth at that moment with that thought. I got to a corner, stopped. On the left were more houses, straight ahead the same. I ran to the right for two blocks. The houses were unpainted, even slovenly, and they looked like havens of the rich. Inside, people were dry, reasonably safe. Some were happy. My chest hurt. I finally got to another corner, lost, Lord, found a Seven-Eleven, came storming inside. A few black faces turned to me with understandable hostility.

"What in the world," said a tall man about my age.

"I need a phone," I gasped. "My car's been stolen."

"You lost," said the tall man. His eyes softened to a kindly shade. "You need a police officer."

And he called one for me. I stood by the door awkwardly and stared out at the rain. In less than five minutes, a police car stopped out front. For the first time, I smelled the store, a friendly mix of coffee and sausage biscuits. The tall man had two friends with him, both men, and they talked softly, laughing.

The policeman was courteous, understanding, helpful. When he got all the information, he even offered to take me home. The periodic static of his radio broke our silence.

"What in hell's a man like you doing in that part of town?" he finally asked. I knew it had been on his mind. I'd told him I was there to see a friend, and he'd just said unh huh.

"A woman I used to know was in a house over there," I said. "She's back in town and I was going to see her."

"Woman," he said.

"That's correct, officer," I said.

"We don't never learn," he said in a deep bass. "And that's just the way it is."

"You telling me?" I said.

"I tell you what," he said.

Jill was propped up in our bed, reading. It was something after midnight. When I came into the house, soaked, downcast, chastised, she merely stared at me over the top of her rimless glasses.

"Well?" she said coldly.

"Jill, the car's been stolen," I said.

"Oh?"

"Please forgive me," I said. I sank into a chair across the room.

"For what?" she asked. "I called you to ask if you'd bring some milk home for the kids' breakfast. You didn't answer."

"Because I wasn't there, but it's not what you think," I said. "It's a long story. Honey, listen, I promise I didn't see Starr tonight," I said. "It was Camille."

The sentence settled between us like smoke from a battle. Her hard expression did not change.

"Well, well," said my wife.

"No, Honey," I said, leaping up and wandering around the room. My shoes squeaked from the water with each step. "She met me at Myrtle Beach, like I told you, but she and my cousin are here, and they're going to kick off a new religion on Friday with this meeting. A dwarf who runs a motel at the beach came with them, and I saw him putting up posters, and I followed him to this really bad part of town, and I parked, and, and I got out in the rain and came up to the door, but they didn't open up, even when I used the password 'Green light at the end of the dock!' And I came around back, and I walked in garbage, but when I came back around front, this skinny guy with only a couple of teeth was stealing my car, and I had to walk to a Seven-Eleven."

I stopped and let the words wander around our bedroom. They came back to me with heavy sarcasm.

"Ford, for God's sake," she said softly. I thought she might cry.

"It's the truth," I mumbled.

"Is it?" she said. "What's happened to you?" Her sadness evolved suddenly into fierceness. She sat up and leaned forward slightly. "You were going to be somebody important, Ford. Remember? You were going to be world-famous. Like Balzac, you said. The only things you ever wanted were fame and love, fame and love. You used to say that to me over and over. Do you remember?"

"Yes."

"We were going to be the stuff of legend," she said. "Do you remember that?"

"I do," I said.

"Well, I held up my end of the bargain!" she shouted. "What happened to you?"

"I've gotten a little lost," I said. "What do you want me to say?"

"What do I want you to say? I want you to say that fame is love. That the fame you want is me and the kids. Why isn't that enough? You're never going to finish that goddamned opera. You've never even been to Oklahoma or California."

"I was in Phoenix once," I mumbled.

"Then write a damned opera about the Phoenix airport!" she shouted.

"You're going to wake the kids up," I said.

"I should be waking the whole world up!" she cried. "I should be telling everybody to beware! The end is near! The end of love is right around the corner!"

"Christ, I'm sorry," I said. "I thought Camille was homeless. I thought she had nowhere to go. I felt bad for her. I didn't know she was just pretending."

"Art is nothing but pretending," said Jill.

A deep silence settled between us for a long time. I took off my squeaky shoes and wet socks. I had never been so tired in my life. Jill finally turned out the light, leaving me soggy in the darkness, so I walked back downstairs. The clock on the mantel reminded me that time was passing.

The next two days slid past like slugs. I moved with the motion of tectonic plates. Camille did not show up at my office, or Clarence, or Mister Josiah. *The Text* lay on my desk like the Gordian Knot. I didn't open it again.

Jill was restrained, but we talked. The kids were excited that my car had been stolen. Everyone at their school was deeply impressed that Kathy and Jay were victims. I had begun to believe that Camille had left for New York.

Late Thursday afternoon, when the warm sun was spangling the old rug in my office, I glanced up to see her in the doorway. She was wearing jeans and a plain blue T-shirt.

"Hi, Ford," said Camille Malone. "How do you like the game

so far? Bet you didn't think I'd still be here."

"Camille," I said, "you're ruining my life."

"No, I'm saving it," she laughed. "I'm saving everybody's life. Did you read *The Text* yet?"

"Parts of it," I said. "It's a confused and confusing piece of garbage." She laughed at me knowingly.

"If you don't understand it, that's okay," she said. "You always were slow, Georgia. It's the blueprint for tomorrow."

Now, I laughed.

"It's a waste of verbs and nouns," I said. "Camille, you always thought of yourself as a goddess. Now you're trying to recreate the altar where you've worshipped."

"Clever," she said. She stretched beautifully and looked around the room. "But I really shouldn't be too hard on you, Ford. You never were more than you were." I stood up and came to her, saw that though life had changed a few geologic eras since we first met, she was still Camille.

"Camille, how can anybody be more than he is?" I said. Miranda Terrell wandered by, saw me standing there with raised voice, saw Camille, and smiled with approval at my obvious discomfort. I ignored her. "What makes you think that you're more than you are?"

"You think I'm more than I am," she said with a smile. She shrugged and walked slowly to the window. "You even found me at the safe house."

"Safe house?" I cried. "Who do you think you are, Patty Hearst? Are Mister Josiah and Clarence the last remains of the Symbionese Liberation Army, Camille?"

She laughed.

"Music and Romance, music and Romance," she said with a mock sigh. "You've never done anything but pretend, Ford." She walked into the office and looked out my window at the green quad. "You think this is anything but pretending? Why else does anybody wind up in a place like McCandless? To pretend, for God's sake. Well, I've found that pretending is the most real thing in the world, Georgia. And the older I get, the more I have to pretend to survive."

"And the older I get, the more I want a firm foundation!" I shouted. "I want life to be what I feel when I see my kids arguing at the supper table, Camille. I want life to fill me up like my wife fills a wine glass on Saturday night."

"Puh-lease," she said, holding her nose between the thumb and index finger of her right hand. "Is this the *Reader's Digest* Condensed Version of the Edgar A. Guest Hour?"

"Okay, okay," I said, knowing I'd been baited into arguing with her. "Look, just forget I got sloppy sentimental. I've been on a journey lately, and I've found that even middle-aged men are redeemable. Perhaps the same is true for middle-aged women."

She smoked and stared at me impassively, but I knew I'd hit a core of pith in the ironwood of Camille Malone.

"*The Text and the Test*," she said blithely. "This is your doing, Georgia. Don't you know you created all this?" She turned and walked quickly out of the room, and when she turned, a light film of dampness covered her eyes. "You created me."

Her words hung in the air. She left the building, descending the stairs to God knows where. I hadn't even had time to blame her for the theft of my car.

Late that afternoon, when I'd finished my classes and I felt as thick and stupid as ever, I walked outside and waited for Jill to come pick me up on her way back from her own job. I sat on a bench in the parking lot behind Roberts Hall, dazzled by the sunlight on the grass. My past and present were an illuminated manuscript, an incunabulum that unwound without much sense. Therefore I was not terribly surprised when my cousin, Clarence Clayton, came scrambling out of a privet hedge, grinning like a fool.

"So, Clarence," I said softly. "Did you find the Philly Stones?" He stood before me in the parking lot.

"Hark! Lo!" he shouted. I jumped.

"Do you have to do that?" I said. "Clarence, Camille's trying to prove something. I'm not sure what. She's not homeless or heartless. Why don't you go back to Georgia and try to start over?"

"Before taking the Test?" he said. "When the world studyeth the Text, they'll take the Test and Camellia will be the Queen of the May."

"What about Fonda?" I asked. "Did she come up here, too?"

"She had to work," he said. He sat next to me on the bench. I chuckled. The late afternoon was God's kiss. Music drifted from the rooms, especially up a slope to the Chapel, where I'd first heard Camille so many years ago. Camille's music did not soothe the savage breast; she *was* the savage breast, and she soothed no one.

"Tell me something, Clarence," I said. "What is the meaning of life?" He turned and looked at me as if I was something to be pitied.

"I missed that when it come around," he shrugged. "I think I was still in the slammer."

"Just as well," I said.

A mockingbird's endless song rose over the hills of North Carolina.

By FRIDAY MORNING, CAMILLE AND HER HELPERS had half-trashed the campus with posters and handbills for *The Text and the Test*. I tried not to worry, but everyone knew something strange was happening, and soon word got out that one Camille Malone was behind it. Those faculty who remembered Camille from her student days weren't surprised.

"She was wild as the March Hare," said Darian McClancy, professor of theory. He was nearly seventy and always wore a bow tie. We sat in the dining hall, at mid-morning on Friday, watching the lovely flow of students around us. "Do you know that once I assigned a simple exercise in chord inversions and she came in the next day with, God, it must have been a hundred pages of them? I gave her an A, but I wanted to have her tested or something. It wasn't right. Then, at other times, she wouldn't do the work at all."

"Dr. McClancy, she's still wild as the March Hare," I said. "She came to my office a couple of days ago."

"Back then, weren't you two...." he began.

"Yes, we were," I groaned. "Or at least I was. She never belonged to anything but Camille Malone."

"Well, there's something to be said for a wild woman, I suppose," he said. I smiled, but he seemed serious.

I met Jill for lunch at the dining hall at the Community College. She was somber and unhappy but trying to understand what was about to happen.

"So she's going to get out there and try to talk about this *Text and the Test?*" she asked. She munched on a carrot stick. "Why would the administration let her do it?"

"They don't think it's very serious, and neither do I," I said. "Even if she's just having a fine old time, it's just too nutty to figure."

"So you're going to stay for this thing?" she asked.

"I've got to, Jill," I said. "I feel responsible. I was the one who somehow got her to come back to McCandless. I was just trying to help an old friend."

"Is that what it really was?" she asked.

"I think so," I said.

"Were you really just trying to do a good deed, Ford? Or were you trying to start over?"

The question hit me with an amazing force. Start over? Humans cannot start over, though we constantly deceive ourselves about it. We can only try not to lose our place.

"Maybe," I said. "But I think now that I know how to separate the various humors in the blood."

"Well," she said. "Are you going to take *The Test?*"

"I have the strangest feeling that I've already taken it," I said.

As the day passed, people all over campus began to drift toward the Circle Beech, throwing Frisbees, singing in groups, roughhousing, generally enjoying a spring Friday under the benevolent shade of these fine old trees. Oddly, I felt compelled to clean my office, and so I did. I threw out styrofoam cups, old test papers I never graded, bales of newspapers, circulars from L.L. Bean, *Time* magazine, and (God) the AARP. By mid-afternoon, my office was cleaner than it had been in years. I had, I believed, come to find comfort in personal disorder: they might find my junk, but they won't find me.

With classes over and nothing left to do, I locked the door and strolled around campus. Here was the Chapel, unchanged in its glory, there was the spot where we had built the snowmen, Wolfie and Constanze, and here was the lake where I'd walked in the moonlight with Nancy.

The loss was permanent, yet repairable.

Students started to head across the quad for the Circle Beech. I was drawn there, too, and so I strolled, hands behind my back.

Kids sipped beer from red plastic cups. The late-afternoon sun spangled the emerald grass. Laughter. Shouts of unmodulated exuberance, young men and women shadowboxing with the spring.

I came to the back of the amphitheatre. The sight before me was nearly comic: crude banners of purple cloth had been hung from two staves on either side of a spot down front where Camille, dressed in jeans and a black T-shirt, was running around, shouting instructions at Clarence and Mister Josiah. Behind them was a bedsheet on which someone had crudely written with what appeared to be mercurochrome: *The Text and the Test.*

I noticed a commotion down to the left and found why the students were here: two kegs of beer and plastic cups. A boy and girl brushed past me, and I saw that it was Starr and a shaggy young man with his hair in dreadlocks. They walked very close to each other, and once, Starr flung a glance over her shoulder at me, but that was all.

A minute later, the crowd started to get quieter, though the mumbling and giggling persisted sotto voce. Camille was smoking a cigarette and nervously scanning the crowd. She paced. Clarence seemed about to come apart. Finally, Camille raised her arms and the crowd fell reasonably silent.

"Now listen to me," she said. Her voice was strong, pleasing. "I am Camille Malone."

"Big deal," said a voice in the back. Everybody laughed. Camille pointed her finger toward the voice.

"I'll have you kicked out, and you won't be able to take *The Test!*" she said.

"What test?" another voice asked. "Would you please tell us what this is?"

"This is the story of your life!" shouted Camille. Everybody laughed. Campus police officers stood back out of the way, relaxed. "This is the time in the history of this glorious country when the people begin to wake up. This is the formation of the Government of Nothing."

"We've already got one of them," said a tall, heavy-set boy. Lots of laughter. Camille began to look mildly amused. What was on her mind?

"The Prime Minister of Nothing will now address you!" Camille shouted. She turned and grabbed my cousin Clarence by his sleeve and jerked him to the front. The crowd saw him, this small man with trousers that didn't come to his ankles, white socks, hair greased back neatly, a white shirt with two pockets. He held what I presumed was a copy of the Text. His hands were shaking so badly he could hardly hold it. I felt so bad for him.

"Howdy," said Clarence with a nervous laugh. "I am...*uh! Hark! Lo!*"

The place erupted in mirth, and Clarence couldn't quite figure it out. Camille held onto one of the banner staves. Mister Josiah was on the other side, feet moving in a secret dance. "I mean, them's words to getteth the attention of the masseth. You read it in the Bible, it's in there."

"What's this test shit?" cried a pretty girl with curly blonde hair.

"Oh," said Clarence, "this here's the bible of the new order that me and this little woman here, Camille, done wrote."

When he said "little woman," Camille almost rushed him. She took a step toward him, stopped, flexed her fists.

He cleared his throat and opened the pages. "This here's from *The Book of Refusals*, starting at verse sixty-three:

63 *We refuse to believe in the Grecian urn because its symmetry is no more than a joke upon gullible people with a true fondness for Melmac.*

64 *We don't know a thing about what makes a peach blow up on them limbs in the spring.*

65 *We refuse to read the libretti of Lorenzo da Ponte, though we may listen to Mozart's music.*

66 *They say our love won't pay the rent.*

He looked up and smiled, but the crowd was starting to be playful, to ignore him, and around the fringes they were leaving. The beer must have run out, because I realized students were geting nothing but a spray of foam. Clarence was clearly losing the crowd by reading from *The Book of Refusals*. Maybe he should have read *The Book of Baseball Statistics*. Camille walked slowly up and took *The Text* from Clarence and screamed at the top of her lungs.

"Quiet!" she yelled. The place began to do as she asked. She shouted it once more.

She walked back and forth and seemed to be thinking. All the shards of conversation fell away, and Camille Malone was left in front of us all, eyes dancing. Finally, she stopped in front.

"People, listen to me," she said. "This earth is no more than Pasiphae, and we are minotaurs. Do you understand me?" No one did, but they were quiet. She went on.

"Do you remember when Artegal kills Pollente in *The Faërie Queene*?" she asked. No one did. "Do you remember Charlotte Corday's act? Why did they do it? Why was Lotis changed into a tree? Have you ever saluted the jewel in the tree?" Clarence looked confused and sad. He walked over to Mister Josiah and mumbled something, and then they both looked confused. "Do you remember what Schopenhauer said about suffering? Can you tell me the plot of any play by James Shirley?"

It wasn't working, and I ached for her. She waved her arms, as if to steady them, but she had already lost. For the first time, I felt pity and compassion: Camille was ill, perhaps manic or just permanently confused about life and love. She wasn't doing this as some sophomoric joke, though the students thought it was. She wasn't even really making fun of them. She was merely returning the arch to its starting point: completing the circle. But for Camille, nothing had ever had such surfaces. Everything was encrypted with deeper meanings. And I was jealous of whatever she saw in that darkness. That was the secret of her hold on me. Perhaps I'd lunged for it when I'd betrayed Jill.

"Wait! cried Camille. "Everything's just beginning, I...." A great change descended over her. She looked around in silence. Most of the crowd wandered off. Those who remained did not seem to breathe. Starr and the boy in dreadlocks left, not looking back, whispering and giggling to themselves. I approved, but sadly.

"What do you believe in?" asked Camille Malone. She waited, as if genuinely wanting to know, but no one said anything. The leaves trembled with a fresh breeze. Their music was restless, heading somewhere. "Do you believe in free beer?"

Well, yes. They went through some backslapping and *yeahs* as Camille showed them something halfway between a smile and a sneer. "I wondered, you know."

Was she about to cry? She stopped and rocked on her white jogging shoes.

"I wondered if I still believed in anything. Nobody else does, so don't feel pregnant or anything." They were silent again. "It's just that once I believed in something. And here was where I believed it."

A bluejay came down and lit on the sign for *The Text and the Test.*

"I suddenly don't feel all that well," she said. "I'm not even sure what I'm doing here. I can't keep things straight. I feel like I'm going to freak or something."

Nobody had a clue who she was or what she meant, but they did not leave.

"I don't believe anything matters," she said, her voice shaky. "This test thing — it's a nontest based on a nontext. I was trying to say something, but nobody's getting it."

She waited then, because she heard what we did: a pianist from somewhere playing Bach, clear, pure. She listened, looked down, waited for thirty seconds until it ended.

"You know, this place is where I live," she almost whispered. "I feel as if I'm supposed to be hearing some message." She laughed unconvincingly. "Anybody know what that message might be?" No one answered. "Well, it's not important."

"What is important?" I blurted. She looked up at me as heads turned my way. I could not believe I had spoken. A wan, disturbed smile appeared on that once-lovely face.

"I don't have a clue, Georgia," she said. "Never did."

"Me neither," I said.

They glanced back to Camille.

"I guess I just wanted to see this again," she said. "I just wanted to see if I was still here." She looked around. "And I am. Maybe...." She started to choke a bit. "Maybe I could do something. I don't know."

The world moved in the breeze.

And so I said out loud what was clearly obvious to everyone there.

"Nobody," I said, "ever forgets Camille Malone."

Heads turned toward me in silence. Camille heard me, looked up with tears spilling to the corner of her mouth. She merely nodded, stood for a moment in our admiration.

The crowd dispersed, laughter coming back with it. I walked down front to Camille where she stood rooted in her embarrassment. Before I got to her, she held up her hand to stop me.

"I quit taking my medicine," she said in painful gasps. "I wanted to see who was there. I thought you wanted me to come to the beach. I never knew where I was, Ford. Everything always hurt. I don't know what I'm doing here, but maybe I will. Maybe I'll take *The Test*. I'm probably the only one who could pass it."

"Camille, are you sick?" I asked.

"I've been sad so long," she said. She looked around at the Circle Beech, and saw its massive girth, moving in the wind but solid into the soil.

I said nothing. She put her finger to her lips, then walked off toward her car, Mister Josiah running along after. I watched until they got in and drove off, feeling sad and without a trace of wisdom.

I walked to where Clarence sat in the grass, looking confused yet not very upset.

"Time's on our side, Clarence," I said. He looked up at me.

"I wrote that," he said with a sigh. "Lot of good it done me."

"Starting a new religion's not very easy," I said. "The old ones are about all we can handle now."

"But I don't have anywhere to go," he said. "Unless I go back to Jamesburg or something. Maybe I could help out your Mama or something."

Was there symmetry here? I began to laugh. Clarence laughed, too, though he didn't seem to know why.

"Her yard does need somebody to look after it," I said. "It's all overgrown and going wild. Maybe she'd pay you to make it look like a home again."

"Now that's a thing to thinketh on," said Clarence Clayton.

We walked slowly up the seats of the amphitheatre, and when I turned one last time, all I saw was a copy of *The Text* lying in a pool of faint sunlight.

THAT AUTUMN, NOT A MONTH AFTER THE STUDENTS had
returned to Asheville, I walked one noon around McCandless,
watching the kids rush to class or indulge in horseplay. I stopped at
a bulletin board in front of Jumper Hall and read a poster:

TONIGHT IN KELL AUDITORIUM
THE MCCANDLESS SYMPHONY ORCHESTRA
IN CONCERT

BEETHOVEN: SYMPHONY NUMBER ONE

RAVEL: DAPHNIS AND CHLOE, SUITE NUMBER TWO

WORLD PREMIERE
THE LAKE ISLE OF INNISFREE
FOR CHORUS AND ORCHESTRA
BY FORD CLAYTON

8 P.M.
TICKETS AT THE KELL BOX OFFICE
OR AT THE DOOR

I took a deep breath and smiled. Rehearsals had gone well, and
I was sure that my piece would succeed. Even Edgar Fuller had
dropped by one rehearsal with praise.

The summer had been glorious among these old mountains. A week after she left, Camille sent a letter to me.

Friday night

Dear Georgia,

I guess sooner or later, everybody's a fool. I'm not sure what I was doing, only that I wanted to come back. But it wasn't McCandless. I wanted to be again who I was then. But I couldn't. I wanted to be who I was back in the sixties.

I still can't believe we wound up at Myrtle Beach, but that's life. Judith and Holofernes, we ain't. I took Mr. Josiah home, and Beaularice was not pleased. In fact, I think she put a curse on me.

The truth? I haven't seen it in so long, we've become strangers, I'm afraid. I've actually been teaching piano here in New York for nine years, making a decent living, of course. Before that, I had a bad nervous breakdown and drifted for a while. I've been diagnosed, and you don't want to know the details. As long as I take my medicine, I'm boring and in control. I quit from time to time. When I heard from you, I hadn't taken it in weeks. I know, I know. Anyway, once a Dada, always a Dada. I also have money my father left me. He was a doctor, remember. I kept telling myself those days at the beach were a vacation.

I'm sorry for everything. But I can't be too sad. I'm moving. And you know what they say, Georgia. A change is always good for everybody. Take care.

Love,
Camille

The same week, we had been watching a *National Geographic* special when the phone rang. Jill's head was in my lap on the couch, and the kids were on the floor. I didn't want to get the phone, but neither did anyone else, so I finally got up and walked into the kitchen. It was my mother in Jamesburg.

"Ford, you must pack an overnight kit and come down here immediately," she said. "I'm on the verge of a nervous breakdown, and you, son, are the cause of it."

"You mean Clarence?" I asked.

"Did you really tell him I would give him work, Ford?" she asked. In the background, Eileen Farrell was in acute distress during a Puccini aria.

"Well, I just said your yard needs cleaning up," I admitted. "Maybe you could pay him minimum wage to trim the hedges back and cut the grass."

"Darling, I cannot understand how you would do this to your mother," she said. "Did you have a relapse in your nervous breakdown?"

"No, I'm fine, and Jill and the kids are home for good, Mom," I said. "But Clarence needs something to do. It's either something like this, until he finds it, or knocking over another liquor store. Besides, I know you have plenty of money."

"Dear, he's been preaching to me from something called *The Book of Ginger*," she said. "He said Ginger nipped the ass off the Calydonian boar. He's ripe for the loony bin."

I smiled. The Text lived, after all.

"Just ignore him," I said. "He's just trying to get out of the labyrinth. You could use religion or music or even calculus, Mom. We're just trying to find the way out."

"I'm thinking of throwing a plugged-in hair dryer into his bath," she said gaily.

"Mom, he'd be autopsied," I said.

"Son, autopsy is a noun," she said. "I'm bereft you'd forget that."

"I wish you'd stop these homicidal daydreams about Clarence," I said. "He's just trying to do his best."

"Well, you're certainly right," she sighed. "Anyway, I think he has a girlfriend who's coming to see him. Perhaps that will take his mind off defacing my yard. Some woman named Fonda."

I had gone back to the living room and grinned through the rest of the *National Geographic* special, only telling Jill about it when the kids had gone to bed.

Fonda had indeed come over to see Clarence, and he in short order had abandoned Mom to move to Myrtle Beach. I got a card from him in early September with a picture of the Gordon House on the front, as it must have looked in 1960. He had taken a job with Mister Josiah. He said Beaularice had read his hand and told him he would someday run a tire dealership. "Now, ainteth that a thing to thinketh on!" he'd scribbled. Fonda, it seems, was keeping her night job, but Clarence didn't seem to mind.

Now, with the crisp chill of October hanging in the air and leaves blowing down the sidewalks of McCandless, I felt a deep calmness that I had survived with the best part of my heart intact.

Jay couldn't believe I'd set to music a poem that talked about bean rows and clay and wattles.

"You might as well have done the Sears Catalog," he said as we were dressing that night.

I was already in my tux an hour before we had to leave, nervous as a water bug. Jill tried to calm me.

"Son, don't make fun of Daddy's music," she said.

Kathy was moaning because she had nothing to wear.

"Sue me," said Jay. "Are we gonna be back in time for the Friday Night Frights?"

Jill went downstairs for maybe three minutes as I sat in a chair in our bedroom, trying to feel the Great Circle of Life embracing me. When she came back up, I knew what she was going to say.

"Ford, she's down there in the kitchen rearranging the dishes and stuff," said Jill.

She was lovely, even gorgeous, in her black gown. Her hair was pulled to one side and secured with a diamond-studded hairpin I'd given her on our wedding anniversary in July.

"I know," I said. "She started doing it before I came back upstairs."

"Go down there right now and tell her to stop, or I'm going to kill her," said Jill. Her eyes were merry.

"Okay," I said. I stood, but instead of heading for the stairs, I came close to Jill and took her in my arms.

"You'll mess me up," she said. A glint rose in her lips.

"You're damn right I'll mess you up," I said. I nibbled on her left ear. "But I'll wait until we're home." I stepped backed and looked at my wife.

"Honey, I just want you to know something," she said. "I'm proud of you. And I know the concert will be wonderful."

I could have waited a lifetime for those words. They were the pay for having survived my descent into the maelstrom. I kissed her again and went downstairs and into the kitchen.

Dad was in the living room trying to fix the leg on a coffee table. He waved cheerily as I passed.

"Dear, glasses should never be stored next to dishes," said Clarice Clayton. "If you plan to have a career as a noted composer, you must pay attention to the amenities of life."

"Mom," I said, "if you don't get out of the kitchen now, I'm going to sell you into white slavery in Morocco."

"Well, aren't we testy tonight," she said with a smile. "I'll chalk it up to artistic temperament." She moved past me with great elegance into the living room.

I left early in my MG, which had been recovered by the Asheville Police in July. They'd found it parked next to a dumpster in a town forty miles away. I had to have it repainted, and now it looked good as new. The family would come later, lovely Jill, bored Jay, elegant Kathy and the eternally Romantic Clarice Clayton.

I would not conduct my piece, but neither would I sit in the audience. I'd be backstage, then I'd come out for a bow after it was over. I parked behind Roberts Hall and walked around campus for twenty minutes, trying to remember it all, finding I couldn't, that it didn't matter.

The students and faculty members in the orchestra started arriving. The long dresses and tuxedos cheered me, turned me into a drumming tub of nerves. Already, I'd begun a symphony, and the work was going so well I could hardly believe it. I was starting to live the life for which I had been chosen.

I was standing in the spot where we'd made the snowmen of Mozart and his wife, when I saw Edgar Fuller half-jogging down the sidewalk toward me. He was not in the orchestra, so he merely wore a black pin-striped suit, but he was still dressed perfectly.

"Edgar, why are you running?" I asked.

"I've been looking all over for you," he said. "It came here about an hour ago. I called the house, but Jill said you'd already left." He took a slip of folded paper from his coat pocket and placed it in my hand. "It looked like something you might want." He slapped me on the shoulder and turned to walk off.

"Thanks, Edgar," I said.

He merely waved. The sidewalk lamps were on. The sun's light had nearly backed west over the mountains. I held the paper up. It was a telegram.

I did not wait. I put it in my pocket and turned on my freshly shined dress shoes and walked beneath the new stars across the campus. I could hear phrases of my music from the Rehearsal Hall on the back of Kell Auditorium. It took me only three minutes to get to the Circle Beech.

I walked down through the amphitheatre's seats, and, in the glow of a lamp, took out the telegram and opened it.

Of course, it was from Camille.

Dear Pyramus,
Read about it in the Alumni Magazine. It's about time you did something worthwhile, Georgia. I am teaching piano lessons to kids here in New Orleans. It almost feels like home. Remember, Hermes invented the lyre on the first day of his life. So may you invent more wonderful things.
Your devoted
Thisbe

I read it twice, then I slowly walked away from the Circle Beech back across campus. A wind arose in the treetops.

Just like Camille. Perfect timing.

About the author

Philip Lee Williams is an award-winning author of four works of fiction. Managing a full-time position at the University of Georgia, he is also an accomplished composer. His previous works include THE HEART OF A DISTANT FOREST (winner of the Townsend Prize for fiction), ALL THE WESTERN STARS (optioned for film by Zanuck Productions), SLOW DANCE IN AUTUMN, and THE SONG OF DANIEL (for which he was named Georgia Author of the Year). Williams lives in Athens, Georgia, with his wife and son.